FORSAKING ALL OTHERS

A damp, gentle breeze kissed Bartholomew's cheeks as he stepped from the lighthouse and stood looking at the moonlit sea. The stars were few and scattered. He breathed deeply of the tangy air and listened to the steady roar of the waves pounding the bluff two hundred feet below, letting the sea's timeless serenity wash over him. Then he turned and climbed the slick wooden stairs to the top of the bluff.

Suddenly he became aware of something moving toward him in the darkness. Coming to a halt, he stood motionless; holding his breath.

Ariah stopped an arm's length away, her lush mouth slightly parted as she gazed up at him. He waited for her to speak, but she remained silent, only the expressiveness of her beautiful blue eyes telling him that she had been hoping for him to come.

"Tomorrow . . ." she began, and let it trail away. "I had to see you."

Common sense and need warred within him. If he so much as touched her, he would be lost. And yet, wasn't he lost already? Hadn't he been lost since the first moment he'd laid eyes on her? "Come here," he said in a low, sensuous growl.

She rushed into his arms. Minutes passed while they embraced, content merely to bask in one another's warmth and closeness, to know their hearts beat as one, their souls enmeshed in the same heated emotions.

Eventually, Ariah lifted her face to gaze up at him. Her hood fell back and the moon streaked her pale hair with silver and gold. She was so beautiful Bartholomew's chest constricted.

And suddenly, holding her was no longer enough . . .

Books by Charlene Raddon

TAMING JENNA
TENDER TOUCH
FOREVER MINE

Published by Zebra Books

FOREVER MINE

Charlene Raddon

ZEBRA BOOKS
KENSINGTON PUBLISHING CORP.

This book is dedicated to my Oregon writing buddies: Dorothy Keddington, Carol Warburton, and Ka Hancock. And to the wonderful friends I made there who helped in researching this book. In particular: Nancy and Carl Hopkins, and Barbara Watkins. With a special thanks to the Tillamook County Pioneer Museum, and all the folks who keep the Cape Meares Light accessible today.

Then there is George W. Higgins, whose father, George H. Higgins, was a keeper at the Cape Meares Light from 1901 to 1909, and whose parents' wedding picture, taken at the light, inspired this story. Thanks, Old Hig, for sharing your special knowledge of the area, your childhood memories, and a ride up the Trask River Road. Most of all, for becoming a dear and very special friend. I will never forget you.

Presentiment is that long shadow on the lawn,
Indicative that suns go down;
The notice to the startled grass,
That darkness is about to pass.
—Emily Dickinson

One

Cape Meares, Oregon, 1891

To Bartholomew Noon the unceasing rumble of the sea and the melancholy cries of gulls were the very embodiment of his loneliness. Constant. Never ending. But loneliness was not the cause of the heavy sense of foreboding that had come over him on awakening that morning. A warning he knew better than to ignore.

In the hope of escaping the gloomy cloud hanging over him, he had hiked the steep trail down to the beach where a man could be alone. Here on the driftwood-littered strand, he could be himself. No one to placate. No one from whom he must hide his innermost feelings in order to keep from being manipulated or tormented. Here, he could ponder his unwonted presentiment without interruption.

Out where the water deepened, a wave of translucent jade crested, curled in upon itself, then broke in a boiling froth that tossed and fumed until its force ebbed. Indolently, it crept toward him until the foam-tipped water encircled his boots, as if to embrace him in empathy and compassion before being sucked back into the gray Pacific Ocean, stealing the sand from under him as it went.

A derisive snort erupted from deep inside Bartholomew's chest as he shrugged off his imaginings. The sea neither embraced nor understood him. What it did do, a few grains at a time, was erode away the land, the same way life with Hester was eroding away his soul.

The sky darkened from gray to black as a storm drew near. Fog, pushed by the wind herding the storm inland, had already obliterated the headland to the south where Hester and the lighthouse awaited him. The air grew more chill. Soon the rain would begin. Resolutely, he thrust his icy fingers into his coat pockets and turned his back on his beloved sea. It was time to see to his responsibilities.

The thick February mist formed droplets on his lashes and the tip of his sturdy nose. Under his keeper's cap, his damp sable hair formed a mass of loose curls.

"Come on, Harlequin," he called to a puffin feeding in the shallow water, "time to go."

The stubby bird scooped up a last mouthful of tiny mole crabs in its garish orange and red beak and waddled out of the surf toward the man, every bit as though it had understood the human command. Awkwardly, it flapped its raven wings, flying barely high enough to reach the man's broad shoulder, but it seemed content there. Bartholomew patted the sleek snowy feathers of its breast as he climbed the bluff that rose above the strand. The wing Bartholomew had mended was nearly as strong as ever. Any day now the bird would rejoin its own kind on the seastacks off the Oregon coast, leaving Bartholomew more alone than ever.

Evergreens draped in moss crowded close around him as he made his way up the trail, and added to the gloom of the foggy morn. Tree trunks, misshapen by ferns that rooted in every gnarl, appeared like phantoms in the drifting mist, writhing and moaning in the rising wind. It was when the track ran close enough to the cliff to offer a last view of the sea that Bartholomew saw the ship.

One second the vessel was there, the next it was gone. The fog congealed to the consistency of Hester's sausage gravy and lay every bit as heavily upon the sea as the gravy did in Bartholomew's stomach. His dark eyes strained to penetrate the ghostly vapor. If he was right, Pyramid Rock lay directly across the vessel's course.

Like a too-tight seam, the fog split apart. In the resultant window, he spotted the ship, heading straight for the hidden rock.

He screamed for the vessel to veer sharply portside, knowing in the more reasonable portion of his brain that he was much too far away to be heard.

The rising wind hurtled the ship closer to its destruction, as easily as a stone cast from a sling. To Bartholomew, the scene played out in painfully slow motion, grating on his nerves like wood beneath a rasp. People were on that ship, people who would die. He wanted to rage at the heavens for allowing such tragedy.

The thought that there might be survivors sent him racing back down toward the beach, until reality brought him to a halt.

At sea level the white-capped waves would hide the ship from him. Even if it did crash, there would be time to fetch horses from the lighthouse station and get back before the sea deposited its victims on the sand. Meanwhile, he could hope he was mistaken about the ship's danger.

But as his mind formed the thought, he saw it happen. Ship and rock appeared to merge and become one as they collided. Then, as though to refuse such a marriage, the cold lifeless stone ejected the helpless mass of wood and sailcloth back out into the sea. Billowing white sails crumpled as the mast snapped and collapsed upon the heaving deck. The wind and the roar of the sea drowned out the splintering of wood and the screams of men, but Bartholomew heard them. In his heart.

For one more moment the ship bobbed uncertainly upon the waves, then sank from view. Bartholomew turned and sprinted up the steep forest trail. The puffin frantically flapped its wings to maintain balance on the man's broad shoulder, then plummeted unnoticed to the mossy earth.

Hester was coming from the garden when her husband sprinted out of the woods and around the fenced compound in which the houses stood. She crept along as though each step were an act of painful labor. With one hand she carried the freshly rinsed ceramic chamber pot she used at night instead of making the long walk down to the cold water closet off the kitchen.

"Where you going in such a hurry?" She waited for him to reach her, her shawl clutched over her flat, pious chest.

"Shipwreck," he said, as he passed her. "Crashed into Pyramid Rock. I'm taking the horses down to the beach for survivors."

"What'll you do with 'em if you find any?" she called after him in the waspish voice she was careful never to use around others.

Bartholomew didn't bother to answer. He rushed into the barn, snatched bridles off the wall and went to work readying the four horses they kept for hauling supplies.

Hester was still standing on the path, her thin face scrunched with disapproval, when he led the horses out into the fog.

"Won't have no putrefying bodies stinking up my house," she said, following him to the back porch of their home.

"Don't worry, Hester, I'll put them in the barn."

He glanced up as a white beam cut weakly through the thickening fog, followed by a red flash. On a good day the beam could be seen twenty-one miles out to sea. But this wasn't a good day. At least Pritchard had not fallen asleep and allowed the light to go out.

"Have Seamus relieve Pritchard, Hester, and send the boy down to help me. Right now I need blankets, and that brandy we keep for emergencies . . . if you haven't drunk it."

Hester blanched, then colored. In her best imitation of refined gentility, which she usually saved for company, she said, "How dare you accuse me of drinking alcoholic beverages? You know I am a member in good standing of The Tillamook Women for Temperance Coalition—even if you have buried me here where I can't get to the meetings anymore."

Her husband tossed her a look of disgust, saying nothing

about the bottle of Dr. Hamilton's Heavenly Elixir he had found that morning under the porch steps. The so-called tonic was mostly alcohol, but Hester had ignored his demand that she destroy her supply. She claimed it gave her strength and made her feel better. Bartholomew no longer cared. It made her easier to live with, if nothing else.

"Yes, Hester. Now get the blankets, please. I haven't time to argue."

"Get them yourself then. You can move faster than me."

The day was nearly gone before Bartholomew was able to head back to the lighthouse station, exhausted and gloomier than ever. Each time he had spotted a head bobbing on the waves, or a body clinging to a piece of flotsam, he had swam out to bring the victim ashore. He built a bonfire to guide survivors through the fog and warm them when they arrived. He emptied one woman's stomach of seawater and dealt with the deep gash her son had received on one leg. He carried or dragged lifeless bodies through the surf to dry land. He rubbed life into the frozen limbs of the living, doled out blood-warming doses of brandy, then loaded everyone—dead and alive—onto the horses for the ride over the headland.

Pritchard Monteer met the cavalcade halfway along the trail and took charge of the extra horse. Slung over its back were two wet, blanket-wrapped bodies, a bright-eyed black and white puffin perched irreverently on top.

"Are you all right, Uncle Bart? Seamus was out playing with those blasted goats again, and Aunt Hester couldn't find him or I would have been here sooner."

Bartholomew had no strength to reply.

Across the rump of the bay mare he rode lay a small shrouded bundle, two dainty bare feet dangling limply from beneath the blanket. A third horse carried a young man in his teens, an unconscious woman cradled in his arms. Two more men rode double on a buckskin gelding, looking as weary as their dark-visaged rescuer.

At the back gate of the compound, Bartholomew dismounted and looped the reins around the rail. He took the woman from her son and carried her to the house while Pritchard helped the others alight. Before Bartholomew could open the door and usher his charges inside, Hester swung the portal wide and stood barring the entrance.

"Where do you think you're taking them?" she asked.

He stared at her with eyes like black ice until she backed away nervously. Then he motioned for the shipwreck victims to go on in and warm themselves at the kitchen stove. Turning to Pritchard, Bartholomew handed over the unconscious woman. The younger, smaller man staggered under the weight his uncle had so easily carried.

"Put the woman in Hester's room, and the boy in the garret. The men can share my room."

Pritchard waited until Hester gave a reluctant shrug before he carried out his uncle's orders. Bartholomew closed the door and pinned his wife with his harsh gaze. His voice was low and deadly calm. "Those people nearly died, Hester. They're exhausted, half-frozen and in shock. The boy lost a lot of blood. Would you truly deny them the comforts of a dry bed and some warm broth?"

"Why can't you put them next door? They'll track up my floors. I just—"

"Hester!" Bartholomew's large hands grasped her shoulders, dangerously close to her chicken-thin neck, and lightly squeezed. She squinted up at him, daring him, her thin lips so pinched they nearly disappeared. Slowly, he loosened his fingers and forced himself to relax.

"There's an extra bed over there," she said with a smug smile, knowing she'd won that last round.

"One bed. Where would the rest of them sleep?"

"The boy can sleep on the floor and Pritchard can share your room till they're gone."

To Bartholomew, Hester's brown-checked shirtwaist gave her complexion a sallow cast and deepened the blue stains beneath her dull, hazel eyes. She wore only dark, somber colors, considering anything brighter to be appropriate only for "loose" women. Yet she insisted on wearing ruffles and ruching and bows that made her look like a gift-wrapped prune. Her values were high, her rules strict, but she tended to twist them to suit her needs. Regarding her with a mixture of pity and exasperation, he said, "You won't mind running next door several times a day with hot broth and whatever else they'll need?"

Hester's eyes yawned wide in astonishment. "Let them make their own broth. Or let Seamus do it, Lord knows he's not worth much else. I'm no scullery maid, I'm your wife."

"Only when it suits you," he muttered.

"What?"

Ignoring her question, he said, "Do you truly think that would be the Christian thing to do—to leave them to shift for themselves in their condition? Or to push them off onto an old man?"

"I daresay a little rest is all they need. You know what the good book says: 'The Lord helps those who help themselves.' " She bobbed her beaklike chin as if dotting an exclamation point.

Bartholomew smiled sadly. "The Bible says no such thing, Hester. But it does say 'Blessed are the merciful, for they shall obtain mercy.' "

Hester's mouth opened, closed, and opened again. "So I didn't say it exactly right, it still—"

"They stay, Hester." His voice was like cold granite. "I'll sleep with Pritchard. You can sleep down here on the sofa, or take the extra bed next door. I don't care. But those people *will* stay in this house, and you *will* care for them until I can get them to Tillamook. Is that clear?"

Her eyes filled with hatred as she glowered at him. Without another word, she stormed into the kitchen, slamming the door in his face. Alone, Bartholomew pressed the inner corners of his eyes with thumb and forefinger. The discreet clearing of a throat brought up his head. Pritchard stood in the doorway to the hall which opened onto the end of the porch.

"Excuse me, Uncle Bart. I had to move some books off your bed onto the floor. The shelves were full. But the folks are all settled in now."

Bartholomew gave a weary sigh. "Fine, Pritchard. Come on and help me with the bodies now."

"What'll we do with the others when they're feeling better?" the younger man asked as they led the horses to the barn.

"We'll drive them to Biggs's place and get him to take them in to Tillamook. From there they can catch a ride to Astoria and go on to San Francisco where they were headed in the first place."

"I think I'd be wanting to stay off ships if I was them." Pritchard shuddered. He wasn't very brave at the best of times, but the thought of having a deck break apart beneath his feet and chuck him into an icy ocean made him want to crawl under his bed and never look at the sea again.

In the barn, as they lowered the last of the victims to the floor, a blanket slipped, exposing the face of a young woman with russet hair and a freckled nose.

"Holy Hector," Pritchard muttered, staring at her.

Bartholomew flipped the blanket back over the girl's face and dragged himself to his feet.

"Pretty little thing, wasn't she?" The boy hop-stepped to keep up with his uncle's long loose stride as he went to tend the horses. "Married, too. At least I guess she was, she's wearing a gold band."

Bartholomew stopped and looked at his nephew. "The other day you were asking me if the Hopkins girl over on Trask River had married yet. What is this sudden interest in the marital state of young females, Pritchard?"

The boy colored. "I . . . well . . . Holy Hector, Uncle Bart, I am a grown man. Why shouldn't I be interested in women? Maybe I'm tired of baching it with old Seamus while you go home to Aunt Hester every night."

"Good hell!" *If the boy only knew.* Pritchard had turned twenty-two a month past. In truth, he wasn't a boy any longer, though he would always be one to Bartholomew. "So, you're thinking of getting married, are you?"

His cheeks bright rose, the young man shrugged and gave his uncle a shy smile. "Actually, I've been doing more than thinking about it. You see, I . . . well, I've been trying to find a way to talk to you and Aunt Hester about this for weeks. I contacted Pa's brother in Portland a while back, the one who's an attorney, and he placed an advertisement for me back East."

"What kind of advertisement?" Bartholomew asked as he turned the mare into her stall.

"For a bride."

Bartholomew stared at him in amazement, certain he had not heard right. "A bride? You advertised for a bride?"

Pritchard filled a bucket with grain. "Uncle Edward wrote to a lawyer friend of his in Cincinnati and asked him to screen applicants for me. It took three months, but now—" he grinned "—she's on her way."

Bartholomew took the bucket and dumped the grain into the mare's feed bin. "Are you telling me they found you a bride— and she's already on her way here?"

"Kind of like getting hit by a wild pitch, isn't it? That's how I felt when I got the news."

Pritchard filled another bucket and took it into the buckskin's stall. Through the haze in his head, Bartholomew heard the grain strike the metal bottom of the bin. A thin cloud of chaff rose toward the loft.

"Uncle Edward's friend knows her and her family real well," the boy said over the partition. "In fact, he and her father are law partners. Her name is Ariah Scott and she'll be coming in on the train next week."

Bartholomew was still standing in the mare's stall, an expression of bewildered astonishment on his face, when Pritchard emerged with the empty bucket.

Pritchard chuckled. "I'm getting married. Plumb throws you

a curve ball, don't it?" His smile faded and his gaze fell. "I . . . uh, was hoping you might do me a favor, Uncle Bartholomew."

Bartholomew frowned. The boy only addressed him by his full given name when he was in trouble or wanted something outrageous. "I can't arrange a leave for you, if that's what you want. You know I have a shipment of pheasants to deliver in Portland next week. The buyers are expecting it and a delay could put us too close to nesting time. Frank Worden is coming to take my shifts, but he can't cover for both of us, and it's too late to change things anyway."

"I wasn't going to ask you to change anything. I was only hoping you could pick Ariah up for me at the Portland train station while you're there."

"Me? Oh no." Bartholomew shook his head, holding up a curry comb as if to fend off Pritchard with it. "There's no reason she can't take the train to Yamhill and then catch the stage like everybody else."

"But the worst part of the trip is between Yamhill and Tillamook. Especially in March. You know that ride over the Trask River toll road is pure hell at the best of times, let alone in spring when it's all muddy and everything."

"Then have her take a steamer up the Columbia and around to Tillamook Bay."

"I suggested that, but she's terrified of boats."

Bartholomew slung his arms across the mare's back, rested his forehead against her side, and groaned. "Can't you have her wait a month, till the weather's better?"

"I don't want to wait another month. I'm a man, Uncle Bartholomew, and I'm looking forward to having a wife of my own. I have needs, like any other man. That's something you should understand, even if it has been a long time since you've had to worry about how to fill those needs."

Bartholomew stifled a bitter retort about the so-called pleasures of marriage. He might have attempted to set the boy straight, except that Pritchard took after his aunt in one way—he saw only what he wanted to see, heard only what he wanted to hear. Clamping a commiserating hand on the young man's shoulder, he said instead, "I do understand. But don't you think the solution you've chosen is a bit drastic? You don't even know this woman. Lord only knows what she looks like."

"No, I don't think it's drastic." Pritchard shook his head so enthusiastically his baseball cap nearly flew off. "You know how lonely it is here. I want a family of my own, a wife I can share things with. And children—I want children." He grinned. "Nine boys. My own baseball team. Wouldn't that be grand, Uncle Bart?"

"Yes, Pritchard, that would be grand."

Suddenly, Bartholomew felt a hundred years old. A yearning so sharp it pierced his being, urged him to hurry back down to the beach where he could lose himself in the roar of the waves and the screams of the gulls.

Loneliness and a man's needs. Had there ever been a day in his adult life when he hadn't suffered those needs?

Maybe one. The night his father died, when a prettier, more amiable Hester had come to his bed to comfort him. One brief moment when he thought he had found heaven.

But that had been a lifetime ago.

Two

The train was already standing on the track when Bartholomew parked his wagon and hurried to the loading platform. The engine puffed steam and noisily belched out black smoke while it disgorged its passengers. People rushed to greet relatives and friends, adding joyous shouts and laughter to the *chug-chug* of the idling train and the rumble of baggage carts on the wooden platform.

For several seconds Bartholomew stood breathing in the hot-metal smell of the engine, mixed with perfume, body sweat, and wood smoke. The air hummed with an excitement he did not share. Pritchard's request that he save the young man's bride from the hazards and discomfort of a stagecoach ride from Yamhill to Tillamook still nettled Bartholomew.

What on earth would he do with her on the long trip home? What could they talk about? Even if the weather remained fair and the road in good condition, they would spend four interminable days together. Days when they would be entirely alone, for Hester had pleaded illness and opted to wait in Tillamook with friends until he returned.

Days of freedom from Hester and responsibility. Days which Bartholomew had looked forward to with the eagerness of a child at Christmas.

And what of the nights that went along with those days? Miss Ariah Scott was a city girl. From what Pritchard had learned of her—which wasn't much—she had never so much as stepped foot out of Cincinnati before. Often Bartholomew stayed with friends when he traveled—the Olwells, the Uphams and the Rhudes—but what if it became necessary to camp out? How would such an inexperienced miss handle sleeping on the road with a strange man? And what would his friends think about him traveling with a young, unmarried woman? He would soon find out.

Several women stood on the loading platform, trunks and satchels stacked at their feet as they waited to be met. Two were elderly. Another proved to have a child hiding behind her skirts.

Then he saw her. Miss Ariah Scott.

Three or four inches taller than Pritchard, her body had as much substance as a puff of air. In spite of the current popularity of the perfect, hour-glass shape, this woman obviously disdained the use of body padding such as Hester used in filling out her figure. Miss Scott's face was long enough for her to wear a halter and was bound to curdle cream.

Bartholomew started forward, feeling both sympathy for and irritation with his idiotic nephew, but before he half reached the horse-faced stick of a woman, she let out a screech and flew into the arms of a tall gentleman. Only partly relieved, Bartholomew went back to studying the crowd.

All the passengers had disembarked from the train, and most had already left the station. A young woman came from the station house and joined an elderly lady. He dismissed her at once as being too pretty to have to resort to an arranged marriage with a man she'd never met. She glanced around, and bounced up and down on her heels with glaring impatience. When she turned his way, affording him a full view of her face, he sucked in his breath at its delicate beauty.

Burrowing into the shadow of an overloaded baggage cart, Bartholomew drank in his fill of her, the way an old seaman would guzzle a tankard of ale after too many months at sea. Her hair was the ordinary brown of a walnut shell. Her form, in a well-made traveling suit the color of hothouse orchids, hinted of fragility. Her face was less than perfect, its shape too symmetrical, the skin too flawless, without even a smidgeon of character. As for its features, the brows were too thick, the nose too small and straight. And the mouth . . . Good hell, that well-defined mouth with its tiny mole perched so enticingly at the tip of one rounded peak fairly begged to be kissed.

But, except for her mouth and the fresh, innocent sort of sensuality he sensed about her, he was at a loss as to explain her appeal. Then he heard the trill of her laughter, like the song of a bird—clear, resonant, *alive*—and he knew. Her face was animated, her hands quick and graceful in their gestures. She was a living, breathing advertisement for youthful enthusiasm. For life.

For the first time in more years than he cared to remember, he was glad to be alive.

Awed by her affect on him, Bartholomew forgot about Miss Ariah Scott. He forgot Hester and Pritchard and the lighthouse station where he was Head Keeper. Had something not burst him out of his trance, he would likely have been content to stand there forever, watching this entrancing creature in her fantastical orchid attire. But at that moment a gray-haired man appeared. With an exclamation of joy the girl rushed toward him. She made as if to hug the man, nearly losing her balance when he quickly backed away.

"Here, here, young woman," the man blurted. "What do you think you're about?"

An older woman hurried over to them. "Anthony, what is going on here? Who is this . . . this female? Tell me at once or you'll be sleeping on the summer porch for the rest of your deceitful life, along with that mutt of yours."

Anthony's hands went up in testimony to his innocence. His irate wife took hold of his ear and hauled him to the buggy, casting the girl a look of contempt as she went. Instinctively, Bartholomew's feet carried him toward the trio, his protective urges coming to the fore. But the girl was already scurrying back to her friend. He turned away so she wouldn't know he had witnessed the embarrassing scene.

"Oh, Mrs. Doughney," the girl wailed when she reached the elderly woman, "why can't I ever think before I act? My mother always told me I was too impulsive by far and that I hadn't a modicum of common sense."

"No harm done, my dear." The woman patted the girl's gloved hand. "You're a bit anxious, is all. Be patient, your gentleman will show up."

"I'm afraid a lack of patience is another of my failings. How am I ever to be a proper wife when . . . ?"

The girl looked up and caught Bartholomew staring at her. Hope blossomed in her eyes. They were so full of eagerness, those eyes, lively and optimistic and innocent. Stunning. The exact shade of forget-me-nots.

Abashed at being discovered spying on her, Bartholomew stepped forward. "Forgive me, I didn't mean to stare. I'm—"

"Are you Mr. Noon?" she asked.

Taken aback, Bartholomew stammered, "Why, yes. That is . . . do you mean to tell me you are—"

"Oh, I knew you'd come." With that Ariah threw herself into his arms.

Bartholomew stiffened with shock, then shut his eyes as his body succumbed to the soft warm feel of her. His arms closed about her. It was heaven. It was hell. His jaw clenched as he fought the urge to snatch her up and run away with her. Resolutely he moved his hands to her arms and set her away from him. Over her shoulder, Mrs. Doughney winked at him. Flushing with embarrassment, he bowed to the girl and spoke with stiff formality.

"I take it you are Miss Ariah Scott from Cincinnati?"

She laughed gaily. "Of course I am. Who else . . . ?" Her voice faltered, her smile fled. "Gracious Sadie, I've done it again, haven't I?" Her hands flew to her face and she stared in dismay, first at Bartholomew, then at Mrs. Doughney. "I've made a fool of myself again. Oh, I am hopeless, am I not?"

"No, my dear," Mrs. Doughney assured her. "I'm sure Mr. Noon finds you as refreshing a change from the usual stiff-necked young misses from back East as I do. Is that not so, sir?"

Bartholomew smiled, glad to be able to switch his attention away from the girl. "Indeed, ma'am. And I am doubly relieved to see that someone was able to convince her to bring along a chaperon for her journey." He awarded the older woman a deep bow. "Bartholomew Noon at your service."

Chuckling, Mrs. Doughney gave an old-fashioned curtsey. "Utterly charming. If your nephew's manners are as gracious as yours, young man, I shall feel satisfied that my Miss Scott has found herself a good husband. I am not, however, her chaperon, but only an old woman lucky enough to have made her acquaintance when I boarded the train at Pendleton for my yearly visit to my son here in Portland."

"And what need do I have for a chaperon, I'd like to know?" Ariah Scott faced them, arms akimbo, a frown marring her pretty face. "It is nearly the twentieth century, after all, no longer the Dark Ages. Although one could hardly tell it from the way women are still being treated in some countries." Looking to Bartholomew she said, "Did you know that Greek women are cast from their homes and left to beg beside the road, or chased down and threatened with death, merely because some man got ahold of them? Even the savages here in the West are more humane to their women than that."

For the first time in longer than he cared to recall, Bartholomew found himself smiling with genuine pleasure. "The fact that a man was able to get his hands on your Greek woman proves the need for good chaperons."

Ariah glared at him. "All it proves is that she was foolish enough to let herself get into a situation she could not handle. Anyway, this is America, not Greece. Women here are taking charge of their own lives every day. Haven't you ever heard of Arizona Mary?"

He shook his head no, but he couldn't help smiling. Miss Ariah Scott was more than beautiful. She was unique. A fiery suffragette in nymph's clothing. And totally irresistible.

"Arizona Mary drove her own sixteen-yoke team of oxen and competed with other male freighters quite successfully," Miss

Scott was saying. "Or what about Charlie Pankhurst who drove a stagecoach for years until she died and people discovered she was a female? And did you know there have been ten female mayors already in the state of Kansas?"

"No, I didn't know that." Bartholomew was now struggling to keep from chuckling. "Were any of them elected to a second term?"

Taken aback, Ariah dropped her hands from her hips and stared at him. "Why, I don't know. There wasn't anything in the article about that."

Mrs. Doughney politely cleared her throat. "Well, this is all terribly interesting, my dear, but now that your young man is here, I believe I shall hire myself a buggy and go on to my son's house. The trip was the most enjoyable I can remember in a long time, but I am quite tired."

"No one is meeting you?" Bartholomew asked.

"No. My son is unmarried, Mr. Noon, and a very busy doctor. I discovered long ago that I was able to reach his home and kick off my city shoes much more quickly if I didn't rely on him to tear himself away from patients in time to pick me up. The arrangement pleases us both."

"May I offer you a ride, then?"

"What are you driving, if I may be so rude as to ask?"

"You may be as rude as you like. I'm afraid I have only a farm wagon, much more useful for hauling supplies than a buggy."

"Of course it is. Unfortunately, it also has only one seat and that one not too comfortable. In front of the station there are men sitting around in nice cushioned buggies, hoping to pick up a few coins by driving old ladies like me to hotels and such. You won't mind, I'm sure, if I give my business to one of them and let the two of you get on your way."

Sudden panic at the thought of being alone with the entrancing child standing next to him assailed Bartholomew, but he managed to project calm. "No, of course not."

"Oh, Mrs. Doughney." Ariah threw her arms about the elderly woman. "I shall miss you so. You've been so kind."

"Nonsense, child. Haven't enjoyed myself so much in years. Waiting with you until your fiancé's uncle came for you was the least I could do." Her eyes sought out Bartholomew and, once again, she winked. "And it was worth it. Mr. Noon is a handsome devil. Should give you an idea of what you can expect in your own young man."

Ariah released her and looked back at him. "You're right, he is handsome. And I should have expected it, from the description of him Mr. Monteer provided in his wire. In my excitement I had forgotten about it until now."

Her gamin's smile made Bartholomew's chest tighten. Surely this had to be a mistake. An awkward, immature pup like Pritchard couldn't possibly be lucky enough to win a nymph as intriguing as the one who stood before him. It was a waste, a crime, an outrage.

Bartholomew thought of Hester and tasted a bitterness so vile he closed his eyes to it, shocked and mortified by the vehemence of his emotions. He felt as though someone had pried open his soul and spewed its contents onto the muddy, horse-befouled street. Frantically, he snatched at his last remaining bit of self-control, at the precious indifference to life he had so painfully, conscientiously cultivated over the years in order to survive.

"Yes, well, I must apologize for leaving you standing so long." He forced a smile. "You're not quite what I expected either."

Mrs. Doughney chuckled and waved a finger at him. "I know exactly what you were expecting, young man. A prune of an old maid, with a bun so tight it could probably hold up her stockings. Am I right?"

The tightness in his chest loosened a fraction as he gazed at the wizened face with its lively, dancing eyes.

"I confess." He awarded Mrs. Doughney a gallant bow, but his gaze was on the girl. "That was exactly what I expected."

Miss Ariah Scott grinned.

Ariah. The name suited her. Light and airy. Perfect for a nymph. He struggled to regain his composure and remember what he was about.

All around them, passengers continuing on to Goble, where train and all would be ferried across the Columbia River before resuming the journey to Seattle, were boarding the train. Soon the platform would be empty except for porters and employees of the Union and Northern Pacific Railroads. And Bartholomew suddenly realized, he too was eager to be away; he could not wait to have Miss Ariah Scott to himself.

"Actually," she was saying, "I never would have guessed you were Mr. Monteer's uncle. You seem much too young. How old are you anyway?"

Bartholomew burst into peals of deep masculine laughter that were rusty from lack of use, and which drowned out Mrs. Doughney's polite warning cough.

"Gracious Sadie!" Ariah blushed prettily. "I truly should have my mouth sewn shut. It's likely the only way I'll learn to stop shoving my foot in it."

Never! he wanted to say. Such delectable lips were meant to be used, though he did have a purpose other than conversation in mind. "I shall be thirty this year, eight years Pritchard's senior."

"An excellent age." Mrs. Doughney gave an approving nod of her gray head. "Old enough to have sown your oats, as they say, and to have made something of yourself, yet still young enough to adjust to the tricks fate plays on all of us, eh?"

Bartholomew glanced at Miss Scott, wondering if she could be one of fate's tricks. Something niggled at his memory. He shrugged it away.

"I'm sure you're right. Now, Miss Scott, if you'll point out the rest of your baggage, I'll get it loaded while you finish your good-byes. We've a long way to go."

"Oh, yes, of course." She gestured to two small crates and a large trunk. "That's it there."

Bartholomew shouldered the trunk as though it contained nothing more than bird feathers, holding it in place with one arm while he squatted to pick up one of the crates.

As he put space between himself and the two women, he chuckled silently, remembering how he had wondered what he would do with the girl during the four long days of the journey home. There was no doubt about what he wanted to do. His hands ached with the need to stroke that smooth, velvet flesh, to explore and discover its secret contours. Thinking about it, four days no longer seemed enough.

He set the crate alongside the boxed-up fancy rosewood étagère Hester had insisted he buy her, then lowered the trunk onto the wagon bed.

Hester. Bartholomew's fantasy burst like the seed head of a giant dandelion, scattered by the wind.

Hester was his wife—till death do them part—no matter how much he might wish things were different. And Ariah Scott belonged to Pritchard.

His shoulders sagged under guilt as weighty as a steam engine. He rested his arms on the sideboard, braced his forehead on a fist, then shut his eyes and tried to banish the image of the girl's sweet tempting mouth, so lush, so—

A warm hand closed over his arm. "Are you all right, Mr. Noon? Is there anything I can do for you?"

Bartholomew looked down to see Ariah Scott standing only a kiss away, gazing up at him with those incredible forget-me-not blue eyes, her luscious lips moist and parted, her concerned expression sweetly, guilelessly intent.

And he plummeted into hell.

Three

Pretending to admire the stately buildings lining Portland's streets, Ariah studied the profile of the man next to her on the seat of the rumbling wagon as it carried them out of town. The only similarities she could see between Bartholomew Noon and the architecture she was supposedly enjoying were their stalwart solidity and craggy surface. Ensconced inside one of the buildings or seated beside the man, a woman would feel safe.

But there, all likeness ended. The edifices lining Jefferson Street were relatively common—Bartholomew Noon was not.

His face put her in mind of a sculptor's work, of sensitive hands armed with clay, dabbing on a bit here, pinching off a tad there, smoothing with the swipe of a thumb, then moving on. It was a face of inconsistencies, a face as complex, she imagined, as the man himself. Dark, brooding, intense. Predatory.

In his ridiculously long wire Pritchard Monteer had described his uncle as a man to whom women generally gave a second glance, and Ariah agreed. Some, no doubt, would even call him beautiful. A few might be challenged to see what it took to make those full, sensuous lips curve in genuine joy. Others, noting his forbidding expression and the sense of barely contained power hidden inside that massive body, would give him a wide berth.

Ariah Scott was fascinated. His full mouth hinted at sensitivity. The brooding sable eyes suggested compassion. Try as she might to give her attention to the passing sights, her gaze was drawn back to him again and again. She kept her hands clutched in her lap, her skirts properly swept aside so they wouldn't brush his muscular thighs, as she resisted the urge to stare, to study, to touch.

"I'm very eager to see the lighthouse." She looked away, desperate to get her mind on something else. "I've never seen the ocean, but I'm terribly excited to think that I'll be living so close to it. Are there many birds? I am an ornithologist, so I'm hoping to spend some time studying the birds there. I hope there'll be sea lions, too. I've always wanted to see one. You'd think any sort of lion would be ferocious looking, but sea lions strike me as enormous pillows with mustaches."

Ariah knew she was prattling and thought at once of the "Hints on Etiquette and Personal Manners," she had read during her train ride. They had been in a book, *Dr. Chase's Recipes, or Information for Every Body,* given her by Aunt Ida. "Be discreet and sparing of your words," it had instructed. She'd completed only the first paragraph of that section and already she'd broken one of the rules.

Actually, Ida was the wife of her father's law partner, Lou Steinberger, and not related at all. But to Ariah the Steinberger's had been "Aunt" and "Uncle" for as long as she could remember, and, in truth, they were the closest thing she now had to blood relatives.

Except for Uncle Xenos.

Ariah's stomach clenched with the agony of a grief—and fear—so new she had yet to come to terms with it. Perhaps, if her father had not died so suddenly, so cruelly, if she had at least dared to attend his funeral, his death would seem more real. As it was, she had found it all too easy to push the painful reality aside for hours at a time during her journey west, to think only of the future the rattling, shrill-whistling train was carrying her to. A future that hadn't existed until a few brief days before her departure.

The hair at her nape prickled as she sensed Bartholomew Noon's gaze on her. Quickly she brought her emotions under control. She wasn't ready yet to talk about her father. Or why she had been forced to abandon everything comfortable and familiar in her life and agree to a marriage with a total stranger. The pain was too fresh, the fear too real.

Out of the side of her eye, she peeked to see if Mr. Noon was still watching her. He appeared so confident and competent, one boot braced on the front of the wagon, his arm resting on his thigh. What would he do if he knew of the danger that even now might be tracking her across the country? Certainly this man appeared strong enough to take on any foe. Even outraged Greek uncles. Squeezing her eyes shut, Ariah prayed that wouldn't become necessary.

"We do see sea lions now and then." His voice seemed to emerge from deep inside his massive chest, a sort of half-growl, half-caress that reached into Ariah and helped soothe her over-wrought nerves.

"Mostly they stay out on the seastacks though," he added.

Grateful for the distraction, Ariah said, "Seastacks?"

Without looking at her, he nodded. "Small islands of rock. Basalt, mostly."

"Oh. I thought sea lions liked to lie on the beach and bask in the sun."

"They do, but spending much time close to shore usually wins them a bullet in the brain."

Ariah gasped and clutched at his arm. "Why? Who on earth would shoot such gentle creatures?"

Bartholomew glanced down to gauge the genuineness of her reaction. What he saw pleased him almost as much as her deli-cate hand on his thick forearm. "Fishermen don't like anything harvesting salmon or shellfish but them."

"That's selfish. Why doesn't someone stop them?"

Her face was so close he could count the spikes of her lashes and see the pale tracery that made the blue of her eyes look like fractured glass. How he longed to cover her small hand with his own, to lean forward and . . .

Bartholomew gave himself a harsh mental shake. The girl

would soon be his niece, for God's sake. And even if she wasn't, Ariah Scott was a fragile, beautifully wrought piece of crystal, shining and pure. He was a clumsy oversized chamber pot. For him to think of her with such heated prurience was immoral.

"Don't the fish belong to the sea animals as much as they do to humans?" Her eyes altered to a periwinkle blue as her anger grew.

Bartholomew took a deep breath and froze his lust with an iceberg of guilt. "The fishermen are only trying to protect their livelihood, can't blame them for that. And the law is on their side. Anyway, until someone manages to see beyond his next plate of steamed oysters and gain enough influence to get things changed, there's nothing that can be done about it."

To his disappointment she removed her hand from his arm, leaving him feeling surprisingly bereft and alone.

For a long moment she stared blindly at the road ahead, her generous mouth pursed. When she spoke, her voice was soft and reflective as though she were merely speaking thoughts aloud. " 'The most vicious acts are done involuntarily.' "

Taken aback, Bartholomew stared at her in stunned surprise. Any female spouting Greek philosophy would astonish him. To hear it from a nymph of a girl like Ariah was both a shock and a thrill. With a grin so broad it used muscles he was sure he hadn't exercised in years, he offered a favorite quote of his own: " 'He who commits such acts is in a worse state than he who knows the good and wills it, but is overcome by passion—' "

" 'For the former cannot help doing evil,' " Ariah finished for him, her eyes dancing with delight. She had been right; his body might look as though it belonged on a wrestling mat or behind a plow, but it contained the soul of a poet. "You read Plato?"

"Some. Who taught you his philosophy?"

Did she dare tell him the truth? Surely it could not hurt to admit her heritage. "My mother. She was born in Crete."

His brows rose again in surprise. "You're Greek?"

"Only half. My father was English."

Bartholomew caught her use of the past tense when speaking of her parents, but he gave it little thought. He was too caught up in the pleasure of knowing he now had someone with whom he could share one of his interests.

"Plato had another teaching you might find fitting," he said.

"What is that?"

"That through the order of nature which God sustains, He sees to it that justice is always done."

Her eyes filled with anguish before she dropped her gaze and stared off into the distance. "I hope He does, Mr. Noon. More than anything in the world, I hope He does."

Her voice was velvet soft, yet vehement. So vehement that he wondered if she were still thinking of sea lions or of something much more personal. Her sudden vulnerability overwhelmed him with a need to protect her, cherish her. But he said nothing.

Soon Portland's bustling streets and thoroughfares were left behind. The road narrowed and became rougher. Houses grew smaller, more rustic, farther apart. Evergreen forests carpeted with ferns, rich green where the sun managed to infiltrate the deep shadows, brought soft exclamations of delight from the parted lips of Bartholomew Noon's young passenger. A few brilliant pink, wild azalea blossoms, brought on by the unseasonably warm weather of the past few weeks, provided a startling comparison to the more somber greens and browns.

Burying her grief in thoughts of her future home, Ariah said, "May I ask you something, Mr. Noon?"

He glanced down and saw with relief that the sadness had faded from her eyes. "Of course, anything you like."

Her gaze rested on the large, bare hands riding relaxed between his thighs, their grip on the reins seeming loose, though she knew he was in complete control. Capable-looking hands, the fingers thick but not overly stubby. Handsome hands, she decided, in spite of the small scars speckling deeply tanned skin. Were the palms tough and hard with old calluses, and how they would feel on her skin?

Flustered by her errant thoughts, she blurted out what was on her mind: "Is . . . is my fiancé, Pritchard Monteer, is he as pleasant to look at as you, or will I find him squat, pock-faced or half-bald?"

Bartholomew gave her a look of surprise, then tipped his head back and bellowed with laughter.

"No," he said when he finally controlled his mirth. "Pritchard's nothing like me. He's shorter, but certainly not squat. Actually, we aren't related by blood. His mother and my wife are sisters."

That brought up her head. "Your wife?"

"Yes."

Why did she find that such disappointing news? "She also lives at the lighthouse?"

"Yes." He cursed himself for the despondent note that crept into his voice. "There are two houses at the station, both new and well equipped, though we have no electricity, or even gas lighting, since we're so isolated. Hester and I live in one. You and Pritchard will share the other with the First Assistant Keeper, Seamus."

"Oh." She seemed to consider this. "Seamus is not married?"

Bartholomew chuckled. "That old seadog? He's well into his sixties, and so salty from his years on the sea that I doubt any woman could live with him. In the same room, anyway," he added, not wanting to alarm her. "Actually, he's likable enough and easy to get along with, as long as you don't mess with his pipe. Or his goats."

"He has goats? Are there other animals there?"

"Two milk cows, four horses, chickens, two goats and my Chinese pheasants."

He felt her gaze on him and couldn't help but look down at her. Her eyes glowed with excitement.

"You raise pheasants?" she asked.

The wagon jolted as the front wheel rolled onto a rock. She clutched at his thigh to keep from being thrown across his lap, and her breast flattened against his arm. His pulse doubled. He gripped the reins hard to keep from reaching for her. The wheel bumped down off the rock and the wagon straightened. Even after Ariah had righted herself and let go of his leg, a few seconds passed before he could speak calmly.

"One of our Oregon judges, Owen Denny, discovered these pheasants in Shanghai when he was consul general there about ten years ago," Bartholomew said. "Denny liked them so much he shipped several crates home to establish them here. I became interested in them about five years ago, but I was too busy tending my father's dairy farm then. That's one of the reasons I took the job as Head Keeper at Cape Meares, so I could start raising them. I sell live birds all over the country, to men who hope to establish them. Shipped a load off to Kentucky yesterday."

"How exciting. I love birds. May I help with them?"

He wished she wouldn't smile up at him like that, those blue eyes radiating such joy, her lush mouth moist and parted. It kept his pulse throbbing with a need he did not dare sate. He leaned farther over his knees to hide the evidence of her effect on him and said, "We'll see."

Bartholomew spent a goodly amount of time studying the lowering sky that afternoon. He didn't like the look of the clouds rolling up from the south. Oregon had been enjoying the warmth of an early spring, but he knew that could quickly change. Now dusk was just around the corner. One more hour could see them at the Olwell place. He wiped a hand down the back of his neck. The image of Nehemiah Olwell's bushy white brows raised to his fading hairline at the sight of Miss Ariah Scott made Bartholomew sweat.

Nehemiah was a Baptist circuit preacher. In good weather, he rode a swaybacked mule to the settlements, bringing The Word where it might otherwise never reach. Nehemiah's sons Joe and Lemuel worked the homestead. Along with their wives and a pack of children as wild as timber wolves, the two younger Olwells shared the house with their parents and an unmarried sister called Toots.

Toots. Bartholomew had had a hunch for some time now that her interest in him was less than proper. The thought—to his shame—had provided fuel for more than one unwonted fantasy on nights when he became overwhelmed by needs his conscience and Hester forbid him to sate.

A nighthawk darted up from the rutted road, startling the horses and eliciting cries of excitement from Ariah. Bartholomew firmed his grip on the reins and brought the team under control. Between the mossy trunks of Douglas firs the sinking sun reflected muted shades of coral and orange off low-banked clouds. Soon it would be dark and he would have to find a place to spend the night.

Miss Scott had made no complaints about the long hours sitting on a hard, bumpy wagon seat. But there was a definite droop to her shoulders, and her straw bonnet failed to hide the bluish shadows under her eyes or the thickly lashed lids threatening to close over those unforgettable eyes. He had to make up his mind; the Olwells or a camp in the wilderness—just the two of them.

As though feeling his gaze on her, she straightened her spine and tucked a wayward strand of hair behind a delicate, seashell ear. Her stomach rumbled. She clapped a hand to it and gave him a wan smile.

Bartholomew made his decision. "There's a stream a little way ahead. We'll stop there."

Though he didn't bother to examine his motives, he didn't lie to himself either. Bartholomew never hedged at looking reality in the eye. If his interpretation tended to be a bit pessimistic, that was another matter.

He wanted Ariah to himself. Nehemiah's disapproval of a married man traveling with a woman who was not his wife was only a convenient excuse.

The thought of spending the night only a few feet away from her, smelling her subtle scent of lily of the valley and femininity, listening to her soft breathing, and imagining what that luscious mouth would taste like, how she would feel beneath his exploring hands . . . Hell, it was headier than a bottle of old Seamus's demon rum.

"I think I hear the stream." Ariah squirmed with enthusiasm. Her arm brushed his, and a charge, like the electric currents they were using in Portland now to create light, sizzled through his body.

"Won't be long now." He smiled, leaning into the current, rather than away.

Ariah returned the smile, causing his insides to tighten. Then her head swiveled as a piercing whistle cleaved the air.

"That's the train to Yamhill," he said. "The tracks pass quite close here."

The team broke out of the trees into a clearing. The wide stream meandering through was easy to spot, shining silver and orange in the last rays of sunlight. Dusk hovered, adding mystery and intrigue to the lonely spot.

Bartholomew brought the horses to a halt well off the road. He jumped to the ground and hurried around the wagon before Ariah could climb down. Looking up at her, he held up his hands. Without a moment's hesitation, she braced her palms on his shoulders and let him lift her into the air.

His hands were so broad they embraced her entire midriff, the tips of his thumbs nearly reaching the under sides of her breasts. His breathing quickened. For several seconds he battled an impulse to pull her against him. If Ariah noticed that he held her longer than necessary before setting her down, or if she heard the wild hammering of his heart, she gave no sign. Her hands slid slowly down his muscular arms, coming to rest lightly below his elbows while she gazed up at him through the fading light.

The sight of those lips so close to his blocked sanity and reason from his mind. Caught up in the romance of twilight and the blazing sunset, Bartholomew lowered his head toward hers.

"Hey! Bartholomew, is that you?"

Bartholomew's head snapped up. His hands fell from Ariah's

tiny waist and he jerked himself away as though caught pilfering coins from a collection box.

A horse and rider appeared out of the darkness along the river bank. Bartholomew stepped out from the wagon for a better look. Then his heart, which had dropped into his stomach, fell the rest of the way to his feet.

"It's me," he said. "How are you, Joe?"

Joe Olwell pulled up a few yards short of the wagon and slid to the ground. A few years older than Bartholomew, he was taller but only half as wide. "Good, by golly. Good as a Sunday afternoon with chicken frying, the kids off chasing roosters and the wife smiling that 'Let's make hay' smile o' hers. Don't get no better'n that, do it?"

Bartholomew chuckled. "I reckon not. But what are you doing here?"

"Fishing, what else? It's Saturday, ain't it?"

Bartholomew nodded and shook Joe's hand. Fishing was Joe Olwell's passion. Every Saturday night found him waist-deep in slow-running water, a pole in his hand and hope in his heart. He didn't do it the easy way like the twins did, with fat wriggling worms few fish could resist. Joe tied his own flies instead. Trout killers he called them.

For Nehemiah and Lemuel—like Bartholomew—it was the pheasants, with their spectacular red eye-patches and iridescent rust-hued feathers, but in Joe's eyes nothing was prettier than a big sly trout.

Ariah stepped out from behind the wagon and Joe gave a soft, wordless exclamation of appreciation.

"What the g-golly dickens you got here, Bartholomew?"

Bartholomew's heart, which had somewhat resettled itself, dropped back down a notch. The fat was in the fire; there would be no way to get out of spending the night at the Olwells now.

"My wife's nephew Pritchard . . . you remember me telling you he came to work at the station as Second Assistant Keeper? He's getting married. This is his bride, Miss Ariah Scott."

Joe snatched his battered hat off his head and gave Ariah an awkward bow, his wide, nearly drooling gaze never leaving her face. She smiled and nodded, her hands clasped behind her back. The heavy knitted shawl she'd wrapped around her to ward off the evening chill parted, awarding the men a view of her slender, curvaceous figure set off by the brightly colored traveling suit.

Bartholomew heard Joe's sharply indrawn breath and sympathized. Although he had had an entire day to get used to the sight of her, his body still reacted to Ariah's beauty and sweetness with shock and sudden heat.

Joe sidled closer and whispered, "What's she doing here with you, Bartholomew? Running away with her, are ya?"

Bartholomew made a sound in his throat that could have been a chuckle but was closer to a choked gasp.

"No, Joe. She arrived in Portland this morning on the train. Since I had to see a crate of pheasants off to Kentucky, Pritchard asked me to pick her up and bring her back with me."

"G-golly dang, if you ain't the lucky one." Louder, he said, "Well now, you wasn't getting set to make camp here, was you? The house ain't no more'n a whisper away. You know the folks'd be hurt if you didn't spend the night."

Bartholomew bit back a grimace and brushed his hand down the back of his neck. "Didn't want to impose, Joe."

"Horse—" Joe flashed a glance at Ariah and didn't finish the colorful expletive. "You know Ma'd never call it imposing, even if you brought half a dozen folks along."

Joe gave the girl another long look and grinned. "And the twins . . . well now, reckon they're gonna consider this 'bout on a par with a Christmas morn."

Bartholomew frowned. He hadn't even considered the twins. They must be seventeen now, blond masculine replicas of their attractive mother, and all rampant sexuality. He took a protective step closer to Ariah, but before he could think of a reasonable excuse to refuse, she spoke up.

"We'd love to visit your family, Mister . . ."

Realizing his lapse in manners, Bartholomew quickly filled in: "Olwell, Joe Olwell."

Ariah blessed them both with a tantalizing smile. "Mr. Olwell, it's very kind of you to offer us shelter for the night."

Joe crushed his hat in both hands. Color suffused his face as he shifted awkwardly on his feet. "Naw, 'tain't nothing. Plain food and a bit of Bible reading from Pa is all, but you're welcome." He backed toward his horse. "Let's get going then."

Joe patted a wicker basket tied to the back of his saddle, along with a two-piece bamboo pole that cleverly fit back together when needed. "Got me the finest passel o' trout you ever seen. Ma'll be waiting with a hot frying pan when we get there." He winked at Bartholomew. "Better'n pheasant breasts fried in fresh churned butter."

Bartholomew let the jibe pass, not feeling particularly jovial at the moment. His fate was set. All he could do was lift Ariah back into the wagon, then follow Joe across the stream and on to the Olwell homestead.

Four

Ariah glanced about, wondering why Bartholomew had brought the wagon to a halt. Then she spotted three small yellow squares of lamplight in the distance and knew they had at last arrived at the Olwell house.

For the last few miles it had been all she could do to keep from slumping against Bartholomew's shoulder and giving in to the exhaustion that demanded she close her eyes and sleep. Strangely, now that they were here, the sight of the house with its warm glow of welcome in the windows brought the itch of imminent tears to the backs of her eyes instead of relief. Her hunger had gone beyond the growling stage. Her body felt as though she had been dragged every bit of the way behind the wagon, and her emotions were riding appallingly close to the surface.

When Bartholomew lifted her to the ground, fatigue and the long hours of sitting caused her knees to buckle. He caught her and held her tightly to him. Joe's voice, as he spoke to a boy who had raced out to take his catch, drifted to them on the brisk night wind. Nearer, beneath Ariah's ear, was the steady, reassuring thump of Bartholomew's heartbeat. She knew she should move away. But his strong arms felt so good around her, comforting, safe, warm.

"Are you all right?" he asked.

Ariah nodded and forced herself to step back. He did not entirely relinquish her, but kept his hands on her slender arms.

"Can you make it into the house on your own?" He bent down, trying to read her face in the darkness.

"I'll be fine. Truly," she added when he did not move. "Go and see to the horses."

"All right. Get into the house. I'll bring your bag."

Guided by the lamplight in the windows, she started toward the dwelling. She had gone only a few feet when she heard the first low throaty snarl. Ariah froze.

"Miss Scott?" Bartholomew's voice came from behind her, along with the clank of metal from the doubletree he had just unhooked. "Why are you standing there like that?"

She didn't answer. Couldn't answer. Her vocal chords were solid ice. As frozen as the blood in her veins. Only her heart still worked, and it was pumping double-time.

Another snarl came out of the night. When Ariah staggered backward, the dog lunged directly onto the path in front of her. Big. Black. Bloodcurdling.

Ariah felt its fangs sink into her flesh, though it had moved no closer. She experienced the pain, the terror, the ooze of blood from the nonexistent wound. In her mind she no longer stood on a dark Oregon road, but on a street near the Cincinnati home in which she had lived until she turned seven. Tremors of horror washed over her. Her mother's panicked wails. The doctor who came, shook his head and left again. Days of waiting, of being watched. Expected to foam at the mouth, howl at the sight of water. Expected to die.

The shuddering of her body and Bartholomew's hand on her shoulder brought her back to the present. But they didn't banish the terror.

Then he saw the dog. "Why, hello, Pudding." He brushed past Ariah to kneel in front of the Labrador.

Ariah sucked in her breath. Her hand inched up to her throat. Bartholomew would be attacked. She should warn him, say something, but all she could think was . . . Pudding?

"How are you, girl?" Bartholomew scratched the sleek dark head. To Ariah's amazement, the dog neither snapped nor snarled. Its tail wagged furiously as it attempted to bestow a sloppy lick on his face.

Bartholomew ruffled the dog's fur, then rose to his feet. In the reflected light from the windows he caught a glimpse of Ariah's face. Stark, staring eyes, grim open mouth. Terror. His smile faded. "Miss Scott?"

Her gaze never left the dog who sat now, perfectly calm, at Bartholomew's feet. He put a hand on her arm and felt her tremble. "Are you afraid of Pudding?"

Ariah didn't answer, didn't move.

"Good hell, woman!" Not knowing what else to do, he pulled her to him, wrapped his arms around her and stroked her back. "It's all right. Pudding is as harmless as a kitten. Believe me."

She shivered and swallowed hard. Tilting up her chin with his finger, he forced her to take her eyes from the dog and look at him.

"Dog . . ." she said in a low quavering voice. "When I was five . . . rabid . . . bit me."

Gently, he replied, "If it had been rabid, you'd be dead."

She made a small jerky movement with her head. "But it was days and days until they knew. The bite festered and . . ." Her voice trailed off.

Bartholomew felt helpless. Never before had he held an hysterical woman in his arms. He wanted desperately to ease her fears. To make her feel safe. He didn't want to let her go. Embracing her was like embracing spring. All freshness and sweet, sweet softness. He thought how different his homecoming would be if this girl were waiting for him instead of Hester. Ariah would greet him with a kiss, and he would take her in his arms and rejoice in the knowledge that she was his, only his. No separate bedrooms, no waking up at night alone and miserable, his soul and body aching for completion.

"Bartholomew?" said a female voice in the darkness.

He whirled guiltily, releasing Ariah and putting space between them at the same time.

In the shadows stood a tall, solidly built woman some years

younger than him, though a good deal older than Ariah. Toots Olwell's gaze went from him to the girl and back again. The rigidity of her body spoke of suspicion and animosity. Anger and guilt warred inside Bartholomew. He had done nothing wrong, except perhaps in his mind, and even if he had done more than that, Toots had no right to accuse him. She was only a friend, like Nehemiah or Joe, whatever else she might wish for. "Hello, Toots. We ran into Joe upriver, and he insisted we spend the night."

Her gaze remained on Ariah. "Kipp said his pa had rode in. Didn't expect to find you out here though."

Bartholomew glanced down at the woman at his side. The terror had left her eyes, but she still looked dazed. Almost against his will, and knowing full well it was an idiotic move, he reached out to draw her near. "This is Ariah Scott. She arrived from Cincinnati today."

Toots's eyes on Ariah were hard and cold. Blast the woman. Hoping to head off trouble, he said, "Miss Scott and my nephew are to be married."

"What's she doing with you then?"

Impatience had him shuffling his feet. How many more times would he have to explain? "I picked her up from the train station. Just now I was reassuring her because she was frightened by Pudding."

Toots snorted. "That dog wouldn't hurt a dang spider."

"Miss Scott didn't know that. She was bitten as a child and is afraid of dogs. Understandably, I'd say."

Toots gave him a hard, protracted glare. "She don't look that scared to me." She turned and started back to the house. "Bring yer carcasses on in, we're about to eat."

"I have to see to the horses." He put his hand to Ariah's back and urged her forward with gentle pressure. "Go with Toots. I'll be along shortly."

Having sensed the other woman's enmity, Ariah preferred waiting for Bartholomew, but she forced herself to follow Toots

Olwell to the door. Pudding trotted alongside, tail wagging, tongue lolling.

The house was a shambling, haphazard affair. As the family grew, rooms had been added to the original one-room cabin, sometimes a step higher or lower than the last. When Bartholomew came in, he found Ariah standing inside the door, abandoned and alone, with over a dozen pairs of eyes riveted on her. Then one of the children discovered him and there was a mad dash as they all raced to leap on him. In the middle of the fracas, Nehemiah's wife appeared in the kitchen doorway near an enormous L-shaped dining table. She had hair as black as soot and a face like a dried peach, all ruddy and wrinkled.

"Food's on, get washed up, the bunch of you," she said. Surprisingly bright eyes swept the room, pausing momentarily on Ariah before zeroing in on Bartholomew. "Bart, you handsome devil you. Where'd you blow in from?"

With children clinging to every limb and hanging about his thick neck, Bartholomew nearly stumbled as he tried to go to the old woman. She strode to him instead, her skirts, as scandalously short as ever, swirling about her calves above oversized work boots. Youngsters scattered, shrieking, as the two adults clasped one another in an enthusiastic bear hug.

"Effie, you old doll, how are you?"

Effie slapped him playfully on the arm. "Watch that 'old' stuff, if you want to eat any of my vittles, boy."

"Okay, young'un." Bartholomew gave her a smacking kiss on her withered cheek.

"That's better." She sidled a glance at Ariah. Not bothering to lower her voice, she said, "She with you?"

"This is Miss Ariah Scott, Effie. She and Hester's nephew are to be married."

"You mean that young scamp, Pritchard? What kinda husband material is he gonna make? All he ever wants to do is play that stickball game."

"Baseball, Effie. It's very popular now, especially back East. He's a good hurler. That means he throws the balls for the strikers to hit. I think he's a better striker than he is a hurler, though. He often hits them clear out of the field, and gets a home run."

She gave an indelicate snort. "Waste of good time, if you ask me."

"Nobody asked." A big man with hunched shoulders and white hair rose from a deep chair by the fire.

Bartholomew withdrew from Effie and crossed the room to shake the old man's hand. "Hello, Nehemiah."

"Hello yerself." Nehemiah motioned to the children who had regathered about the fire. "You young'uns do as yer grandma said and get washed. Rest o' ya go on in to eat." He glanced at Ariah. "Bartholomew, like to have a few words with ya, if ya don't mind."

Ariah heard the hint of censure in the old man's tone. The rigidity in Bartholomew's shoulders as he followed Mr. Olwell from the room suggested that he, too, expected some sort of lecture. Because of her? She wished she could eavesdrop, but Effie was already dragging her toward the kitchen.

Toots handled the seating arrangements so Ariah wasn't surprised to find herself at the opposite end of the table from Bartholomew, between drooling twin teenage boys. The other woman took the seat next to him, then proceeded, following a lengthy prayer from Nehemiah, to fill his plate as though it were her right. Bartholomew accepted the dish in silence and avoided meeting Ariah's gaze.

And still she felt Toots's animosity. It radiated toward her like the smell of the fried fish and the draft from the ill-fitted window at her back. Throughout the meal, Ariah kept one eye on them, wondering what was between the two. It confused her to realize how much it disturbed her to think they might be lovers. It was none of her concern who Mr. Monteer's uncle bedded. Yet she liked Bartholomew. Knowing he was involved in that way with Toots Olwell would mar the respect she now held for him.

Toots was not unattractive. Her curves were generous and well distributed, her face was soft and feminine. But there was a crassness about her, in her speech, even in the way she ate her food—open-mouthed and oblivious to drool. Ariah firmly believed, no matter how outwardly obnoxious, everyone possessed some pleasant trait, something likable. But Toots was a challenge. Right now she reminded Ariah of the frigate birds who steal their food from others, rather than find their own.

After the supper dishes were washed and Nehemiah had finished the evening's Bible reading, he dismissed the family and ordered a pallet made up for Bartholomew in the parlor. Miss Scott, he said, could share Toots's bed. Toots stiffened. Her eyes, on Ariah, filled with resentment.

The thought of spending any more time with the woman than was absolutely necessary tied Ariah's stomach in knots. "Oh, please, I don't want to put anyone out." She glanced about the large room until she spotted the couch in front of the fire. "I could sleep on the couch, it looks more than adequate."

"Toots's bed would be more comfortable," Effie said.

"Truly, I'd prefer the couch," Ariah insisted. "I've inconvenienced people enough already, having to rely on Mr. Noon to get me to my new home and everything."

"But she's a guest, Ma," Toots protested. "I can sleep on the couch as easy as she can."

"Wouldn't be fittin' fer either one o' ya to sleep in the same room with Bartholomew, and you know it, girl." The room echoed with Nehemiah's stern baritone.

Eight-year-old Mark insinuated himself in front of the old man. "Bartholomew can sleep in my bed, Grampa. And I can sleep on the floor between my bed and Johnny's."

"Please, can he, Grampa?" Johnny pleaded.

Nehemiah frowned. Giving in was too much like relinquishing his position as head of the family, something that would be happening all too soon now that he'd passed his seventieth birthday. Effie, his dear sweet Effie, would call it a sensible compromise, but as far as he was concerned, compromise was only another of Satan's hand tools.

"Staying with the boys would suit me fine, Nehemiah."

Bartholomew ruffled first Mark's hair, then Johnny's. "I promised them a story before they went to sleep anyway."

"Very well," Nehemiah said with a sigh.

"Good, that's settled." Effie rubbed her reddened hands together with satisfaction. "Toots, fetch Miss Scott some bedding, then get to bed. Come on, Nehemiah, tomorrow may be Sunday and a day of rest, but you still need your sleep."

Mark tugged on Bartholomew's hand. "Come on. I wanna hear the story 'bout how you saved the people from the ship that sank."

At last everyone went to bed and Ariah found herself alone. Except for the slightly off-key sound of Joe's wife singing a lullaby to two-year-old Elly somewhere at the back of the house, all was quiet. Ariah retrieved her nightrobe from her satchel, turned out the lamps and moved to a dark corner to undress, in case someone felt a sudden need for a glass of water or something. She had stripped down to her underwear when Toots came in with another quilt.

Toots dumped the bedding on the couch and ran her gaze up and down Ariah's slim figure. Tiny tucks alternated with strips of Platte lace beneath the square neckline of Ariah's combination chemise and drawers. Matching tucks and lace decorated the legs. Over this undergarment Ariah wore a short Paris corset of black Italian cloth trimmed with embroidered insets.

"Fancy." Toots rested her hands on her own curvaceous hips and thrust out her ample, uncorseted breasts. "Too bad you ain't got more to fill it out with."

Ariah gave her a startlingly beautiful smile. "Yes, but I'm young. Seeing you gives me hope that in another five years or so I may be equally as well endowed."

Toots's hazel eyes widened, then narrowed. Her lips drew back from her teeth in a snarl. "Why, you little—"

"Toots." Effie stood in the doorway. "Run along, dear, and let Miss Scott finish getting ready for bed."

After a last scowl in Ariah's direction, Toots stalked from the room. Effie sighed and shook her head as she watched her daughter go. Then she turned to Ariah. "Here you are, dear. I brought you a pillow."

Ariah thanked her and bid her good night. Finally dressed in her nightrobe, she went to gaze out the window. So much had happened that day, and it had been far too long since she'd had a moment to herself. She needed time to think, and to remember.

Bartholomew let himself in through the back door off the kitchen—a different door from the one he'd used to leave the house—and headed up the hall, pausing at the parlor doorway. The look he'd seen pass between the twins when it was decided Ariah would sleep in the parlor gave him a convenient excuse to make certain they weren't spying on her as she undressed. The thought that he might be the one to catch her half-naked caused the blood to curl and heat low in his abdomen. He ignored the guilt niggling at his conscience and peeked inside the room.

Folded quilts lay on the couch, but there was no sign of Ariah, or the twins. The lamp was out, the room dark. Then he detected movement by the moon-washed window and saw her gazing out at the cloud-streaked sky.

Hair tumbled down her back to her knees in gentle waves, a wild array that made him want to tangle his fingers in it, bury his nose in the fragrant tresses. In the shadowed light he saw that she wore only a nightrobe of muslin with lace high at the neck and about the wrists.

Virginal. Except that he could barely detect her form through the thin fabric, silhouetted against the moonlit window.

Her shoulders rose slightly as she took a deep breath, and the cold glass fogged as she exhaled. With a finger she wrote her name in large letters, the way a child would, then paused to study her work. Again her finger moved through the condensation, this time drawing four letters: *P-a-p-a*. Papa. Her head bowed until her forehead rested against the pane. She laid a hand carefully, lovingly, over the two words. He had to strain to hear what she whispered brokenly: "Oh, Papa, what will become of me without you?"

Not thinking about what he was doing, Bartholomew crossed the room. He forgot Nehemiah's earlier lecture. He forgot Hester and the rules of propriety. He saw only Ariah, knew only that she needed him. When he put his hand out to touch her, she jumped and whirled about to look at him with alarm in her moist, stricken eyes.

"I-I thought everyone was in bed," she said.

"I went to check on the horses. I didn't mean to startle you." His hand tightened for an instant on her shoulder. "You were crying."

"No." Her back straightened, and she lifted her head. "I was just thinking of my father, and wondering if anyone's filled the bird feeders at home."

"You've lost your father, haven't you?"

For a single heartbeat her head bowed; then she forced it back up again. "I . . . yes, two weeks ago. It was sudden. I should be wearing mourning, but my father made me promise not to. After all, I'm about to be married and . . ." Her voice trailed off as she stared miserably out the window.

"Is that why you agreed to marry Pritchard, because you're alone now?"

She looked at him, her eyes surprisingly dry, and for a moment he thought he saw fear in their blue depths. But how could anyone as gregarious and optimistic as Ariah Scott be afraid of anything?

"Shouldn't I have?" she said.

"No, it isn't that. Pritchard's a fine young man. But there must have been dozens of fellows in Cincinnati you could have married. Men you knew."

His compliment brought a small smile to her mouth, and a bit of the sadness left her eyes. "One or two, perhaps." It was a lie; no man had ever asked for her hand, but she wasn't about to tell him that.

"Only one or two? Cincinnati men must be blind then, as well as stupid."

Her cheeks flushed a delicate shade of rose, like the dawn sky when it first begins to color, and she turned quickly back to the window. Bartholomew lifted his hand. It hovered above her head, aching to stroke her tawny mane, then fell to his side. If he were to touch her at that moment, he feared he wouldn't be able to stop.

"You're much too kind, Mr. Noon. I don't blame you for questioning my motives out of concern for your nephew. I assure you I intend to be a good wife to him."

"I've no doubt of that." An image of Hester's locked bedroom door intruded into his mind, along with the inexplicable certainty that Ariah would never do the same. "He's a very lucky man. Actually, it was you I was concerned about. It must take a great deal of courage to travel alone clear across the country to put your life into the care of a stranger."

His sensitivity brought emotion surging back into her. How could he be so perceptive as to know exactly what was on her mind? She longed to tell him of her fear, to bury her face against his chest and take what comfort he might offer. But that would be the coward's way out, and unfair to Bartholomew, as well as to his wife.

Swallowing her tears, she put her back to the window and to the dreams in which the moon invited her to indulge. The smile she forced to her lips was wistful, but her voice was steady.

"There's nothing left for me back home, Mr. Noon, except loneliness. At least here I have the excitement of new surroundings and the challenge"—she thought of her exhilaration a few weeks past when she had received notice that she had been accepted into the Cincinnati Society of Ornithologists and her voice faltered, but she forced up her chin and continued—"the challenge of a new career."

Bartholomew's brow lifted at her choice of words. He'd never thought of marriage as a woman's career choice before. Ariah Scott was definitely different from the women he'd known in

Tillamook, or in Corvallis where he'd attended the university for almost a whole term before his father's paralysis forced him back to the farm. He thought of the free spirits he had met on campus, carrying banners and cursing the traditions that kept women tied to home, hearth and husband. Ariah was intelligent and independent. She might not follow any traditions but her own, yet he was sure she would never scoff at the beliefs of others or try to force them to think her way.

Good hell. He'd only known her a day, and already he was half in love with her.

He took a strategic step backward. "I admire your optimistic outlook on life, Miss Scott. I'm sure no matter where you are, you'll make a niche for yourself and create your own happiness. I'd best let you get to bed now. The boys are waiting for me."

"First, I think I'd better . . . ah . . ." A slow flush reddened her cheeks. "Could you possibly direct me . . . ?"

Bartholomew hid a smile. "The necessary's out back. Come on, I'll point it out and make sure Pudding behaves herself. You'd best put on a coat, it's cold out."

She looked down and gasped with the sudden realization that she had been standing there talking with him dressed only in her nightdress. She clasped her arms over her breasts and glanced up, but he had his back to her as he made his way to the kitchen, giving no indication that anything out of the ordinary had happened between them. Ariah snatched up her cloak and followed.

When she rejoined him after using the necessary, he saw her back to the parlor where her bed awaited, said good night, doused the lamp and vanished down the crooked, darkened hall.

Ariah snuggled into the warm quilts and wondered what Effie had meant about Mr. Monteer not making good husband material. A fondness for baseball was hardly a good reason to scorn a man as a husband. She hoped he would be gentle and sensitive like his uncle. Bartholomew Noon had the most compassionate eyes she had ever seen. Eyes as dark as the thick Greek coffee her mother had brewed on holidays, sweet with honey and rich with secret meaning.

An image of Toots Olwell sneaking into Bartholomew's bed crept into Ariah's mind. At least, with him sleeping in the boys' room, the woman wouldn't be doing that tonight. Ariah yawned. As she drifted toward sleep, she imagined him lifting the covers to welcome her, then taking her into his strong arms. She felt the warmth of his huge body, watched his lips descend toward hers, and something strange and mysterious and wonderful stirred deep inside her.

Lying in Mark's child-sized bed, his feet hanging off the end of the mattress, the boys snoring softly in the darkness, Bartholomew thought of Nehemiah's lecture on temptation. The old man was right; spending so much time alone with a woman who didn't belong to him was a risky business. He'd felt it strongly, standing in the dark alone with Ariah Scott. The girl aroused his emotions more than any woman he had ever known, giving him visions of what might be and making him all the more dissatisfied with what was. It was perilous. It was wrong.

A sense of helplessness, so strong that he wondered if it could be another presentiment, haunted him. Then, like a driftwood log rammed into his solar plexus, reality struck home.

The sense of doom he had felt the morning of the shipwreck—the same day Pritchard had announced his forthcoming marriage—had had nothing to do with that tragedy. No, the threat of succumbing to an infatuation for another man's woman, this was what he was being warned about. This was the debacle he had to prevent.

Silently he prayed that the clouds crowding the sky outside the bedroom window would pass on and leave a dry, open road to get him and his much too attractive ward home as quickly, as safely and as innocently as possible.

Five

Nehemiah insisted on praying for their safe journey as Bartholomew and Ariah prepared to take their leave of the Olwells the next morning. The sky had cleared, and the day promised to be fair.

Bartholomew bowed his head, but instead of closing his eyes, he studied Ariah's demurely folded hands. Tiny hands, as delicate as the fairyslipper orchids he'd seen in the woods near the lighthouse.

As the wagon pulled away from the house, he leaned close to Ariah and let the rattle of chains and the rumble of wheels cover his words. "Be thankful we escaped after only one prayer. It's Sunday so the family will spend the entire day listening to Nehemiah read from the Bible and pray over everything from sin to the laying of the hens."

Ariah clapped a hand over her mouth to stifle a giggle. Bartholomew's eyes sparkled as he smiled down at her. He didn't try to analyze his unaccustomed feeling of joy.

That evening, as they pulled back onto the road after eating supper at the inn in Yamhill, the morning stage from Portland barreled past in a cloud of dust. Ariah coughed and fanned her hand in front of her face.

"By the time we get to Fairdale, the passengers on that stage will be at the Mountain House digesting the venison or salt pork and cabbage they get for supper," Bartholomew said when the dust settled.

"How much farther is it?"

"Nine miles. We've already come over fifteen since leaving the Olwells." He sidled her a glance and added, more casually than he felt, "Of course, if you'd taken yesterday's stage from Portland you'd be in Tillamook now, instead of having another forty-five miles to go."

"I'm glad you picked me up instead. The stage looks dreadfully dusty and uncomfortable."

"Are you?" he asked with an intensity that seemed to sizzle in the air between them. "It should have been Pritchard."

"Perhaps," she said. Then she smiled with a warmth he felt all the way to his heart, and added, "But it's been a lovely trip, and I've enjoyed your company."

Something tightened in his chest, making him quickly glance away. Her answer had meant too much, and he desperately wanted to kiss her for her kindness.

Ariah caught the intensity of his expression before he turned away and knew she had pleased him. He was such an emotional man. Yet proud. If he were a bird, he would have to be none other than an eagle, the most magnificent of all. But there was too much sadness in his eyes; and she wished she could wash it away.

After a while she said, "Mr. Monteer's wire didn't say why you were picking me up instead of him."

He searched her eyes for disappointment but saw only curiosity. "Mostly it was bad timing. The only way a keeper can leave the station for more than a day or so is to arrange ahead of time for a man to fill in for him. I had already arranged for my trip and couldn't cancel. Shipping the birds later would have interfered with mating season. I'm sorry he didn't explain it to you."

Her full lips quirked in a wry, sad sort of smile. "It was all rather sudden."

Too sudden, he wanted to say.

"It doesn't really matter," she said then. "I've enjoyed getting to know you, Bartholomew."

The sound of his given name on her lips stroked him like a caress. He swallowed a surge of emotion and busied himself driving the wagon as darkness settled over them.

That night was spent at The Mountain House in Fairdale. By noon the next day it was raining, a gentle mist that seeped beneath their oil slickers. The temperature dropped ten degrees, forcing them to huddle together on the wagon seat, sharing body heat but very few words. From Fairdale the road went straight up, zigzagging across the snowy mountain face to the summit, seventeen miles to the tiny store and inn operated by the Rhude family. When the rain turned to snow Ariah and Bartholomew joined the Rhude children in an impromptu snowball fight before retiring to the rooms allotted them for the night.

Late the next afternoon, as the road plunged down the mountain, along with the South Fork of the Trask River, a battle more turbulent than the storm pelting them with icy rain was taking place in Bartholomew's head.

Two more miles would bring them to the turnoff for John Upham's farm. It would get them out of the weather sooner, and off a rough, muddy road that was rapidly becoming treacherous. The last thing he wanted was to risk Ariah's safety, yet he found himself mentally dragging his heels at the idea of stopping with the Uphams.

What it came down to, if he were honest with himself, was that he simply didn't want to share her with one more person. Or explain again why they were traveling together. Tomorrow they would reach Tillamook and the home of the Ketchams, where Hester was staying while he was gone. The next day after that would see them home at the lighthouse station. There would be no more time alone with Ariah then, and Bartholomew wasn't ready for that.

Without warning, the lead horse on the left, slipped and went down on one knee, nearly dragging down the sorrel next to her.

Ariah cried out and clutched her cold hands to her mouth. Bartholomew yanked back on the reins. "Whoa. Easy there, Snowdrop. Get up, girl, come on now."

The mare struggled several minutes before managing to stand firm on all four feet. Bartholomew wrapped the reins around the brake and climbed down. Twenty yards below, the South

Fork of the Trask, swollen with snowmelt and rain, roared and tumbled and swirled. One slip and he would plunge to his death.

Ariah held her breath as he slogged through the slick muck, talking to each of the horses and stroking their trembling necks until they were calm enough to continue on. When he went to haul himself back up into the wagon, Ariah reached out to help, as though her puny weight could keep a hundred and ninety pounds of muscle, bone and sinew from falling into the watery abyss below.

Seated in the wagon again, he gazed down at her for a long time, lost in those bottomless forget-me-not eyes, his heart so full he thought it would burst from his chest. She was so close that he could feel her quivering with fear and cold inside her wraps.

How long had it been since anyone had looked at him with such concern? Not since '78 when his mother died, he supposed. Or was it six years later, the night he buried his father, when Hester crawled into his bed to comfort him? Guilt and a desperate kind of need had driven him to marry her the next day. Ever since, she had been berating him for not providing a better life for her. And punishing him with a locked bedroom door. The result was a brooding, cynical man who expected little from life and gave little in return.

Until Ariah entered his life and made him feel again.

Now, staring into her sweet, delicate face, he didn't try to fool himself into thinking that she loved him. It wasn't that simple. Ariah Scott cared about people. Hell, she had more concern for *animals* than some people did for humans. But that didn't lessen the gratitude he felt for the caring he saw in her eyes at that moment. Instead, he drank it into his soul, like a dry sea sponge takes up water, and felt a tiny part of himself come back to life, the part all the years of nursing sick parents had drained, the part Hester had nearly killed.

The urge to take Ariah into his arm, to try to absorb her into his starving body, to lay his claim on her and make her his, was so strong he shook with the effort to hold himself still. He couldn't speak. Didn't dare speak. Didn't dare move. Except to give the reins a flick and shout "Gee-up."

The wagon eased into motion and the world took on a semblance of normalcy, until a rear wheel skidded in the slime and began to slip toward the embankment on the river side. Ariah clasped her hands once more over her mouth and buried her face against his shoulder.

"Steady, steady," Bartholomew crooned to the horses.

The wheel wobbled, then sank back down into an old rut carved by frequent use. Ariah let out her breath, straightened and dropped her hands to her lap. Gazing down at her, his control once more in place, Bartholomew flashed her an encouraging smile.

"We're all right." He laid his big gloved hand over her smaller one and gave it a squeeze. "I've driven this stretch a dozen times in weather like this, and as you can see, I'm still here to tell about it."

She peeked up at him from under the hood of her slicker and bravely returned his smile. He debated whether or not to explain their options and let her choose. The ideal, as far as he was concerned, would be their own camp along the river. Alone. Foul weather precluded that; they had no tent, nothing to give them shelter except the wagon and a gutta percha tarp which wasn't nearly good enough. The only other option, besides John Upham's place, was Trask House, five miles beyond. The Crenshaws would undoubtedly be curious about his traveling with a young woman, but they'd be too busy taking care of customers to do much prying, so Bartholomew would have Ariah mostly to himself. Until bedtime anyway. It was more than he'd have at John Upham's.

The question was, How bad was the road ahead? Darkness impeded his view. He couldn't allow his need to be alone with Ariah to place her in danger. Bartholomew cast her a glance out of the side of his eye, his mouth a hard straight line as he struggled with his conscience. The right thing would be to stop at John's as he'd said he would. The right thing would be to stop thinking of Ariah Scott as *his*.

Good hell, was that what he was doing?

There was no denying it; his need for her was becoming as great as that for food or breath. He had tried to fight it, but from the moment he'd first laid eyes on her, his soul had been soaking up her sweetness until he could think of nothing else. She was like an addiction now, worse than morphine to a wounded soldier.

His indecision carried them past Upham's. The road grew steadily worse. The instinct to survive took over his thinking processes, though he spared a moment now and then to curse himself for not getting Ariah to safety when he'd had the chance.

Two miles past Upham's the wagon rounded another bend and rolled toward an inward curve where memory told him a bridge crossed a rocky ravine. Full dark was upon them and Bartholomew's vision in the driving rain was nil.

Suddenly the lead horses pulled up short. Whinnying in panic, they tried to back into the horses behind them. Cursing under his breath, Bartholomew took firm hold of the reins and strained to see what was scaring them while he brought them under control. He could see nothing of the bridge or the road ahead. The flooding river was roaring so loudly he had to shout into Ariah's ear to be heard.

"Can't see what the problem is. Have to get down and take a look."

Ariah kept her terror in check as she watched him set the brake, secure the reins and climb down. He soothed each horse with a pat on the rump as he made his way past. Watching, Ariah prayed that should he slip, he would be able to grab hold of the traces and keep from plummeting into the swirling, raging waters below.

Mud sucked tenaciously at Bartholomew's boots as he worked his way to the lead horses. The wind lifted the hood of his slicker from his head and whistled shrilly in his ears. He swiped rain from his eyes and squinted into the murky darkness, seeing nothing. He dug a match out of his pocket and struck it on a bit of metal on the undercarriage that he hoped was dry. The match flared to life, creating a dim circle of light.

He peered into the rain and swore.

Where the old wooden trestle should have been—mere inches from where he stood—the road ended in a torrent of water and debris that plummeted wildly down a rocky gorge into the river below.

The bridge was gone.

Six

Bartholomew blinked against the onslaught of rain, and shouted, "Bridge is washed out. I'm going to back the wagon up, in case part of the road goes, too. Keep a firm grip on the reins while I direct the horses from down here."

Ariah retrieved the reins from the brake handle with trembling fingers and nodded to let him know she understood. Rain poured down his face, slowing when it reached his jaw where his beard was coming in thick and dark, even though he'd shaved that morning. The moisture pooled at the tip of his strong chin, then dropped onto his yellow slicker to merge with the water already beaded on the sleek surface. Beneath her slicker Ariah's heart pounded with fear. Adrenaline hummed in her veins, demanding action. Somehow she had to hide her panic and help Bartholomew. Later there would be time to think about how close they had come to falling into that chasm and the raging water below. How easily they still could.

Time and terror sat on her shoulders like twin gargoyles of doom, weighing her down as she struggled to catch the orders Bartholomew bellowed and the wind tried to snatch away. The thought of backing the wagon around the curve on this slippery road was even more horrifying than trying to turn it completely around. On one side was the sheer rise of the mountain, on the other, the drop-off to the river, with barely enough room for a rider to get by. She tried to remember if they had passed any spots along the way wide enough to turn around in and found her mind a blank.

The horses continued to whinny their fright, but Bartholomew's calm voice and sure hands kept them under control. The wagon jarred as the wheels fought to break out of the old ruts and go straight instead of following the curve of the road.

Ariah's breath caught. She craned to see how close they were getting to the edge. Wind whipped rain into her face. She blinked to clear her eyes. Beyond the end of the wagon everything was black. At any moment she expected to feel a wheel drop over. If that happened, she must contain her terror and jump off the far side. But hysteria was already threatening, making her skin prickle.

Then the wagon jolted again, nearly throwing her off the seat. The rear wheel lifted. When it dropped back down she felt it slide, jerking the wagon closer to the ravine. Her stomach hung, as if in midair, and for a moment, sickeningly, it seemed she was already falling.

"Bartholomew!"

Moisture filled her mouth as she screamed. His slicker was a pale yellow blur in the distance. Still clinging to the reins, she scooted along the wagon seat to the far side, preparing to jump. Above the sound of the rain she heard a faint rumble. The rear of the wagon on the river side dipped suddenly.

"It's going!" she screamed. "Bartholomew!

The wagon jerked to a sudden halt, tumbling her backward. She scrabbled frantically to grab onto something and screamed again and again.

"I've got you, I've got you."

A thick arm came around her waist. She found herself crushed against Bartholomew's broad chest, and murmured a silent prayer of thanks.

"I'm sorry," he mumbled as he frantically pressed his lips to her cool, wet skin, covering her with desperate kisses. "Oh, God, I nearly lost you. The edge crumbled and the wagon almost went over. God help me, if I'd lost you I would have died."

His lips felt amazingly warm on her cheek. Warm and alive. She wrapped her arms around him, ignoring the stiff slickers bunching up between them. The roar of the water faded. Fear receded. Time hung suspended. They were safe, and together.

"You're shaking." Bartholomew couldn't tell if she was crying or if it was only rain pouring down her cheeks. He pulled the yellow oilcloth back onto her head and tucked her hair inside. His throat felt tight. The possibility of her plunging into the river made his knees weak, his stomach queasy. All he could think was Thank God, thank God.

Too soon Ariah was lifted into the wagon. Cold and desolation set in the moment he let go of her. Her eyes clung to his dark face. If he stepped out of sight, she would die.

He had to shout to make her hear him. The world and the storm had returned. "Put whatever you'll need for the next few days into your valise. We'll have to leave the wagon here."

"Where will we go?"

"I have friends two miles back. We'll ride the horses, it won't take long."

As she gathered together what they would need, her ears searched out the faint clink of metal and the nervous snorts of the horses as Bartholomew unhitched the team. She needed these confirmations of his presence. She stuffed the oilcloth-wrapped leftovers from their noon meal into her valise along with a change of clothing. Then, on impulse, she fished among her dresses until she found a framed photograph of her parents and a beaded bag that contained her old baby brush and spoon, swaddled in her mother's hand-crocheted dresser scarf. To lose those, should the wagon end up in the river, would be more than she could bear. Bad enough to leave behind her books and the gaily colored plates her mother had brought from Greece. But the bag would only hold so much. For a moment she stroked the satiny glazed surface of a plate and gnawed her lip as she eyed Bartholomew's battered leather satchel.

By craning her neck, she could see that he was still busy with the horses. Knowing her mother would scold her for her impulsiveness she tucked first one plate, then another among his garments. By the time she'd fit in all four, protected by Bartholomew's shirts and—she blushed to think of it—his underwear, the bag was so full it nearly refused to fasten shut.

"Are you ready?"

Ariah whirled guiltily at the sound of his voice beside the wagon. "Yes."

"Good, can you ride bareback?"

"I-I've never ridden a horse before."

"You'll have to ride with me then. Hand me the bags."

With a rope he had scrounged from the wagon he tied the two bags together, frowning in puzzlement as he hefted his own. Then he slung them across the mare's broad rump, like saddlebags. After fetching his rifle from beneath the wagon seat, he mounted, positioning himself well back on the mare's rump. He laid a folded blanket over the harness gear to make a more comfortable seat and helped Ariah on. While she arranged her skirts to cover her legs, Bartholomew slid his arms around her waist and took up the reins.

Ariah could have sworn it took them a week to travel the two miles to the Upham place. The dampness and cold had seeped into her bones, chilling her thoroughly inside and out. Her bottom and her inner thighs ached. She comforted herself with thoughts of hot coffee and a warm bath when they reached Bartholomew's friends.

While they rode, Bartholomew told her how he and John Upham had grown up together in Tillamook.

"Heaven only knows why we became friends. John used to complain of what a bore I was, because I always had my nose in a book." Bartholomew chuckled. "All he cared about was having his own farm someday. The only true common ground we shared was animals; him to raise and profit by them, me to doctor and shelter them."

"Doctor them?"

"Yes. I wanted to go to veterinarian school. After my mother died, I went to Corvallis University to complete my schooling, but a few months later my father was gored in the spine by a bull. It left him paralyzed, and I had to return home to take care of the farm."

"Didn't you have brothers or sisters to help?"

"Two brothers, one sister, but they were all married and gone. Hester was there to see to the house and most of the nursing, though. She came shortly before my mother passed away and stayed on as housekeeper for my father."

"I see."

Bartholomew glanced down and saw the question in her unforgettable blue eyes. He smiled ruefully. "I was young and full of resentment. Hester had had a rough life. It seemed to create a bond between us." He shrugged. "Anyway, I married her."

A mile or so down a track that veered off from the road, they came to a log house. No light shone from the windows. Ariah moaned in dismay. "No one's home."

"It's all right, the door won't be locked."

Ariah resisted the urge to kiss the puncheon floor on which she found herself standing when she stepped inside. Within a few moments, Bartholomew had a kerosene lamp lit. The light spilling across the floor gave a welcome sense of comfort and cheer.

"You'd best get out of those wet clothes." He added a log to the small blaze he'd got started in the fireplace. "I have to get the horses in the barn. Maybe there'll be something there to tell me where John and the family are."

Ariah was holding her hands out to the blaze and studying several framed photographs displayed on the mantel when she noticed a paper propped against a vase. "There's a note here addressed to you.

Bartholomew carried the letter to the lamp and turned up the light.

Bart,

Sorree we could not be hear when you come back. Littil Johnny look a bad fall from the barn loft and brok his leg bad. We ar taking him to Doc Woolsey. Mak urself to

hom and if we do not get back in tim mabe we will see
you on the road.

Yore friend
John

    P.S. Shood be hom tomoro but we wood be gratful if
you cood feed stock.

Bartholomew chuckled and handed the note to Ariah. "Since
spelling has nothing to do with the price of hay or the produc-
tion of cheese, John pays little attention to it. The way he looks
at it, it's pure foolishness to waste time worrying about silent
e's when the only sensible way to do it in the first place is
phonetically."

With the Uphams in Tillamook—on the other side of the
washed-out bridge—Bartholomew and Ariah would have the
house entirely to themselves. Bartholomew felt as though he had
been given a thousand silver dollars.

Ariah handed back the note, then pulled the pins from her hair.
She bent from the waist, letting the wet strands hang over her
face to the hearth while she finger-combed them in the heat of
the fire. Steam rose from the thick tresses and even from her
skirt, filling the room with the smell of damp wool and lily of
the valley.

Bartholomew clenched the paper tightly to keep from plunging his own hands into the fire-tinted mass of her hair, so absorbed in the sight that he was barely aware that she had spoken.
"What?"

"You usually stay with them, don't you?" she repeated.

He walked closer, drawn to her like a bee to pollen. "Usually.
I'd stopped on my way in to Portland so they knew I'd be passing
by again on my way home."

"Then it was because of me you didn't stop this time?"

She looked up and he saw the distress in her eyes. Cursing
silently, he said, "The inn was only a bit farther. I thought you'd
prefer the comfort of a bed." He gestured to the single bed in the
corner behind a bright calico curtain, and the ladder that led to

the loft overhead. "Here we would have been sleeping on the floor."

The lie was a small one; Olivia would never allow a lady to sleep on the floor. She'd have put John there instead and shared the bed with Ariah. With relief, Bartholomew watched the frown ease from Ariah's brow.

"I feel a tad guilty enjoying their home when they aren't even here," she said with a smile.

"Don't. John would skin me alive if I hadn't felt at home enough to stay. Olivia will be sorry to have missed you, though. She loves getting to visit with another woman, it's a treat out here where they're so isolated. You'd best get into dry clothes now. I'll see to the horses."

After he was gone, Ariah went into the bedroom. She placed her valise on top of the high bed and sat down to test the firmness of the mattress. What she wouldn't give to take a bath, climb beneath those lovely quilts and sleep for twelve hours straight. She didn't think she'd ever been so tired. But she needed to wipe up the mud they'd tracked in, then fix them something to eat.

When she discovered a bucket of water on the floor next to a washstand that matched the bed, she decided to compromise with a spit bath. The bowl on the stand held pinkish water. Beside it was a crumpled towel stained with blood. Olivia Upham's son must have suffered more than a simple break in his leg. Ariah scrubbed the towel to keep the stain from setting, then tossed the water outside.

When she finished bathing, she picked up the clean chemise and drawers she had set out. For a moment she stared at her corset, wishing she didn't have to bind herself up in it again. She detested corsets. How much more comfortable it would be if she could simply don her nightrobe and a wrapper. Would it be so very wrong? The impulse was too much to resist. Seconds later, primly covered by a blue, scotch-gingham wrapper that matched her eyes, she went out to prepare a meal.

When Bartholomew reentered the cabin his gaze went instantly to Ariah, who stood at the table, setting out bread, cheese and apples left over from lunch.

"I put on some coffee," she said. Lamplight fell on the long, loose braid that hung down her back as she turned to take cups and plates from the sideboard. Except for their night at the Olwells' when he had found her staring out the window in her nightdress, shrouded in shadows, he had never seen her hair uncovered and unbound. Now he saw that it was not so much brown as a rich dark honey. His fingers itched to free it from the braid and to stroke the fine golden tresses.

"Good, I could use something warm to drink."

The wrapper hugged her hips, making it abundantly clear that she wore no petticoats or corset. He stumbled over the wolf pelt spread in front of the hearth, too busy staring at Ariah to see where he was going.

"Do you want to change into dry things before we eat?" she said. As she swung toward him he detected the movement of her breasts beneath the thin garment. Desire slammed into him like a fist.

"Maybe I'd better."

He rushed off to the bedroom, where he could take several deep breaths and get control of himself. Fresh water waited in the basin on the washstand. Considering his state of arousal, he hoped it was good and cold. With his mind on cooling his ardor, he thrust a hand inside his bag in search of a shirt, and cursed as his fingers rammed into something solid. When he drew out the plate, he frowned in confusion. Then he noticed the Greek lettering on the back, and smiled. Later, wearing a clean shirt and trousers, his control reestablished, he took a seat at the table, saying nothing of his discovery.

In the awkward silence that accompanied their meal, he became increasingly aware of the popping of burning logs and the clink of china. One of Ariah's front teeth slightly overlapped the other and he found himself oddly charmed by that. He wondered if the enticing little mole on her lip would taste of the tangy cheese he was slicing. A shudder ran over him, causing him to jerk his hand. The knife clanked against the dish, bringing her gaze to his hands, then his face.

"I'm sorry, it's not much of a meal," she said. "There's food in the larder, but it seemed dishonest to take it somehow."

"Don't worry about that. John and Olivia would want us to help ourselves to whatever they have. That's the kind of people they are."

Ariah smiled. "I should have known that."

"Why?

"It simply stands to reason. They're your friends, so they're bound to be gracious and generous. Like you."

Without thinking, he said, "Hester might argue that."

She cocked her head and gazed at him a moment before saying, "Then she doesn't know you very well."

He stared at her. "You think you know me that well?"

The tip of her tongue emerged to lick away all traces of cheese from her fingers. "Well enough to know that you're compassionate, as well as sensitive."

"Passionate, perhaps," he said softly. *Hester would call it lust.*

Her gaze dropped to her plate. "I'm afraid passion is something I know little about. Carnal passion, that is."

Bartholomew sank back in his chair, legs weak, stomach quivering. How he longed to be the one to teach her. Ariah Scott was definitely not like most women. Hester would have cut out her tongue before she would have uttered the word carnal or any of its synonyms. According to Hester, sex had only one function—to produce children. Since she had been thirty when they married, and too old for child bearing, she claimed there was no need for them to share a bed. In frustrated rage, he had pointed out what a hypocrite that made her—considering her past. Forgetting her new role as a genteel woman, she cursed him in language that would have made old Seamus blush. Then she installed a lock on her door. And learned that locks can be broken.

His appetite gone, Bartholomew pushed aside his plate and rose to his feet. He crouched in front of the fire and prodded the embers with an iron poker.

Alone at the table, Ariah gnawed her lip, kicking herself once again for opening her impulsive, tactless mouth. Somehow she had offended him. She considered apologizing and decided it might be best to leave matters alone. "It's late, I guess I'll go to bed."

"Take the one down here," he said tonelessly. "I'll sleep in the loft."

In spite of her exhaustion, sleep eluded Ariah. She was still awake, lying on her stomach in the big feather bed and hugging the pillow beneath her head, when she heard Bartholomew bank the fire, then climb to the loft overhead.

Bedsprings squeaked beneath his weight. A boot thudded to the floor, then another. Softer sounds followed, the rustle of clothes, a sigh.

Ariah rolled over and stared up at the ceiling, trying to picture him in his nightshirt or whatever he slept in. Did men sleep the same way women did? Sprawled on their stomachs. Or on their sides, drawn up in a ball, like a child. She smiled in the darkness at the thought of a big man like Bartholomew Noon curled up like a toddler, his hair in his face, all sweet and innocent. Soon she would know exactly how men slept. As Mr. Monteer's wife she would share his bed. She would sleep beside him and learn at last what it was husbands and wives did together in the sanctuary of their marriage beds.

Once when her mother had friends visiting, Ariah had caught enough of their whispered conversation to know they were discussing the mysterious subject of marital relations. She heard their stifled giggles, saw one of them shudder in revulsion. Later she had asked her mother what it was that men and women did in bed. Demetria Scott had smiled, gently chided her ten-year-old daughter for eavesdropping, then explained that the marriage bed was where babies were created. It wasn't until years later that Ariah realized she still did not know *how* babies were created.

Soon, now, she would find out. Fear and excitement rushed through her at the thought. What if she didn't like this act done in the secrecy of a marriage bed? Once she found out what was expected of her, it would be too late to back out. No woman should have to go into such a binding commitment that blind. It wasn't fair.

Overhead the springs creaked loudly as Bartholomew turned over. He mumbled softly and thrashed about. Then she heard a sharp whack, followed by a curse.

Ariah sat up. "Bartholomew? Are you all right?"

The only answer was another thud and the cracking of glass. Or china. Her mother's plates!

Ariah shoved the bedding aside and hurried to the ladder, forgetting her wrapper in her panic. Holding up her gown with one hand, she climbed the wooden rungs until she could poke her head above the loft floor. Sitting on the far side of the bed, rubbing the top of his head, he was barely visible.

"You've hurt yourself!"

He started to rise, mumbled an oath, and plopped back down on the bed, yanking the covers over him as she stepped up onto the floor. "What in thunderation are you doing up here?" His voice held frustration and alarm.

"I heard something fall and I was afraid . . ." On the floor lay a broken china cup that matched those in Olivia's sideboard downstairs. A cup—not a bright, hand-painted plate. Her eyes moved back to him. He was still rubbing his head. Stepping closer, she said, "Here, let me look at it."

He jerked and pulled the covers higher. "Good hell, woman, are you always so impulsive? To barge into a man's sleeping quarters like this?"

"Yes." She paused, uncertain now of her welcome. "My mother always said it was my worst trait."

"Your mother was right."

"I'm sorry, it was only that I . . . Oh dear, you really will think terribly of me, but I'm afraid I've done something absolutely unpardonable. You see, I couldn't bear the thought of leaving my mother's precious plates behind, in case something happened to the wagon and just now, when I heard something break—"

A noise startled her into silence, something sounding oddly

like laughter. She stepped nearer, and yelped as her head brushed something hanging from the ceiling.

"Watch out." His voice held undeniable humor. "Little John has paper stars hanging all over the place. There's a moon too, and a few planets, I think."

Her hand found the dangling object. Her fingers made out the five points of the star, as well as the dry, rough texture of cheap paper. "Gracious Sadie, this ceiling is so low . . . No wonder you cracked your head. And look how short that bed is, you must be miserable there."

"I'll make out. Go back downstairs to your bed." *Before I pull you into this one.*

"No. I'll take this bed, you take the one downstairs. Come on, get up."

"I can't. Not until you get out of here."

"Why?"

"Because I'm not dressed."

Ariah lifted her eyes to the ceiling and sighed. "Mr. Noon, it's too dark in here for me to even see you in your nightclothes, and since the situation in which we find ourselves is not exactly the usual, I think we can dispense with worrying about such small matters of propriety."

Bartholomew couldn't help it, he laughed. "I'm afraid you don't quite know what you're saying."

"And why not?"

"Because I'm not wearing any nightclothes."

"You mean . . ." She retreated a step, then whirled around as realization sank in. "Oh. Oh, dear."

"Yes, oh, dear is right."

Ariah thought of his big, masculine body with its wide shoulders and narrow waist. She'd seen a picture once of a Greek statue of a male nude and couldn't help wondering if he would look as virile and shockingly beautiful as the statue. For one whole second she battled the sinful urge to peek at him over her shoulder. Then she gathered herself together and boldly turned to face him. All she could see were his shoulders and arms above the blanket he held. Resolutely, she shoved aside her disappointment.

"Very well," she said with a sigh. "I will return downstairs while you dress. Then we will trade places."

He found her waiting for him below. Dressed but carrying his shoes, he paused, his face close to hers as he grinned. "You are the most impetuous, unpredictable woman I've ever met, do you know that?"

Ariah heard the humor in his voice and faked a pout. "Am I truly that bad?"

He chuckled and moved closer. "No, not bad at all. Not to me, anyway. It's refreshing to find a woman who doesn't feel she needs to go into a swoon every time she's faced with something slightly . . . improper."

A delicious shiver ran down her spine as his breath wafted over her face. The warmth of his body so intimately close to hers heated her blood. She put out her hand, intending to push him away, and found her fingers tangled in the springy hair that covered his chest. She made a choked sound and jerked her hand back, but not before he'd seized it with his. Her breath caught as she stared up at him in the dim light from the banked fire.

For a long moment he gazed at her, his eyes dark, enigmatic, intent. Then he lifted her fingers to his mouth and lightly kissed each one. His voice was hoarse and ragged. "You'd best get to bed."

"Yes." Reluctantly she withdrew her hand, then turned and began to scale the ladder, agonizingly aware that he stood below, watching.

Bartholomew exhaled as she vanished from sight. He ignored the guilt that plucked at his conscience for having stayed there, admiring the flash of ankle and calf as she climbed. Painfully aware of the hardness of his body and the surging of his blood, he went to the bed and crawled beneath the covers. At once he was assailed by the scent of lily of the valley and he groaned. How on earth would he ever get to sleep surrounded by her smell and the image of her small body lying where he now lay?

<h1 style="text-align:center">Seven</h1>

The next morning Bartholomew rose early. He dressed and got fires going in the stove and fireplace, trying to be as quiet as possible to let Ariah sleep. When he returned from milking the cows, he stepped inside to the sounds of splashing coming from behind the bedroom curtain.

"Bartholomew? Is that you?"

The sound of his given name on her lips flooded him with warmth. "I brought the milk, where do you want it?"

"The milk? Why, I don't know. Is there something I'm supposed to do with it?"

A true city woman, Bartholomew thought with a grin. "It has to be strained and separated. When I get back from feeding the stock, I'll show you." He headed for the barn.

Dressed in a fresh shirtwaist and a draped wool skirt in emerald green, she searched for ground coffee and found only beans. Remembering how, as a child, she had occasionally helped the cook by grinding the coffee for her, Ariah searched out a grinder and set to work. By the time Bartholomew reappeared, the coffee was ready and a pot of oatmeal seasoned with cinnamon was steaming on the stove.

"Smells good." He closed the door against the chill of the rain and stood for a moment, savoring the odors and the feeling it gave him to find her there fixing his breakfast.

Ariah fetched a small tin of milk left by the Uphams in a cold box set in the kitchen window, and they sat down to eat. He said nothing about the lumps in the porridge or the chunks of half-ground coffee beans floating in his cup. Afterward, Bartholomew helped with the dishes, then showed her how to strain the milk.

"What if the cloth slips when you're pouring it?" she asked.

"Then you start all over."

Ariah faked a moan. Actually, she was enjoying sharing this chore with him. Then she remembered that he had said there were cows at the lighthouse station. "Will I have to do this after I marry Mr. Monteer?"

"Hester does it now, but I imagine she'll expect you to take your turn. There's butter churning and egg gathering, too."

This time Ariah's moan was not faked. She wasn't at all sure how well she would do at such tasks. Being outdoors was much more appealing to her than slaving over a hot stove. Or a butter churn. "Maybe I could just do the egg gathering, that sounds rather like fun."

His eyes sparkled with humor as he smiled down at her. "Enough to help me raid the henhouse in the rain? I still need to feed them."

She grinned back. "I'm not made of sugar, so I won't melt. Besides, I love the rain."

"Then let's go."

They wore their slickers, and Ariah sported a pair of little John's work boots on her dainty feet.

Inside the henhouse, Ariah reached out to stroke a ruddy Rhode Island Red perched on its nest. "Oh, they're pretty." The hen cackled shrilly, flapped its wings and pecked her hand. She jumped back, slipped on the fresh droppings that covered the dirt floor and would have fallen had Bartholomew not caught her about her trim waist.

"They aren't pets, you know." He set her upright, chuckling at the disgruntled look she gave him.

"Does that mean they have to be so unfriendly?"

In a flurry of feathers, the hens flew down from their roosts, startling her, as he filled the feed bin. She backed into a corner while the flock quarreled at her feet, pecking and squawking as they fought for the food.

"Go ahead and collect the eggs now," Bartholomew told her as he finished pouring out the feed.

Leery about turning her back to the ruckus going on at her feet, Ariah kept one eye on the chickens as she checked the nests. She exclaimed over each small brown egg as though it were a prize and nestled it carefully in her basket.

"I can't wait to see your pheasants," she said, as they left the coop.

"I should have taken you for a walk at the Olwells, we might have caught sight of a few. Nehemiah and I set a bunch loose there a few years ago, and they've done well." He chuckled. "In fact, last spring one of the pheasant cocks ousted the white leghorn rooster from the henhouse and took over its flock. Made Joe madder than two cats with their tails tied together."

Ariah frowned. "Gracious Sadie! How would two cats get their tails tied together?"

Bartholomew blinked as he stared at her, then broke into his rusty, deep-throated laugh, charmed almost as much by the expressive way she used her hands when she spoke as he was by her naiveté. "I'm afraid that's one of the ways boys sometimes entertain themselves."

"But how could they? It would be so cruel."

Bartholomew sobered, thinking of locked doors and broken promises. "There are a lot of cruel things in life."

Ariah's own thoughts turned solemn. "Yes, there are," she murmured, as they picked their way across the muddy yard to the barn where he'd promised her a glimpse of a litter of new kittens.

Bartholomew regretted souring the mood and was glad for the distraction of the kittens. Ariah sat on the hay-littered floor and gathered the five tiny balls of black and white fluff onto her lap. When one escaped back to its mother, it was thoroughly licked as though to erase the smell of human contact.

"When I was a child I used to dream of living on a farm with lots of animals." Ariah rubbed her nose against a cold wet kitten nose. "Have you always lived in Oregon?"

Bartholomew grinned. "You asking me or the cat?"

She feigned a look of exasperation. "You, of course."

"In that case, yes, I grew up here. I wasn't born here though. My father was easily bored and moved around a lot. He married my mother in Pittsburgh, where he was working as a barkeep in her father's inn. They had my brother John there."

With a scoop of his big hand, he rescued a kitten from tumbling off Ariah's knee and returned it to her. The kitten snuggled into the soft mounds of her breasts, and his stomach jackknifed as desire shafted through him.

"How many brothers and sisters do you have?" Ariah asked, unaware of the cause of his silence.

He flushed red, even though she hadn't noticed where he'd been staring. To get his mind off her bosom, he went to sit on an upended bucket while he inspected a broken harness he'd found on a hook.

"Three brothers, one sister. I never knew Richard, though. He died before I was born."

The kittens fell asleep in Ariah's lap. The mother, deciding perhaps that she wasn't going to get her brood back, crawled into the soft cradle of Ariah's lap and began to purr. Certain he knew how the cat felt to be in such a delicious spot, and feeling himself harden at the thought of placing his own head there, Bartholomew bent lower over the harness.

"Would you believe I was born in a covered wagon—during a stock stampede and in the middle of a thunderstorm?" he said, his voice a bit strained.

Ariah giggled and flapped a hand at him. "No. You're teasing me."

He held up a hand, palm out. "Honest Injun. Ma always teased me about having had violence bred into me because of it. She liked to call Calvin and Mary and me her 'three little bluffs,' because they were born in Council Bluffs and I was born near a place on the Overland Trail called Scott's Bluff. Every time she said it, Pa would ask, 'Does that mean John's the only honest one in the bunch?' "

They laughed. Ariah went back to stroking a silky kitten nestled against her chest, and he found himself fantasizing about testing the softness of her breast himself. Suddenly he could sit there no longer. Two minutes more and he would have her on her back. He hung up the harness and rose to his feet. "Do you believe the morning's gone already? I'm hungry."

Halfway back to the house, Ariah came to a dead halt. He followed the direction of her gaze and saw the Uphams' old yellow dog trotting their way. "That's just Bones. He's old and even more harmless than Pudding."

Ariah edged closer to Bartholomew anyway. "Does everyone have a dog out here?"

Enjoying her nearness, he put his arm around her. "A good dog is invaluable on a farm, keeps small varmints like possums and raccoons away from the chickens and warns a man if there's bears or wild cats about."

The dog stopped a few feet away, lifting its nose to whiff their scent. Bartholomew hunkered down and ruffled the dog's fur. Looking up at Ariah, he said, "Let him sniff your hand so he'll know you're a friend."

Not wanting him to think her a coward, she summoned her courage and edged a hand forward. Bones craned his neck, nostrils flaring. His pink tongue came out and swiped at her fingers. She yelped and yanked back her hand.

"See? He likes you." Bartholomew stood and gave her arm a reassuring squeeze.

Bones sat at her feet, tongue lolling, his thumping tail splattering mud everywhere as he seemed to smile up at her. Studying the mangy dog, Ariah said, "I believe I still prefer cats."

To her chagrin, the dog followed them to the house. Safely inside, Ariah hung her slicker on a hook. When she sat down at the table to take off her muddy boots, not particularly eager to mop the floor again, Bartholomew knelt in front of her and removed her boots himself—something he'd never thought to do for Hester. But even if he had, his wife would have found some reason to complain about it.

There had been a time when he'd tried very hard to make

Hester happy, until he'd decided that some things simply weren't possible.

He set the muddy boots aside, then sat down to remove his own. In her stocking feet, Ariah padded over to the stove to pour them hot coffee. The ordinary chores they performed made living there with her seem natural, right. He found himself wishing it were for real.

Seated in front of the fire, Ariah curled cold fingers around her warm cup, a wistful expression on her delicate face. "It must have been nice to have so much family. All I ever had was Mama and Papa."

"No aunts or uncles or cousins?"

"No. There was Uncle Lou and Aunt Ida, but they weren't truly related to us. Lou was Papa's law partner."

Bartholomew tossed down the towel and joined her at the table. "Law partners. Pritchard said his uncle heard about you through an associate. Was it this Uncle Lou who talked you into accepting Pritchard's proposal?"

"Actually, it was my idea. I acted as a secretary at the law office, so I first opened and read the letter from Mr. Monteer's attorney. When my father died, I remembered the letter. To leave Cincinnati and start a whole new life in new country seemed like a good way to put the past behind me, so I wrote and accepted."

"Why couldn't you have stayed on with your friends?"

"It was a complicated situation, Mr. Noon."

He walked to the fireplace. "This morning I was Bartholomew. I liked hearing you use my given name."

She glanced up and tried to smile. "I'm sorry . . . Bartholomew."

"Never mind." He knelt and poked at the logs. "Ariah, are you in some sort of trouble?"

Her eyes widened in alarm. "No, no, of course not."

Swiveling toward her, he caught her gesturing hand in his. His gaze on her face was grave and questioning. "If you were, I'd want to help."

Afraid she would start crying, or disgrace herself even worse by throwing herself into his arms, she retrieved her hand and got up to start lunch.

Bartholomew watched, white-knuckled from gripping the back of the chair to keep from going to her. If she were in trouble, it was Pritchard's business, not his. The thought didn't help, knowing how inept and insensitive the boy was. He studied the gentle curve of her back and the graceful arch of her head as she investigated a cupboard. How he longed to kiss that slender white neck. He imagined her turning in his arms and offering up her lips.

His blood heated and surged. His heart galloped like a stampeding steer. He gave a silent snort of laughter at the futility of it all; here he was suffering for the love of a woman he could never have, even if by some miracle she were to return his affection. He had never regretted his marriage more.

"Bartholomew?"

His head jerked up at the sound of his name.

"Will you tell me about Mr. Monteer? What he's like, I mean."

Bartholomew ran his hand down the back of his neck and grimaced. "Pritchard? He's young, twenty-two as of January thirtieth. Not tall . . . About your height, but nice looking." The words tasted like gall in his throat.

"Effie said he likes baseball," she prompted.

"With a passion. I doubt he thinks of much else."

Ariah smiled teasingly as she tried to open a can of beans with a knife. "You make him sound rather . . . shallow."

With a sigh, Bartholomew went to open the can for her, trying to think of something more complimentary he could say about his nephew. "He's healthy, honest, and he'd never hurt a soul. I'm sure he'll try his best to make you a good husband."

Their hands brushed as she took the open can from him, and excitement coiled low in her abdomen. After setting the beans on to warm, she mixed flour with baking powder and milk for biscuits. Her hopes for a happy life sank as she considered Bartholomew's lackluster description of her future husband.

Pritchard. How odd that she'd never thought of him as anything but Mr. Monteer, yet Bartholomew's given name came so naturally to her. She supposed it was understandable. After all, she had yet to meet Pritchard, while his uncle had come to seem like a good friend. She slid a glance to where he was slicing bacon on the sinkboard.

Few men were as handsome as Bartholomew Noon. It was more than his dark good looks and muscular body; he was intelligent, sensitive and caring; virtues Ariah cherished. Even his dark, brooding enigmatic side, which would put most people off, attracted and intrigued her. She didn't waste time being shocked by the fact that she wished he weren't married, but it did disturb her to realize she was already forming a dislike for a woman she had not even met.

"Tell me more about what it's like living at the lighthouse," she asked as she slid the pan of biscuits into the oven.

Bartholomew laid the bacon in a hot pan. The lighthouse; here was something easier to describe than his nephew. He launched into the task with enthusiasm. "The light itself sits at the tip of a finger of land that juts out into the ocean. The keepers' houses sit a thousand feet back. There's a barn too, and a large vegetable garden."

"Are there flowers?"

"Only the few that bloom on their own. Hester doesn't believe in wasting time on something that can't be eaten."

"What about trees?"

He chuckled. "There're plenty of those, a whole forest that covers the rest of the cape. Spruces, mostly. Hemlock, elderberry bushes, alders."

Ariah's face lit up. "How lovely. Are there wild animals in the forest? And birds?"

"Deer, wild hogs, rabbit, possum, a bear or an elk now and then. Over toward Netarts Bay there are wild cattle, little runty red mullies that originally came off a Spanish ship wrecked on Cape Lookout years ago. And lots of birds," he added.

"Oh, I can't wait to see it all."

Bartholomew's smile faded. He busied himself turning the bacon and tried not to think how much he dreaded going home. Hester would watch him like a starved vulture. He'd hardly dare speak to Ariah. And the thought of Ariah living with Pritchard, sleeping with him . . . Bartholomew's hands shook and a strip of the bacon fell to the floor. He scooped it up, rinsed it under the pump and plopped it back into the skillet. The hot fat popped and splattered.

Ariah put her hand on his arm. "Why, you're trembling. Have I upset you?"

Bartholomew forced his lips into a facsimile of a smile. "No, I was just distracted, wondering how long it would take to get the road repaired. It won't be an easy job, and they'll have to wait until it quits raining to even get started."

She removed her hand from his arm and stirred the beans. "Who will fix it?"

For a moment, he didn't answer. Ordinarily he would go himself and see what he could do, though he knew men from town must be aware of the problem and already forming plans. But right now, the last thing he wanted was to leave this house. Not as long as Ariah and he had it to themselves.

Her scent drifted to his nostrils, and his insides tightened in reaction. He wanted desperately to feel the texture of her skin, to taste those perfect lips. Perhaps it would be best if the rain ceased immediately so they could get out of there sooner. Otherwise, he wasn't certain how long he could keep from giving in to his urges. The black, iniquitous urges he had been fighting for years, but which had never reached such a burning fever pitch as now.

The next two days followed the routine set that first day. Bartholomew rose early to start the fires and tend the stock. Ariah bathed in his absence, then made breakfast. Afternoons were usually spent talking. Sometimes they argued, expressing differences of opinion on some point of philosophy as espoused by Plato or Socrates, or on the merits of Spenser's sonnets versus those by Shakespeare.

Tonight was no different.

"Have you read Emily Dickinson?" Ariah was seated on the floor in front of the fire close to Bartholomew's knee, he in Olivia Upham's rocker, his long legs stretched out before him and crossed at the ankles.

He shook his head. "I've heard of her, but I haven't run into any of her work yet."

"Oh, you'll love her, Bartholomew. She's wonderful, so fresh and unique. I have a volume of her poetry in the crate back at the wagon. When I get it open, I'll read you some of my favorites."

"I'll look forward to it."

Without thinking, he tangled his fingers in her hair. The rain had ceased for an entire hour that afternoon, and they had taken advantage of the lull to get out in the fresh air. Her hood had caught on the knot of hair on top of her head, pulling it loose when she'd removed her cloak after they had returned. He supposed she hadn't bothered to put her hair back up because it would soon be bedtime. Whatever the reason, it hung now in a glorious mass he couldn't resist touching. He brought a strand to his nose. It smelled of spring rain and lily of the valley. She glanced up with a shy smile.

"Your hair is like silk," he said in that half-growl, half-caress of his. "Thick, soft, shredded silk."

Lashes as lush as her hair lowered over blue eyes, but she did not move or protest.

"It reminds me of my mother's," he went on. "I used to brush it for her the last few years she was alive, when she no longer could. She enjoyed it, I think."

The lashes lifted, impaling him on twin shafts of brilliant blue.

"Was she ill a long time?" she asked.

"For years, actually. Apoplexy. At first it was mainly her memory that was affected. Sometimes there was temporary paralysis. By the end, she didn't even recognize me anymore, she didn't know any of us."

"And you took care of her?"

"I was the only one left by then. Except for Pa." He spread Ariah's hair over his lap like a shawl, running his fingers through it over and over. "Brushing it seemed to calm her. It was as long as yours, only dark, with a white streak that ran from one temple clear to the ends. She always asked me to plait it for her at night. I enjoyed doing it." To lighten the mood, he bent forward and gave Ariah a teasing smile. "Would you like me to plait yours?"

She cocked her head in a coy gesture he found slightly flirtatious, and entirely captivating.

"Do I appear to be incapable of caring for my own hair?"

"Yes," he said with a grin. "You look like a wood nymph, helpless and fey and in need of a keeper."

Her hair dragged sensuously across his lap as she drew it away. Her gaze was hooded by half-lowered lashes, her lips a pouty smile that exposed her teasing nature. "But you're a lighthouse keeper, not a nymph keeper."

"How do you know?" Bartholomew grabbed the ends of her hair and tugged gently. "Come back here and I'll show you what a good keeper I could make you."

Her laughter spilled over him with the softness of Oregon rain, as melodic as the song of a white crowned sparrow. "No," she said. "I'm not sure I trust you."

"Are you afraid I might tickle you or something?"

"Oh, no. I wouldn't allow you to tickle me."

"How are you going to stop me?"

He lunged for her, and they tumbled onto the thick wolf pelt covering the floor, rolling and giggling as he tickled her. She slapped at the big hands that seemed to be everywhere at once; her waist, her back, under her arms.

"You're cruel," she gasped. "Stop."

"Oh, no, you're my nymph, and must submit to my power."

"Never."

She rolled to escape the fingers digging under her arms, and

Bartholomew suddenly found himself cupping a soft, round breast.

Ariah went stone-still.

Bartholomew's breath caught. His grin vanished.

Ariah stared up at him, eyes wide with shock, lips moist and parted. Mere inches away. The pulse at the base of her neck fluttered with the mad velocity of a hummingbird's wings, and he knew with sudden and inexplicable clarity that she wanted his kiss as much as he wanted to give it. Filled with wild exhilaration, and tense with the knowledge that his control was already thin, he lowered his mouth to hers.

The kiss was light, a mere brushing of lips. Testing, tasting. He pulled back to take in her expression and found her eyes closed. Without opening them, she lifted her chin, as if in invitation.

Bartholomew moaned and succumbed.

Her lips quivered as they met his. He shifted his head to one side and deepened the kiss. Lily of the valley and the even headier scent of woman filled his nostrils. She tasted as sweet and fresh as exotic fruit plucked straight from the vine. Passion fruit, ripe and yielding. His senses reeled with the ecstasy of it. His hand tightened on her breast. The small husky sounds she made deep in her throat sent the flames of his passion soaring. He traced the luscious outline of her lips with his tongue, finding and exploring the texture of the exquisite little mole that had haunted him since the first moment he'd laid eyes on it. Then he nudged her lips farther apart and dipped his tongue inside. She gasped at this invasion and tried to move away, but he held her fast.

"Open for me, sweet nymph," he whispered against her lips. "Let me taste you."

A shudder racked her body as she surrendered to his demanding tongue. He swept the satiny inner surface of each lip and traced her teeth, finding and worshiping the crooked one he had come to adore. He groaned. "Ariah, Ariah, if I don't have you, I'm going to die."

Her voice came back low and tremulous. "What do you mean . . . have me?"

Bartholomew stared down at her flushed face. He had forgotten how innocent she was, forgotten his marriage, forgotten everything but his blind, wretched need for her.

"Good hell," he muttered. "What have I done?"

Eight

"Bartholomew?"

Ariah reached for him. Her skin prickled in the cold draft left in his wake as he pulled away from her and rose to his feet.

"I'm sorry, it never should have happened." He lurched to the door as though in pain, and took down his coat. "Go to bed and forget about it."

"I don't want to forget it, I want to understand." Ariah dragged her passion-drugged body to a sitting position and tried to shake off her confusion. "You say that if you can't have me, you'll die. Then you jump up and leave? What were you talking about?"

"Go to bed, Ariah." His voice was harsh. He pulled a slicker on over his coat and flipped the hood over his rumpled hair. "Forget it ever happened."

She stood up and stepped toward him, both hands held out. "How can I, when I don't even know what it is I'm supposed to forget?"

The door slammed shut behind him.

"Oh . . . *oh, hell!*" Ariah stamped her foot and swung back toward the fire, hugging herself against the chill that had swept in through the open door.

Blinded by rage and mortification, Bartholomew stomped through the rain and mud, seeing little and heading nowhere in particular. What had gotten into him? A few minutes more and he'd have taken her. He'd have stolen her innocence and in the process committed adultery. Not only against Hester, but in a very real sense, against Pritchard as well. He was scum. The most misbegotten, immoral lecher there ever was.

Hester knew it. Had from the beginning. All the years he had watched her move about his father's laudanum-scented house, with lust in his eyes and curses in his soul, she had known. And used it against him. Then, one scant day after he succumbed to his need for her and made her his wife, she locked him out of her room. Laughing from behind the door. Until he kicked it in, ripped the gown from her body, and all but raped her.

He hadn't touched her since. For several years she had mocked and ridiculed him every waking moment of the day. Her complaints were continual. The house he provided her wasn't grand enough, the furnishings not rich enough, her place in society—as his wife—too lowly. To admit that the needs of his body had for a time occasionally brought him low enough to consider going to her room and finishing what he'd started that night so long ago filled him with shame.

Now, heaven forgive him, he'd nearly allowed his vile lechery to ruin an innocent girl. Bartholomew's self-loathing at this moment could not have been more profound had he actually done the foul deed.

And still, he ached for Ariah.

The Upham house appeared dark when he finally returned, half-frozen and exhausted. Cautiously, he pushed the heavy door inward. A lamp shone weakly from the table where she had left it for him, turned low to conserve fuel, but Ariah was nowhere in sight. Breathing a sigh of relief, he eased the door shut and removed his outer garments, one eye on the loft in fear that she would hear him and come down. For a long time he crouched in front of the fire, until his toes and fingers quit tingling and his body stopped shaking.

Later, tucked beneath the warm quilts on the big feather bed, he stared into the darkness, imagining how it would feel to have her small body snuggled against him, their legs entwined, her head on his shoulder and her breath warm on his naked skin.

On a low groan, as his body reacted to the vision, he rolled over, closed his eyes and sought the oblivion of sleep. But even there she haunted him, dancing just out of reach in the midnight mist, covered only in diaphanous veils that fluttered behind her like ghostly wisps of sea fog.

The next morning, though tired and listless, he made sure he was out of the house before Ariah awoke, taking his rifle with him. The rain had ceased during the night. By the time Bartholomew had saddled Snowdrop, using John's tack, and ridden to the main road, the dawn sky had begun to lighten. He rode slowly, more eager to keep himself busy and away from the cabin than to reach his destination. Once, he shot at a deer grazing at the edge of a meadow. Hunting wasn't his greatest talent; the bullet passed a good six inches over the buck's back. The deer jumped, spun about at the same time, and disappeared into the brush.

The steep, curving road was in as bad shape as he had expected. The saturated earth had given way in more than one location, leaving the exposed side ragged as a saw blade. Mud slides and boulders half blocked the road in spots. He skirted the rubble, glad he would not have to get the wagon past these obstructions as well as the one that had forced him to abandon everything in the first place. When he rounded the last curve and saw the wagon waiting, exactly as he had left it, he smiled in relief.

Human tampering had not been his concern—no robberies had ever been reported on the Trask Toll Road. But a boulder or a slide could easily have bowled the wagon into the river thirty-five feet below. Only a few rocks lay about the wheels. The tip of a sapling that had been ripped from the earth rested across the tarp covering the wagon bed.

After dismounting and securing the reins, he dragged the sapling aside and flipped back the tarp to check for damage. Satisfied that nothing had been harmed, he refastened the covering, then walked beyond the wagon to the gaping chasm where the bridge had once been. The South Fork of the Trask was higher than he'd ever seen it, and more turbulent. A few beams from the old bridge could be seen jammed along the bank, but the rest had been washed away.

He studied the hillside above the road. The nearly vertical slope would be difficult to manage on foot, impossible on horseback, and in these mountains, any attempt to circle around the hill could take days and would likely only get them lost. There was nothing he could do but return to John's and wait for the rain to stop and crews to rebuild the bridge.

No doubt, John, worrying about his stock, would be among the first to cross the new span. Weeks could pass before that happened, however. He swung himself into the saddle and headed back to the house.

Inside the cabin he found the fire blazing and coffee warm on the back of the stove, but no Ariah. Pierced by a loneliness stronger than any he'd ever endured before, he left the carcass of the rabbit he'd managed to shoot on the way back, snatched a cold biscuit from a plate on the table and went back outside.

"Ariah? Ariah, where are you?"

The quiet seemed to mock him. Alarm skittered down his spine. Had something happened to her?

His long, swift strides ate up the ground as he checked first the outhouse, then the chicken coop. He was about to throw open the barn door when he heard the dulcet, slightly husky tones of a woman's laughter.

Ariah's laughter.

For one heartbeat Bartholomew froze, mesmerized by the sound and impaled on a sudden shaft of jealousy. Who in hell could she be laughing with in there? With his pulse pounding erratically and his blood heating the way he was becoming used to, the way it always did when she was nearby, he swung open the door and stepped inside.

"Oh, don't you like it up there?" Ariah crooned softly somewhere within the gloom of the unlighted barn.

Bartholomew paused while his eyes adjusted to the dimness. Then he saw her.

With her hair loosely knotted at the top of her head so that it puffed out around her face, Ariah lay sprawled in the hay, her legs drawn up beneath her skirt in a not too ladylike pose that exposed delicately turned ankles above little John's boots. High overhead, a kitten dangled from her fingers, mewing plaintively. Captivated by the sight, he watched her lower the kitten and nuzzle its silky head beneath her chin. He could almost hear the kitten purr, could almost feel Ariah's satiny skin against his own face.

The urge to throw himself down beside her, to drown her in kittens so that she was too busy hanging onto them to resist his caresses, carried him three paces closer before he clenched his fists, tightened his jaw, and slowed to a casual stroll. But every step he took toward her weakened his resolve to control his yearning for her and end the intimacy growing between them. Dry hay crunched beneath his feet. Ariah glanced over and saw him.

"Bartholomew." She sat up, hugging the kitten to her breasts. "Where have you been all day? I was worried when you didn't even come back for lunch."

His full, sensuous mouth lifted at one corner. "Yes, I can see how worried you were."

Kissing the kitten's pink nose, she said, "I had to find something to do to keep from going crazy waiting for you." The ball of fluff wriggled out of her grasp, climbed onto her shoulder and teetered there under her hand while she rose gracefully to her feet, wearing a bewitching smile.

She had missed him; he saw it in her eyes. She had worried about him. Suddenly, spring invaded the dim, musty barn, filling it—and him—with invigorating lightness. He wanted to run through the woods with her, climb trees, hunt frogs, anything and everything. He felt seventeen again, energetic and eager and terribly in love.

"Come exploring with me," he said, plucking a bit of hay out of her hair.

Like dust motes, her laughter floated upward to the thick beams overhead. "You're crazy, it's too muddy."

"All right. Then feed me."

The kitten batted at a honeyed wisp that had come loose from Ariah's hair. Keeping her eyes on Bartholomew, she rescued the strand from the tiny claws. Something in his husky voice made her go shivery inside. She set the kitten down and preceded Bartholomew from the barn. Douglas firs shielded the house from the ugliness of the muddy farmyard. As they passed them, Ariah, always on the lookout for birds, pointed out a small gray form hopping about the lower branches. Its black-hooded head distinguished it from the more common sparrows flitting about. "Look!" she cried. "A dark-eyed junco."

Bartholomew smiled. "We call them Oregon juncos."

Lifting her brows at that, she said, "Oregon doesn't own them, you know. We have them in Cincinnati, too."

"Not with *black* hoods and chestnut mantles, you don't. The Western variety is officially known as an Oregon junco."

Across the track that led from the road past the house to the barn and other outbuildings red-winged blackbirds squabbled over territorial rights in a cattail bed.

"They're beginning to nest," Ariah said.

"It's spring."

His warm gaze seemed to pierce her soul. For a moment she felt the same heady sensation women had been feeling since the dawn of time, hearing their mates call for them. Soul to soul. Heart to heart. A call she wanted badly to answer.

She had awakened thinking of his kiss and longing to experience it again. What had he meant when he'd said he would die if he didn't have her? Had he enjoyed the kiss as much as she did? It had been her first, if she didn't count the wet, awkward smack Ian had given her on her twelfth birthday. But Bartholomew had surely kissed many women, besides his wife.

The thought of Hester Noon renewed the guilt that had

plagued Ariah after Bartholomew's flight from the cabin the night before. She had kissed another woman's husband. Worse, she hoped to do it again. Not something her mother would have taken lightly—for all her modern thinking on an unmarried woman's need to know about physical relations between men and women. Demetria Scott had taught her daughter the difference between love and carnal sin. But knowing the danger an unknown act presented to her immortal soul did nothing to kill Ariah's desire for Bartholomew.

Ariah glanced up and caught him looking at her with the intensity of a hawk too long without food. In that instant a truth larger than life bore down on her with brutal clarity. Right or wrong, whatever the consequences, all that was happening between her and Bartholomew Noon was meant to be.

Ariah believed strongly in fate. When her father lay dying, and she recalled the letter from Mr. Monteer's attorney explaining his client's need for a bride, she realized at once that fate had something else in store for her, something that waited in a faraway land called Oregon. Now she knew what that something was.

The air around them seemed to thrum like a hive of aroused bees as she and Bartholomew walked to the house. Every time he touched her or took her hand to help her over a slick spot, Ariah felt a spark ignite deep inside her. She caught herself seeking ways to touch him. A tingling spread low in her abdomen and her heart raced. Not new sensations; she'd been experiencing them at one level or another ever since she'd arrived in Portland. She needed no one to tell her, however, that they had nothing to do with the city, or even with Oregon. It was the man beside her. Bartholomew.

Ariah had known few men. None very well. Would she feel similar sensations with Pritchard Monteer? Somehow, deep inside, she knew she wouldn't. It was Bartholomew who was her fate, Bartholomew who would know her love.

Thick, ominous clouds crowded the sky, adding to the darkness of twilight. Their breath came in silvered puffs as they trudged up to the house where Bones lay sprawled on the porch. The temperature was dropping. After they shed their mud-caked boots and outer garments, Bartholomew rebuilt the fire that had burned to glowing red embers in their absence.

"Gracious Sadie!" Ariah exclaimed behind him. "Ugh! Bartholomew, someone's left a poor dead creature here."

He turned to see her staring aghast at the bloody, skinned carcass of the rabbit he had left on the drysink.

"I thought it would make a nice rabbit stew," he said with amusement.

Ariah shuddered visibly. "You don't expect *me* to . . . to touch it, do you?"

"Tell you what," he said, chuckling, "I'll take care of the rabbit. You find some vegetables to put with it."

Soon the smell of simmering potatoes, carrots, onions and meat filled the air. While they cooked, Ariah sat at the table, Dr. Chase's book propped open in front of her, though her gaze spent more time on Bartholomew's back as he sat oiling a harness than it did on the page. When the food was ready, she set the book aside and called him to the table. Except for a request for the salt or an idle comment about the food or the weather, they ate in silence. He was sopping up the last of the gravy from the stew with a half-charred biscuit when Ariah said, "We're both orphans."

It was the last thing Bartholomew expected to hear. "What did you say?"

She rose from the table, leaving her half-empty plate, and went to kneel in front of the fire. Her hair was damp and tangled. He watched her pull out the pins, watched it fall about her shoulders to the floor as she sat back on her heels. She combed it with her fingers, plucking out a leaf or a pine needle now and then to toss onto the flames. Firelight limned her perfect profile, lending her a nearly classic beauty that made his breath catch in his throat.

"You and I are both orphans," she repeated.

He waited, amazed to realize that he knew her well enough

now to be certain that her words—so seemingly bizarre and out of the blue—would make sense eventually. She was leading up to something. Sleet clattered softly against the window, like the drumming of fingernails on wood.

"In New Guinea," Ariah was saying, seeming about to go off on another tangent, "there is a bird called a bowerbird because it builds a bower for its mate by stacking twigs against a sapling until it looks like a tepee. He carpets the floor with moss, then decorates it with colored pebbles, iridescent beetle wings and flowers. When a female comes along, he dances about with an orchid in his beak to entice her inside. Some bowerbirds even paint the walls inside with wads of leaves soaked in berry juice."

He said nothing to this, only waited patiently. When she continued, her voice was low and wistful.

"I could tell you any number of such romantic tales. How the male whooping crane bows to his potential mate. How he dances in synchronized steps and stances, turning his movements into a graceful water ballet. At the end the male becomes so exuberant he leaps completely over the female. Then there are the trumpeter swans who literally dance on top of the water. Or the great crested grebes who dance together with bits of weed from the bottom of the lake dangling from their beaks. I could even tell you exactly how the birds go about the actual mating."

Her hands lifted once and fell back to her lap. "But I haven't the foggiest notion how humans go about the same thing."

Silence engulfed the room.

Bartholomew dropped his last bite of biscuit on his plate and swallowed. As he had expected, it all made sense now. A painful, gut-wrenching sort of sense he wished desperately he could ignore.

Ariah felt heat rise in her cheeks as she waited, barely breathing, for his reaction. As the seconds ticked by and the hiss and pop of the fire began to sound louder and louder, she grew angry. Clenching her fists, she swung to face him.

"Why is something as essential to every living being as human reproduction shrouded in such absurd secrecy? Am I some sort of idiot that no one thinks me intelligent enough to handle such information?"

Bartholomew's dark face flushed. "No, of course not."

He rose so abruptly from his chair that it teetered on one leg before settling back on all four. At the stove he filled his cup with coffee, took a swig and choked on the hot brew. Ariah rushed to pound him on his back.

"There," she said, as if everything were absolutely normal between them. "Are you all right now?"

"Yes"—he coughed again—"thank you, I'm fine."

"No, you're not. You're shocked and probably appalled." Spinning about, she paced to the fire. "Human reproduction is not a subject a well-bred woman—especially an unmarried one—allows to enter her head. We are expected to pretend that such activities do not exist, and to swoon at the mere hint of anything so vulgar as bodily functions. But being women does not make us less human than men."

With one hand on her hip and the other slicing sharp-edged toward his chest, she advanced on him, eyes flashing, nostrils flared. "Nor does it mean that we don't experience the same needs men do. And since we are the ones who must carry the babies and endure the pain of delivering them into the world, it seems to me we have at least as much right, if not more, to fully understand the entire procedure *before* we're committed to it."

Completely flummoxed, Bartholomew wiped a hand down the back of his neck, then along his chin, dark with new stubble as it was every evening. In the quiet that filled the room following her tirade, he could hear his beard rasp against his callused fingers. He glanced at Ariah who was still glaring at him, defying him to argue against her assertions. She obviously intended to force an answer from him, and Bartholomew was at a loss as to how to get out of it. Finally he cleared his throat and, carefully keeping his gaze on neutral territory, said, "Didn't

your mother have any conversations with you on this subject
when you were coming of age?"

"*Mana*—my mother—died, if you will remember, when I
was only thirteen."

He sighed, taking a seat in the brocade wing chair that faced
the rocker in front of the fire. "Your father then?"

"On my seventeenth birthday, *Patera* told me it was time I
gave some thought to what type of man I wished to marry.
When I explained that it would help me to make my decision
if I knew more about what would be expected of me in the
marriage bed, he did a lot of hemming and hawing, then announced that he had urgent work to do in his study."

A corner of Bartholomew's mouth lifted in a wry smile. He
knew exactly how Jeffrey Scott had felt. Unfortunately, Bartholomew didn't have a study in which to escape.

"Ariah, I truly don't think I'm the person you should be having this discussion with."

Her hands gestured wildly as she paced in front of the fire.
"Then who is? I might have asked Effie if we'd stayed there
longer. She seemed very kind and open. But before I felt I knew
her well enough, we were leaving."

Once again, Ariah wished she knew what the Fates had in
store for them. Obviously, it wasn't marriage. Not now, anyway.
Which meant that, in the meantime, she would indeed have to
become Mrs. Pritchard Monteer. She whirled to face Bartholomew.

"Within a few weeks, I will be married, yet I haven't the
slightest idea what to expect." She knelt beside his chair, her
blue eyes reflecting more fear now than anger as she stared up
at him. "Is it so awful—what happens in the marriage bed—that
everyone is afraid to tell me?"

"No, no . . ."

"Then why won't you explain it to me?"

She gripped his thigh with both hands, her upturned face
filled with frustration. "*Mana* made me promise never to marry
for any reason except love, because then everything would be

beautiful for me, she said. Her parents tried to force her to marry a much older man, you see, one she'd never met, but she had already fallen in love with my father.

"They were so happy, Bartholomew. Sometimes I felt left out because they were so wrapped up in each other. I did very well at entertaining myself. I read a lot and played fantasy games with my dolls. But I still got lonely. There were friends to play with, but I didn't go to school; I always had a governess. After my mother died, the only friends I had were Andrea and her brother, Ian, who lived next door. Andrea and I used to speculate about what the big secret was about marriage, but she didn't know any more than I did. Ian was younger and a brat. Even if he had known, I wouldn't have asked him."

Ariah sat back on her heels. "When I was fifteen, I started helping *Patera* at his office, as *Mana* used to do. The two other clerks were men, of course, and older than me." She grimaced. "I suppose even if I had been a man, they wouldn't have been friendly since the boss was my father. And the last three years I rarely had occasion to speak to other women, except for Aunt Ida and our cook, Enid."

Bartholomew broke in to ask, "Couldn't you have spoken with one of them?"

Ariah giggled at the thought. "Aunt Ida would have fainted and Enid would have quit."

Her face became serious again. "I suppose I never worried much about any of this before because I always assumed it would be the same for me as it was for *Mana*." Ariah's hands lifted expressively, then fell. "Whatever went on in their marriage bed, she obviously enjoyed it."

Bartholomew squirmed in his chair, his face going to deep rose beneath his tan. He tried to think of someone more appropriate for her to talk with, and wished, for the first time since their arrival at the Upham place, that Olivia were here instead of in Tillamook. He quickly banished the thought of Hester, who believed only women of the lower classes spoke openly of bodily functions. The introduction of such a subject would be taken by her as an intimation that she was of that class, something she could not abide because it was far too close to the truth, in spite of the airs she put on to convince everyone of her fine breeding.

"The problem is"—Ariah recaptured his attention—"I'm not marrying a man I know, one I'm in love with. That's why I need to know what's going to happen. And my mother would agree. Don't you, Bartholomew?"

He started as she laid her hands once again on his knee. "Yes. I suppose I do, but what I really think is, your mother must be very disappointed right now."

Disappointed?" Ariah blinked. "Why?"

"Because you're about to do exactly what she begged you not to do."

"You mean marrying a man I don't know." She frowned. "But I'm sure *Mana* would understand."

"I'm afraid I don't understand."

She stared up at him a long time. "If I tell you why I must marry Mr. Monteer, will you answer my question?"

To hide his consternation, he picked up his cup from the table next to his chair and took a sip. He pursed his lips, cleared his throat, then cleared it again, feeling like a bear with his hind leg in a trap. "Ariah, if your mother had thought it best for you to know, she would have told you herself."

Ariah beat her fists against her thighs. "But she died. I know she would have told me if she'd lived long enough. When I asked where babies came from, she was very forthright in her answer. She explained that men plant a seed in a woman's womb, here"—Ariah pointed to her stomach—"and that the baby grows there until it's ready to be born. But I was so young, it wasn't until after she was gone that I began to wonder exactly how the man went about planting the seed. That is what happens in the marriage bed, isn't it, Bartholomew? Seed planting?"

Bartholomew rubbed his hand over his quivering mouth, uncertain whether to laugh or cry.

"Well, is it?"

Heaving a sigh, he nodded. "Yes, that's what happens in the marriage bed. Seed planting." Leaning his forearms on his thighs, he bent toward her. "But, Ariah, there's a good deal more to it than that, and you'd be much better off learning about it from . . . from your husband." He had started to say *From the man you love,* but the notion that that man would not be him brought such pain to his chest, he nearly couldn't go on.

On her knees again, she placed both hands on his arms and looked him in the eye. "You're my friend, Bartholomew. I've come to feel close to you, safe, comfortable. I want you to be the one to tell me."

"Good Lord." He ran a hand across his eyes, feeling the iron teeth of the trap slice through his flesh. That he had taken the Lord's name in vain was a grave indication of the chaotic state of his emotions. He needed time to think.

"The deal was that you tell me first why you have to marry Pritchard."

Letting her breath out in a huff, Ariah sat back again on her. heels. "All right, but you must promise that you won't repeat a word of what I say to anyone without speaking to me first."

With a weary lift of his hand, he said, "I promise. Now get on with it."

Nine

With great care, Ariah arranged her skirts, fussing with the folds as she tried to decide how best to explain her situation to Bartholomew. Her brow wrinkled in concentration and her teeth worried her lower lip. How much should she tell him? Would he feel honor bound to tell his nephew? What would she do if Mr. Monteer decided he wanted no part of her and the danger that might follow her to his isolated lighthouse on the Oregon coast? She would be alone then, with nowhere to go and no one to protect her.

Bartholomew attempted to hide his impatience by downing the last of his coffee, then going to the stove to refill the cup, but she wasn't fooled. That dark look was on his face, as though he were already dreading her words, knowing he would not like them. When he returned to his seat, she cocked her head, glancing up at him from under her thick, stubby lashes. Her decision was made. She could not risk losing the safety marriage with Mr. Monteer promised. A half-truth would have to suffice.

"To understand," she began, "you need to know a little of how Greek people think. I told you my mother was to have married another man. Her family had already paid her dowry in household furnishings. Land is a better dowry, but they had barely enough for their crops and the goats they raised. Anyway, the marriage was all arranged. Until *Mana* told her mother that she was carrying me."

At her last words, Bartholomew, who was taking a sip of

coffee, choked, spewed brown liquid over his white shirt and sat forward again.

"No, I'm not illegitimate." She grinned at the shock on his face. "*Patera* would have married her sooner, but it took time to arrange everything since he was not a citizen. I know most people would consider it scandalous that she gave herself to him a bit early. Goodness, back home, if they knew you and I slept alone in the same house together, I would be ruined, regardless of the circumstances. But *Mana* said when you're in love"—*the way I'm beginning to think I love you*—"then propriety and the rules of society become stuff and nonsense. She never regretted what she did, and she told me never to let love slip past me, to trust in my heart, grab hold of love and let it take me where it would."

Bartholomew shook his head at the rapt expression on her lovely face. "Even so, surely she warned you against allowing men to take liberties with you. Didn't she tell you that some men would say or do anything to get what they wanted from you?"

"Yes, but she said I would know when it was right and when it was wrong."

Good hell, had there ever been a more innocent woman? Part of him was appalled, but another part was completely enchanted. He couldn't help himself; he took her chin in his hand and drew her closer, his tone gruff. "You allowed me liberties, little nymph, and you know full well that it was wrong."

"It didn't feel wrong."

No, it had felt more right than anything he had ever known, but he didn't dare say it aloud. He let her go and sat back. "I believe we've digressed from the subject."

"Oh yes." She made herself comfortable, her knees drawn up, skirt spread out about her, her toes in their black stockings barely peeking out from under her hem.

"In eighteen twenty-one," she began, "when the Greeks fought for freedom from the Turks, the women of a small mountain village went to the top of a high cliff and, holding hands as though they were at a wedding feast, jumped to their deaths rather than face dishonor at the hands of Turkish soldiers. You see, to the Greeks nothing is more important than honor. A disgraced woman brought shame on the entire family. It didn't matter to my mother's family that *Patera* loved her and wanted to marry her. She was promised to another man, a Greek man, who already had her dowry. That was all that counted. Her grandfather . . . the head of the family, was a tenacious old man who insisted, out of sheer stubborn pride, that she be forced to honor his agreement with her Greek fiancé. They would simply pay the man more dowry to accept the coming baby as his."

Ariah's tone became more grave, her expression somber. So far, all she had said was true. Painfully true.

"So, with the aid of a sympathetic aunt, my father stole *Mana* away. A lot of Greeks were emigrating to Egypt then to find jobs constructing the Suez Canal. *Patera* hoped that their leaving Greece would put an end to the matter and they would be left in peace. He never dreamed anyone would come after them. But my great-grandfather sent one of my uncles to bring her back and to punish Father. It took time to discover where they had gone, more time to get a passport and follow. Through my father's embassy, he learned my uncle was on his way, and once again they fled. Eventually, *Mana* and *Patera* ended up in France where I was born. When Uncle Xenos tracked them there, they escaped to Britain, then to America.

"*Patera* changed his name from Scott Jefferson to Jeffrey Scott. For a while he worked as a store clerk to throw my uncle off. But it upset him to see my mother living in near poverty when his chosen profession could allow them to live better. Uncle Lou worked for the owner of the store. When he found out my father had been trained in the law, he convinced him to become his partner. I was eleven then. So much time had passed, they were sure they were safe."

Ariah sniffed and Bartholomew saw wetness gleaming on her cheeks in the firelight.

"I don't know why it took Uncle Xenos so long, but two weeks ago, he showed up at papa's office. When *Patera . . ."* She swiped at her eyes to cover the fact that she had almost said too much, almost told Bartholomew the truth. She leaped to her feet and began to pace, her fingers knitted tightly together as she forced herself to go on.

"When Uncle Xenos learned that *Mana* and my father were . . . gone, he asked where to find me. I'm an orphan now, Bartholomew, unmarried and alone—except for my Greek relatives. He meant to take me back to Greece and marry me off to advance the financial situation of the family and make up for what my mother deprived them of. What else could I do but run? If I must marry a stranger, I prefer him to be American"—she thumbed her chest—"and of *my* choosing."

When she turned to face Bartholomew, she saw shock in his sable eyes. Then the heavy dark brows came down over them, giving him an icy black look that would have sent her uncle racing back to Greece where he belonged.

"Your uncle would have forced you to go with him?" He came to his feet and towered over her, stiff with rage and something else she could not identify.

Ariah froze, hypnotized by the intensity of his gaze. He looked at her and the anger drained out of him as he took her in his arms, gently cradling her head against his chest.

"He won't take you anywhere," he whispered while his thick fingers brushed the moisture from her checks. "I'll see to it, I won't let anything happen to you."

Bartholomew squeezed his eyes shut as the reality of his promise splintered through him. It would not be up to him to protect her. She would be Pritchard's wife, not his. The anger, and the fear of losing her that had overwhelmed him on hearing her story, surged back to submerge him in a vicious whirlpool of emotion, a vortex of agony and hopelessness. He loved her beyond anything, but he could never say it, could never claim her as his. Many times in his life he had wished he could start over, be reborn. Now, he wanted simply to die.

"I'm scared, Bartholomew."

Her words dragged him back up out of the pit of self-pity he had been digging himself.

"Not of Uncle Xenos," she added, "but . . . how can I marry when I don't know what will happen to me on my wedding night?"

Bartholomew held her to him so tightly that she whimpered. The thought of her sharing a bed with anyone other than himself plunged him lower into the maelstrom of pain threatening to drown him. Gritting his teeth, he eased his grip on her. She needed him. Lord knew, Pritchard would be no help to her if her uncle did come to claim her. The boy was a coward when it came to standing up for himself, let alone anyone else. And if the matter should become physical, Pritchard would be the first to duck and run, leaving Ariah to fend for herself.

Bending his head, he pressed his face into her hair, breathing in her scent as though it could keep him sane and strong. "Don't be afraid, nymph, I won't let anyone hurt you . . . ever."

"Will you tell me then?" Her arms were wrapped about his waist, her words muffled against his chest.

Distracted by the feel of her soft breasts pressing against him, he planted fiery kisses atop her head. All he would have of her was now, this brief respite heaven had granted him by destroying the bridge and isolating them in John Upham's empty cabin. He'd be damned if he would give up one moment of it unnecessarily—or pass up the chance to enjoy what he could of her before he turned her over to Pritchard. Ruthlessly he shoved down the guilt that arose with that thought. He lifted her face, intent on kissing her sweet lush mouth.

"Bartholomew? You promised you'd tell me."

"Tell you what, nymph?" His lips were a mere breath from hers, his hand exploring the gentle curve of her waist.

"About seed planting."

Bartholomew went completely still. The painful reminder of

her innocence was like a bucket of ice water dumped on the searing need of his body. He sucked in air, let it out slowly, then put her from him. Her cheeks were damp, her lips parted and her expression anxious. One look told him there would be no putting her off. He nudged her toward the rocking chair.

"Sit down."

While she sat, he turned away, staring into the fire as he tried to compose himself and formulate some sort of coherent answer to her question. Finally, he faced her.

"Have you ever seen dogs mate?" He cursed himself as soon as he said it, appalled at the crude and animalistic image such an analogy would create in her mind.

"No." She tipped her head, frowning in puzzlement.

Bartholomew ran his hand down the back of his neck and sucked in another deep breath. "Forget about that. Do you know the physical differences between males and female?"

"Certainly."

"Good, then—"

"Men are larger and more muscular," she said, totally serious, "and, of course, they don't have breasts."

His relief vanished. He sighed. "I'm afraid there's a bit more to it than that. Haven't you ever seen a male infant, helped change his diaper, perhaps?"

"No. I love babies, but I've never been around many."

"Lord help me," he muttered. This was going to be more difficult than he'd expected. Sweat broke out on his brow and he thought it quite possible—humiliatingly so—that he might faint, from mortification alone. How did one make an indelicate subject delicate enough not to frighten a gentle and innocent girl like Ariah? He frowned.

"Ariah, a man's . . . privates differ from a woman's. Do you understand?"

Unconsciously, her hand slid to her lower abdomen. His gaze followed and he nodded. "Yes. A man's privates are made to fit inside a woman's, and that is how he . . . plants his seed in her."

The sweat was running down his face by the time he finished, and he knew he must be as red as a boiled lobster. Certainly he felt hot enough to be on fire. Worse, his contrary body chose this time to renew its earlier arousal. He sat down and crossed his legs, unable to look her in the eye, knowing that the moment the words were out, her gaze had no doubt become riveted to his groin.

"Gracious Sadie, I already knew that much." Ariah flapped her hands dramatically. "I watched a pair of mallard ducks mate once in the pond at the park back home. The drake climbed onto the hen's back and thrashed around until I thought he would drown her. When he jumped off and came ashore I saw his . . . privates. What I don't understand is how he got such a limp, stringy looking little thing like that to go inside her. And where, exactly? I couldn't see any openings on that hen."

With both hands over his face, Bartholomew scrunched down in his chair as though it could swallow him whole and deliver him from this horror. He felt an hysterical urge to laugh, and knew if he succumbed he would likely cry instead. After a long moment his hands dropped and he heaved a loud sigh. Eager to get this outrageous conversation over with, he blurted, "The hen's privates are under her tail feathers, which she moves aside so he can reach her."

Ariah pursed her lips as she considered this. "Okay, but how did he get that floppy little—"

Bartholomew held up his hands. He wasn't at all sure he could endure her description of male attributes again. "That part of him changes when he becomes aroused. It becomes . . . firm. After he has . . . planted his seed, it becomes limp again."

Ariah rose to her feet. She walked the length of the broad, rock fireplace, turned slowly and came back. "I cannot imagine that merely getting excited could make something that flaccid get firm enough to—"

"Take my word for it, Ariah. Please. It does."

"Very well." Pivoting, she paced back the other way. "Now,

I know this is done in bed—people do it in bed, I mean—and I assume they must be at least partially nude."

Bartholomew closed his eyes and squirmed in the chair as his overactive imagination conjured up an image of her lying naked in his bed.

"But," Ariah continued, oblivious to his discomfort, "does the woman lie there on her stomach, flat out, with him on top of her? Or does she get on her knees with him behind? And where exactly does he put his . . . privates? I thought it must be where I bleed each month because *Mana* told me that was where the baby would come out, but the image of a man trying to reach there from behind like that seems terribly awkward to me, Bartholomew."

When there was no answer, she turned. "Bartholomew?"

He no longer occupied his chair. She found him staring out the far window, beyond the lamplight, one hand braced against the window frame. He appeared tense, agitated. "Are you all right, Bartholomew? Have I upset you? I know I'm a failure as a proper Victorian woman, but—"

He tipped his head back and guffawed. The deep husky sound seemed to reach inside to stroke lightly down her spine, over her hipbones to her pelvis. She froze where she was, her teeth worrying her lower lip as she watched him.

"I'm fine," he said, his mirth fading. After a long while he turned to face her, still hidden in the shadows. "Humans are not limited to only one position for reproduction, Ariah." It helped, he realized, to keep the conversation as clinical as possible. "The most common position, however, is lying down, with the man on top and the woman facing him, stomach to stomach rather than back to stomach. And your assumption about the entrance used to enter the woman's body is correct."

Ariah said nothing to this. When several moments of silence had passed, he released his breath and turned back to the dark window, as exhausted as if he had taken on an entire harem alone, satisfying all but himself.

Ariah was recalling her childhood eavesdropping and the revulsion of her mother's friend. "Does it hurt?"

Good hell but she was innocent. How would she react if he told her that it was hurting him like hell right now, that it hurt more *not* to plant her damned seeds than if he could. But that was him, and he knew that wasn't what she was asking. "The first time for a woman is slightly painful, I'm told, but the discomfort doesn't last more than a few seconds."

"Only the first time?"

"Yes."

"Is it done often, or only when conception is desired?"

Her voice held neither shock nor revulsion. Only curiosity, and perhaps puzzlement. Was it done often? Bartholomew saw his mouth form a wry smile as the glass cast back his dim reflection. If she were the wife and he the husband, he would never want to leave bed at all. He'd bury himself so deep inside her sweet body that nothing—and nobody—could ever tear them apart.

It was the wrong thing to think. He had nearly gotten his body under control. Now the hunger, the need that was becoming more desperate every day he spent near her, was approaching overload. He saw himself as a volcano ready to erupt. The whirling flow of heat inside his body made his head reel. His stomach muscles tightened until he could feel them quiver with the effort to contain himself. He tried to wipe the sweat from the back of his neck, but his palms too were wet, accomplishing nothing.

"Bartholomew?"

His gaze flicked back to meet hers. One night. If he could only have one night with her. Twenty-four hours in which to sate his body and soul. To explore every inch of her; each curve, each plane, each hidden nook and valley that promised such heady treasure, such joy. Surely then he could be happy the rest of his days. Twenty-four hours to fill himself so full of her that when the need arose, he could simply crawl inside himself, find her there waiting for him, and gorge himself once more on the sweetness of her that would always belong to him. Only to him.

"How often depends on the man and wife," he said finally, his voice ragged and hoarse. "It is a pleasurable experience, Ariah, very pleasurable. At least, for most people." Hester invaded his mind, but he quickly blanked her out. "Much too pleasurable to limit it to procreation only. And in any case, one instance does not guarantee conception."

"I see."

Her expression was such that he wasn't sure she saw at all, though she seemed content with what he'd told her.

"It's getting late," he said. "You'd best get to bed."

"Yes. Thank you, Bartholomew, for your honesty." A slight frown marred her forehead as she headed toward the ladder. When she passed him, she paused, sending him a bright smile. *"Kali nikhta"* she said. "That's Greek for good night."

"Good night, nymph."

His soft reply followed her all the way to her bed. Her head was so full of the images conjured by his words that she was in bed before she knew it. He had made everything sound simple and reasonable, even . . . pleasurable. His word. Her hand stole to the vee of her legs. The thought of his naked body stretched out on top of hers, rubbing against her, caused fiery tremors to splinter through her body. She flushed and felt a tingling between her legs. But would she ever be naked in a bed with Bartholomew? It was Pritchard Monteer who would be her husband. Bartholomew already had a wife. Hester.

Jealousy stabbed deep. Ariah struggled to cast it out. She had no right to be jealous. No right to feel resentment toward a woman she'd never even met. Did he love Hester? Did he enjoy lying with her? An unexpected wetness dampened Ariah's cheek. She wiped it away, rolled onto her stomach and tried to think how enthralled she would be living beside the ocean. How good it would be to have her own house. And a husband.

Her marriage to Pritchard would be happy, as her mama's marriage had been with *Patera*. And someday she and

Bartholomew would be together. It was fated to be so, she was certain. Yet she could not erase the bleakness that invaded her soul, and the harder she tried, the more impossible it became.

Below, in the Upham's big bed, Bartholomew listened to her toss and turn, and wondered if the source of her disquiet was the same as his. Lord knew, the cure was simple enough. Bartholomew's body was painfully ready, and he was definitely more than eager. The knowledge that this particular fantasy would never come true brought a tightness to his throat that he had not felt in a very long time.

At first Bartholomew thought the noise was only John and Olivia arriving home. It was the sweet hot feel of Ariah curled up tightly against him that told him he was dreaming. Then a devil in black began chasing Ariah, screaming retribution in a foreign tongue.

Bartholomew raced through the night, trying to save her, lost in fog so white and solid he could feel it brush past his body. Cold, like ice on his naked skin. John appeared, smiling, talking about cows and roads that vanished into the river. Suddenly the black devil was gone and Ariah was nowhere to be seen. Bartholomew was in his bed, slick with sweat, heart pounding still. He glanced around. Everything seemed normal, except for a scraping sound, like boots being cleaned of mud on the metal blade John had attached to the wooden steps outside the door.

Someone was out there.

Bartholomew struggled to fully awaken. He wasn't dreaming anymore, yet he sensed danger. Danger for Ariah. Her uncle; had the man tracked her here? Was Xenos trying to take Ariah away? Bartholomew's feet tangled in the covers as he tried to leap from the bed. He had to stop Xenos. He couldn't let her be snatched from him. Xenos would have to kill him first.

The latch jiggled as it was lifted from outside. A chilly draft wrapped around Bartholomew like ghostly arms as he tumbled out of the warm bed. The intruder was opening the door. Fear prickled Bartholomew's skin. He grabbed up the first thing that came to hand and lunged, half-stumbling, toward the door.

The wooden portal swung inward and a cloak-shrouded form carrying a lantern entered, along with the icy wind. Bartholomew raised his weapon and prepared to crash it down onto the intruder's head.

Then the hood of the cloak was thrown back and he found himself staring down at Ariah.

She set the barely lit lantern on the table and slipped the cloak off her shoulders. Her dark-honey hair shone golden in the dim light, and her white nightrobe appeared almost yellow. She stepped in front of the lamp to hang up her wrap. The glow penetrating the thin fabric of her gown outlined her figure in exquisite detail. Bartholomew gasped and she glanced up.

"Bartholomew? Is that you?" The light barely reached his corner. She stepped closer. "What are you doing there in the shadows?"

Anger replaced his fear. Before he could ask her what the hell she was doing wandering about in the middle of the night by herself, she looked at his still upraised hand.

"Why are you holding your boot up like that?"

Her gaze dropped, following the line of his body. Her mouth fell open, and she stared in shock. Bartholomew lowered his arm and saw the boot he held—the lethal weapon he had intended to protect her with. His focus widened, taking in his bare feet on the cold puncheon floor—and everything in between.

He was naked. Naked and partially aroused as he was most mornings.

"Bartholomew!" she said again in a breathy whisper. Her gaze darted up to meet his, only to fall once more to his exposed body. "Is that your privates? Is that what you put inside . . . ?"

She glided closer, sending his pulse soaring and causing more blood to rush to his loins.

"Oh." One hand moved to cover her mouth as she watched his body react to the fresh stimuli. She looked up at his face. "But you're not at all like a mallard."

Bartholomew wanted to laugh. To cry. He wanted to throw himself down a hole. He wanted to pick her up and haul her off to the bed. He did nothing. His entire body seemed to have turned to granite.

Ariah passed her glance over him, starting with his wide shoulders with their rippling muscles, the dark carpet of hair on his chest, his taut abdomen that inescapably led her gaze back to the apex of his legs. He was beautiful, and so potently masculine. Simply looking at him caused heat to curl deep inside her. One tentative finger reached out to stroke the satiny hardness. It jumped and she let out a soft cry of wonder, then reached for him again.

Bartholomew snatched her hand away with a hard jerk that did the opposite of what he had intended and brought her smack up against him. He let out a groan and held her away, his hands on her arms. "It's sweet torture when you touch me like that," he said, wincing as his voice cracked.

"But . . ." She tried to free her arm, wanting to touch him again, to explore the heat, the incredibly smooth texture, the strength and power she had sensed beneath the taut skin.

"No," he said. "Don't move, just stay there and let me breathe."

He needed to get control, of himself, of the situation. It was everything he could have dreamed of; the empty house, him, her, only her thin gown to keep their bare flesh from coming together . . . and a bed waiting nearby. His body begged him to act. His conscience railed at him to wait. Hoping his agony didn't show in his voice, he pushed her toward the ladder to the loft. "Go up to bed, Ariah. I'll take care of the lantern."

She resisted for a moment. "Bartholomew—"

"Go, we'll talk tomorrow."

She didn't want to wait until tomorrow. Nor did she want to talk. Her body was feverish and full of urges she didn't understand. She ached and didn't know why. But she knew Bartholomew could explain. Knew instinctively that he could ease her agitation. She tried to make out his expression in the dim light. His face was dark, intense, forbidding. He looked in pain. Caused by her?

Swallowing the lump that formed suddenly in her throat, she turned to the ladder. With her foot on the first rung she paused, hoping he would call her back. When he didn't, she chanced a look over her shoulder. He hadn't moved, just stood there watching her, his face as hard and inscrutable as the worn wood beneath her hands.

"Go on," he said.

After one long last glance at him, she did as he told her.

Alone again, Bartholomew turned to the wall, pressing his face into a rough, peeled log, welcoming the pain that obliterated at least part of his agony.

Ten

The following day was fraught with tension. When his porridge was lumpier than usual, Bartholomew cursed and slammed the bowl so hard on the table that the salt cellar bounced up and landed in his mush.

"Good hell, woman." He leaped to his feet and snatched up a towel to wipe off the mess that had splashed onto his hand. "A child could make porridge in his sleep. Why can't you do it wide-awake?"

Ariah, where she stood at the stove, jumped at the banging of the bowl behind her back. At his angry bellow, the basket of freshly gathered eggs she had been sorting so she could scramble the two largest for him, fumbled from her hands and plummeted to the floor. Eggshells and gooey clear liquid splattered onto her skirt. She glared at him as she knelt to mop up the mess. "Who says I'm awake? I hardly slept a wink last night."

"And you're blaming me for that, I suppose?"

Her eyes stung with unwanted tears. She lowered her head and busied her hands with the rag she was using to sop up the eggs. "If the noose fits, go hang yourself with it."

Bartholomew clenched his hands, torn between shaking her witless and kissing her until she fainted from lack of air. "All you have to do is pay attention to the one thing you're doing," he said, "instead of trying to cook, read that confounded book of yours, and mend your skirt at the same time."

Ariah stood up so suddenly she swayed with dizziness. He reached out to steady her and she slapped his hand away. "I have better things to do with my time than stand around watching porridge thicken."

"Yes, the same way you have better things to do than grind the coffee until it's the proper consistency, or roast it first as you're supposed to do."

She looked at him blankly. "I'm supposed to roast it?"

Bartholomew stared back at her, his face like black thunder, terrifying and beautiful at the same time.

"Is there anything you do know how to do?" he asked.

Ariah had no argument; he was right in everything he said. Her mouth quivered. "I'm very good at identifying birds."

The urge to laugh at her inane statement fled as he watched tears pool at the corners of her eyes, then spill over. Damn! He slammed a fist on the table hard enough to rattle the dishes, then stalked toward her. He couldn't stand to see her cry. She flinched when he drew near. The black anger fled his face as guilt lacerated his heart. His voice softened. "I'm not going to hit you. Come here."

He drew her into his arms, cursing himself for losing his patience. It wasn't her fault that his need for her was chewing him to bits more efficiently than the coffee grinder did beans, or that he couldn't sleep anymore, could barely force himself to eat. His control had been stretched to its limits and then some. With his every nerve jangled, he found himself white-knuckled more often than not in his effort to keep his hands off her.

Why hadn't he insisted she take the train to Yamhill and then the stage? *Because I had no idea she'd turn out to be the most precious creature I'd ever laid eyes* on. But he had known within five minutes of meeting her. He should have put her on the train right then. It was his weakness that had created this disaster. Now he had taken out his mounting frustration on her and she was soaking his shirt front with tears. His arms tightened around her. "I'm sorry, nymph, I'm sorry. Please stop crying."

Desperate to please him in any way she could, she made an

heroic attempt to stem the flow. After a few hiccuping sobs, she succeeded. He stroked her back and buried his face in her hair. Lily of the valley pervaded his senses, along with the warmth of her body and the softness of the breasts pressed against him. His body reacted with vigor.

"Oh, hell!" Bartholomew thrust her away. "There's only one cure for this."

Painfully aware that what he was about to do was *not* the only cure, but simply the only one available to him, he wheeled toward the door and snatched up his coat and rifle. A few brief seconds later he was gone.

Ariah listened to the crunch of his boots in the frosted mud and the mutter of his curses as he headed for the barn, and vowed to grind this night's coffee as fine as flour. She'd fix him the best dinner she could come up with—Greek food, the one thing she did know how to cook—and she'd make certain nothing was undercooked or burned because of her damnable lack of domestic aptitude.

Her resolve firm, she hurried to the rocker where she had left Dr. Chase's book. Making herself comfortable in Olivia's chair, she thumbed through the recipes in the cooking section, searching for instructions on baking an apple pie, remembering his mentioning to Effie that it was his favorite.

Through a misty rain that was half-sleet, Bartholomew rode to the washed-out bridge where he held a shouted conversation with two men on the far side who had come from Trask House to investigate the damage. Tomorrow a crew would begin cutting trees for the new bridge. If they waited for the rain to cease, it might take weeks. He wasn't the only one needing to get through. He promised to do what he could on his end to help, and departed.

Now, riding up the track to the house, he watched the smoke curl up from the chimney and tried to quell the eager churning in his gut at the thought of seeing Ariah. Then she was there, framed in the open doorway, waving to him. His heart did a backflip. His pulse doubled. He paused long enough to tell her he would be in as soon as he'd taken care of his horse. She called back that supper would be ready when he finished. He saluted and rode on.

The 18,000-candlepower lamp of the Cape Meares light could not have outshone her smile. It seared its way straight into his heart, making him feel lighter than he had all day. He tried to ensure his control with a severe lecture about the danger of letting himself forget that Ariah Scott belonged to Pritchard, and would never be his.

"Got a deer liver for you," he announced as he stepped inside with a hide-wrapped packet.

Ariah hurried over. "Look at you, you're soaked and covered with mud. Here, let me help."

"What's that I smell?" He leaned close, grinning while she hung up his coat. "It's certainly not burned bacon."

"No, it certainly is not."

"Then what is it? I didn't think you knew how to make anything but lumpy oatmeal, burned bacon and canned beans."

She swatted him indignantly upon the arm. "My rabbit stew wasn't so bad."

"*Your* rabbit stew? I'm the one who skinned that rabbit and cut it up. You didn't have the slightest idea what to do with it. Except to scream your head off over the blood."

"I did not scream my head off."

"You nearly fainted."

"It *was* a grisly sight." Stiff-backed she marched to the stove where she stirred the contents of a large soup kettle, filling the room with a delicious aroma. "Well, today no one helped me. I made rice pilaf, fried zucchini and a sort of meatless *moussaka*."

"Moose-aka? What in heaven is that?" Bartholomew reached for the long-handled spoon, intent on sampling her fare, but she smacked his hand with it instead.

"It's a casserole made with eggplant and lamb, only I didn't have any lamb."

"I'm relieved to hear that you didn't go out and slaughter any of John's sheep. I'd hate to have to explain to him when he gets home why he's short one."

Ariah gave a disgruntled humph!

Bartholomew chuckled. "When do we eat this feast?"

"As soon as you stop making fun of me and sit down."

He sat. Ariah brought him a bowl of soup and waited, her hands tangled in her apron, while he took his first bite. Onions, chunks of potato, carrots, canned tomatoes and oregano floated in a delicious clear broth that smelled like heaven and tasted like ambrosia after his long, cold ride. With a sound of pleasure, he scooped up another spoonful. Pleased, Ariah fetched a bowl for herself.

"I brought you something," he said, watching her. She was wearing a wool skirt in Christmas red, plaited at the sides, and a plain red shirtwaist that made her skin glow and deepened the rosy tinge of her full lips.

"A surprise?" Ariah brought her bowl to the table and sat down across from him.

"Sort of." He broke open a biscuit—not burned for once— and slathered butter inside. "I thought you might like something to read besides that one book of yours and John's worn Bible, so I brought back your carton of books."

"Oh, do get it, Bartholomew. Now. I can't wait to open it."

"Now? Can't it wait until after supper?"

His spoon never stopped moving as he scooped the delicious soup into his greedy mouth. She wanted to insist, but knew it would be silly to let the meal she had worked so hard on get cold. "Very well, but hurry and eat then."

The tension of the morning was forgotten, and both of them were so glad, they were willing to do anything to prevent a return. Bartholomew nodded toward the book lying near her plate and asked what she found so interesting within its pages.

"Nothing. I had hoped to find something about birds. There

is a farriers' section, after all. But nothing for birds. A big medical section discusses the treatment of wounds, illnesses and such, though. For people, I mean."

"The way you've been studying it, I expected more than medical advice for horses and humans."

"There's a great deal more, actually; information for merchants and saloon keepers, tanners, blacksmiths, barbers and gunsmiths. Even beekeepers. There are recipes for everything from biscuits to mouth glue to home remedies for gout. Mostly I've been reading the part on etiquette and personal manners."

Bartholomew smiled. "And have you learned anything?"

She gave an exasperated sigh. "Only that I'm hopelessly uncivilized. I can't seem to remember to hold my handkerchief by the center and let the corners form a fan, instead of balling it up in my hand. I hate wearing gloves, I dance abominably, and I tend to blurt out whatever's on my mind without thinking beforehand. I'm afraid I'll never be able to memorize all the rules of proper behavior, let alone execute them."

Bartholomew burst into laughter. "I think the best thing you could do is toss that book into the fire. Or at least ignore that section." He leaned across the table and framed her jaw with his large hand. "Don't change, little nymph, you're much too delightful as you are."

Ariah barely breathed, praying he would kiss her again. "Am I?"

Words tumbled into his head, words about honesty, freshness and generosity. Words about love. Words he didn't dare speak. He let go of her and looked down at his empty bowl. "How about some of that moose dish?"

Disappointed, she filled his plate and set it before him, then reclaimed her seat. He breathed in the aromas, wondering which scent belonged to which tasty-looking food, before forking a bite into his mouth. Ariah waited, her lips slightly parted to reveal the tip of a rosy tongue, as though she, too, were tasting her creation.

"Ummm." He licked his lips. "Delicious, nymph."

She smiled, her frustration of a moment ago forgotten. "Do you truly like it?"

"It's wonderful. You'll have to . . ." He'd started to say she should teach Hester how to make it, then clamped his mouth shut, knowing his wife would never welcome cooking advice from anyone as young and lovely as Ariah. And, in truth, he didn't think he could bear having his memories of this special time tarnished by any sort of involvement on Hester's part anyway.

Ariah frowned. "It would be much better with lamb added, of course, but—"

"No, no, that isn't what I started to say at all. I was only thinking how lucky Pritchard was."

The lie seemed to satisfy Ariah, but the light went out of her eyes. The meal resumed in silence. After a dessert of apple fritters, which Ariah served with an apology because she hadn't found a recipe for apple pie, Bartholomew insisted on washing the dishes. The least he could do for such a delicious meal, he said. While she dried the last of the dishes, he fetched in the crate he'd left on the porch and set about opening it.

Soon an assortment of books in bindings of deep rich shades—burgundy, hunter green, rosy brown and ebony—lay scattered over the wolf pelt in front of the fire. Ariah, sitting on her heels, tossed their protective India-rubber coverings aside and rifled through the embossed, leather-bound tomes, her eyes alight with pleasure.

"Here it is." She held up a slender volume. "Emily Dickinson's poems. Remember? I told you about her."

Bartholomew nodded, but Ariah was already flipping through the pages and didn't see. He was seated on the floor, his back braced against the wing-backed chair, his long legs stretched out in front of him.

"Emily died a spinster, but some believe she had a lover once." Ariah glanced up from under her lashes, a coy, almost seductive look that made his knees go weak. "I like to think she did. Every woman should have a lover once in her life, don't you think?"

"Definitely," he murmured, smiling.

"Here's one of my favorites." With her face suitably sober, she read: " 'Because I could not stop for Death, He kindly stopped for me; the carriage held but just ourselves . . . and Immortality.' " She paused to look at him. "There's more, but it's not very romantic, is it? I fear Emily suffered a bit of melancholia."

"Why don't you find something a bit lighter? Then I'll recite you one of my favorite verses."

"All right." Excited, Ariah squirmed into a more comfortable position and leafed through the thin book. When she found what she was looking for, she lowered her voice to give it what she hoped was a sensual huskiness. " 'The rose did caper on her cheek, her bodice rose and fell, her pretty speech, like drunken men, did stagger pitiful . . .' "

Bartholomew's gaze fell automatically to Ariah's prim shirtwaist which rose and fell with the swift rhythm of her breathing. His pulse quickened.

" '. . . What ailed so smart a little maid, it puzzled me to know, Till opposite I spied a cheek that bore another rose, just opposite, another speech that like the drunkard goes . . .' "

Bartholomew leaned closer, longing to kiss her flushed cheeks and the full lush lips that now imprisoned his gaze.

" 'A vest that, like the bodice, danced to the immortal tune, Till those two troubled little clocks ticked softly into one.' " Ariah's gaze lifted as she finished. Her breath caught in her throat at the passion in his dark eyes. Feeling awkward, she closed the book. "Now you."

"Very well." He took her hand and gazed intently into her eyes. " 'My beloved spake, and said unto me, Rise up, my love, my fair one, and come away. For, lo, the winter is past, the rain is over and gone; the flowers appear on the earth; the time of the singing of birds is come, and the voice of the turtle is heard in our land.' "

Entranced by the deep hypnotic resonance of his voice, Ariah watched the movements of his mouth and wished she could feel it pressed to hers again.

" '. . . and the vines with the tender grape give a good smell. Arise, my love, my fair one, and come away.' "

After a moment of silence, she said, "That was beautiful. Who wrote it? I've never heard it before."

"It's from the Old Testament, actually."

The soft expression on her face and the warmth of her gaze fanned the coals of need smoldering deep inside him. Ruthlessly he ignored the voice in his head that had more than once, since he first heard it at the age of five, accurately warned him of disaster and danger. He was beyond fear. Lord, he was even beyond caring. In the blue of her incredible eyes he saw a need as strong as his own and that was all that mattered.

Slowly he drew her toward him. Ariah held her breath, her bones turning to water as she waited, willing him to do whatever he would with her. He settled her across his lap, half-turned toward him, then lowered his head to hers and took her mouth in a tender, lingering kiss.

Against her lips, he whispered, "Here's another one: 'How delicious is the winning'"—he nibbled his way to her ear—" 'of a kiss at love's beginning' "—nipped the lobe—" 'where two mutual hearts are sighing' "—returned to her mouth—" 'for the knot there's no untying.' "

Her mouth opened on a sigh and he filled it with his tongue, pillaging her sweetness like a love-starved pirate. His searching fingers tangled in her hair, scattering pins everywhere. When the honeyed mass came tumbling down, he spread searing kisses across her cheek to her temple, then buried his face in the silken tresses, inhaling their scent.

Ariah moaned and squirmed, wanting more of his mouth, of his kisses. She savored his taste, with its hint of coffee and oregano; the sleek texture of his lips, and the slightly rougher one of his tongue as it explored her mouth, creating a tingle that vibrated all through her. One hand slipped around his back to discover the taut muscles and uneven ridge of his spine. The other hand went to his shoulder, en route encountering the hard bulge of his biceps. His apparent strength both unnerved and excited her.

Bartholomew's lips reclaimed hers, hotter and more demanding now, one hand cupping her head, the fingers entwined in her hair. Need roiled inside him like breakers on the sand. He felt the undertow pulling him under, drugging his senses. Instinctively, he came up for air.

Ariah's full lips were as red as wild cranberries in October, plump with passion. Her blue eyes deepened to the color of gentians on a stream bank. She was so lovely it brought a lump to his throat merely to look at her. The feel of her in his arms was like an aphrodisiac. Emotionally, the miracle of being able to hold her was more than he'd hoped for. But physically, he was aroused beyond anything he had ever known. If any man were to try to take her from him at this moment, he would find himself in a fight to the death.

She moaned and tried to draw his mouth back down to hers. He gladly surrendered. Mentally, he was doing his best to ignore the scoldings of his conscience.

You're touching what doesn't belong to you.

Defiantly, he caressed her waist, above the gentle flare of her hip, and noted with joy the lack of a corset.

Thou must not covet.

His thumb slid to the undercurve of her breast.

Think of Pritchard.

He swallowed her gasp of shock and moved his hand to cup her fullness.

Think of Hester.

Her moan of pleasure nearly undid him. When he brought his thumb across the peak of her breast, she went wild. Her lips nipped his, her tongue delved, and her breast lifted to press more intimately into his hand.

The adulterer shall surely be put to death.

Tearing his mouth from hers, he lowered his head and laid

claim to a nipple through the fabric of her shirtwaist. He heard her rapid, hissing intake of air and felt the shudder that shot all the way to her toes. In one easy move, he eased her from his lap and stretched them both out on the wolf pelt to give himself easier access to her treasures. While he caressed one breast, he suckled the other through the thickness of her shirtwaist and chemise. There was a certain lack of satisfaction to it, yet he was unwilling to let her go long enough to get rid of the barrier.

The rubbing of the moistened cloth on her sensitized flesh created sensations Ariah never imagined could exist. Needs spiraled inside her that she felt helpless to understand or satisfy. They frightened and thrilled her at the same time.

"Bartholomew?"

"Hmmm?" He switched breasts.

"I feel . . . strange. What are you doing to me?"

"I'm loving you, nymph, don't you like it?"

"Oh, yes, very much." She stroked his rugged face and felt the intriguing scrape of evening stubble on her palms. "But I-I want something . . . more. I simply don't know what."

His chuckle was hoarse. "I know what it is you want, little nymph." He inched upward to kiss her. "And, oh, Lord, I want it, too. You've no idea how much."

The sight of her sweet mouth was more than he could resist. He kissed her again, a long, intoxicating kiss that heated his blood to fever pitch and created images in his head of her lying naked beneath him, his body united with hers, knowing it would feel right in a way nothing in his life ever had before.

He drew back and his hand went to the buttons down the front of her shirtwaist.

"Is all this a part of seed planting?"

Her voice was tremulous. Whether from fear or excitement, he wasn't sure. "Yes, nymph."

"But there's more?"

"Much more."

Ariah's expression left him uncertain as to her thinking. She appeared confused, unsure. He hesitated. And into the void leaped his conscience.

She's a virgin. To take her innocence could ruin her life.

That was something he could not do. Would not do. He had no right. Uttering a sigh of frustration, he ran his thumb over her swollen lips. Then he forced himself to move away.

"Bartholomew? What is it?"

Avoiding her gaze, he hauled himself to his feet and went to the door. The rustling of fabric told him that she also had risen.

"Bartholomew, please. What have I done?"

He turned to face her and she saw in his eyes the wild, dark emotions ravaging his insides.

"You've done nothing. It's me. I had no right to touch you that way." His voice broke and he glanced away. "Forgive me. Forgive me."

Eleven

"Don't go, Bartholomew," Ariah pleaded as he headed out the door. "Not again."

Bartholomew heaved a tormented sigh and turned to look at her. Her lips were swollen from his kisses, her cheeks flushed, her hair and clothing mussed. She looked as though she'd just gotten out of bed, so incredibly sensual that his heart cartwheeled into his stomach at the sight of her. He knew he should close his ears to anything she might say. His need for her was too great, and he was too weak to offer much resistance.

"Listen to me, Ariah—"

"No, please, Bartholomew. You can't go off and leave me like this. I-I feel so odd, sort of . . . panicky inside. Parts of me ache, only it's a 'needy' sort of ache. I simply don't know what it is I need." She placed his hand on her breast. "Except . . . maybe for you to touch me some more."

Her breath wafted over him, sweet and warm, as she moved up on tiptoe to brush her lips across his. Bartholomew groaned. How could even God expect him to maintain control when she pressed her lush, soft body to him this way, her slender arms wrapped about his neck? Her words had glided down his spine like heated honey, straight to his groin. It might be the devil who created this wicked need in him, and no doubt Bartholomew would go directly to hell if he succumbed, but meanwhile, the feel, the scent, the sight of her, offered a heaven any man would die for.

He buried his head in the wealth of hair at the crook of her neck. His arms crushed her against him, lifting her off the floor. His voice was a harsh, ragged whisper.

"Don't do this to me, nymph. If I touch you anymore, you'll soon find me buried inside you and nothing will ever be the same after that."

"You mean because I'll have your seed inside me then, and I might have a baby?"

His groan this time was loud and agonized. "Oh, God." With his hands under her arms, he lifted her high and nuzzled her flat stomach. She could barely hear his whispered words: "What I would give to see that."

Then he set her back on the floor and moved away to stare morosely into the darkened bedroom. "Go to bed, Ariah, where you'll be safe. Where we'll both be safe."

After a moment of silence she said, "Is it because of Toots?"

Taken aback, he turned to look at her. "Toots?"

"Yes. Is it because you're already planting seeds with Toots that you don't want me?"

"Good hell, no! Where'd you get such an idea?"

She shrugged. "She looks at you as though you were chocolate cake and she was starved."

Her insight startled an abrupt chortle from him. "She may be hungry, but I'm no chocolate cake," he said wryly. "At least, not for her." Then his voice hardened. "And no, I'm definitely not, now or ever, planting seeds with her."

Ariah grinned. "Then—"

"Then nothing, Ariah. Go to bed. There'll be no seed planting tonight."

Without a word, she went up the ladder, surprising him with her rare show of submissiveness. Feeling a hundred years old, with a thousand-pound sack of grain on each shoulder, Bartholomew turned out the lamp. Then he went into the bedroom and undressed. Above him, the floor creaked. Fabric rustled as Ariah removed her clothes. An agony so deep he thought surely he would die of it, twisted his insides.

How could she have ever thought he might prefer Toots Ol-well to her? The idea was ludicrous.

Footsteps approached the ladder overhead. He glanced up to see her descending. The sight of her bare feet and ankles beneath the flounced hem of her nightrobe, and the knowledge that under the thin fabric she was as naked as he, sent hot blood pumping afresh to his groin. Hope slammed into his heart like an anvil. He tried to block her from view with tightly shut eyes and hold himself stone-still as he stood naked beside the bed, thankful that he was hidden in the darkness. When she spoke, he opened his eyes to see her silhouetted in the opening to the bedroom.

"I still ache, Bartholomew. Are you aching, too?"

He tipped his head back and laughed, a ragged throaty sound. "Yes. God, yes, I ache."

"Then maybe—"

"There is no maybe, Ariah. If I do what you want, you will be ruined. There'll be no marrying Pritchard or any other man then, not unless you lie to him or he wants you badly enough not to care that someone else has already taken your virginity."

The thought of anyone else having her, before or after him, made his throat swell painfully. He was drowning, his chest bursting for want of air. How could he walk away from what she was offering him? How could he not? Lord knows, if he were Pritchard and she confessed to having been less than vir-tuous, he would still marry her—and gladly. But if he made love to her tonight, there would be no way he could ever allow any other man to touch her. She would be his and no one else's.

Could he leave Hester, take Ariah somewhere new and start over? Bartholomew squeezed his eyes tight against the urge to cry. There was no question of his answer. Hester was his lawful wife. No matter what she had done to him, he could not turn his back on his responsibility to her. That was something for which he could thank his father.

Responsibility, trust, obligation. To Jacob Noon there were no excuses for not fulfilling every duty, no matter how trifling or unpleasant, and Bartholomew well remembered the few times he had erred and the thrashings that had embedded that principle deep into his being. The dulcet softness of Ariah's voice brought him back to the present.

"It's fate that brought us together, Bartholomew, and fate will decide our future. All we can do is grab onto what joy is offered us along the way."

His chuckle was harsh and without humor. "And how do we do that without taking fate into our own hands, Ariah, because that's what we'd be doing. Once your virginity is gone, there's no getting it back."

She mulled that over. "I don't think I could lie to a man I intended to marry. But he wouldn't know unless I told him, would he?"

"He'd know the minute he bedded you."

"How?"

"When a man enters a woman for the first time, he breaks a thin membrane that bleeds. Even if he couldn't feel it when it broke, he would know from the blood on the sheets."

For a long moment she was quiet. When he realized she was coming into the bedroom, Bartholomew threw himself into the bed and jerked the covers up to his waist.

"Is it the breaking of the membrane that makes it hurt?" she asked from the side of the bed.

"Yes. After that there is no more pain, not if the woman is aroused."

"But isn't it because I am aroused that I ache so?"

Bartholomew groaned. Would she never cease torturing him? "Yes, Ariah. Now go to bed. The ache will go away."

She pressed her hands to her breasts. "Is there no other way to ease it?"

He stared at her a long time, while thoughts and images tumbled chaotically in his mind. "Yes, if a woman trusted a man."

"I trust you."

Beneath his heated gaze, in the dim light that filtered in from the other room, her fingers went to the buttons that ran from her high, lace-trimmed neckline nearly to her navel. With each freed button she teased him with a glimpse of newly exposed flesh, the pale swell of a breast, a hint of shadowed undercurve, a promise of erotic mystery. Only the tremor in the fingers exposing her beauty to his avid gaze revealed her nervousness.

When she started to push the garment off her shoulders, Bartholomew reached out and yanked the gaping fabric closed.

''Be certain, nymph. What you're offering me is a gift I would treasure to the end of my days, but once you're married to Pritchard"—*heaven forbid, could he endure that?*—"and your curiosity is sated, you may find it awkward to have me living close by."

"I am certain, I can't say why. It's not curiosity. I only know that it is right, no matter how it seems."

Gently she removed his hands, and the gown, as white and shimmering in the darkness as moonlight on a tranquil sea, slid weightlessly down her body to pool at her feet. She looked like a Greek sea goddess cresting a wave of purest white foam. Sweet innocent seduction in human shape. Bartholomew groaned in joyful agony; the gods had given him back his dream, one he knew he would pay dearly for someday.

"Come here, nymph."

She stepped out of the gown entangling her feet, and stood close to the bed. Bartholomew spread her luxuriant hair over her breasts like a satin fan. Then he allowed himself the bliss of stroking the lustrous length of it as it followed the contours of her breasts, her tiny waist and rounded hips, to the feathery ends at the apex of her thighs.

"You're so beautiful," he whispered huskily, "more beautiful than a sunset on the sea . . . or a rainbow in the mist of a waterfall." He lifted her onto the bed. Slowly, as she knelt beside him, he pushed the wealth of hair behind her shoulders, revealing her small, full breasts. "More beautiful than anything."

His voice was hushed with awe, his touch feather light, as though she were made of fine crystal. For a long moment, he studied her. Then, with a strangled moan, he pulled her to him in a fierce embrace. "Nymph, my sweet nymph."

Frantic kisses rained on her face. He kissed her eyes, her temples, each dainty ear and, finally, her lips. He drew back to look at her again, and she smiled. A lump hardened in his throat as a tide of emotion overwhelmed him. Bartholomew had never believed in miracles. Until this moment life had been a duty to be gotten through, like watching his mother waste away before his very eyes, or ignoring his paralyzed father's growing hatred every time he helped the man take care of his most private needs. Or like honoring his marriage vows, even though Hester had violated hers the day after the wedding.

But having Ariah in his bed—this was a true miracle. One he accepted with a reverence so deep it filled his soul, bonding him to this small woman, regardless of their situation. No matter what happened tomorrow, he would worship her all the days of his life.

"Bartholomew?" Her hand caressed his cheek, loving the rough feel of his burgeoning beard. "Are you all right?"

He swallowed salty liquid along with the emotions choking him. Nothing must get in the way of what he meant to do for her this night. "I've never been more right," he said.

He kissed her with all the finesse learned in his days of freedom at the university so long ago—though this kiss was like nothing he had known then or ever before, for this kiss was born of love as well as of passion. Tender, fiery, giving, demanding. He put his all into it, tamping down his own needs as he sought to show her what she meant to him.

When his lips finally left hers, Ariah's breathing was as ragged as his. Sensations similar to those she had experienced the evening before racked her body. She was at a loss to understand them. But she did know how special she felt as Bartholomew gazed at her with fire-hazed ebony eyes, as though she were a rare and precious pearl.

"Your skin is so translucent, smoother than silk." His fingertips drifted over a breast. "Softer than otter fur."

Blood sang in Ariah's veins as, like every woman before her, she became aware of her power over a man. He wanted her. She could see it in the glazed expression on his rapt face, feel it in the slight tremor in his hands. And she wanted desperately to be whatever he thought her to be—beautiful, precious, desirable.

His grip loosened, allowing her to move against him. She gasped as her breasts brushed the lawn of dark hair on his chest. Excitement ignited a fire in the deepest regions of her being. Childlike in her uninhibited enjoyment, she rubbed herself over his body and heard his throaty chuckle.

"You like that?" he asked.

"It feels like . . . like the lightest sort of tickling, only better. I can feel it all the way from here"—she touched her breast, then her groin—"to here."

Bartholomew's insides jackknifed with desire. "That's the way it's supposed to be," he said in a hoarse whisper.

"Does it feel that way to you, too?"

"Yes, only I might put it a bit more strongly."

"More strongly?" She rubbed her breasts against him again. "I can't imagine anything stronger than this."

He laughed wolfishly. "You'll do more than imagine it before I'm through, little nymph."

She coyly cocked her head and her smile became slightly crooked, like the tooth he had come to adore. "What kind of nymph am I? A dryad, a nymph of the trees and woods? Or a naiad, a river nymph with the gift of prophecy, the patron of poetry and music." Her voice lowered seductively. "The fertility nymph."

Bartholomew groaned. "Heaven forbid. No, you're a sea nymph, one who assists sailors in need."

"Ah, a Nereid." She ran her finger along his lower lip. "Are you a sailor in need?"

He nipped her finger, delighted with her teasing play. "Desperately in need."

Suddenly she was the shy innocent again. She ducked her head and her tone was hesitant, almost apologetic. "I'm afraid I don't really know how to help you."

Charmed, Bartholomew kissed the finger he had captured. "I'll teach you."

He kissed all her fingers, then stroked her palm with the tip of his tongue, until she uttered a startled "Oh!"

"What is it?"

"Your tongue on my palm."

"What about it?"

"It shocked me . . . I mean, sort of the way it happened when, as a child, I'd run along the carpet, then touch the brass doorknob and my hand would go all tingly and almost numb. Except, then it was more like pain. This felt good, like having my hair brushed or when you kiss me."

Bartholomew smiled. "Then you liked it?"

"Yes."

He put his tongue to the soft unprotected skin of her inner wrist and felt her shudder. "That's only a beginning, nymph, only one raindrop in the storm I'm about to unleash in you."

He pushed her gently onto her back and turned onto his side next to her, supported on one elbow while he slowly nibbled his way up her arm.

" 'Had we but world enough, and time,' " he whispered, dipping his tongue into the depression inside her elbow, " 'this coyness, lady, were no crime. We would sit down, and think which way to walk, and pass our long love's day . . . I would love you ten years before the Flood, and you should, if you please, refuse till the conversion of the Jews.' "

He worked his way to her shoulder and across to the curve where her neck began, tasting the sweet, musky flavor of her. She smelled of wood smoke and herbs and her own special, arousing brew of scents.

Bartholomew's hand on Ariah's waist was hot, yet soothing. She shut her eyes, more than willing to do as he asked and give herself over to him. Her lips parted and her breathing became more rapid as he bombarded her with one new sensation after another, tactile and auditory.

" 'A hundred years should go to praise thine eyes, and on

thy forehead gaze . . .' " He kissed the tender spot beneath her ear, slid his tongue around the contour of the ear, then kissed each eyelid. " 'Two hundred to adore each breast . . .' "

The mere mention of her breasts sent a thrill of anticipation down Ariah's spine. Eagerly she waited to see what he would do next. And he did not disappoint her.

He gently suckled first her lower lip, then the upper, a hint of what was to come, though she was too innocent to catch it. He increased the pressure of the kiss until her lips parted and he could mate his tongue with hers.

Ariah gasped when she felt his hand on her breast, and he drank it in. Her arms came around his neck, and she clung as though she would never let him go. He drank that in too. But he had more to show her, so he disentangled his mouth from hers and moved to the breast he had warmed and firmed with his hand. Her body jerked at the first shock of what he was doing, then arched to make her more accessible. When he began to suckle, she moaned. Talons of need sank into him at the sound, hardening his body even more, but he shrugged them aside. He cradled a breast in his hand, stroking it with his thumb while he took the nipple of the other between his teeth and gently tugged.

Ariah lay perfectly still, afraid to move lest he cease this marvelous thing he was doing to her.

Between kisses he continued to whisper: " '. . . an age at least to every part, and the last age should show your heart. For, lady, you deserve this state, nor would I love at lower rate.' " His head lifted and he gazed at her with dark, passionate eyes. " 'But at my back I always hear Time's winged chariot hurrying near: And yonder all before us lie deserts of vast eternity.' "

Only the widening of Ariah's eyes acknowledged the stroke of his hand down over her stomach and onto her thigh. His fingers dipped daringly between her legs where her skin was like softest velvet and so sensitive that she cried out.

The rush of sensation flooding over Ariah, pooling at the tip of her womb, was so intense she thought she might die of it.

But as his hand moved upward, closer and closer to her most private place, her breathing became so rapid she had to pant to get enough air into her lungs, and she knew what he meant when he said he had more yet to show her.

" '. . . Then worms shall try that long-preserved virginity,' " he whispered, " 'and your quaint honour turn to dust, and into ashes all my lust. The grave's a fine and private place, but none, I think, do there embrace.' "

Bartholomew's mouth came down hard on hers in a burning kiss. His tongue swooped inside, drinking in her subtle flavors. Her untutored response as she parried tongue thrusts with him and lifted her hips against his hand drove him higher. He could hear the blood pound in his ears, feel his body—trapped beneath the bedclothes—demanding release. He left her lips to trail kisses along the sensitive underside of her jaw, then down to the depression at the base of her throat, while his fingers searched out the moist softness at the joining of her legs.

Ariah moaned his name and writhed under his touch, wanting more but not knowing how to go about getting it. When she felt something firm push into her, she gasped. "Bartholomew! Is that . . . ? Are you planting seeds?"

He chuckled. "No, nymph. It's only my finger. I'm not going to plant any seeds in you."

"Why not?"

"Because when"—he couldn't bear to speak Pritchard's name now—"when I get you to the lighthouse, you may be more knowledgeable about the physical side of marriage, but you'll still be the virgin I promised to deliver."

"No, I want you to be the one to—"

"Quiet, little Nereid. Trust me. You're only frightened because you don't know what to expect. I'm going to show you and, at the same time, give you enough pleasure to banish your fear of the marriage bed. I can do that without ruining you."

"Don't you want to plant seeds in me?"

The innocent passion in her blue eyes as she stared up at him and the hurt in her voice nearly drove him over the edge. "Oh,

God, yes. There's nothing I want more at this moment than to sink myself into you, to become one with you. But it would be wrong. You're promised to another man, my own nephew, for hell's sake, and I . . ."

He sighed and hugged her tightly. "Please, trust me, let me show you what pleasure I can. You like it when I touch you, don't you?" he asked, needing to be certain he was not allowing himself to be blinded by his own need.

"Oh, yes. It's odd, the way it makes me feel . . . sort of shivery, but hot at the same time. I want to . . . to move, to do something, only I don't know what, and another part of me is afraid to move for fear you'll stop and the feeling will go away."

"I'm not going to stop, not unless you ask me to. And the sensations you're feeling are going to grow more intense. Go with them, nymph, let them take you where they will."

"I think I'm a little afraid."

Fear that he was frightening her, rather than reassuring her, struck him to the core. "Why?"

"Because when you hold me and touch me and kiss me like that, I have a strange desire to climb right inside you, to become part of you, as though I were losing hold of myself."

Relief made him chuckle. "And simply becoming an extra foot or a third ear?" She slugged his arm, but he saw her smile.

"Don't laugh at me," she said. "You asked, and I only tried to answer honestly."

"I'm not laughing at you, I'm laughing because I feel the same way."

"You do?"

"It's normal when you feel passion for someone to want to become part of them. That's why it's called mating."

For a long time she said nothing, but he could tell she was thinking hard.

"Does that mean if I touch you, you'll feel the same way I do?"

He shivered, merely thinking of her touching him. "Yes, I'll feel the same."

As if to test him, she put her hand on his chest. She studied his face as she combed her fingers through the hair there and massaged firm muscles. When her hand moved lower and the fingers slid under the covers hiding his abdomen, his eyes closed and his mouth tightened.

"Did I hurt you?" she asked.

A strangled sound, half-grunt, half-laughter, was her answer. "No, nymph, no more than my touch hurts you." To prove his point he spread his thick blunt hand over the concave flesh between her hips, the tips of the fingers nesting in her hair.

Ariah's lips parted in a silent moan and her eyes half closed. "I'm convinced."

"So am I." He kissed her. "I'm convinced that you are the most delectable, most seductive nymph I've ever known."

Ariah frowned. "How many nymphs have you known?"

Bartholomew ran a finger over her swollen lips, following it with his tongue. "Only you."

"But you have . . . planted seeds with other women, haven't you?"

"I am married, Ariah."

"Besides her, I mean."

He sighed, seeing that she was serious. Yet he was pleased by her jealousy. "There were other women before my marriage, yes, but none that meant anything to me."

"Do I mean something to you?"

"Oh, Ariah. Sweet, innocent Ariah." He rested his forehead against hers, wondering how to answer without making things worse between them. "Don't ask that. Not because you mean nothing to me—that's not true—but because neither of us is in a position to allow the other to be more than a friend."

Ariah twined her arms around his neck. "But you're already more than a friend to me, Bartholomew. I love you."

Bartholomew moaned. Her words were like a killing shaft of sunshine, driving deep inside him and making his heart sing even while it sank beneath a weight of fear for what the future would bring them.

"Don't say that, nymph. I'm the first man you've ever really known. You might want to take your words back someday."

"Never. Love me, Bartholomew. Show me the pleasure you promised." Her voice vibrated with emotion. "For this one night, let's pretend tomorrow doesn't exist."

With gladness tinged with guilt, he acquiesced, kissing her eyes and tasting their saltiness. " 'Let us roll all our strength and all our sweetness up into one ball,' " he whispered, " 'and tear our pleasures with rough strife thorough the iron gates of life. Thus, though we cannot make our sun stand still, yet we will make him run.' "

And with that, he shoved aside the bedclothes and brought her full against him, thigh to thigh, breast to breast, eager mouth to eager mouth.

Twelve

To Bartholomew the feel of Ariah's supple body pressed against his was more beautiful than the sea with the waves whipped high by the wind, and more intoxicating than wine. He had been wrong when he'd decided years ago that hell and life on earth were the same thing; there was a heaven, after all.

Ariah's thoughts were not so precise, but she would have agreed that this was indeed heaven.

For long moments, simply the embrace was enough. Then Bartholomew's mouth searched out hers, and his hands began to move in slow, indolent circles over her warm, supple body. His fingers traced the tapering line of her back to the flare of her hips, climbed the stairstep of her spine to gently massage her slender shoulders and arms. They explored the swell of her breasts where her body was compressed against his, then moved lower to find matching dimples above the firm roundness of her buttocks.

Ariah had no such freedom to investigate his body, but her awareness heightened with each minute that passed. An awareness of heat, of hard corded muscles, of strength, power and blatant virile masculinity. Then he rolled over and she found herself pinned beneath all that muscle and heat and power. It occurred to her that she should feel crushed. Instead, she felt like a gosling tucked beneath its mother's protective wing. Secure, sheltered, cherished.

Bartholomew shifted to the side and renewed his titillating caresses. Ariah daringly began her own explorations. She adored the way the dark hair on his arms tickled her palms, and longed to see if the thick wedge on his chest would do the same, but she gladly settled for the ecstasy of that rough texture gently abrading her breasts. The bunching of his powerful muscles beneath her hands as he moved over her—his lips following the trail his hands had blazed—sent butterflies flitting through her veins. She became lost in a hurricane of sensation that swept everything else aside and made rational thought impossible.

Bartholomew's hands and lips were everywhere, burning her even while they worshiped her. Her heart rose into her throat, its staccato rhythm thunder in her ears. Her body ebbed and flowed beneath his touch, eagerly responding to his every entreaty, whispered or implied. Ariah's senses spiraled upward, higher and higher, until she thought she would disintegrate from so much pleasure. She resisted in the same instant that she grabbed for more, her blood pumping every bit as hotly and as fiercely as his.

Bartholomew hadn't thought it would be this difficult to hold back. To give without taking. He trembled with the effort it took to restrain, to control. Her ardent, guileless responses were more seductive than the most erotic performance of a master courtesan. With Ariah there was spontaneity. *Shared* rapture, *mutual* bliss. He took none of it for granted. Though his body demanded release, he clung to rigid control. His pleasure would have to lie in the knowledge that he had given her all she could endure. There would be no other joy for him. And he would keep driving her higher, farther, closer to the edge, until she screamed for mercy.

In her mind, Ariah was already crying out for release. She simply didn't know how to put her need into words.

Every pulse point in her body throbbed. In her temples. In the lips he had suckled and nipped and kissed until they felt bruised. At the base of her throat. In the breasts he had fondled and laved and nursed to hard, pulsating points. Even behind her knees. And between her legs. Especially between her legs, in that dark, humid, secret grotto which his wondrously clever hand was, at that very moment, stalking.

The fingers delving into her heat, seeking out her core, were feverishly hot, but not as hot as Ariah. With a wordless whimper, heedless of her own actions, of anything and everything except the need sweeping her on toward a misty, rainbow horizon, she arched against him. Instinctively, her legs parted and when he found her, she closed around him like a clam, as though frightened that he would steal whatever pearl she might have to offer, then run away, leaving her in empty agony.

But Bartholomew stole nothing and gave everything. Like the sail of a ship he hoisted her up and up, until at last she reached the tip of the tallest mast.

Her cries found voice, ragged, strangled words of wonder and ecstasy that set the blood in his loins throbbing, hot and heavy, with each triumphant beat of his heart, nearly taking him over the edge with her. As her body spasmed beneath him, plummeting her over the peak, he murmured throaty reassurances and approval.

Her eyes flew open, wide with astonishment, twilight dark with the last draining dregs of passion he had ruthlessly wrung out of her. Watching, Bartholomew smiled from a mask of restraint that stretched his lips taut across his teeth in a grimace that might have frightened her if she hadn't been too lost in his spell to grasp the reality of what she was seeing.

He saw her eyes glaze, saw the lashed lids drift shut, heard her sigh of repletion. Burrowing his face in her hair, he drank in the scent of her passion, acute, pungent, arousing, and he groaned with the torment of having to deny his own raging need.

For a long time, Ariah floated on a velvet sea, riding the gentle waves like a gull, sated and sluggish after a feast.

Nothing in her life had ever prepared her for what she had experienced moments before. She felt lost in a world of fantasy and confusion. Questions stirred sleepily in her mind, but she ignored them, giving herself up instead to the call for rest. Curling herself tighter into Bartholomew's warm body, she slept.

* * *

The first golden fingers of dawn were piercing the lace curtains at the window like crystallized needles of light when Ariah awoke. The pillow under her head was rock hard, yet amazingly warm. Experimentally, she moved her hand from beneath her cheek out over the odd surface, marveling at its downy surface. Velvet-encased stone.

Through the blur of her sleepy gaze she saw a forest of dark hair on a gently rolling plain that pulsed with a beat similar to that of her heart. Her fingers tunneled into the forest, finding it pleasantly ticklish and silky soft. Memory stirred, but she made no effort to catch it.

Then she became aware that her entire body was wrapped around that same velvet stone on which her head lay. And she was shockingly naked. Slowly she brought up her knee, tracking a landscape of warmth and hardness. When her leg encountered a protuberance that was particularly hot and rigid, she was startled to feel it move beneath her. Someone groaned and she lifted her head.

Only inches away, Bartholomew Noon stared back at her, his eyes dark with indecipherable emotions, his mouth a tight slash across his bristled face.

"Oh!" Ariah's eyes opened wide.

"Good morning," he said, the slant of his mouth crooking up at one corner.

At once she realized that she lay in the bed, curled about him, his body as shamelessly naked as hers. Memory crashed over her like a tidal wave, and she blushed to her toes. When she tried to extricate herself, his arm tightened around her.

"It's too late to run," he teased.

She stared at him, noting the purplish blue tinge beneath tired eyes and the taut flesh stretched across his forehead and over his firm jaw. Obviously, while she had slept the night away—done in by the incredible experience he had given her—he had lain awake, holding her and . . . and what?

"You haven't slept," she said. "Are you upset? Are you wishing that I . . . that I had stayed in the loft?"

The dark eyes closed. "No, I wasn't wishing you'd stayed away." His voice was a hoarse whisper, tight, hinting of pain. "Only that I had found you seven years sooner."

"But I was only a child then."

"Yes, I suppose you were."

His large hand pressed her knee firmly down on his hot flesh. His eyes squeezed shut, his expression became one of near rapture, then he nudged her leg lower down his body. When his eyes opened she saw regret, need, and pain in their ebony depths. Suddenly it became clear exactly on what her knee had been residing. She let out a small gasp and turned a bright shade of rose. "Oh! I-I didn't mean to . . ." she stammered in embarrassment. "I didn't realize what—"

Bartholomew gave a husky laugh and hugged her tight. "I didn't mind, believe me."

Her blue eyes wore a haze of concern. "But you looked as though you were in pain."

"It's a pain I'm well accustomed to." His face sobered, and the tortured look returned to his eyes.

"Why? What causes it?"

He glanced at her in surprise, then smiled and shook his head. "I keep forgetting how innocent you are."

"Not as innocent as I was yesterday."

He chuckled, but his voice held regret. "No, you'll never be that innocent again."

"I'm glad." She looked at him from beneath lowered lashes, shyly, but with a saucy tilt to her smile. "I enjoyed last night."

Bartholomew tucked a finger under her chin and lifted her face for his kiss. "For that, I'm glad."

"But did you? Enjoy last night, I mean?"

"Yes, nymph, I enjoyed it more than anything in my whole life."

"Even though you planted no seeds?"

His chuckle was brief and terse. "Even though."

Silence stretched between them like a drawn bow, while Ariah idly combed her fingers through the hair on his chest.

"What is it, little Nereid? I hear the whir of unasked questions spinning in your brain."

She cleared her voice, but several more seconds passed before she finally spoke. "I was only wondering . . ."

"Wondering what?"

"If you felt everything I felt last night?"

His hand stroked her cheek as he gazed into her curious eyes. "The purpose of last night was to show you part of what happens between a man and a woman in the marriage bed. What I felt doesn't signify."

"But—"

He cut her off by covering her mouth with his, brushing his lips over hers, once, twice, then returning to deepen the contact. With his tongue, he traced the generous curves of her mouth, teasing the corners and the tiny mole on her upper lip until she opened to him. When her tongue darted out to spar with his, desire ripped through him in a hot, searing flash that brought a groan from deep in his throat. His breath came out in a ragged sigh.

Ariah squirmed closer, loving the feel of his body against hers. Her knee rose higher. Only when Bartholomew's hand blocked its travels did she realize where she had been aiming—that hot, firm, intriguing protuberance she had encountered before.

"If you want to kill me," he whispered against her mouth, "it would be kinder to use a knife."

"My knee hurt you that badly?"

"No, but that kind of touch incites the wolf chewing at my innards because it can't get at you."

"A wolf?" Her brow puckered with confusion. "That wants to eat me? I don't understand, Bartholomew."

He laughed. "Of course you don't. Never mind."

Bartholomew tried to bring her face back for another kiss, but she jerked away.

"Don't be condescending, Bartholomew. You're suffering for

some reason, something that has to do with me, with what we did last night, and I need to know why."

Bartholomew sighed heavily. "There is some . . . discomfort when a man becomes fully aroused and is then denied release. Don't worry about it, nymph. I can handle it."

"What do you mean . . . release?"

"It's what happened to you last night, when you went over the edge. When your pleasure became so intense it bordered on pain, then gave way. When a man reaches that point his seed is released into the woman's body."

"Oh, I understand now. You weren't inside me, so you couldn't release your seed. Your body—the wolf—was primed, and now it's punishing you for cheating it."

Bartholomew's chuckle was dry, hollow. "A very apt description."

Ariah levered herself onto an elbow. Staring down at him, she stroked his bristled face with her hand. "I don't want you to suffer because of me, Bartholomew."

Gently, he ran a fingertip along the well-defined contours of her full mouth. "It was worth it."

"But isn't there some way—"

His hand moved quickly to the back of her head, pulling her down for a kiss and effectively cutting off her words. "We already discussed this," he said against her lips. "I won't take your innocence and ruin you for marriage, Ariah."

Her mouth thinned, but she said nothing. After a moment she drew away, rolled to the edge of the bed and sat up. Reluctantly, he let her go, watching as she rose to her feet.

Her body was even more beautiful in the light of early morning than it had been in last night's darkness. Her back was straight, the spine gracefully curved. From her shoulders her form narrowed in a vee to her tiny waist, then flared gently into femininely rounded hips and firm buttocks. She slipped her gown on over her head, obstructing his view. But the damage had already been done. Hot blood shot through his body to pool between his thighs. He gritted his teeth against the need to pull her back down on the bed. To sheath himself in her tight heat and know the ecstasy of loving her, a rapture he knew would surpass anything he had ever experienced before. His hands coiled into claws and his body tensed, ready to spring like the ravenous wolf gnawing inside him.

Caging the wolf of his own sensuality was more difficult than he had ever imagined as he lay there watching her slip from the room, leaving behind a void that was bigger than the bottomless sewage pit in which he had lived for years.

When she was gone, he buried his head beneath his crossed arms and struggled to find some island of peace in the chaos of his brain, an oasis in which to take refuge until he could rebuild the walls of blessed apathy that had protected him and kept the wolf in a harmless stupor, before Ariah Scott came to set it free.

Ariah opened the cabin door onto a world of blue skies and fleecy white clouds. In the east the sun shone round and yellow as a gold coin. Chirping sparrows skipped about in the frosted grass searching for seeds, and the cheerful song of an American goldfinch drifted on a gentle breeze to her ears.

"Bartholomew," she called urgently. "Bartholomew, hurry, come look."

Fear slammed into him, sending adrenaline pumping into his heart. He leaped from bed, yanked on his trousers and arrived at the door, barefoot and shirtless.

Ariah stood on the porch, beaming up at him.

"Look, isn't it beautiful?" She lifted her face to the sun, eyes closed, nostrils flaring as she inhaled the fresh brisk air. "I can almost fancy that I smell the sea."

Bartholomew smiled, unable to resist her contagious joy, in spite of the fact that the sun's warmth was minimal, the earth was still slick with frosted mud, and she had yet to realize the consequences of the change in weather. But he knew, and inside, a part of him died.

"But at my back I always hear Time's winged chariot hurrying near."

<h1 style="text-align:center">Thirteen</h1>

Bartholomew pulled the wagon off the road onto a grassy meadow and brought the horses to a halt. He made no move to get down, merely sat there staring at the reins in his hands as though he didn't recognize the narrow strips of rawhide or know what to do with them.

Ariah put a hand on his arm. "Bartholomew, are you all right? Why have we stopped?"

He shifted the reins to one hand and put the freed one over hers. Ever since they had left John Upham's place, shortly before dawn, they had been taking advantage of every excuse they could find to touch each other.

With the arrival two days ago of sunny weather, Bartholomew had spent the days helping to construct a new bridge. When he returned that first night, he brought with him three young men who had been waiting at a very crowded Summit House which was already full with stage passengers and other travelers eager for the bridge to open. Since the oldest of the men was the cousin of an old friend in Tillamook, Bartholomew felt obliged to offer them lodging, in spite of his reluctance to give up his time alone with Ariah.

Yesterday, Bartholomew had come home alone; the bridge was finished and the three young men had gone on to Tillamook. Alone again, Ariah and Bartholomew felt awkward with each other, haunted by guilt over what had happened between them, and torn by the desire to do it again. Supper that evening was quiet and strained. Bartholomew was washing the last of the dishes and trying to convince himself he preferred to sleep alone that night, when a wagon pulled into the yard. The door burst open and John Upham bustled inside, carrying his son whose leg was in a plaster cast.

"I knew you'd be here, Bart. Damn glad to see you," John had said setting the boy down.

Olivia had smiled sweetly. "We told Hester you would be here, safe and fine, but she fretted something awful."

The eyes of the elder Uphams then fixed on Ariah, and her face flushed guiltily. Everything changed then. Bartholomew's marriage could no longer be ignored, and an invisible wall rose between him and Ariah.

Now, sitting there in the wagon beside the road, Ariah was grateful for whatever private time she might have left with Bartholomew. At every curve in the road she had stiffened with the fear that around that corner, they would find Tillamook—and Hester—waiting for them like a vulture over carrion.

As though he had read her mind, Bartholomew gently kneaded her fingers. "These last two days have been hard."

"For me, too." She leaned her head on his shoulder.

Bartholomew had spent his boyhood in Tillamook. It was home. For the first time in his life, that thought filled him with dread. He forgot the early days of pranks and highjinks with his brothers and sister. Swimming in the river, crabbing in the bay. Every stray cat and dog in the neighborhood—and a few who weren't strays—geese, ducks, a tame turkey, even a jackass, trailing after him as though he had a pocket full of meat bones and dried apples. Which he did.

First John married and moved away, then Mary and Calvin, leaving behind fifteen-year-old Bartholomew to shoulder chores they had all once shared. He had never blamed them. They'd had no way of knowing Martha Noon would fall victim that same year to a series of strokes. For Bartholomew happiness ended with his mother's death. No more hugs. No more apple pie secreted away just for him. No more laughter. No more love.

With the work and responsibility for an entire dairy farm on his young shoulders, following his father's paralysis, Bartholomew had found little pleasure to enliven his days as an adult. Only the sensuous sway of an older woman's hips. The softness of a breast pressed into his shoulder as she reached across him to place a platter of meat on the table. The feminine glance that stayed a moment too long upon his generous mouth. Hester.

Already, as he sat in the wagon beside the road, he felt his wife's grip on him tightening. Sucking his soul dry. Stripping his life once more to the barest of bones. Duty. Honor. Responsibility.

Celibacy.

Panic raced through his veins, urging him to run. To take Ariah and disappear. Fight for your happiness, it seemed to scream in his ears. How he wished he could.

Without looking at Ariah, he nodded toward the curve in the road. "On the plain beyond that curve lies Tillamook. We'll be at Reverend Ketcham's house in half an hour."

Ariah's fingers tightened on his arm. "Oh, Bartholomew. Suddenly I feel afraid."

He looked at her, his mouth crooked in a wistful smile. "You? My outrageously impetuous nymph?" He ran a finger along the curve of her lip, pausing to explore the tiny mole that begged for his kiss. "I can't imagine you afraid of anything."

She wanted to tell him that she wouldn't be, if he could always be beside her, but saying so would only increase his pain. Instead, she put out her tongue and tasted his finger.

"Ariah, my sweet Ariah." He gathered her into his arms, and she clung to him with a tenacity that told him all he needed to know of her feelings. After a while, he drew back. Her eyes glittered with unshed tears. He caught her chin on the edge of his hand and kissed her softly. Then he put her away from him, took up the reins and flicked them against the horse's flanks.

As the wagon jolted into movement, Ariah faced forward, her back ramrod straight, her hands gripping the edge of the wagon seat. Up ahead lay her future, and while part of her trembled at what it might bring, her youthful optimism and quick, curious mind burgeoned with hope.

"That girl ain't nothing more than a slut."

Hester Noon snapped a dead twig off a rhododendron bush and viciously crumbled it between her thin fingers.

Bartholomew shoved his hands into his trouser pockets to keep from striking the woman. "Hester, I'll not allow you to speak of Miss Scott that way. She's your nephew's fiancée. How do you think he would feel to hear you call his bride such names?"

"She won't be his bride. Not if I have anything to say about it."

Bartholomew closed his eyes. Once, he had enjoyed Hester's soft Southern drawl. Since their marriage he heard it only when company was about. Otherwise, her voice rose to a whiny shriek he had come to detest. Pain throbbed at the back of his head. The woman would not rest until she created trouble between Ariah and Pritchard. The boy was not strong willed. He not only allowed his aunt to walk all over him, he almost seemed to kiss her feet as she did it. Bartholomew let out a snort of disgust and strode several feet away. His nerves were more tightly laced than Hester's corset, and he felt a need for action, preferably something violent.

He glanced up as a flash of yellow caught his eye. Ariah stood at the library's French doors, taking advantage of the light to study one of the reverend's books. An avid collector of seashells, Ketcham had recently published a work of his own entitled *An Analytical Key for the Collection and Identification of Oregon Seashells*. Obviously fascinated, Ariah was spending a good deal of time perusing the reverend's excellent library of books on Oregon wildlife.

Bartholomew didn't blame her. If he could, he'd bury himself in a pile of books as well. Anything would be better than listening to Hester rail at him for something he had no control over. Turning, he walked back to his wife. The light was fading fast now that the sun had gone down. He was tired and eager for his bed. It was the only place he could be certain Hester would leave him alone. "Marrying Miss Scott is Pritchard's decision, Hester. It's none of our business, and I won't allow you to interfere."

"Like thunder it ain't my business. My brother entrusted him to me when he let him come all the way here from Missouri to live with me. And I'm not gonna let Otis down."

Bartholomew stepped closer and pinned her with a look that could fell trees. "Otis had no choice in the matter, and you know it. Pritchard came without his parents' knowledge, let alone their permission."

"But Otis let him stay, which proves that—"

"It proves only that your brother was smart enough to know when he was licked. What good do you suppose it would have done for Otis to order Pritchard back? Good hell, woman, the boy's of age. He can go where he pleases."

"He needed a mother figure in his life, what with Euphronia dying when he was so young, and he chose *me* to come to."

"Poor fool that he is." Bartholomew started for the house. He'd done all the arguing he intended to do. Inside was a woman as sunny as the dress she wore, and he meant to absorb as much of her sweet spirit as he could, even if it was from across a silent and forbidding room.

Hester had different ideas. She grabbed his arm. "What do you mean by that? I done my best by that boy. He loves me."

Bartholomew whirled to face her. His dark eyes sparked like obsidian striking stone. "He fears you, Hester. No more, no less. You interfere with his marriage and I'll see to it the reverend and all your other friends here learn the more colorful parts of your past."

"No!" She backed away from his cold implacable glare until she came up against the rhododendron bush and could go no farther. Bartholomew kept coming, his enormous shoulders blocking out what was left of the fading sunlight.

"You seem to think you can bind all of us to you through

fear, Hester, but don't delude yourself into believing that that is the same as love."

Hester made a sound of derision. "I'd certainly never make that mistake with you, Bartholomew. There's no love in you, threatening me like that."

He leaned over her, forcing her back into the shrub until her thin face was framed by the thick, leathery leaves and he caught their faint scent. "Not for you there isn't. But you never let that stop you from sinking your claws into me seven years ago, did you? Only it was honor that was my downfall. Not fear. Maybe you should keep that in mind; fear is a much stronger incentive than mere obligation."

Her eyes were huge, the irises as green as the rhododendron leaves, and dilated with a fear he knew she would never acknowledge.

Through Bartholomew's shirt Hester could see the muscles of his upper arms and shoulders flex as he clenched his fists. He had the strength to snap her in two, and God knew she'd given him plenty of provocation. Yet she could not resist egging him on a bit more.

"And what about lust, Bartholomew? How far would you let your filthy lust drive you? To that harlot's bed? Did you take what she no doubt offered you, cuckolding my poor foolish Pritchard before he's even bedded her himself?"

He struck before his brain even registered the urge. Her hand flew to her cheek, then fell as she straightened to face him. The red imprint of his hand on her flesh shamed him even more than the heated night he had spent with Ariah in his bed. His gaze lifted to meet hers, and for an insane moment he thought he saw passion blaze in her eyes.

"Well." Hester brushed leaves from the ruffles that capped her sleeves as they would on a child's pinafore. "We know now you aren't above hitting a defenseless woman, don't we?"

An apology was forming on his tongue, but before he could get it out, she added, "First time I've ever seen you act like a man. About time, I'd say."

Stunned, he watched her circle Anna Ketcham's herb garden and enter the house through the kitchen. Then a movement took his gaze back to the French doors off the library. A flicker of yellow skirts. Ariah had seen.

Mortified, Bartholomew hurried to let himself in through the French doors, only to find the room empty. He took the back stairs two at a time and got to the upper hallway in time to hear the door to Ariah's room click shut. Glancing about to make sure no one was around, he knocked and called her name. There was no answer. He turned the knob, found it unlocked, and quickly let himself inside. Ariah was seated in the nook built into the small bay window that overlooked the back yard. Her hands were clasped around her knees, her feet hidden under her skirts.

"Bartholomew, you shouldn't be here." She leaped to her feet and flew across the floor to him.

He took her hands in his, drew them to his chest and held them there. "You saw, didn't you?"

"Yes."

Her gaze never wavered, showing neither disgust nor disapproval. He dropped her hands and clutched her to him in a tight embrace. "Woman, woman, woman, you are a treasure."

The words came out like a sigh. He felt at home in her arms, happy and at peace. How could he give her up? How could he go back to Hester? To live day after day with her freezing contempt, her bitter, negative outlook, her whining complaints.

Ariah belonged to him. How could he stand by and let Pritchard have her? Pain knifed through him until he thought he would die. Wanted to die. Viciously he shoved aside his tortured thoughts. Ariah would never be his, and he had best get used to the idea.

Setting her away from him, he stared intently into her eyes. His voice was harsh with self-contempt. "Would you believe me if I told you I never hit a woman until today? I've never lost control with Hester before, but—"

Ariah placed her fingers over his mouth, shushing him. "I know. It was because of me, wasn't it?"

He opened his mouth to lie to her and found that he couldn't. "You'd have to be homelier than the south end of a two-ton sow to escape her jealousy, Ariah."

She turned away. "Maybe, but we both know I deserve her enmity, don't we?"

He shook his head as he moved to the window and braced a hand against the frame while peering into the gathering darkness. "She's always been a bitter, spiteful woman. No doubt I'm partly to blame."

"I don't believe that. I've wondered a thousand times about your marriage, about what your wife was like. But once I met her, I felt I understood."

He swung about to stare at her, astonished by her gentle tone.

"She doesn't like herself very much, Bartholomew. She sees her own self-loathing in your eyes, and she hates you for it. What she needs is kindness."

"Huh! Kindness." He threw himself down on the window seat and gazed gloomily out at the vacant garden. "When she first came to live with us, she seemed so vulnerable, so . . . defeated. I felt sorry for her. Pa said I had the damn-fool notions of a female. He was right. I saw Hester as a tragic heroine, suffering the injustice of an unfair world."

He chuckled, but there was a dark edge to the sound. "When Pa died and she realized I wouldn't need her anymore, that she'd be without a home again, she—"

He sprang from the bench and went to the door. Matters were bad enough. He didn't need to give Ariah more reason to dislike Hester. Or to pity him. With his hand on the knob, he paused. "Don't trust her too much, little nymph. Hester never forgets, or forgives."

Ariah's trepidation mounted as they boarded the *Henrietta I* off Front Street, and the boat put-putted up Hoquarton Slough.

Her stomach roiled as the boat moved beneath her. She looked over the side at the dark water and fought the terror. The slough didn't look like much more than a stream, but it widened once it merged with the Tillamook River. It broadened even more before emptying into the bay.

She hadn't expected the inlet to be so big. The spot Bartholomew pointed out as Bay City on the north bank was merely a dark blur. The south bank, where ferns and elderberry shrubs crowded the cliff face, was much closer, but not close enough to soothe Ariah's fear. If the boat had sunk in the river she might have had a chance to get to shore, but here, it appeared hopeless. The water was gray and murky, making her shudder as she wondered what lay beneath its riffled surface.

Up ahead, mist shrouded the spit which separated ocean from bay. The sky was overcast, somber and threatening. Gulls wheeled overhead, their melancholy cries filling her with loneliness. She shrugged her cloak more snugly around her slim shoulders, trying to cast off the dread that had descended on her as the time grew near to board the boat.

"It looks entirely different when the tide's out," Bartholomew said as he came to stand behind her.

"You mean the ocean tides affect the water clear in here?"

At his wry chuckle, she glanced at him over her shoulder. Hester, dressed in stiff black bombazine, her skirt so covered with black ruffles and bows that she looked like the inside of a hearse, was scowling in their direction from her seat at the back of the boat where she was guarding her new étagère.

Ariah had been shocked by her first glimpse of Hester. The woman had looked a good deal older than Bartholomew, and she was gaunt, with limp hair and a mouth that turned down at the corners. The guilt Ariah had experienced before meeting Hester had quadrupled. Ariah now heaved a silent sigh. She must try harder to win the woman's friendship. For Bartholomew's sake.

"At low tide this is all mud flats, with only a few channels of water meandering through." Bartholomew waved his hand to indicate the entire inlet. "Travel has to be carefully timed with high tide or you could find yourself up to your knees in muck, dragging the boat across."

Ariah directed her gaze back at the murky water. "Is this actually seawater then?"

"With five rivers emptying into the bay, its pretty much of a mixture." Bartholomew looked down at her white-knuckled hands gripping the railing, and his expression softened. "How's the stomach? Are you still queasy?"

"Yes, very much so. I suppose you think me silly for being afraid of boats."

"I don't think it's boats you're afraid of, but drowning."

Ariah smiled. It was good to have him there beside her, safe and reassuring. "You're right, of course. Once when I was seven, my father took us out in a rowboat on the Ohio River. To me the water seemed so vast and the boat so small. I felt more vulnerable in that boat than I ever have, before or since."

"And you still do."

"Yes. I still do."

They were gazing at each other, smiling, content simply to be near one another. Ariah, conscious of the magnetism between them, the spark that always seemed to ignite when they got close, yearned for him to take her in his arms. The comfort and safety his presence offered wasn't enough. She needed to touch him, and to know he felt the same need. But that could never be. Hester would see to that.

"What are you two looking at?"

At the sound of Hester's querulous voice, Bartholomew casually stepped aside and said, "I was explaining that the waters of the bay are made up of fresh water from the rivers, as well as seawater."

Bartholomew glanced back out toward the sea, feeling the excitement that always came with his first glimpse of the ocean after a trip inland. He tried to pretend Hester wasn't there, but he sensed her presence, the way he sometimes sensed danger. "Are you feeling well, Hester?"

"Of course I am, what are you incinerating?"

"I'm not *insinuating* anything, Hester. Anyone can suffer sea sickness. It does not mark you as a—"

"I said," she interrupted in a voice slightly less genteel than the one Ariah had heard so far, "I ain't ill. You won't have the fun of seeing me rolling around in the bottom of this boat, moaning and groaning like a sick dog."

"Hester—"

Hoping to avert an argument, Ariah interrupted, voicing the first thought that came into her head: "Are there any dogs at the lighthouse?"

Hester sniffed inelegantly. "Most certainly not. Dogs are not only obscurantly filthy but appallingly odoriferous as well. I won't have one near me."

"Been studying the dictionary again, Hester?"

Bartholomew's words were so soft Ariah wasn't certain she heard them, except that Hester was glaring at him as though she wanted to shove him overboard. Then, with a rustle of her black bombazine skirts, she pivoted on her heel and cautiously made her way to her fancy new knickknack shelf. Ariah turned back to the railing, her grip on the weathered wood tightening as the boat struck a swell and rocked. As she scoured the morning mist for a glimpse of the dock at Barnagat, she could still feel Hester's malevolent gaze on her spine.

How much did Hester's nephew resemble her? Ariah's fear of the water was edged aside by new qualms as her thoughts turned to her approaching marriage.

Last evening, after leaving Ariah in her room, Bartholomew had placed their belongings in the care of the boat service and had sent a message to Pritchard to meet them in Barnagat at the next high tide with the horses. Then he'd paid his brother Calvin a visit at the old Noon farm and returned the wagon and team he had borrowed for the trip to Portland. Any moment now the *Henrietta I* would break out of the mist to pull along-side the small wooden dock of a town that was little more than a post office, a school and a few scattered homes. When it did,

Ariah would at last meet the man she was to marry. The man who would lie beside her every night for the rest of her life.

Her stomach heaved at the thought. She closed her eyes and prayed: *Please, Lord, at least let us like each other.*

"I'm relieved to see that Pritchard got my message."

At the sound of Bartholomew's voice, Ariah opened her eyes. The mist surrounded them now, making the rocking boat seem as though it had been lifted into the clouds, a sensation that only added to her nausea. But there, not more than fifty yards in front of them, was the dock. A string of horses waited nearby. Back from shore stood a small building silhouetted against a backdrop of evergreen trees as dark and somber as Hester's black dress—the Barnagat post office.

A slender young man exited the building and ran toward the dock, waving his arms. Ariah's heart picked up speed. Was this her future husband?

Children, brown as berries, with black hair and eyes, scrambled up from their seats on the dock and yanked in their fishing lines as the boat nosed in. But Ariah saw only the young man. He was slight, with light hair and eyes. Nothing like Bartholomew.

The thud of wood against wood abruptly brought her gaze back to the boat. Directly in front of her the dock bobbed up and down alongside the boat. Up, down. Up, down. Instantly, her stomach revolted. She sucked in a deep breath of salty sea air to banish the nausea. A keen wind was whining inside her head, in her ears. Someone was yelling "Uncle Bart, hey, Uncle Bart," but the sound was distant and hollow.

"We're here, Ariah. You can get out of the boat now."

She recognized Bartholomew's voice and felt the warmth of his hand cover hers. She swallowed hard, focused on that large familiar hand until the queasiness ebbed, then glanced up. He smiled gently.

"Let go, nymph. You're safe now."

But she couldn't let go. The entire world was whirling about her, spinning faster and faster.

There was a rustle of stiff fabric, followed by Hester's strident voice. "What's the matter with her, Bartholomew? She's blocking the way. I want to get out. And you have to get my étagère safely onto the dock at once."

"She's lost all her color, Hester. I think she's going to be sick."

Ariah saw Bartholomew's lips move, faintly heard his voice. Her stomach was fishtailing inside her. As long as she could keep staring at him and avoid looking down, she could fight the sickness and the fear. She tried to breathe slowly and deeply, but all she could do was pant. Strong fingers were prying her hands from the railing. Inside her head she was screaming *No! No, I'll fall overboard.* But no sound came from her lips.

"Is this her, Uncle Bart? Is this her?"

Ariah knew the voice belonged to Pritchard Monteer. At last, the time was here for her first glimpse of her intended, if only she could get her eyes past the water to look up. But she couldn't.

"Get that girl away from there, Bartholomew. I told you I want out of this boat. Now."

Ariah's mouth was watering. Her stomach began to convulse.

"I'm doing my best, Hester. Brace her so she doesn't fall when I get her loose."

"Me? You brace her, you brought her here."

"What's wrong with her, Uncle Bart? She's turning green."

Ariah was losing her grip on the railing as her fingers were pried away. The boat was spinning now. Everything inside her head was going round and round. She had to throw herself toward the center of the boat or she would fall overboard. One hand came free and they began on the other. She couldn't hang on much longer. *Left, throw yourself to the left, so when you fall you'll still be in the boat.*

"Easy, Ariah, everything's all right. Hold her, Hester. I can't do this all by myself."

"Uncle Bart?"

Ariah's other hand came free. Shapes and colors flashed

around her. She looked down, trying to find something to focus on, an anchor to hold her steady. The side of the boat bobbed up, then down, up, then down. Every time it went down, she saw black shoes and navy blue trouser legs on the dock. Bile rose into her throat, tasting of spoiled fish guts. Ariah gagged it back. She was falling.

Left, fall to the left.

She lurched to the side and was caught by a strong arm around her middle, accidentally squeezing her stomach.

Ariah vomited.

A woman screeched. Ariah caught a glimpse of stiff, black ruffled skirts, before she fainted.

Fourteen

The lighthouse station at Cape Meares was everything Ariah had hoped for, and more.

Although only two miles from Barnagat, the trip took a good hour by horse. More than once panic stole her breath as her horse slipped and she feared they would tumble backward down the steep trail.

Creeks trickled through the forest, like blood vessels in a hand. Seeps lay in every hollow, scenting the air with musty dampness, and giant Sitka spruce and hemlock enclosed the travelers in a fantasy world where branches reached out like petrified wraiths with arms clothed in tattered green velvet.

Ariah gasped at the sight of a full-grown tree sprouting from the top of what looked like a thick wall encased in moss, in which ferns and smaller trees had taken root.

"Look," she whispered in reverent amazement. "It's eerie, yet so beautiful. But why would anyone build a wall here?"

Pritchard gave the specimen a quick glance, and shrugged. "That's not a wall, it's just an old fallen tree."

"They call them nurse logs," Bartholomew said from his place in front of Ariah. "Rain, fog and the humus provided by the rotting tree make a perfect breeding ground for moss and seedlings."

"I feel as though I've arrived in some strange new world . . . another planet—or one of the stars, perhaps," she said. "One where fairies dance naked in the moonlight and weave the fog into gossamer veils of silk."

Bartholomew chuckled. "Have to be the moon, a star would be too hot. And the fairies would be green and have antennae under those veils." He turned in his saddle to wink at Ariah. "Now, if you spot any nymphs getting ready to dance naked in the moonlight, let me know."

Hester snorted. "Lot of foolish talk, if you ask me."

Suddenly, they broke into the open. Before them stood a barn and two houses, their white paint and lead-colored trim sparkling in the sunlight. Beyond the buildings a finger of land stretched away into the distance, the top of the lighthouse barely visible at its tip. All else was the sea. Billowing clouds mirrored the ocean's grayness, making it difficult to discern where water left off and sky began. Excited, Ariah prodded her mount into a trot, past Bartholomew to the nearest edge of the bluff, where she reined in and slid to the ground.

Never had she expected it to be so beautiful, so awesome. Worked into a white froth, waves battered against sheer ragged walls that formed tiny beachless coves directly below. The water receded, then humped like a spitting cat, to try again. Each wave was unique. Some crashed angrily, spewing froth high into the air, others rolled in with calm precision and but a kiss of foam. Evergreen trees grew to the very edge of the plant-bedecked cliff face. Water streamed down the rough mossy sides. The sea whispered a husky lullaby, accented by the raucous cries of gulls.

Two monoliths stood off the point of land like dark, sinister guardians. Seastacks, she thought, recalling Bartholomew's words about the rocks where sea lions, seals and birds took refuge. The wind flattened her skirts against her legs and snatched her bonnet from her head, leaving it to flap, from the ribbons around her neck, against her back. The action of the water and the gusts rocking her body were miserably reminiscent of the movement of the boat. Nausea threatened, but she swallowed it down. Beneath her feet lay good solid earth. She couldn't drown here.

"Aren't you afraid you'll fall off?"

Ariah whirled at the sound of the voice. Pritchard stood behind her, well away from the edge. His dark, double-breasted coat, with its gleaming brass buttons and the insignia on its collar, stood open to reveal a matching vest. On his head, instead of his keeper's cap, he wore what appeared to be a little round box, upside down, with a stiffened flap over his eyes like an awning.

"Is the ground unstable?" she asked.

He shrugged. "Not when it's dry. But you could lose your balance, you know. Sometimes the wind stops so suddenly you don't realize you've been leaning into it until you fall over."

She looked down at the swirling water so far below, and shuddered. Her retreat from that place was almost as hasty as her mad race to it. Pritchard's hands were clasped behind his back when she joined him. He rocked on his heels, down, up, down, as though ill at ease.

"We had an unusual introduction, didn't we?" she said.

He grinned boyishly. "I don't recall any introduction at all."

Ariah smiled and held out her hand. "In that case, hello, I'm Ariah Scott."

"And I'm Pritchard Monteer."

He took her hand in his and fidgeted with her slim fingers, seeming uncertain what else to say. His own fingers were small and, like his face, unmarked by life. When he spoke, the words came out in a rush, as though he were afraid he wouldn't get them out otherwise.

"I set the wedding for Saturday next. Reverend Ketcham has agreed to perform the ceremony . . . if that's all right with you," he added hastily, meeting her gaze with anxious eyes. "You do still want to get married, don't you?"

She felt an odd urge to straighten his collar, check behind his ears, then take him to the kitchen for cookies. The hazel eyes might have been Hester's, except that his reminded Ariah of soft summer grass instead of tundra and icy glaciers. His brown hair was slick with pomade and parted down the middle, the way John Upham wore his. Only Pritchard's refused to lay flat. It curled at the temples, like the wings of the angel *Patera* put on top of the Christmas tree each year. The memory brought a stab of pain to her heart. Deftly, she withdrew her hand.

"Don't you want to get to know me first?" she asked, thinking of the humiliating moment in the boat when she'd lost control of her heaving stomach. Bartholomew—dear, thoughtful Bartholomew—had taken them to a house where an Indian woman had helped her clean up and change. Warm tea and a bit of rest had put her to rights. "I might do worse things than vomit on your poor aunt, you know."

His cheeks flushed with color. "I thought young ladies didn't discuss such unseemly subjects as bodily functions."

"Stuff and nonsense. If I can get sick in public and still be a lady, then surely I can talk about it."

Thinking that over, he smiled. "It does seem rather silly that just talking about something natural and necessary should dictate what kind of person you are."

"Of course it's silly. But the world is full of ridiculous ideas. Like women being suited only to raise children, when they could become perfectly fine doctors and lawyers."

Pritchard frowned. "But if all women took such notions, what would happen to the world? Nobody'd have any babies."

"Don't be absurd. A career would not necessarily preclude motherhood. Besides, not all women would want to be doctors or lawyers. There would always be plenty who preferred to stay home and be fat three-quarters of every year."

Her reference to the state of pregnancy again had the color rising in Pritchard's cheeks. Swallowing her amusement, Ariah suggested they join the others.

"Holy Hector! Aunt Hester will box my ears." He started back toward the houses, taking her horse with him. "There's unloading and putting away to do, and she said to tell you she expects you to do your share."

"I'm sorry, I never meant not to help." Ariah hurried to catch up with him. "It's only that this was my first glimpse of the ocean and I was carried away. But I'm going to love it here, I know I am."

He came to a halt so suddenly that she nearly ran into him. The mare whinnied in protest. "Does that mean you'll marry me?"

She glanced at his eager, smooth-skinned face and wondered if kissing him would be as pleasant as kissing Bartholomew. He was no taller than she was. All she had to do was lean forward.

Pritchard gasped as her lips briefly met his. "Holy Hector!" He took her by the arms and pulled her fully against him. His nose sideswiped hers as he sought her mouth. It was a wet, awkward kiss, and she found herself shoving at him to escape.

When he finally released her, he took off his cap, tossed it into the air and let out a whoop of joy. He ran a few paces toward the houses, then turned. "I've got to go tell the others. We're going to have fun, you and me, wait and see. I'll make you glad you married me, Ariah, I promise."

Wondering exactly when she had agreed to marry him, and doubting the predicted happiness, Ariah picked up the reins of the forgotten horse. Could she be happy married to Pritchard Monteer? An image of Bartholomew, lantern light highlighting the hard muscles and curves of his naked body, danced into her mind.

Uncle Xenos would come after her. She knew it with a surety she could credit only to female intuition. It was difficult to believe her own uncle could kill her. Yet the memory of her father's bloodied and battered face argued that Xenos was capable of anything. If she didn't marry Pritchard, what would she do? Run someplace else? Keep on running the rest of her life, or until Xenos caught up with her?

The mere thought of getting back on that boat and enduring another ride across the bay was enough to stiffen her resolve to see her original plan through. Marriage was the only sure answer, and she had only one candidate to choose from.

Her decision made, Ariah lifted her gaze to the house that would be her new home. Bartholomew stood in the yard behind the fence, staring at her somberly. Beside him Pritchard was waving his arms in excitement as he passed on the good news. Ariah didn't look to see how Hester took the announcement. It didn't matter to her how Hester felt. Ariah's only interest was in the man still standing by the gate. Even from where she stood she could tell that his knuckles were white from gripping the wooden pickets. The same gentle hands that had strummed her body until it sang with unbelievable ecstasy now curled into angry fists. She wanted to go to him, to deny Pritchard's claim and assure him she would never belong to any man but him. But she could never be his; Bartholomew Noon was already married.

Bartholomew's gaze fell away. His head bowed; then he released the pickets, turned and stalked off between the houses toward the barn. Ariah sucked in a deep shaky breath and let it out in a rush, feeling as if she had just been doomed to hell.

Pritchard waved and called for her to come. She went, but her feet dragged as though she were towing solid steel anchors behind her, rather than a docile mare.

Hester eyed the girl standing in the kitchen doorway and wondered how long it would take to tear out the mass of hair piled on top of Ariah Scott's head, golden strand by golden strand. The girl's skin was flawless now, but it would age, the same way Hester's had. Hester only hoped to live long enough to see it. No, she didn't. She wanted Ariah Scott out of her life much sooner than that. Tomorrow. Yesterday.

"Is there anything I can do to help with breakfast, Mrs. Noon? I do want to make myself useful here," Ariah said.

"How about milking the cows then?"

Taken aback, Ariah stared at the woman. "Milk the cows?"

"You know how, don't you?"

"No, I'm afraid I don't."

"You know how to churn butter? Make jelly? Plant beans?"

"No, I—"

"What the hell use are you going to be around here, then?"

"I can learn how to do those things, can't I?"

"Yes, you can," Bartholomew said from the doorway to the porch. "But there isn't any rush. Is there, Hester?"

His wife caught the threat in his tone and glared back at him. Damn the man for interfering again.

"I'll show you how to do the milking tomorrow after you've had a chance to get your sea legs," Bartholomew told Ariah. He pulled back a chair at the table, indicating that she should seat herself.

" 'T'ain't necessary," Hester put in, determined to keep them from spending more time together. As long as Bartholomew provided the physical comforts Hester desired, and did nothing to prevent her from attaining the status she wanted in the community, she had never cared what he did. Knowing how he was about his precious honor, she had felt safe as far as other women were concerned. But with the arrival of the slut sitting at her table now, everything was different. "She can feed the chickens and accommodate the eggs instead," she said.

Bartholomew gave his wife a satisfied smile, ignoring the misused word. "Fine. Now, what's for breakfast this morning?"

"There's porridge," she said, pouring him a cup of coffee. "Or I could fry you a mess o' eggs."

"Eggs sound wonderful."

Ariah jumped to her feet. "Can I get them for you?"

Scowling, Hester jerked her head toward the pantry set between the kitchen and dining room. "They're in there. You want me to fry you up some, too?"

Ariah opened her mouth to say yes, then glanced from the glowering woman to the pan of prepared mush on the stove. "No. porridge will be fine for me, thank you."

Hester watched her husband's gaze follow the girl from the room as Ariah went to fetch the eggs, and her insides churned. Never had Bartholomew looked at her with such reverence and longing. Not even in the days before their marriage when he had been so hungry for her body she could almost smell his lust.

She had known the minute he got back from Portland that Bartholomew had feelings for the little tart. Feelings no married man ought to have. Now Hester speculated on just how far things had gone while the two of them were holed up at the Upham place so long.

If Miss Uppity Scott figured to have Pritchard and Bartholomew both, she was goin'ta have to rethink her plans, because Hester had some plans of her own to effect. The girl had already taken all she was goin' ta get off'n Hester Noon. Bartholomew could threaten her all he wanted about interfering between Pritchard and his bride, but there were more ways to scrape hair off a skunk than one, and back in the hills of Georgia, Hester had learned them all.

That afternoon Ariah came on a strange structure tucked among the trees near the barn, a roofed framework of chicken wire which seemed to house an unusual growth of plants. As she stared inside, a bird as big as a chicken, with a long, trailing tail, burst from the shrubbery inside, squawking loudly. Startled, Ariah leaped backward.

Aroused by the commotion, other birds scurried off through the grass. Most were dull, unremarkable brown hens, but the males were magnificent. From the tips of their beaks to the ends of their pointed, cross-barred tails, they were at least three feet long. Deep tawny chestnut with blue-black bellies and rich gold-mottled flanks. The iridescent black of their heads appeared emerald green one moment, sapphire blue the next, depending on how the sun struck the feathers. Each eye was marked with a brilliant red patch, and the necks were ringed with a band of white. Bartholomew's pheasants.

As exotic as their homeland China, as handsome as the stained-glass windows of a cathedral, they were breathtakingly beautiful.

"You like my pheasants?"

She jumped again. "Bartholomew!"

He stood a few yards behind her, leaning indolently against an alder tree, his smile as warm and welcoming as the sunny faces of the yellow violets blooming at his feet.

"They're magnificent," she said. "Easily the most striking birds I have ever seen."

Perched on his shoulder was another bird, as outlandish and nearly as colorful in its own way as the pheasants.

Seeing the direction of her admiring gaze, he said, "This is Harlequin. He's a horned puffin. They winter on the seastacks with our tufted puffins sometimes. I think this fellow must have flown into the lighthouse. Ever since I mended his broken wing, he's been trailing after me as though I were his mother."

"A broken wing. Oh, poor little bird."

Harlequin eyed her warily as she reached to pet him.

"The wing has mended quite well, actually," Bartholomew said. "I expect he'll be flying off any day now to join the spring migration."

The puffin evaded her touch, moving closer to Bartholomew and pecking at the collar of his shirt.

"But he's your pet. Can't you keep him?"

"He's a wild creature, Ariah, born to fly free."

Ariah watched the affectionate way the bird nibbled on Bartholomew's ear lobe. "But he seems so content with you."

"Yes, I'm worried about that. I've given him too much attention. If he doesn't go with the others when they migrate, he'll stay here and become a cripple—no longer a normal puffin but not a human either. He'd be better off dead then."

The tender way he stroked the satiny blue-black feathers exposed his affection for the bird, and made her want to feel the snowy white breast herself. Instead of feathers, when she went to pet Harlequin, she met Bartholomew's hand. His fingers curled around hers, gently caressing them while he stared at her, their eyes saying all they didn't dare express out loud.

"I was about to feed the pheasants." He indicated a bucket of grain sitting at his feet. "Want to help?"

"Yes. Please."

He set the puffin on the roof, unlatched the door and waited while she stepped inside. Their hands brushed as they reached into the bucket for grain at the same time. A delicious excitement zinged along Ariah's veins and her heart thrummed. When the bucket was empty they left the pen and he fastened the door securely against the severe winds that frequently buffeted the promontory. In silence they watched the birds scratch for the feed on the mossy ground. After a while Ariah felt his gaze on her and she looked up.

"Is everything all right?" he asked.

She knew he was referring to her small bout with Hester that morning. "Yes, don't worry about me. Please."

He cupped her cheek in one big hand and stared intently into her eyes, his expression so stark with longing that she wanted to wrap her arms around him and smother him with kisses. Her body swayed close enough to feel his warmth and set her heart afire. But Hester's enmity toward her was making life difficult enough for him as it was, and Ariah had no wish to worsen matters.

"Tell me more about your pheasants," she said to distract them. "My mother had an old book on Grecian birds, and there was a cock in it called *phasianos ornis,* the Phasian bird, but I suppose it was of a different species."

He ran his thumb over her lips and gave her a bittersweet smile that told her he understood, that he, too, wished things were different. Then his hand fell away and his tone took on a brisk businesslike quality.

"The Greeks got the Phasian birds at Colchis on the river Phasis hundreds of years ago," he said. "You're right about there being various kinds. Back east they've been importing black-necked pheasants from England for years, trying to establish them in naturalized colonies, but none survived."

He nodded toward the birds in his pen. "These Mongolian ringnecks are the first successfully naturalized in America. I got my start from a fellow in Yamhill County who rescued some of Judge Denny's 1884 shipment when early snow threatened to kill them off before they could be established."

"Mongolian ringnecks?" Ariah bent to peer closer at the proud birds. "But these aren't *Phasianus colchicus mongolicus.* These are *Phasianus colchicus torquatus.*"

Bartholomew hunkered down beside her and stared into the pen. "What are you talking about?"

"The torque on Mongolian pheasants is quite narrow and not as white as on the *torquatus.* See how wide and snowy the collars are on these? They're darker in coloring too, and your full-grown cocks have blue shoulder patches. The Mongolian shoulder patches are white."

"You're right about the coloring, but—"

"There is no 'but,' Bartholomew. Come, I have a copy of the 1789 *Systema Naturae.* You can see for yourself."

She took his hand and tugged him to his feet. Together they walked to the house. "I'll be right back," she said, leaving him in the hall at the foot of the stairs.

"I'm counting on it," he answered. Grinning like a lovestruck school boy, Bartholomew leaned against the wall and watched her climb the three steps to the second landing, then continue upward to the second floor.

At a sound, he turned to see Hester step into the hall behind him. She hadn't come from the kitchen, where he had expected her to be at this time of day, but from outside. One look told him that she had seen him come from the pheasant coop with Ariah. What else had she witnessed? The way his eyes had devoured Ariah, as though she were a chocolate sweet? The way their fingers tangled over the grain bucket? The bittersweet moment when he'd cupped her face in his palm and fought off the urge to kiss her? He was going to have to be a good deal more careful in future, if he wanted to keep his life from becoming more unpleasant than it already was.

"Miss Scott claims that my pheasants are of a different species than what they're called here in Oregon," he said, refusing to buckle under to his wife's accusing stare.

"That so?" Hester looked as though she had been eating green persimmons. "Don't know why that should surprise you. Damned little snippet thinks she's Queen Tut."

"It's *King* Tut, Hester. And in case you have any plans to tumble Miss Scott from her throne, remember what I threatened to do if you caused trouble for her and Pritchard."

Bartholomew moved past her into the parlor and sat down on the sofa facing the fireplace. After a moment, Hester followed and began polishing the new rosewood étagère he had bought her in Portland. A small fire burned merrily on the hearth. Though it was March and virtually spring, the coastal winds still had a bite to them. Bartholomew braced his forearms on his thighs as he held out his hands to the heat. The floor creaked overhead, telling him that Ariah would soon come bouncing down the stairs.

No doubt Hester would linger, pretending to dust the ugly knickknacks already crowding her new prize. Bartholomew much preferred plain, serviceable shelves to anything so fancy and useless, but he had known that its French name would thrill her. Material objects held only one value for Hester—their ability to impress guests. The one exception was a collection of fine china cups and saucers she kept in the dining-room sideboard, unused.

"Here it is, Bartholomew." Ariah sailed into the parlor. Unaware of Hester's presence, she plopped down on the sofa and spread the open book upon his knee with easy familiarity. A slender finger stabbed at the page and the smile she gave him could save gallons of kerosene, could he but figure out how to transfer its power to the great lens in the light-tower. "See," she said. *"Phasianus colchicus torquatus,* more commonly known as the Chinese ringneck pheasant."

She leaned closer to lift his hand from the book so she could turn the page. "Now, here's *The Phasianus colchicus mongolicus,* Mongolian pheasant. Can you tell the difference?"

"Good hell. I'll have to write my buyers and inform them of the correct name." He chuckled, forgetting his wife's presence. "You know I'm going to be well roasted over this. I'm supposed to be an expert on pheasants."

"Oh, but you are." Ariah put her hand on his. "It's not your fault you were misled by—"

The sound of china shattering on the hardwood flooring brought both their heads around. Hester knelt to gather the remnants of the porcelain figurine she had been dusting. Her face was a study in anger, an emotion Bartholomew knew had nothing to do with the loss of the knickknack.

"Oh . . . Hester." Ariah stood, moving away from the woman's husband. "How sad! It appears that an exquisite Meissen figure is broken."

Hester grunted but said nothing.

"I was showing Mr. Noon a volume on birds," Ariah went on. "Do come and join us, the illustrations are quite lovely. The artist was the Duke of Stansbury. I've read that he was a well-respected ornithologist in Britain, as well as an artist."

"No, thank you," Hester said in her loftiest voice. "I have more constrictive methods for occupying my time than pursuing bird illustrations."

Ariah grimaced at the woman's misuse of words. Hester set the broken china pieces on a table between two windows while she fussed with the fronds of a live fern, as though uninterested in the other occupants of the room. Ariah approached her, hugging the book to her breasts as she searched for a way to appease the woman.

"You have a real way with plants, Hester. That's a lovely fern. My mother would have begged you for a start of it."

"Don't waste *my* time on such foolishness. Bartholomew put it here." She swatted the fronds she had been fussing over a moment before. "With an entire forest full o' green stuff out there, I don't compromise the rationing behind bringing 'em into the house."

To see Hester trying to be something she wasn't seemed pathetic to Ariah. The woman must have some good points; everyone did. "A lovely plant such as that adds to your parlor and to the fine furniture, Hester. It emphasizes your good taste." Ariah was hoping Hester would realize that she had merits of her own.

"Huh! You're as . . . as unenlightened as he is. 'Tain't 'parlor' no more, though you'll never perseid him to admit it. It's 'living room.' And as to my *fine* furnishings, there aren't two pieces in the room that match. Sofa's rococo, and mahogany. That lady's chair is Louis XV revival, and these side chairs are Eastlake, made o' walnut." She flashed her husband a look of resentment. "Can't furnish any room proper on a keeper's wage."

Bartholomew came to his feet. "Hester, a Perseid is a group of meteors that can be seen around the second week of August. Now, if you ladies will excuse me, I have work to do in my office. Thank you for showing me the book, Ariah."

Wishing she could slap him for his lack of understanding and consideration, Ariah handed him the volume. "Here, read it at your leisure, Mr. Noon. I have a smaller field guide I use most of the time, so I won't miss it."

He nodded as he accepted the book, sensing her disapproval and wishing he could call back his callous words. Baiting his wife did little to ease the tension between them and made him feel small.

In his office he sank into the armchair behind his desk and pressed the book to his face. The leather binding radiated the warmth of Ariah's body where she had hugged it to her breasts. Lily of the valley pervaded his senses.

To have Ariah living there in his home until her wedding was proving to be both heaven and hell. Her presence haunted him no matter where he went, even in the water closet. Lily of the valley and that youthful effervescence that was the essence of her. At times, like now, he could close his eyes and pretend that only he and Ariah existed, living in the same house, talking, laughing, eating together. If only he could literally take her to his bed at night, as he did in his imagination every time he crawled between the sheets, life would indeed be heavenly.

But no matter how beautifully he dreamed it all, Hester always managed to intrude, with her sharp, shrewish voice and her constant complaints, to bring him back to reality.

Heaven and hell. And he wasn't at all certain that having Ariah married and settled in her own home was going to make life easier. How would he ever get used to the idea of her sleeping in another man's bed? To accept that it would be Pritchard, not him, who could lose himself in the joy of her sweet body each night, then wake up next to her in the morning and know that every day of the rest of his life he would be as happy.

Plato had preached that the health of the soul was more important than that of the body, that vice was worse than death, and to do injustice was worse than to suffer it. Bartholomew could concede the latter, but as for his state of health, he was beginning to believe that even his soul would be a good deal more sound if he could only immerse himself in the holy vessel of Ariah's body.

Surely if God had intended for man to do without sexual release, He would not have made the human body to crave it so badly that one feared to go insane without it. That even death might be preferable to going on without some joy, some love.

Fifteen

At Hester's prompting, Ariah had spent most of her time the last few days scrubbing her future home. Even though the house was only a year old, the care given it by its two bachelor residents left a lot to be desired. Hester's main objective, of course, was to keep her husband and their young guest apart. Bartholomew knew it was for the best, yet the loneliness and sense of loss he felt threatened to overwhelm him. Life had lost meaning.

Now Friday had arrived. Tomorrow Ariah and Pritchard would be married. The thought engendered an agony in him so deep that Bartholomew thought surely it would kill him. In truth, he almost wished it would. Only the strength gained from years of enduring unendurable situations, and hiding his emotions behind a wall of apathy, allowed him now to enter the lighthouse and greet his nephew civilly.

Pritchard was waiting for him. Nothing unusual; the boy was always eager to be relieved of his turn at watch, but since Ariah's arrival, he was more impatient than ever. Bartholomew couldn't blame him. Still, it irritated him.

Today the boy was fidgeting with a rope, creating a hell of a snarl as he tried to work a lanyard knot. Likely Seamus's doing. The old sailor was always trying in his inimitable way to turn Pritchard into a worthy seaman—the best any man could be, to Seamus's way of thinking. A waste of time, Bartholomew thought. Where Seamus was a plodding old workhorse, Pritchard was a young sea otter, expecting always to float along in life, playing in the waves while his mother fetched supper to him.

Pritchard looked up at his uncle's entrance. "Afternoon, Uncle Bartholomew."

Bartholomew nodded and eyed the boy warily. The last time his nephew had addressed him by his full name, it had been to ask him to pick up Ariah at the train station.

"Any problems with the light?" Bartholomew asked, careful not to invite personal disclosures.

"No. Looks like a storm's brewing, though." Pritchard gave up on the rope and tossed it onto a battered sea chest.

"Not uncommon for March." Bartholomew headed for the circular metal stairs that led to the lamp, hoping he had incorrectly judged his nephew's pensiveness. He made it to the third step.

"Uncle Bartholomew, may I ask you something?"

Cursing silently, Bartholomew halted. "What is it?"

"I was wondering if, well . . ." He turned away to pick at a bit of peeling paint, obviously ill at ease. "Aunt Hester thinks I should look into Ariah's past. She says a young woman as pretty as Ariah isn't likely to marry a stranger unless there are . . . extenuating circumstances."

Bartholomew clamped his jaw tight on the foul words that came to mind on learning that his wife was at the bottom of whatever trouble was brewing.

"I'd rather not ask Ariah outright. It would seem rude, don't you think?" Pritchard flicked a fleck of paint from his fingernail as he sat down at the desk where the keepers kept their logs. "But Aunt Hester does have a point, I suppose, so I was wondering if Ariah said anything to you . . . during the trip back from Portland . . . that might explain why she agreed to marry me."

Bartholomew came to stand in front of the boy, pinning him with his penetrating gaze until Pritchard squirmed in his seat.

"Pritchard, I know you don't like to think ill of your aunt, but in this case"—Pritchard opened his mouth and Bartholomew silenced him with a raised hand—"take my word for it, Hester is acting out of jealousy. Miss Scott lost her father recently, leaving her alone in the world. What else can a young woman in such circumstances do but marry? She is only eighteen; she needs someone to take care of her."

Pritchard nodded, but Bartholomew could see he was still worried. If the boy had more insight, he would know that Ariah Scott was too independent to marry simply because she was alone. Bartholomew didn't dare tell Pritchard the truth. If Hester learned of the possible trouble from Ariah's uncle, she would use that to terrify her nephew into sending the girl away. Bartholomew couldn't risk that. To have her living next door as another man's wife would be hell, to see her walk out of his life forever would be unbearable.

"You don't believe she could have gotten herself . . . you know, in trouble?" Pritchard asked.

"Absolutely not. Speak with her, give her a chance to defend herself. I would call that being fair, not rude. And I have confidence that you will know whether she's lying or not."

It wasn't true; Bartholomew wouldn't bet a broken seashell on the boy's ability to detect a lie from anyone. Pritchard certainly never recognized his aunt's prevarications. But the play on the boy's ego might defeat this latest attempt of Hester's to prevent tomorrow's wedding.

Pritchard grinned. "You're right, Uncle Bart. I'll speak to Ariah tonight." He glanced at the floor between his feet as color seeped into his cheeks. "She is beautiful, isn't she? I couldn't be more pleased, really. There's a sort of sweetness about her that makes it difficult to think of her doing anything very improper."

The idea of Ariah as a prim, decorous maiden might have made Bartholomew smile, if Pritchard's intimate, proprietorial tone hadn't balled his hands into fists. He turned back to the stairs and began the slow ascent, his jaw clamped tightly on his temper. But his escape was not to be so easy.

"Wait," Pritchard called, "I wanted to speak with you about something else."

Bartholomew closed his eyes and rubbed the back of his head where a headache was brewing. "What is it?"

Pritchard was on his feet again, nervously pacing the small space between the desk and the door. Panic bolted through Bartholomew as his sixth sense warned him of the extremely personal nature of the boy's dilemma.

"I don't know how to say this but"—Pritchard lifted a hand impotently and let the rest out in a rush—"I've never been with a woman, so I need some pointers or . . ."

Good hell. "Are you saying you don't know how—"

"Holy Hector, Uncle Bart, I've been around animals and I've heard men talk enough to know how it's done. But how do I approach her? I mean, will she know what to expect, or must I explain it to her first? Should I wear my nightshirt or . . ."

Bartholomew's heart sank at the thought of his nymph being subjected on her wedding night to the inexperienced gropings and probings of a man who was, thanks to Bartholomew, more innocent than she was herself. For her sake, he must give the boy some guidance, but it would be the most appalling chore he had ever encountered.

Pritchard was chewing on a fingernail, staring at the floor and speaking as if to himself. "I suppose if the light was out, I could get into bed naked. She'll surely wear a nightrobe." Looking up, he added, "Do I take it off of her or does it all have to be done with our nightclothes on? Will it be all right if I touch her?" Pritchard's young face was a mask of confusion and misery. "I don't want to scare her, Uncle Bart, but I've never seen a woman. Naked, I mean. And I want to see her. I want to touch her."

Each word was like a knife paring Bartholomew's heart into pieces. He kept to the shadows, knowing the blood had drained from his face, leaving him as pale as the whitewashed walls around him. Memories flooded his mind: the softness of Ariah's full breasts, the taste of her rosy nipples, the scent of lily of the valley, the sweet heavenly heat between her thighs. Instantly, his body reacted, sending blood rushing to his groin. Then the image changed to Pritchard, pawing her with clumsy, ignorant hands, Pritchard crawling over her . . .

Bartholomew shook his head to banish the nightmare images, and sucked in a deep breath for control.

"She'll have some idea what to expect, Pritchard. Simply go slow with her and make certain she's aroused before you—"

"Make sure she's aroused? But I understood proper women felt nothing but revulsion when a man took them."

Bartholomew sighed. "Do you think they're less human than men are? They're capable of the same pleasure in sex as we are. They merely require more attention before they're ready."

Pritchard frowned, seeming nonplussed. "But how will I know when she's ready?"

Bartholomew seethed inside at the necessity of having such an intimate discussion with the man destined to be Ariah's husband. If Bartholomew had a son, he would one day be required to have a similar talk, but this was a different situation. And, since he would never have children of his own—something else for which he grieved—he felt no need to practice.

"You test her with your fingers," he said in a cold quiet tone that might have warned a wiser man that he was nearly out of patience.

Pritchard's brows rose to his hairline. "You mean . . . *feel* her? *Down there?*"

"Yes, Pritchard, that's exactly what I mean."

"Feel for what?"

"The natural lubricating moisture supplied by her body in preparation for mating. If it isn't there, kiss her, pet her more, whisper that she's beautiful. Do what comes naturally. And in future, leave me out of it."

With that Bartholomew stomped up the stairs, not waiting to see if the boy had more questions. His footsteps on the metal rungs echoed hollowly in the octagonal tower until the door below slammed shut. Then he stopped and, tightly gripping the railing, closed his eyes and prayed for strength.

When Ariah came out onto the back porch, Pritchard was tossing a baseball straight up in the air and catching it as it came down. The moment he saw her he hurried over, letting the ball thud to the ground and bounce away.

"Ariah! I was hoping you'd come out."

She looked at him in surprise. "Of course I came out. You asked me to, remember?"

"Yes, but . . ." He let the words trail off and feasted his eyes on her delicate face. Then he grabbed her hand and pulled her along with him behind the house. Pushing her up against the woodshed he clamped his mouth hard on hers. Ariah shoved against his chest and twisted her mouth away.

"Pritchard!"

"Ah, Ariah, don't scold. I had to. Besides, you kissed me that first day so you must like it."

"I'm not objecting to your kissing me, only to your hurting me."

"I'm sorry, I'll try to be gentler."

He bent his head as though to kiss her again and she turned aside, her hands still pressing against his chest. "Pritchard, what would your aunt or Bartholomew think if they saw us?"

"But we're almost married. We will be by this time tomorrow."

"Even married people don't kiss in public."

Pouting, he said, "We aren't in public; we're behind the house. Our house. Aunt Hester is doing mending, Uncle Bart's on watch at the light and Old Seamus is sleeping. There isn't anyone to see us."

"That's not the point."

"Then what is the point?"

Ariah wasn't sure how to answer. The reality was that she didn't enjoy his hard, wet kisses, but she didn't want to hurt his feelings by saying so. "As you said, tomorrow we'll be married. Surely you can wait that long."

"Holy Hector, Ariah, I've waited a lifetime already. Is one kiss so wrong?"

Ariah heaved a silent sigh. "No, I suppose not. Very well, but let me kiss you so I can show you how I like it."

He nodded eagerly and bent his head closer, lips slightly puckered, eyes closed. Ariah placed her hands on his shoulders and let him put his at her waist.

"Open your mouth a little, and let your lips go soft."

He did. Ariah put her mouth to his. For one heartbeat it was as though she were kissing Bartholomew. Her pulse skittered into high speed, her nerves tingled. His breathing was already rapid, but as her tongue dipped into his mouth to taste him, he moaned and pulled her so tightly against him she could feel his arousal through their clothes.

The taste was wrong. The body was wrong. Then a hand insinuated itself between them and dug painfully into her breast. Ariah's daydream of Bartholomew vanished abruptly. She wrenched her mouth away.

He was staring at her intently, panting slightly. "You know how to kiss awfully well. How did you learn that?"

Taken aback, she said, "I merely wanted to see how you tasted."

"You did?" He moved closer, grinning. "I liked tasting you too."

He drew her hard against him again and she let him kiss her, hoping he would forget his question about her expertise. Hester's shrill, irascible voice calling her name broke them apart. Reluctantly, he let her go.

"Aunt Hester must need some help. You really should pitch in a little, you know. She says it's a lot more work, having another person in the house, and I don't think she's as well as she pretends to be."

Ariah's mouth fell open and she stared at him aghast. "You

mean milking cows, churning butter, doing laundry and helping with the cooking isn't enough?"

"You did all that?"

"Yes, I did all that, this morning and every other morning since I arrived. I also keep my room clean, wash all the dishes and help with the dusting and sweeping. On top of all I've been doing to ready our own quarters."

Pritchard shrugged. "I don't understand. Why would Aunt Hester complain like that if you were helping all along?"

"Maybe what she truly wants is for me to do all her chores and mine too," she retorted.

"Now, Ariah, don't be like that. Aunt Hester's old, you know, and as I said, I don't think she feels well."

At Hester's renewed screech, Ariah swallowed the tart answer on her tongue. "I have to go. Good night, Pritchard."

"Can't we go for a walk after you see to whatever she wants?" he called as she hurried away.

She did not answer. No doubt he wanted to get her off alone again so he could maul her some more. Ariah shook her head, scolding herself for thinking that way. He was going to be her husband in less than twenty-four hours. If she couldn't deal with his small intimacies now, what would she do once he got her in his bed?

A sense of heaviness came over her such as she'd felt only once before in her life—the day Uncle Lou told her that her father was gone and she didn't dare go home for fear Uncle Xenos might find her. She had pushed the heaviness aside then by thinking of the adventure ahead of her, traveling clear across the country, seeing new things and living in a new place. Now the adventure was over. At least here she would be near Bartholomew. She couldn't embrace him, or feel the wondrous sensation of his hands moving magically over her body, but she could talk with him, see him. And in time, surely she would learn to enjoy Pritchard's kisses, Pritchard's hands on her.

For some reason, that last thought brought on an overwhelming urge to weep.

* * *

" 'Twill be rainin' 'fore daylight," Seamus said as he entered the lighthouse. He hung up his coat, took his pipe from his pocket and prepared to light it. "Wind's in the south."

Bartholomew didn't need to hear the rest of the saying. 'When the wind's in the south, the rain's in its mouth.' Nor could he argue the matter. Seamus was right; tomorrow would be cold and wet. Not the best portent for Ariah's wedding day.

"Think it'll blow hard?" he asked as he finished a notation in his logbook.

Seamus went to the barometer hanging on the wall. " 'When the glass falls low, prepare for a blow. When it rises high, let all your kites fly.' " He took the corncob pipe from his mouth and tapped the stem against the glass of the barometer. "Says here 'twill be a kite day."

Bartholomew smiled. "Except for the rain, you mean."

The stooped old man answered with a noncommittal grunt. The sweet scent of tobacco filled the air. Bartholomew returned his pen to the inkwell, blotted the page he'd been working on and shut the book. Seamus began his watch the same way every day: hung up his coat, lit his pipe and checked the barometer. Yet if there was a person alive who needed no instrument for telling the weather, it was this thin, bent old man with baggy pants and a corncob pipe sticking out from under a ragged, bristled mustache.

"Well," Bartholomew said, rising from the chair at the desk, "it's been a quiet night so far."

Another grunt came from Old Seamus as he shuffled up the stairs to check the kerosene level mind adjust the appropriate weights, even though he knew it was the last thing Bartholomew did before signing out at the end of a watch, and therefore didn't need doing. Bartholomew took no offense; it was the same way he started out his own watch each day.

A damp, gentle breeze kissed Bartholomew's cheeks as he stepped from the lighthouse and stood looking at the moonlit sea. The stars were few and scattered, hiding like naughty children behind nearly invisible clouds in the dark sky. He breathed deeply of the tangy air and listened to the steady roar of the waves pounding the bluff two hundred feet below, letting the sea's timeless serenity wash over him. Then he turned and climbed the slick wooden stairs to the top of the bluff.

He had traversed nearly half the thousand-foot distance that separated the light from the keepers' houses when he became aware of something moving toward him in the darkness. He thought he detected the faint rustle of fabric. Coming to a halt, he waited, holding his breath. His heart beat erratically inside his breast while adrenaline pumped swiftly through his veins. He was afraid to hope that what he suspected might be true; he wanted it too badly. Then the beam of the light swung past and in its glow he saw her pale face, framed by the dark hood of her cloak. His heart soared.

Ariah stopped an arm's length away, her lush mouth slightly parted as she gazed up at him. He waited for her to speak but she remained silent, only the expressiveness of her beautiful blue eyes telling him that she had been waiting for him.

"Tomorrow . . ." she began, and let it trail away. The word and all it implied hung between them like a hangman's noose, ominous and deadly. "I had to see you."

Common sense and need warred within him. If he so much as touched her, he would be lost. And yet, wasn't he lost already? Hadn't he been lost since the first moment he'd laid eyes on her? "Come here," he said in a low, sensuous growl.

She rushed straight into his arms. Minutes passed while they embraced, content merely to bask in one another's warmth and closeness, to know their hearts beat as one, their souls enmeshed in the same heated emotions that had been shared by men and women since time immemorial.

Eventually, Ariah lifted her face to gaze up at him. Her hood fell back, and the moon streaked her pale hair with silver and gold. She was so beautiful Bartholomew's chest constricted. And suddenly, holding her was no longer enough.

He led her to a patch of salal bushes that would shield them from view as the light's beam passed over them. He spread her cloak over the damp grass and lay down beside her. Their first kiss was light and tender, the second long and greedy. Her hands pulled at his clothes, while he caressed her breast through the thin muslin of her nightrobe and kissed the hollow at the base of her throat as though it held the very nectar of life in its shallow depths.

She unfastened his coat and shoved it off his shoulders. His shirt followed. While he worked at the tiny buttons down her bodice, she buried her face in the curly hair on his chest. Her tongue dipped to taste his skin. Then she nipped at a small masculine nipple with her teeth.

Bartholomew abandoned his effort to unfasten her gown and yanked it off over her head. The cool night air on her bared breasts puckered the nipples. He warmed them with his hot breath until they were as hard and swollen as a certain part of his own anatomy, one Ariah was at that very instant trying to free with small, inexperienced hands.

The feel of his feverish body pressed to hers, bare flesh to bare flesh, brought a moan from Ariah that seemed to scald his groin.

His brain cried warnings. His conscience pleaded for control. But his body demanded gratification.

Ariah couldn't get close enough. She wanted to crawl inside his skin, where she would be warm and safe, and no one could ever dislodge her. Once, he had worshiped her with his hands, with his mouth. Now she had an overwhelming desire to do the same for him.

Bartholomew groaned. His entire body trembled. The pleasure of her innocent touch was so intense he feared he would lose control then and there. When he could bear no more without exploding, he took her hands, kissed each palm, then rolled her onto her back. With her arms stretched out to the sides, giving him complete access to all her riches, he once again paid homage to her beauty, and to the passion she roused in him.

Too soon, they were both spiraling into the heavens, lost to the ecstasy they inspired in each other.

"Please," she whispered huskily. "I want to feel it all. I want you inside me as you should be."

Dear Lord, he wanted that, too. She felt so good; hot, wet, eager. Nothing in his life had prepared him for the intensity of his desire for her, of his love for her. A love too strong to allow him to ruin her, to deprive her of her honor on her wedding night. He knew he had taken too much already.

Go ahead, ruin her. Then she'll be yours, only yours; for no one else will want her.

Conscience warred with desire. He could have what he wanted, what they both wanted, then let Pritchard marry her. The boy was so innocent he'd never know, but Bartholomew would. His conscience would haunt him forever. Worse, once he had made her his, he wouldn't be able to let another man touch her.

"Bartholomew?"

The urgency in her voice brought him back to himself in time to sense the first quivers of her release. Almost frantic in her efforts to become one with him, she spread her legs and dug her nails into his buttocks, trying to pull him into her. Her cheeks glistened with wetness and her voice shook with silent sobs.

"Please, Bartholomew. Show me how, help me."

"No, sweet nymph. This isn't the way. Trust me."

Gently, he closed his teeth over a turgid nipple and drew it into his mouth. Ariah writhed as he suckled her, her hands kneading the strong muscles of his shoulders, her low throaty whisper calling his name over and over. The storm swept her up in its maelstrom, as wild and powerful as the first time he had shown her this path to ecstasy. Bartholomew explored and teased and tasted and stroked until she was a mindless mass of seething emotion.

When he felt her stiffen, then give in to the sweet spasms of final rapture, he groaned, gritting his teeth against the overwhelming urge to sink himself into her moist heat and find his own much-needed release. No sooner had her body gone limp in his arms than he felt her hands burrow between them to fondle his fevered flesh. His entire body stiffened and he sucked in air with a loud hiss.

"God, nymph, don't." His hand closed over hers.

"Let me, Bartholomew. I want to give you the same pleasure you've given me."

He moaned, sorely tempted. Although he had stopped her from caressing him, he was still much too aware of her small, soft hands cradling him. His voice was hoarse, his breathing ragged. "Any more pleasure and I'll explode right in your hands, little Nereid."

"Would that be bad?"

He tried to chuckle, but the sound was tortured. "Not for me, but you might find it a bit messy and unpleasant."

"Nothing connected with loving you could be unpleasant. Let me love you the way you loved me."

In spite of his efforts to resist her, she pushed his hand away and gently stroked his straining flesh. It was heaven. It was hell. Only the hot moist honey of her body closing around him, drawing him deeper and deeper inside her, could compare to the ecstasy her hands were bringing to him. He was so lost in it, he didn't notice when she changed position. When her wet tongue touched him, swirling languidly around his hardness, he almost came apart.

He jerked from her grasp and rolled onto his back, grateful for the coolness of the air which helped him regain the control he had so nearly lost.

"Bartholomew?" Ariah put her hand on his damp chest. "Did I hurt you?"

"No." His laugh same out choked. He took her hand in his and brought it to his lips. "Just the opposite, I'm afraid."

"You mean, you liked it?"

"Of course I liked it. What fool wouldn't? But I told you what the results would be."

"And I told you I don't care."

Before he could stop her, she scooted down and took him in her mouth, suckling him the way he had suckled her breasts. The delicious tremors of a climax began to coil inside him. If he didn't pull away now he would be lost. Yet he couldn't. There was only one other choice.

Taking hold of her arms, he drew her up beside him. Then he rolled toward her so they lay on their sides facing each other. At the merest pressure of his hand, her legs parted and he slipped into the hot, moist valley at their apex. So close, so close.

Her legs clamped tightly about him. The increased pressure on his engorged flesh intensified the rapturous sensations he was experiencing as he thrust into that slick, wet heat. His lips pulled back over his clenched teeth as he strained to keep from taking that extra proverbial inch and burying himself inside her. In his mind, he *was* inside her. It was enough.

He stiffened as a rainbow of sensation burst inside him. Good Lord, he had never felt anything like it. The pleasure was so intense he doubted he could survive it. But he did.

For a lengthy time, they lay there entwined, happy both in mind and in body. Bartholomew roused himself enough to draw the cloak over them against the chill of the wind. Ariah's small sigh fanned the hair on his chest as she curled closer into his embrace.

"What are we to do?" she asked finally. "I can't marry Pritchard. It wouldn't be fair to him, feeling as I do about you."

He was too human not to take delight in her words, but he was also too realistic to accept them. "Will you leave here, then? Run like your parents did, from continent to continent, until your uncle finally catches up with you and marries you off to some wealthy old man?"

The words were too true to be anything but cruel.

"You and Pritchard might have a better chance at happiness somewhere else," Bartholomew said tonelessly. "But you must marry him—you haven't any choice."

He didn't say that he couldn't bear her marrying anyone else. A better man than Pritchard Monteer might one day win her love, thereby stealing it from Bartholomew, something he could not endure. Though he couldn't speak this truth to her, neither could he deny it to himself.

"What happened tonight can never happen again," he said. "From now on, I will be Uncle Bartholomew, nothing more—"

"And nothing less," she finished.

There was no more to be said. He cleansed her of the evidence of his passion with his handkerchief, then helped her to dress. Silently they walked to the house. At the back porch, he whispered for her to go on in; he would wait a while, just in case. She started up the porch steps, then hurried back for a final kiss—likely the last she would ever have from him.

When finally the door was closed behind her, Ariah wearily turned to the stairway. There, on the steps, stood Hester.

Sixteen

"Out kind of late, aren't you?"

Hester drew herself upright. Standing as she was on the steps above Ariah, she loomed larger than life to the nervous girl.

"I-I thought I heard Bar—Mr. Noon's puffin crying, so I went out to see if it was hurt." Ariah prayed Hester had not seen her and Bartholomew together, and that he would not suffer because of her impetuous act in going to him that night.

"And was it?" Hester came down one step toward her. "Is that why you came back with my husband? I suppose you went to tell him about his precious bird?"

Hester's face was a mask of malevolence. Ariah told herself it was only her guilt that made her see murder in the woman's cold hazel eyes. Yet she could not deny her fear.

"Yes, I . . ." Ariah stopped herself. At any minute Bartholomew would come through the back door, unaware of their predicament and the lie she'd told to explain her being out in the middle of the night. There had to be a way to warn him. "I think he's looking for the bird." She cocked her head as if to listen. "No, I hear him coming now."

Ariah swung open the door. "Mr. Noon? Did you find Harlequin?"

Bartholomew appeared on the porch, his brow furrowed as he silently asked what on earth she was doing.

Aware of his confusion, she said, "I was telling Hester how I heard your bird crying and that you were looking for it to make certain it wasn't hurt. Did you find it?"

His gaze moved past her into the dimly lit hall. His eyes narrowed with a wariness that made him look every bit the eagle Ariah had once dubbed him.

"Harlequin's fine. Perhaps you heard a gull. Their cries tend to sound very forlorn."

"Yes. Perhaps that was it." Ariah moved aside as he stepped inside and shut the door behind him.

A scowl twisted Hester's thin lips as she silently greeted her husband. He could tell there would be no breakfast in the morning. Hester would plead exhaustion and keep to her bed all day, whining and demanding attention as punishment. Bartholomew cared nothing for that; he was used to her machinations. His only worry was for Ariah. Hester always took revenge on those she felt had wronged her.

"Thank you for your concern, Miss Scott." He gave Ariah a polite nod, making certain to keep his mouth a straight line, all emotion swept from his face for Hester's benefit. "Don't let us keep you any longer from your bed. It was kind of you to worry over my pet, but tomorrow is your wedding day and you'll want to be well rested for the festivities."

Hester's scowl transformed into a ghastly caricature of a smile aimed at Bartholomew, though her words were for Ariah. "Yes, you should save *some* of your energy. My nephew is young and in the prime of manhood. You'll likely find tomorrow night even more exhausting than tonight's . . . adventure."

Bartholomew cursed wordlessly as Ariah blanched. With a mumbled good night, she hurried up the stairs to her room in the garret. Bartholomew hung up his coat and cap, banked the fire and put out the lamps as he headed for his own bed.

He had expected Hester to lay into him with nasty, heated words, but she said nothing, merely watching him with her icy glare, arms crossed over her flat chest, squashing the ruffles that ran up and down the buttoned closure of her wrapper. He behaved as though all were normal, but, inside, his heart thudded like nails hammered into a coffin lid. Had she seen him guide Ariah behind the shrubs? Had she waited for them to reappear, knowing what they must be doing there?

Those moments among the salal were the most beautiful of his life. Time had stood still while the world spun on its axis. Nothing would ever be the same again. Certainly Bartholomew would not.

He climbed the stairs, went past Hester's room into the one she called her sitting room, which sat between his bedroom and Ariah's. The *slap-slap* of Hester's slippers on the wood floor behind him, informed him she had followed him upstairs. Even knowing she was there, he could not stop his gaze from going to Ariah's closed door. No light shone beneath it. No doubt she was in bed.

What would Hester do if he went into Ariah's room instead of his own? If the door had a lock that could keep out Hester and the rest of reality, he would be tempted to do exactly that.

Shaking off the heaviness that suddenly overcame him, he walked into his room and shut the door. At least in the privacy of that room he was spared Hester's hostility, and he could dream of Ariah. Tomorrow she would be married, but in truth, she would be no farther out of reach then than she was at this moment. Or so he told himself as he tried to fall asleep in the wee hours of the morning—the morning of Ariah Scott's wedding day.

In spite of his late hours, Bartholomew arose early, his sleep having been tormented by images of Ariah in Pritchard's arms, by nightmares of the boy's clumsy handling of her as he took the virginity Bartholomew had so carefully, and painfully, preserved.

Old Seamus had predicted true; it was raining, a gentle shower that drenched Bartholomew thoroughly as he made his way to the pheasant's pen for the morning feeding. He rounded the corner of the barn and saw through the mist a dark hooded figure huddled before the door of the pen. A familiar figure that elevated his blood pressure and set his heart thrumming.

Ariah looked up as he reached her side. Her face was wet with more than rain. Her eyes held horror, disbelief, pain. Then he saw the source of her grief. On the ground lay the limp, sodden body of his puffin. The tiny raisin eyes, with their black horns above, were dull and sightless, the red webbed feet loosely folded. The feathers Harlequin had kept so meticulously groomed were now matted and muddy from the rain. Bartholomew hunkered beside Ariah and tenderly lifted the bird in his hands. Its head dangled limply, the neck obviously broken.

In a heartbeat the image in Bartholomew's mind changed from a small colorful seabird to a plump domestic goose, its pure white feathers blood-splotched, its long slender neck drooping lifelessly—Midas, his childhood pet. The gander had trailed after him like a faithful dog, raiding Bartholomew's pocket for corn, protecting him, even from his own father when the man was bent on whipping him. Jacob Noon had shot the goose for its interference. Midas, the one living creature whose love young Bartholomew had never had to share, the way he'd had to share the love of his mother and siblings.

Now Harlequin. Why must everything he loved die? His gaze met Ariah's and he remembered his casual comment to her that the puffin would be better off dead than domesticated. Fate—or someone—must have overheard.

Aside from Bartholomew, Ariah was the only person who ever came to the pheasant pen. The significance of that fact was not lost on him. Anyone else might believe she had killed the bird, when in reality the act carried a subtle message that he had best stay away from her. However afraid Hester might be of her husband, she had gotten her revenge. Next time, it would be Ariah who would be the target of that woman's malignity.

The rainstorm had turned into a full-fledged squall by the time Reverend Ketcham and the wedding guests rode up from the bay to the station. Upstairs in her room, Ariah heard their arrival above the wail of the wind and the drumming of raindrops on the garret roof. The four members of Pritchard's baseball team who had accompanied Reverend and Mrs. Ketcham began shouting for the groom the moment the horses emerged from the forest. Pritchard's reply was no less boisterous or merry.

Ariah's insides twisted with pain. Not one friend, not her father, not her mother, not a single loved one would be there to hear her say her vows.

When she was a child her mother had often described what her wedding would be like if the ceremony followed the ancient traditions of Demetria's Greek village. That would be the kind of wedding Demetria should have had, instead of a rushed civil ceremony her church refused to recognize.

The cooking would have begun the week before, and would have included six huge wedding cakes frosted with crosses, lovers' knots, wild roses and doves, then studded with almonds for fertility. A secret pocket in Ariah's dress would have held scissors, a padlock and a comb, to protect her against the evil eye. A long black tunic with a red stripe, topped by a black satin apron embroidered in gold, would have gone over her dress, and on her head would be a flowered wedding kerchief with coins sewn to its corners. The whole village would have followed the wedding party to the church, singing wedding songs. Bride and groom would be crowned with rings of ribbon-looped orange blossoms. The groom would stamp on her toes to underscore his dominance, and she would spend her first night as a married woman, not with her new husband, but with her mother-in-law, to dramatize whose property she had truly become.

Ariah gave a wan smile. She was grateful there would be no foot stomping today, but she might not have minded sleeping with Pritchard's mother tonight instead of him.

Bartholomew appeared at her door. She gazed at him across the room, almost as pale in the glow of a single lamp as the ecru satin and lace dress she'd brought from Cincinnati. "Since you have no male relative to escort you down and give you away, Hester insisted I do it," he said.

She blanched even paler, and he gave her a grim smile.

"Aye, she knows the irony of making me give you over to Pritchard. She sees it as particularly appropriate." He came a few steps closer, then stopped, as though afraid to trust himself any nearer. "You're beautiful, little nymph."

Ariah tried to smile, but there was no happiness inside her. *Take me away, Bartholomew. Take me somewhere where we can hide and forget the rest of the world exists.*

Bartholomew closed his eyes to the entreaty in hers. She couldn't know how difficult this was for him. How desperately he wanted the same thing. One more second and he would crumble at her feet, as thoroughly destroyed as the puffin that now lay under the earth.

"We'd best go down," she said, taking his hand.

He started, as much from her touch as from her voice, not having heard her cross the room. He flashed her a silent, loving message of gratitude for her understanding. Then he led her from the shadowed room. As they walked toward the small party waiting for them in the living room, she trembled and he wondered if she could feel him quiver as he fought the urge to make off with her. To give her what comfort he could, he laid his big hand over her small one, where it clutched the crook of his arm as if that were a lifeline.

Standing next to the stern reverend, Pritchard was all teeth and glowing eyes. On the reverend's other side stood Hester, a grim, rigid flagpole fluttering with ruffles and bows. To Bartholomew these people appeared more like a gleeful firing squad than a wedding party. An appropriate image for the doom in his heart.

It took all Bartholomew's strength to force himself to relinquish Ariah's trembling hand to Pritchard. Before he could step away and take his place with Hester, Ariah gave him a tremulous smile that looked too much like a final farewell, then murmured something in Greek. The reverend began the service, ending any chance Bartholomew might have had to ask for a translation.

Her voice was barely audible above the raging storm as she repeated her vows. Pritchard's came out loud, cocky, and disgustingly pleased. A hundred times Bartholomew licked his lips in preparation for halting the ceremony. A hundred times his conscience and his heart argued the rightness of letting her go through with it.

It's me who should be marrying her, not Pritchard.

But you're already married.

To the wrong woman. Hester doesn't love me.

She needs you.

Ariah needs me. And I need her.

You have a responsibility to Hester.

To hell with my responsibility. Do I owe nothing to Ariah? To the woman I love?

You are legally bound to Hester, as Ariah is now legally bound to Pritchard.

The last words startled him from his inner debate in time to hear Ketcham announce Ariah and Pritchard man and wife. The words went through Bartholomew like a purge and left him weak and shaking. When Pritchard pasted a wet, noisy kiss on his bride's pale lips, Bartholomew had to clench his hands behind his back to keep from tearing the boy away from her. He thought he would be sick.

The guests crowded around the bride and groom to offer congratulations. Pritchard shook the reverend's hand and accepted a hug from his aunt while Mrs. Ketcham congratulated Ariah. Then Pritchard turned to Bartholomew and held out his hand.

"Congratulate me, Uncle Bart. I'm a married man."

Bartholomew stared down at the outstretched hand. His eyes flicked up to meet Ariah's gaze over Mrs. Ketcham's plump shoulder. The virginal color of Ariah's dress magnified the blue of her magnificent eyes. Forget-me-not eyes that would never again turn violet in passion. At least, not for him. His soul shriveled inside his breast. His entire life did not pass before his eyes—only ten special days spent in a cabin on the Trask River Road—but he felt suddenly dead, certain nothing would, or could, arouse him to pleasure again.

"Aren't you gonna shake Pritchard's hand, Bartholomew?"

Hester's voice held amusement, and he cursed himself for allowing enough of his emotions to show to entertain the woman. Forcing a smile, he took Pritchard's hand.

"Of course," Hester added maliciously, "you'll want to kiss the bride, too."

He couldn't. One touch and he would snatch her up in his arms and flee.

As though understanding what he was feeling and wanting to help, or perhaps feeling the same trepidation herself, Ariah stepped into the arms of one of Pritchard's baseball cronies. Nothing would do then but that the others have their turn, and Bartholomew was saved.

Someone opened a bottle of wine, glasses were filled and a toast proposed. Pritchard, hanging onto Ariah like a barnacle, was chided and teased unmercifully. "Don't let him throw you any curve balls, ma'am," one of his friends told Ariah with a lewd wink. "Hey, Prit, you sure you know how to find home base?"

Bartholomew bent to sniff a bouquet of flowers Anna Ketcham had brought, hiding his outrage and frustration in the sweet petals. Pritchard was urging his chums on their way "so they wouldn't miss the tide." Knowing he was only trying to get rid of them so he could get on with his wedding night, their jokes became even more bawdy.

"Tryouts start in a couple of days, Prit, so take good care of that bat of yours."

"That'll be Mrs. Monteer's job now."

"Yeah, stroke it real easy now, ma'am."

The entire scene ate at Bartholomew's innards with the tenacity of tannic acid. He was contemplating knocking the eagerness from his nephew's face, as well as the proprietorial arm from around Ariah's waist, when he caught Hester's smug, knowing glance.

"She's outta your reach now," his wife hissed, too low for the others to hear. "Not as far as I woulda liked, but I know you well enough to believe you'll keep your distance, now she's married."

Bartholomew sent her a killing smile. "And you're vastly relieved, aren't you, Hester? Now you can stop being afraid that I'll overcome my conscience and divorce you in order to have her. But then," he added, unaware how prophetic his words would become, "we never know what the future will hold, do we, dear wife?"

With a strength that grew out of his hatred for Hester, he went then to Ariah and, after a quick glance at his wife to make sure she watched, kissed Pritchard's new wife.

"Be happy," he whispered against Ariah's full sweet lips, drinking in her scent and savoring her taste for the last time.

With the impulsiveness he had come to love in her, she threw her arms around his neck and hugged him tight. "I will," she whispered back, "as long as I can bolster my spirits now and then with a glimpse of you."

Ariah had not meant to lie to Bartholomew, but as her husband dragged her through the rain to the solitude of their own house, she wasn't sure happiness with him was a viable possibility. Pritchard was singing a vulgar song, obviously far from sober. If the Fates were with her, he would fall asleep the moment he crawled into bed, and leave her alone.

But the Fates were a contrary lot. Beneath the roof of the back porch, he grabbed her to him for another wet kiss, his hands running down her back to her buttocks and pressing her even closer to his male hardness. "My very own wife." He giggled drunkenly. "Come on, wife, let's go to bed."

Ariah blushed hotly and tried to ease herself away. The idea that everyone knew what would take place within the next hour, mortified her. At least Hester had refrained from voicing any of her coarse double entendres, but Ariah knew tomorrow would be another day. Pritchard opened the back door, swung her into his arms and carried her into the hallway. He almost dropped her as he set her on her feet.

"Don't think I can carry you all the way up."

She had barely caught her balance before he was towing her upstairs to their bedroom. The two keepers' houses were identical with one exception; the room off the vestibule, which Bartholomew used as an office, here belonged to the Second Assistant Keeper, along with a bedroom directly above, reached by box stairs off the first-floor room. The rest of the upstairs was the First Assistant Keeper's domain. But, having no need of so much space, Seamus had kindly offered to take the smaller quarters. The kitchen, dining and living rooms downstairs were shared by both assistant keepers.

The instant they were inside the master bedroom her new husband yanked off his coat, vest and tie, and threw them on the floor. Ill at ease and uncertain what he expected of her, Ariah remained by the door. "Get undressed," he said, grinning. Then, "Never mind, I'll do it."

He fumbled with the buttons on the back of her dress while he kissed her so hard her tender lips were ground against her teeth until she tasted blood. The fastenings resisted his clumsy fingers, and she heard fabric rip as he became more insistent. Buttons clattered to the floor.

"Wait, Pritchard, let me—"

"Can't wait, been thinking of nothing but this since the first time I saw you."

His breathing was ragged, his hands demanding. Her dress floated to the floor in tatters. Seeing that she had no choice, she hurriedly undid a few inches down the front closure of her combination chemise while Pritchard yanked down her petticoats, ending in a crouch at her feet. Ariah shuddered as his hands slid up her naked calves, beneath the lace-edged legs of her chemise, to the garters that held up her stockings.

"God, you smell good." He pressed his face into her stomach, his fingers hooking into the tops of her stockings and drawing them downward. "Lift your feet."

Balancing herself with one hand on his shoulder, she did as he asked. He freed her feet from the fine-knit stockings, then ran his hands back up under her chemise. She reached to stop him at midthigh. "I should use the water closet first."

"Do you have to?" he whined.

He forced his way under her restraining hands but before he could attain his goal, she jerked away. "Yes, I have to. I'll be right back."

"Hurry. I'll wait in bed."

Ariah ran down the stairs, wearing nothing but her half-opened chemise, and praying that Old Seamus would stay at Bartholomew's a while longer. The old man had filled in for Pritchard during the wedding, but had since been relieved by Bartholomew until his regular midnight watch.

The thought brought a clear image of Bartholomew to her mind, the way he had looked as he'd relinquished her to Pritchard. *Why, God? Why couldn't I have married the man I truly love? Why did he have to be married already?*

Had she made a mistake in marrying Pritchard? Would she have been better off going somewhere else? Perhaps fate would have been kind enough to give her time to find some other man she might be happier with . . . before Uncle Xenos caught up with her.

Confused and miserable, Ariah locked herself inside the cold, drafty water closet in the woodshed off the kitchen. With her arms braced against the door as if to hold off an attack, she laid her forehead on her crossed arms, and cried until Pritchard came down and pounded on the door.

"Go back upstairs this instant, Pritchard, or it'll only take longer for me to finish." As soon as his footsteps faded and the door to the kitchen closed, she pulled herself together, completed her business, and went back upstairs.

Her husband was in bed as promised. The lamp was turned

Wish You Were Here?

You can be, every month, with Zebra Historical Romance Novels.

AND TO GET YOU STARTED, ALLOW US TO SEND YOU

4 Historical Romances Free

A $19.96 VALUE!

With absolutely no obligation to buy anything.

YOU ARE CORDIALLY INVITED TO GET SWEPT AWAY INTO NEW WORLDS OF PASSION AND ADVENTURE.

AND IT WON'T COST YOU A PENNY!

Receive 4 Zebra Historical Romances, Absolutely _Free!_

(A $19.96 value)

Now you can have your pick of handsome, noble adventurers with romance in their hearts and you on their minds. Zebra publishes Historical Romances That Burn With The Fire Of History by the world's finest romance authors.

This very special FREE offer entitles you to 4 Zebra novels at absolutely no cost, with no obligation to buy anything, ever. It's an offer designed to excite your most vivid dreams and desires...and save you almost $20!

And that's not all you get...

Your Home Subscription Saves You Money Every Month.

After you've enjoyed your initial FREE package of 4 books, you'll begin to receive monthly shipments of new Zebra titles. These novels are delivered direct to your home as soon as they are published...sometimes even before the bookstores get them! Each monthly shipment of 4 books will be yours to examine for 10 days. Then if you decide to keep the books, you'll pay the preferred subscriber's price of just $4.00 per title. That's $16 for all 4 books...a savings of almost $4 off the publisher's price.

We Also Add To Your Savings With FREE Home Delivery!
There Is No Minimum Purchase. Plus You Get a FREE Monthly Newsletter With Author Interviews, Contests, and More!

We guarantee your complete satisfaction and you may return any shipment...for any reason...within 10 days and pay nothing that month. And if you want us to stop sending books, just say the word. There is no minimum number of books you must buy.

It's a no-lose proposition, so send for your 4 FREE books today!

YOU'RE GOING TO LOVE GETTING

4 FREE BOOKS

These books worth almost $20, are yours without cost or obligation when you fill out and mail this certificate.

(If the certificate is missing below, write to: Zebra Home Subscription Service, Inc., 120 Brighton Road, P.O. Box 5214, Clifton, New Jersey 07015-5214

4 FREE BOOKS!

Yes! Please send me 4 Zebra Historical Romances without cost or obligation. I understand that each month thereafter I will be able to preview 4 new Zebra Historical Romances FREE for 10 days. Then, if I should decide to keep them, I will pay the money-saving preferred publisher's price of just $4.00 each...a total of $16. That's almost $4 less than the publisher's price, and there is no additional charge for shipping and handling. I may return any shipment within 10 days and owe nothing, and I may cancel this subscription at any time. The 4 FREE books will be mine to keep in any case.

Name _______________________________________

Address_______________________________Apt. _________

City_______________________State________Zip ___________

Telephone ( )_______________________________

Signature ___________________________________
(If under 18, parent or guardian must sign.)

LF1095

Terms, offer and prices subject to change without notice. Subscription subject to acceptance by Zebra Books. Zebra Books reserves the right to reject any order or cancel any subscription.

TREAT YOURSELF TO 4 FREE BOOKS.

AFFIX STAMP HERE

ZEBRA HOME SUBSCRIPTION SERVICE, INC.

120 BRIGHTON ROAD

P.O. BOX 5214

CLIFTON, NEW JERSEY 07015-5214

A $19.96 value.
FREE!

No obligation to buy anything, ever.

low, but not low enough to prevent her from noticing that he was naked above the waist; the covers hid the rest.

"Could you douse the light?" she said.

"Do I have to?" he said in a little boy whine.

"Please? I'm not accustomed to undressing in front of men."

"I should hope not."

Grudgingly he did as she asked. In the darkness she slipped out of her chemise and into the nightrobe on the back of a chair. She'd given Pritchard some of her things yesterday. Then, taking a deep breath, she went to the side of the bed, lifted the covers and slid in next to her husband. Immediately he reached for her and swore in disappointment at the feel of the gown covering her from chin to toes. "Can't you take it off?" he asked.

She almost answered with the same words he had used earlier when she asked him to douse the lamp, but stopped herself. What did it matter if she were naked or not? It would not alter what was to happen, or make his unwanted invasion of her body more palatable. So she took off the gown and endured his rough exploration of her body, the same way she endured his breath, rancid from the wine he had drunk—by holding her breath and mentally listing the various families of birds.

Accipitridae, vultures, hawks, harriers.

Pritchard squeezed a breast and she gasped from the pain.

Alaudidae, larks.

His nose butted hers as he tried to kiss her. Her mouth was already sore from the bruising pressure of his, her inner lip torn, but she resisted the urge to turn aside. His tongue sliding over her lips made her stomach lurch.

Why did Pritchard's touch revolt her when Bartholomew's filled her with delicious sensations? Was it only Pritchard's roughness? Should she ask him to be more gentle? Guilt for wishing he were Bartholomew kept her silent.

Much too soon, he was shoving her legs apart and clambering on top of her.

Caprimulgidae, nightjars. *Cathartidae,* new world vultures. *Certhiidae, chamaeidae, diomedeidae.* The Latin names pounded through her head, faster and faster and still she could not block out the fear and revulsion.

The hand groping between her thighs held no tenderness. It felt as if a vulture were tearing at her flesh.

"You're dry," Pritchard panted into her ear, making it sound like an accusation. "Uncle Bart said you'd be wet."

To learn that Bartholomew had discussed her so intimately hurt even more than her husband's inexperienced probing. She fought back tears.

"Uncle Bart said wait, but I can't." His voice was raspy, his breath coming in gasps. His fingers dug at her, desperately seeking the lubrication necessary for his entry into her body, until she cried out in pain.

"I'm sorry," he muttered brokenly. "I have to . . ." His rigid flesh demanded entrance. He grunted and groaned as he tried to force himself inside, battering at the ungiving barrier of her virginity.

Ariah bit down on her lower lip to keep from crying out. The pain was worse than she had expected. The embarrassment and indignity increased her suffering until she longed to scream. Pritchard stiffened. A high, keening moan issued from inside his throat. Fluid washed over her. Then he collapsed on top of her and went still. In silence, while tears ran down her face, Ariah thanked the Lord.

Seventeen

Midnight. The sky was so black there was no discerning where it ended and the sea began, where the sea ended and land began. It didn't matter.

Bartholomew left the lighthouse, secure in Seamus's good care, and started up the stairway to the upper level of the bluff. The wind tore at his slicker, slapping the heavy, oiled fabric against his legs. Like a trickster, a gust swirled to lift off his hood. He felt the cold rain dribble onto his face and kept going.

Nothing seemed to matter, not the rain, not the wind, and, most especially, not him. He was nothing, less than nothing. He no longer wished he could be reborn, only that he could cease to exist.

His boot slipped on a slick wooden step and he began to fall. Only instinct and his hands on the rails kept him upright, though one knee crashed painfully into the stair. He welcomed the pain. It helped hold back the images haunting his brain.

Images of Ariah—and Pritchard.

The wind was so fierce that to keep from being swept away he had to cling to the cable strung along the board path to the houses. He blinked water from his eyes and swiped a hand down his streaming face. Far ahead, a thousand miles at least, a pinprick of light beckoned. His house? Ariah's? Was it her bedroom window still alight? Hers and Pritchard's?

A keening gust knocked him to his knees. He shoved himself back up and danced sideways before his grip on the cable reined him in. Old Seamus had warned him it was bad out. 'Twould be easy, the old seadog had said, to be blown clean off the bluff and drowned in the swirling black brine below. The edge of the bluff wasn't more than twenty-five feet from where he stood. How tempting to simply let go, to let the storm end his pain.

Somehow he made it to the compound. The gate squeaked as it swung open. The light that had guided him home came from his own porch. The assistant keeper's house next door was dark. He walked around to the north side where he could see the windows of the master bedroom. They, too, were dark. He stood for a long time, staring up at the windows and wishing with all his heart that the wind that night had been stronger.

Hours later, Hester flung open the office door and stared at Bartholomew as he sat behind his desk. His dark hair, always curly from the dampness but usually neatly combed, looked to her like one of his dratted birds had nested in it. A tracery of red colored the whites of his eyes, and fatigue deepened the lines in his face. His slicker lay in a puddle on the floor. On the desk stood an empty bottle of whiskey.

"What do you want, Hester?"

Weariness and dejection weighted his voice.

"You been up all night, haven't you?" she said. "Frettin' over that . . . that . . ."

The rich brown of his eyes turned to ice, promising a retribution as lethal as a shark's bite if she used her favorite foul name for Ariah Scott. No, it was Ariah Monteer now. A smile as sweet as three-day-old fish guts curved Hester's lips. Seeing Bartholomew tie his insides into knots over Pritchard getting under that girl's skirts instead of him was almost worth having the slut as part of their family.

"She belongs to Pritchard now," Hester taunted, "and I aim to make blame sure you don't never get *your* hands on her."

Tense moments passed as he studied his wife. Her drab, overly beribboned dress hung on her like an ill-fitted sail. "You should see Dr. Wills, Hester," he said tonelessly. "You've lost weight. Makes you look like an old hag."

"Ain't nothing wrong with me that getting away from this gawdforsaken bluff wouldn't cure."

He smiled. It felt good to goad her into a temper. Maybe a good fight would make him feel better. "Are you sure? I can tell by the way you hobble around here that your feet are hurting you more."

Her eyes widened at that.

Bartholomew's smile spread into a self-satisfied grin. "You didn't think I was aware that you were having trouble with your feet, did you? Or is it your legs now too? And you've been drinking enough water to sink a steamship. Not to mention that demon moonshine you call a tonic. You spend half the night on that thunder mug of yours, and three-quarters of the day in the water closet. What's wrong with you, Hester? What sins are you atoning for with your health?"

Rigid with anger, she sneered back at him. "You're the one been sinnin'. Lusting after that girl like a ruttin' bull. That's always been your albatross, hasn't it? Lust. It eats away at you like the rot of dead flesh. You married me so you could pant and rut in my body night after night, but I put a stop to that, didn't I?" Her laugh was shrill, with an edge of dementia. "And you ain't never forgiven me, cause lust is what you live for."

In a dramatic gesture, she flung one arm into the air, her other hand on her padded breast. "They which lusteth after flesh shall not inherit the kingdom of God."

" 'But the fruit of the Spirit is love,' " he answered in a voice as calm as hers was shrill. "That's something you've never known, isn't it, Hester? Love. I might have come to love you, if you hadn't locked the door on me. But your spirit has been consumed by bitterness. All that's left of you is a shell, like the ones that wash up on the sand, still slimy from the snail that abandoned it. Your own shame made you afraid to let anyone love you, and now no one ever will. You can be sure of that."

"Damn you, Bartholomew Noon. Damn your"—she searched for a word foul enough for her intent, big enough for her pride—"execrable hide. I hope that lousy piece of flesh hanging between your legs shrivels up and falls off for lack of use.”

He broke into rich peals of laughter. Hester’s gaunt face flushed and she fled the room, leaving the door open behind her. Bartholomew’s laughter ended as abruptly as it had begun. He sank back in his chair, drained by more than the unpleasant encounter. Hester was right; he’d slept little during the long, lonely night. Every time he’d closed his eyes, scenes of Ariah with Pritchard had flashed onto his inner eyelids in three dimensional color, like the double-imaged cards in the stereoptic viewer Hester had bought in Tillamook. There was no denying it. He loved Ariah, and it was eating him up to think of her being bedded by that awkward cub, Pritchard. It was worse even than Hester had described.

With a sigh he dragged himself to his feet. For a time, he gazed out the window toward the lighthouse. It was a fine day. The storm had passed on, leaving clear skies. Far out over the sea a cormorant soared on the wind, a graceful black arc against the azure sky. Closer lay the spot where, only two nights ago, he had worshiped Ariah’s sweet body, with his mouth, with his hands. Would she forget what they had shared, now that she was married?

Restless with his troubled thoughts, he wandered into the living room to stare out at the house that now sheltered her. She had skipped her usual chores this morning. Was she all right? Had Pritchard misused her?

He didn’t hear Hester come to the doorway.

“If it pains you so much to see that girl wed to my poor nephew, why don’t you resign your post here?” she asked. “We could move back to town and you could run for mayor. Old Duncan’s already said he ain’t gonna run again.”

Without turning around to face her, he said, “I’ve told you, I’ve no intention of moving back to town. I’m happy here, with the sea and my birds.”

“And your slut over there in Pritchard’s bed,” she retorted. “What about me? Doesn’t my happiness matter? I hate it here,

Bartholomew. That's all that's wrong with me. If you're really worried about my health, move me back to town and just see how healthy I can get."

"You forfeited your right to my concern the day you locked me out of your room, Hester. I've spent my entire life looking after the welfare of others. Now I'm going to see to my own, wherever and however I have to."

Hester snorted. "Like in that trollop's bed? I'll see you in hell first."

He turned and pinned her with his hard penetrating gaze. "You've done your best for seven years to make my life a hell, and you've done a good job of it. But no more. I no longer care what you do, Hester."

His attention switched back to the house forty feet from his own, dismissing her as though she were a bug on the wall. Hester had always known he didn't love her—not even when he'd married her—in spite of the way she'd worked her fingers to the bone, cooking and cleaning and caring for his paralyzed pa, and for him, too. She wasn't good enough for Bartholomew Noon. No, she was hill people, looked down on all her life because she'd had the misfortune to be born into a family of poor white Southern trash.

If she could be honest with herself, she would have to admit it was his very lack of love for her that drove her to his bed the night his father died. That and the need to secure her future. He had wanted her body; oh yes, the same way Lenny Joe had, back when she was sixteen. Lenny Joe had run away to avoid paying for what she'd given him. But not Bartholomew. She'd made sure Bartholomew didn't get away. And she'd made him pay for his filthy use of her body.

The way she'd always wished she could've done to Lenny Joe.

Ariah closed the cover of Dr. Chase's book and went to the stove to check the roast she was browning for supper. She'd had enough of the doctor's "Hints on Housekeeping." "Do every-thing in its proper time. Keep everything to its proper use. Put everything in its proper place." Simply reading the words put a constricting steel band around her chest. The good Dr. Chase obviously didn't believe in enjoying life. She imagined him ly-ing awake at night, unable to sleep until he'd thought up a new rule to live by.

She turned the roast, then glanced around the kitchen. The room needed something bright to make it more cheerful. She considered moving her mother's decorative plates from the din-ing room where she'd hung them, then decided against it. Every room in the house needed dressing up. She'd ask Pritchard for yellow gingham for kitchen curtains and a matching tablecloth.

When Hester had set her to righting the house that was to be her new home, Ariah had been appalled at what she'd found. Dirty dishes overflowed the sink onto the work space, mingling with ancient editions of the *Headlight-Herald,* empty cartons, spilled food, and tin cans filled with dottle from Seamus's pipe. Piles of ashes and wood chips waited under the stove to ignite the entire house. Dried food crusted the tabletop. Greasy fin-gerprints marred the walls.

The furniture was still dull and unpolished. The family of mice she'd discovered in the pantry refused to budge, and the scent of tobacco, rancid grease and wood smoke clung stub-bornly to everything in spite of her scrubbing. Ariah doubted anyone had dusted, polished or swept since the house was built the year before. She was sick of grimy windows and rebellious dust balls.

For two self-indulgent hours after Pritchard left that morning to relieve Seamus, Ariah remained in bed, pondering her situ-ation. Her usual optimism was in a dreadful slump. No matter how she scrutinized the matter, there seemed no answer to her dilemma. She was in love with one man, married to another. Pritchard's favorite subject next to baseball was himself. He had never heard of Plato, called Shakespeare a fop, and insisted that the only birds worth bothering with were those that made good eating, like ducks, geese, robins and Bartholomew's pheasants. His hands on her body left her cold as the sea in winter. His kisses had the appeal of the four-inch greenish yellow slugs in the forest.

Was this how Hester felt toward Bartholomew? Was that why she'd locked him from her room the day after they were married? No, that wasn't possible. Gentleness and sensitivity were second nature to Bartholomew. He could have been no less tender with Hester than he had been with her.

Bartholomew. Ariah closed her eyes against the sting of tears. She would not give in to her need for him. How could she ever face him again? To see the pain in his eyes, because of what he and everyone else assumed Pritchard had done to her in bed last night would be more than she could endure.

She had bled after Pritchard's battering of her, but only a spot. And when she had examined herself, curious about this very intimate, very sore, part of her body which could inflame men almost to violence, and which, under Bartholomew's gentle talented hands, had given her a glimpse into heaven, she found the precious membrane still firmly in place. If she had her way, it would stay that way. At least until she and her new husband could come to some sort of understanding and develop some basis for mutual regard.

From outside came the clear, flutelike notes of bird song. Out the window she could see a bird, yellow as a buttercup, perched on the porch railing. She gasped at its beauty, but before she could note its unique markings, it flew off toward the forest north of the house.

A strong need to be outside, to explore that tantalizing wall of greenness so alive with promise, had assailed her the moment she arrived. Now the urge overwhelmed her. If she kept the house between her and anyone who might be watching, surely she could reach the trees without being seen. She didn't want to be spotted. Hester would be angry with her for not doing chores, and Bartholomew. . . .

In a defiant bid for freedom, Ariah snatched her shawl from a hook by the back door and fled the house.

A flutter of pink as bright as a wild rhododendron blossom caught Bartholomew's eye. He yanked the lace curtain aside and peered closer. Someone was running toward the forest beyond the compound, fleet-footed and dressed in billowing folds of pink. Ariah.

His heart soared as he watched her slim vibrant figure vanish into the forest, taking the old Indian trail that led to the beach this side of Barnagat. If he circled through the trees from behind the barn, he might intercept her, and Hester would never know. He let the curtain drop and forced himself to walk to the back door with a calmness that belied the excitement surging through his veins.

Like a mother's arms, the woods enveloped Ariah in their soft, shadowed world. The serenity sank into her spirit, soothing her. Like a sponge, the lush layers of moss and evergreen needles absorbed the sounds of her footsteps on the narrow, winding Indian trail that was as ancient as the Sitka spruce towering overhead.

The rest of the land was densely carpeted in multiple shades of green. Trees, logs—even the bogs—were verdant with moss and lichen, making forays off the trail treacherous. Except for the path, there wasn't a square inch of ground or bark naked of growth. Ferns as tall as her waist lifted feathery fronds to the filtered sunlight that prevented total darkness beneath the towering trees. Tripetaled trillium blossoms, fading from white to rose as they aged, mingled with thimbleberries and false lily of the valley. Broad leaves hiding small spikes of tiny white flowers scented the air with a vanillalike aroma. Everywhere Ariah looked she saw a land as primeval as the day God created it. Formidable, forceful, enduring, yet soft as velvet, it encompassed her like Bartholomew's embrace.

A loud caw brought up her head in time to see a bird flash

past in a blur of blue and black. There was no sign of the yellow
bird she had seen on the porch. She was crouching at the side
of the trail, examining a sprawl of redwood sorrel with rose-pink
blossoms the exact shade of her dress, when her flesh prickled
as though caressed by unseen hands. Slowly she rose to her feet
and turned. He stood not more than thirty feet away, his dark
hair gleaming in a shaft of sunlight. He looked at home there
in the woods, among the wild, aromatic vegetation and the rich,
fertile earth. Primal. Ariah let out a glad cry and ran toward
him, but he held up his hands.

"Don't try to come closer." Bartholomew gestured to a low
spot between them that was dank with stagnant water and bright
with large blossoms that looked like sheaths of yellow satin
encasing golden phalluses. "There's a bog here."

They stared at each other across the smelly morass, while
insects buzzed and tree frogs belched from hidden nooks.

"Are you all right?" he asked finally.

She nodded, wanting desperately to throw herself into his
arms and tell him how awful her night was, but she knew it
would only make him feel worse, and was afraid she would
burst into tears and make a fool of herself.

He found her more seductive, surrounded by the lush wild
greenery, than ever. His wood nymph. Her hair, hanging loose
over one shoulder, made his fingers itch to caress its silky
strands.

"I saw a Steller's jay," she said lamely.

He smiled. "Did you?"

She shrugged. "We don't have them back East. What are
those odd flowers called?"

"Skunk cabbage. Because of the stink."

Another long silence yawned between them. There seemed
so much to say, and yet so little. The important messages were
evident in their eyes: longing, need, sorrow. Finally, he lifted a
hand, then let it fall uselessly to his side. "I'd better get back.
It will be time for me to relieve Pritchard soon."

Ariah bit her lip to keep from begging him to stay. He backed up a step, then another, and still she said nothing, only stood staring at him and trying not to cry.

Bartholomew forced himself to turn away. He had gone only a half-dozen feet before he wheeled about to find her where he'd left her. "What was it you said to me in Greek, before the ceremony, when I gave you over to Pritchard?"

Her words came slowly, soft and rich with emotion. "I said 'We have eaten bread and salt together.' It means that we have shared food, suffered hardships together, discovered mutual joy, and nothing can break the bond that ties us." Her voice broke as she added, "Not even death."

Ariah returned home a short while later to a house reeking of smoke, to find Hester flapping her apron over a scorched roast.

"Have you got a cerebellum in that head o' yours?" Hester railed. "You could've indicted the house on fire, going off and leaving meat on a hot fire like that."

Ariah rushed to the pot where she'd left the roast browning. The meat was black char on one side, raw on the other. Hester had moved it to the sink and opened the windows to air out the room. "I'm sorry, I—"

"Save your worthless exculpations. Knew you was a useless piece the moment I laid eyes on you, but Pritchard had to have you. Well, let me tell you, Miss High and Mighty"—Hester hovered so close Ariah could smell the tonic the older woman was always sipping—"you best make him happy or—"

"Hester." Bartholomew stood in the open doorway, his dark eyes like chips of obsidian, cold and dangerous.

Hester started at once to defend herself. "She went off and left a roast on the stove. She—"

"Hester!" He moved to the sink and studied the roast. "Only one side is burned. Cut that part off, the rest should be fine." The raw side was speckled with a reddish brown substance. He scooped some on his finger, sniffed, then tasted it with the tip of his tongue. "You used cayenne on this?" he asked Ariah with a grimace.

"Cayenne?" she repeated. "What's that?"

A small tin sat near the sink. He picked it up and showed it to her. "You didn't use this on the roast?"

"No, why would—"

"What's that filthy thing doing in here?" Hester screeched, pointing to a barn cat calmly licking her tail.

"That's Toots. I locked her in the pantry so she would catch the mice in there." Ariah went into the passage between the dining room and the kitchen. The door to the pantry stood open. "I don't understand how she got out."

"I believe I do." Bartholomew tossed the tin of cayenne pepper into the air and caught it deftly with his other hand, his hard penetrating gaze on Hester.

"Why are you looking at me that way?" Hester retorted. "She's the numskull who can't tell cayenne pepper from regular, and can't be trusted to do a simple thing like season a roast."

"But I didn't put the pepper—"

"It doesn't matter, Ariah. Simply wash it off." He turned to his bristling wife. "Come along, Hester. You can get back to your own business now."

"Speaking of minding your own business, what're you doing here?"

"I was heading for the light and saw the smoke. Come on now, I'll walk you back to the house."

When she opened her mouth to argue, he said softly, "Or do you wish to cancel that little bargain we made?"

With uncharacteristic meekness, Hester left through the back door. Turning back to Ariah, he cocked his head toward the cat. "Toots?"

Ariah stifled a grin. "She's always hungry, and good at catching . . . mice"

His eyes softened to charcoal. He chuckled, then he was gone, leaving her to wonder about the bargain he had made with Hester and why she suspected it had something to do with her.

* * *

Bartholomew left Hester at the porch of their house and went on to the light. Dreading the sight of Pritchard's smug, satisfied face, he opened the door and closed it softly behind him.

"Evening, Pritchard."

The young man jumped halfway out of his chair. "Oh! Uncle Bart." Pritchard settled himself at the desk and went back to staring at the logbook lying open in front of him.

Bartholomew frowned. Something was troubling his nephew, but he had no intention of asking what. He started up the stairs, taking them two at a time until he heard Pritchard call out. Gritting his teeth, he peered at the young man over the curved metal railing. "What is it, Pritchard?"

"Could I speak with you a moment?"

The nervous edge in the boy's voice did not bode well. Feeling like a crab in a baited cage, Bartholomew retraced his steps. Pritchard avoided his uncle's direct gaze—another bad sign—giving all his attention to the barometer on the wall.

"I was wondering if . . . do women who haven't . . . you know, virgins . . . is it always . . . difficult the first time?"

Bartholomew's shoulders slumped. He didn't want to hear this, didn't want to learn how miserable Ariah's wedding night might have been with an inexperienced, insensitive cub like Pritchard. "I'm afraid I've had very little experience with virgins, Pritchard."

"You mean except for Aunt Hester?"

Bartholomew's pause might have been answer enough for a more discerning man, but Pritchard only stared at his uncle, waiting. "Yes," Bartholomew finally said, "except for your aunt. If you are referring to the initial tightness—"

"Initial tightness?" Pritchard's laugh contained both relief and fear. "Yeah, well, that gets easier . . . doesn't it?"

A question formed in Bartholomew's mind. A question he did not want to ask. He had known a man once who had claimed an inability to consummate his marriage until his wife's hymen was surgically removed. Bartholomew hated to think of Ariah having to endure such pain and embarrassment.

"It's like learning to be patient, I suppose," Pritchard added hopefully. "Each time gets easier?"

"It's a simple matter of learning control, Pritchard."

Pritchard tried again to laugh, but it came out hollow and desperate. "Yeah, without that, a poor fellow would find himself making a mess on the sheets like a thirteen-year-old, instead of . . . where he ought to. Glad I don't have to worry about that. It would be"—his Adam's apple bobbed as he swallowed hard—"humiliating."

Bartholomew cursed wordlessly. On the one hand, he was thrilled to think that the boy hadn't been able to take what he coveted himself. But on the other, Pritchard's fear of losing control was bound to cause more problems. Guilt ate at Bartholomew as he fought the urge to enhance Pritchard's fear, rather than easing it.

Abruptly, Pritchard shoved the logbook into a drawer. "I'd best get home." He tried for a grin that came out more like a grimace. "I have a wife waiting for me now."

Before Bartholomew could utter a word, the young man bolted out the door.

Eighteen

Her toes were black. Hester could see them peeking out from under her skirts after she'd kicked off her shoes.

She poured the last of the hot water into the tub, set the kettle back on the stove, then tested the temperature with her elbow; her hands couldn't seem to tell blistering hot from warm anymore. She checked to be sure she had soap, a towel and her clean nightrobe. Locks clicked as she secured the three kitchen doors. The sound was followed by the rustle of fabric as she removed her clothes. She wobbled a little as she stepped out of her undergarments, her strength uncertain, as was common lately.

Only after her clothing had been hung over a chair back, and she stood naked as God made her, did she allow herself a good look at her feet. It was as she had feared; they were blacker than ever. Heels, arches, toes. Black as midnight. And icy cold. They looked dead. A shiver ghosted over her.

Ever since Bartholomew returned from Portland, she had worn the new, tan, Paris kid, button boots he had brought her. Again and again, she had scrubbed her feet raw. Still, they were black, and she could no longer blame the dye from her old black shoes.

There was no escaping it; God was punishing her. How could He be so unfair? Hadn't she suffered enough for her sin? She had been so young when Lenny Joe took her, she had barely known what he was doing to her. Since then, she had spent her life keeping her body pure. 'Course, there was the one time when she had gone to Bartholomew's bed, but surely that didn't count; they were married the next day. Only adultery and fornication outside of marriage counted as sins.

Whatever turned her feet black must be what caused the cramps in her legs too, and the constant pain and cold in her feet. Could it explain her unquenchable thirst? The loss of weight, no matter how much she ate? The nausea and diarrhea, the blurred vision, the sores that refused to heal?

Hester propped a foot on her knee so she could see it better. There was a red spot on her heel that was puffy and sore. She bent closer and saw that a blister had burst open. From the new shoes, she supposed. It looked more painful than it felt, but then, she'd noticed lately that her feet, like her hands, weren't worth a tinker's damn for feeling anything.

She climbed carefully into the tub and sank down into the warm water. Could Bartholomew be right? Was she being punished for denying him her bed? She had promised to love, honor and obey, but why in hell did that have to mean letting him rut in her body whenever he damned well wanted to? But maybe if Bartholomew had her in his bed, he would stop lusting after Ariah.

He had snuck off to the woods that day, and Hester reckoned that was where Ariah was, 'stead of tending to her cooking as she shoulda been. Wedded one day and already meeting in the woods with the wrong husband. Hester knew better than to count on her dolt of a nephew to put a stop to it; he was too gone on his new wife to see her for what she truly was—a sneaky, husband-stealing slut. Hester would have to see to everything, just like she always did.

Next door Pritchard glanced at the mantel clock for the hundredth time since supper. Twenty after nine, finally; surely that was late enough for going to bed. He set aside the stiff new padded baseball mitt he'd been rubbing with mink oil. These new mitts had only been out a year now, and most of the players still used the old unpadded ones, with a raw beefsteak inside to protect their hands. As soon as he had enough money saved, he'd order him a pair of the new shoes they were making with heel- and toe-grips for traction. He rose and made a display out of yawning noisily and stretching as though very tired.

"You ready for bed?" he asked Ariah.

Seated on the living-room sofa, she took another stitch in the skirt she had managed to tear somehow on her jaunt into the woods that day. Her husband had been unusually quiet all evening. She had begun to hope he was too exhausted to want to make love. Yet, as she looked up at him, she noted with a sinking heart the telltale bulge in his trousers. Quickly, she averted her gaze. "You go ahead. I wanted to finish my mending first. I'll be up in a moment."

He pulled a face and whined, "Can't you do it tomorrow? I want you to come up with me *now.*"

Ariah glanced anxiously toward the vestibule and the closed door of the First Assistant Keeper's sitting room. "Shhh! Seamus will hear. He's only in the next room."

Pritchard listened and caught the low baritone of the old man's voice raised in one of his sea chanteys:

> "Around Cape Horn we've got to go,
> To me way, hay, o-hio!
> Around Cape Horn to Call-eao,
> A long time ago!"

"He's singing, he can't hear us." Pritchard tried to take her hand and pull her up off the sofa. "Besides, what's wrong with wanting my wife to come to bed with me?"

Ariah blushed and jerked her hand away. "There's nothing wrong with it; you simply don't speak of such intimacies loudly enough for others to hear."

"I said he couldn't hear us. Come on."

She longed to avoid the scene she knew was coming once they went upstairs, yet she couldn't abide his whining. Why couldn't he have gone up and fallen asleep as she had hoped he would? She sighed. What was the use of trying to put off the inevitable? She'd best get it over with.

"Very well." She secured her needle in the fabric and tucked it into her sewing box. "I'll put Seamus's meal out for him and be right up."

Pritchard grinned and hauled her to her feet before she could further object. "Let him get his own meal. Come with me now."

He nearly dragged her up the stairs, but his steps slowed as snatches of his conversation with Bartholomew came back to him. He wanted to bed Ariah so badly, to learn how it felt to actually be inside a woman, but he was terrified he'd go off too soon like he had last night. If he humiliated himself again, would she make fun of him in front of everyone, the way Jimmy Caine's wife did, until the poor man was so impotent even the fancy whores in Portland couldn't get it up for him? The thought wilted the hardness in his trousers.

As they entered the bedroom, he let go of her hand. She shut the door and leaned against it, her gaze on the floor as though she'd grown shy. He took off his jacket and hung it on the back of a chair, then lowered his suspenders and took off his shirt. Still she stood there, hugging the door. Thinking she might be worrying about the pain that would come when he entered her, he went to her and took her into his arms. He breathed a sigh of relief when he managed to kiss her mouth without bumping noses. "I'll try to be more patient tonight. You're so small, I don't want to hurt you."

At that she glanced up. "I'm already sore."

"You are?"

"From last night."

"Oh."

"Would you mind very much if we waited?"

Her request came as a bitter disappointment, but there was comfort in it as well; he couldn't fail at something he didn't try. "For how long?"

"We've known each other such a short time, Pritchard. You

still seem like a stranger to me. You must understand how it is for a woman. All our lives we're told over and over to guard our innocence, that letting a man touch us is wrong. Now suddenly I find myself married and expected to eagerly give my body to someone I don't even know. It's not that easy to tell my body it's all right now. In my heart I feel confused, and a little scared. I need time."

He let go of her and stepped back. "But I'm no stranger, I'm your husband."

"I know that, Pritchard." She struggled to remain calm, knowing everything would be lost if she let her temper get the upper hand. "And I want to be a good wife to you. I want to make you happy. But can't we start slowly, the way it would have been if we'd met in town and you'd courted me for a proper length of time?"

"Does that mean I can't even kiss you anymore?" He flung his arms into the air in a gesture of pure frustration. "Are you going to move back to Aunt Hester's?"

"No." Feeling guilty and thinking to pacify him, she laid a soothing palm on his bare chest. "We're still married—and we'll still live together—though it might be easier on you if I slept in the other room for now."

Pritchard stared at her, trying to think. When she was this close and touching him—God, her hand on his bare chest had nearly caused him to explode—his mind couldn't function properly. He'd never be able to lie beside her without going crazy wanting her.

"It will work out best in the long run, Pritchard, you'll see. And when we are ready to consummate this marriage, I promise you'll find it easier than it was last night."

Was she right? Would it be easier after some time had passed? Once they got to know each other and felt comfortable together? It did make sense. If he got more used to having her around, to being able to kiss her and touch her whenever he wanted, then surely he'd be better able to control himself when she was ready to return to his bed.

"All right," he said, slumping down onto the mattress. "But for how long?"

With a natural instinct for bargaining, she pursed her lips and pretended to consider. "How long does a man usually court a woman before they get married?"

Pritchard came to his feet in a rush. "Holy Hector, you want me to wait a whole year? Ariah, I don't—"

She held up her hands. "I was thinking more like two months, Pritchard."

Two months sounded a heck of a lot better than an entire year. He might be able to survive that. And maybe if he was nice to her, later he could convince her to cut it down to one month. Or even less. "All right, two months."

She smiled and kissed him on the cheek. "I'll move my things into the other room."

"I don't want the others to know," he said as she opened a drawer and snatched out a handful of lacy underwear.

"What we do in the privacy of our own home is no one's business but our own, Pritchard."

"Good."

Feeling more relaxed—and more hopeful—than he had all day, he watched her take her clothes into the bedroom across the hall. What he had to do was think of this as getting hired onto the Cincinnati Red Stockings. A man always started out on second string until he'd proved himself. But if that dream ever came true, Pritchard intended to make sure he was moved to first string before the season was half over. He would do the same with Ariah. Hell, he was going to be so nice to her, she'd be begging him to let her come back to his bed within a week.

"Hey, Ariah," he called, following her into the other room. "You're from Cincinnati. Ever see a Red Stockings game?"

She paused in the act of hanging her dresses in the wardrobe. "A Red Stockings game?"

"Yeah, they were the first professional baseball team. They had a one hundred and thirty-game winning streak once. I think they're still the best team in the league."

"I'm sorry, I've never been to any baseball games. Do you play them here?"

He moved out of the way so she could pass back through the doorway. The change of subject had helped him lose the aching need in his groin. "Not with only five people to work with; it takes nine men to make up one team. You don't know anything about baseball, do you?"

Untroubled by the disdain in his voice, she moved her mother's hand-crocheted dresser scarf to the other room and spread it lovingly over the dresser. Then she set out her brush, comb, hand mirror and the photograph of her parents in its ornate silver frame. "No, I'm afraid I don't."

"Then I'll have to teach you. If we're going to produce our own team, you'll have to understand the game."

Ariah whirled to stare at him. "Produce our own team? Are you saying you want nine children?"

He grinned "Sure. Don't you?"

"I don't believe I've ever even considered the idea."

"Well, you better start, and soon, too. We don't have a lot of time to waste, you know. If you give me a bunch of girls, it'll take that much longer to come up with nine boys."

Her mouth dropped open as she realized what he was saying. She might have to bear more than a dozen children in order to come up with nine boys. When would she have time to read or study ornithology?

Pritchard walked back to his own room, feeling a great deal more cheerful than he had when they'd started upstairs. He'd speak to Uncle Bart tomorrow about getting some time off so he could take Ariah to Portland or Astoria for a good baseball game. The team he played with in Tillamook during the summer was too amateurish. He had a feeling his wife would not be impressed by anything but the best, and it was important that she share his fondness for the game. A lot more important than those books she was always reading, or her silly birds.

He might even see if he could wangle a tryout while they were in Portland. He had no intention of remaining a lighthouse keeper all his life. This job was only temporary, until he could get onto a professional team. Baseball was his life, after all, and he was the best hurler and striker the National League would ever see. All he needed was a chance to show them.

In the meantime, it might be a good idea to go into Tillamook and pay a visit to Nettie Tibbs on the far end of Hoquarton Slough. He'd heard that for half a dollar Nettie would teach a man everything he ever wanted to know about sex. A man didn't have to worry about pleasing that kind of girl. He could let himself go off as fast as he needed to, and he wouldn't have to take a bath first either. Once he'd learned the ropes, he'd feel a whole lot more confident bedding Ariah.

All he needed now was an excuse to go into town—without his new wife.

Down at the light, Bartholomew was finding the night much too long. He polished brass fittings until his fingers were raw. He performed one arm push-ups. When it was still light enough to see without carrying a lantern, he ran up and down the stairs, his hard heels clattering on the metal steps until the tower rang with their echo. After dark he studied Dante's *Inferno* until the words blurred and his eyes ached. By the time Old Seamus relieved him at midnight, Bartholomew was exhausted enough to sleep, in spite of Ariah Scott Monteer.

Or so he had hoped. But when he lay alone at last in his narrow bed, he found his eyes wide open and his entire body tense with frustration. Had Pritchard succeeded tonight in deflowering Ariah? Had she suffered from his efforts? Or, worse, enjoyed them?

The knock on Bartholomew's bedroom door came as a surprise. Only serious problems with the light would bring someone to his door in the middle of the night. Yet there was no storm, and he had doubled-checked everything before he'd left. The light was in perfect order. Had something happened to Seamus? Or could it be Ariah? Had she fled Pritchard's bed and come to him for protection or solace?

He leaped from the bed and yanked on his trousers. When he opened the door and found Hester on his threshold, dressed only in a nightrobe that looked virginally white in the lantern light, he was too astonished to speak.

"May I come in?" she asked with a smile that might have been seductive, had she been capable of the necessary passion.

Bartholomew eyed her warily. "What's wrong? Are you ill?"

Hester's smile waned and her lips grew thin, a sure sign of annoyance, but her tone remained light. "No, merely . . . lonely."

Another shock. To his knowledge, Hester had never needed any company but her own. His mind was so befuddled with suspicion and puzzlement he didn't think to step aside so she could enter. He simply stood there, staring at her.

"Pritchard's wedding started me thinking." Hester squeezed past him into the room she had never before entered, except to clean it. The quality of her soft, Southern drawl warned him that her visit was anything but casual. She was up to something.

"I've been a good wife to you; even you can't deny that." She ran a fingertip along the dresser top as though to point out its cleanliness. Then she picked his shirt up off the foot of the bed and folded it. "I've kept your home clean, served you good hot meals and made myself useful in the barn as well as the garden." She laid the shirt on the dresser and turned to pin him with her gaze. "I'm sure you believe me extravagant with your money, but most wives of our station spend a good deal more than I do on clothing and furniture."

Her emotionless hazel eyes held an accusation she kept from her voice. Bartholomew almost smiled. Whatever she wanted, she was desperate to achieve her goal, desperate enough to sacrifice her prudish pride. Curiosity overcame his distrust of her unorthodox visit, but he refused to aid her by asking leading questions. He remained mute instead.

As though she sensed his amusement, her lips tightened. She switched her gaze to his mussed bed.

"The only place you can say I failed you is here. I"—her voice faltered, but he couldn't tell if that was faked—"I've decided to rectify that maleficence—tonight."

"I think you mean malfeasance, Hester."

"Whatever."

She turned and he saw that she had unbuttoned her gown. With a shrug of her shoulders, it slipped free, slithering down her candlewick-thin body as if she were warm paraffin. He averted his gaze from her thin, unappealing form, and heard her climb into his bed. Stunned, he stood frozen for several heartbeats, unable to think. Of all the stunts he might have expected from her, this he would never have believed her capable of. Finally the shock wore away and with the resumed functioning of his brain came illumination—and anger.

Whatever was wrong with Hester she was scared enough to want to make sure she wouldn't be punished for denying him his marital rights. It appalled him to realize how much pleasure her fear gave him. He was becoming as embittered as she was.

"Get up, Hester. This won't make you well again."

She watched him stare at the floor so he wouldn't have to look at her. Damn him! He'd had his little slut in the woods. Now that the girl was wed to that fool Pritchard, Bartholomew figured he could go off fornicating whenever he wanted. Hester knew he reckoned his wife no better than white trash, and old now to boot. What did he care if he condemned her to the Lord's awful retribution? But she'd get even, and she'd find a way to get rid of Ariah Scott Monteer, too.

With as much grace as she could manage, Hester left the bed and drew on her nightrobe. Then she went to stand before the husband to whom she had given seven years of her life.

"You ungrateful bastard. After all the care I gave that foul-mouthed father of yours, and then you. All you ever cared about was that lump of flesh 'tween your legs. Only a whore like her would like having it rammed into her. Does she like to put her mouth on it the way I've heard other whores do?"

Bartholomew pretended not to understand. It was safer that way. Otherwise, he was afraid he'd kill her. "I haven't been to any whores, Hester."

"Your precious Ariah's a whore, if'n you admit it or not."

His hand came off the doorknob and balled at his side. "Shut up, Hester, before you regret your ugly words."

A thrill surged through her at the razor edge hidden in his soft voice. His dark eyes had hardened to flint, the way they had in the Ketcham garden when he'd struck her. She smiled. At least she could still wrest some passion out of him, after all his years of apathy.

"I could never regret anything I said about your beloved trollop." She pressed closer until he sucked in his breath at her fruity stench. "No words are ugly enough to describe *her* kind. Did you take note of the nice odor in the kitchen when you come in tonight? She brung me a bouquet of wildflowers. To thank me, she says, for savin' her roast. Stupid little bitch put a skunk cabbage smack in the center. Thinks she's so smart, bringin' cats in the house, taunting me. Well, we'll see who gets the last laugh."

"Now, Hester—"

"Don't you 'Now, Hester,' me! Save yer threats for somebody as cares. You say one word 'bout my past in town and I'll tell everyone about the whore you forced your own nephew to take on just so you could keep her around. Does she beg for your filthy touch, Bartholomew? Does she pant for you like a bitch in heat?"

The urge to knock the leer from her face, to thrash the ugliness out of her soul, was so great he could almost feel her flesh give under his hands. But he'd given in to the dark side of his soul once, and had found it too bitter to bear. Now he saw how her eyes blazed with a strange sort of eagerness that reminded him of her passionate response the day he'd hit her. Swiftly he clamped down on his emotions, and smiled.

"You're a sick woman, Hester, in more ways than one, and you know you have more to lose than Ariah if it comes to hanging out dirty laundry. Even Pritchard will refuse to back you on this one. He's quite smitten with his new wife." He leaned back against the door as if bored. "I'll take you to see Dr. Wills tomorrow. I suspect you have a fever. You're sweating, in spite of the chill in tonight's air, and you smell like rotten apples."

Her face blanched, then flushed red as a starfish. "If I'm sick, it's because of you . . . you and your filthy need to rut on any female you can find."

"That's not true, Hester. I've no need, or desire, to *rut* on you." He gripped her arm and guided her out of the room. "I'll take you back to your room. High tide will be about dawn tomorrow. Be ready to leave an hour before that."

"I told you, I don't need no doctor for what ails me, Bartholomew Noon, and I won't let that man put his hands on me. He ain't nothing but a lecher like you, using doctoring as an excuse to gawk at a woman's naked body."

"Don't you want to go to church? It is Sunday tomorrow."

She straightened at his mention of church, and fear entered her eyes. "Yes, yes, gotta go to church. Lord's riled enough at me, mustn't make it worse."

Bartholomew pushed open the door to her bedroom and led her inside to her bed.

"Don't turn out the lamp," she said as she crawled under the covers. "Can't stand the dark . . . devil hides there, waiting an' waiting. And make sure there ain't no cats in here. Be just like that slut to put a stinking cat in here, to rile me."

"There aren't any cats, Hester. Go to sleep now."

She curled into a fetal position, her back to the wall. Her eyes scoured the shadowed corners of the room. The air stank of urine, with a sweetish scent to it he'd never noticed before. He feared she was more ill than he'd suspected. Her stubbornness about seeking treatment would kill her, unless he did something to prevent it. Unbidden, the thought came to him that this might be his chance to be free of her. All he had to do was ignore her condition, and wait.

The temptation lasted no longer than one tick of the clock on her bedside table before he thrust it aside.

Feeling more weary than he had at the end of his exhausting watch at the light, he closed Hester's door and returned to his bed. Dawn would come early tomorrow, along with the tide, and the night was already half gone.

Please, God, let me sleep and, in sleep, escape the torture of imagining Ariah in bed with Pritchard.

Nineteen

The shack sat amidst a tangle of bog birch and elderberry shrubs, shaded by a single maple tree. A thin stream of smoke curled upward from the chimney, telling Pritchard someone was home. He was trying to work up the courage to go up and knock on the dilapidated door when it opened and a young girl emerged with a basket of laundry.

Pritchard guessed her age to be in the neighborhood of fifteen, though there was a definite sensuality in her walk and movements. Her hair was so pale it was almost white and seemed to shimmer even on this cloudy day. Then she turned toward him, and he sucked in his breath at the sultry beauty of her face.

"Hullo," she said, spotting him on the weedy track that led to the house. Lips so red he thought she must have been eating cranberries curved in a smile that made his toes curl and his groin sizzle with a rush of heat.

The girl set the basket of wet laundry down on the grass near a drooping clothesline. With her hands on her aproned hips, she sauntered toward him. "You lookin' fer me?"

Pritchard gulped and stammered, "Yes, I mean . . . no. I was looking for Nettie Tibbs."

Her head tilted to one side as she studied him with friendly amber eyes. "I'm Nettie. Don't I know you?"

As he watched her glide closer, he realized she was older than he'd guessed—at least seventeen—but since he'd expected a woman reputed to be so experienced in sexual matters to be a good deal older, her claim to be Nettie Tibbs took him by surprise. He eyed her warily, wondering if she could be trying to fool him. "You sure you're Nettie?"

Her laugh was low and husky. "Ain't nobody else living here an' answering to that name but me." She stood close enough now for him to catch a subtle scent of roses. The bodice of her threadbare dress fit her like skin, making it difficult to keep his eyes off the lush roundness of her large breasts. His body hardened and began to ache.

The girl laughed again and moved even nearer, hips swaying, her gaze traveling brazenly down his body to his groin. "So, you gonna tell ol' Nettie what you want with her, or do I have to guess?"

Pritchard blushed to the roots of his mouse brown hair. "I, uh . . . I heard . . ."

"You're cute, you know that?" She interrupted his stumbling discourse. "You wanta come in for some coffee? Or if you need somethin' to calm them nerves o' yours, I got some wine inside."

He ducked his head in an awkward nod of acceptance. "That would be . . . nice."

There was only one chair inside the small one-room shack, sitting next to a wooden table with a broken broomstick grafted onto a shattered leg. The only other furniture was a large bed, covered with a pieced quilt, a washstand holding a chipped basin, and a chest of drawers. The mere sight of the bed made Pritchard nervous. He edged toward the chair, only to be cut off by the girl.

"Sit yerself right here." She patted the edge of the bed. "I'll fetch the wine. It ain't fancy, but it's wet."

She moved to a set of crude shelves on one wall and took down a tall green bottle. Pritchard watched as she removed the cork and half-filled two glasses. She carried them to the bed and sat down beside him. "What's yer name?"

"Pritchard."

She sipped her wine, her eyes never leaving his face. "You look familiar, but I don't remember a-meeting you afore."

"I just moved here last summer from Missouri. I'm a keeper at the Cape Meares light."

"A keeper! You mean them they call wickies?" Her golden eyes lit up, and she smiled. "Bet that's excitin', sitting up there in yer tower an' watching all them big ships go by, and whales an' ever'thin'."

He shrugged and tried the wine. It was acrid and thin. "I wouldn't exactly call it exciting."

Nettie leaned toward him, one finger playing with the insignia on his collar. "What do you do for excitement then? Come into town and look up little ol' gals like me?"

"No! I've never . . . I mean, I don't . . ."

She chuckled as his words trailed away and his cheeks bloomed like roses. "Don't be embarrassed. I'm right glad you came."

"You are?"

"Sure." Her hand slid down his chest and inside his coat to stroke his chest through his shirt. Since he was only supposed to be playing poker with the men from his team, he hadn't worn a vest or any neckwear. Nettie toyed with a button as she smiled up at him, her face so close now that all he would have to do to kiss her was to bend his head. But she didn't wait for him to work up the nerve.

"You are really cute." She touched her mouth to his.

He sucked in his breath as a warm breast brushed his arm. When his lips parted, her tongue darted inside. He thought he would melt to a puddle of bones right there on her bed. His body was blazingly hot, so hard and uncomfortable he could barely stand the pressure of his need. Nettie moved away and his heart plunged in disappointment, until she set their glasses on the floor, then reached for his coat.

"You look kinda warm," she said, as she pulled off his coat. "I'm gonna make you real comfortable, 'cause I don't want you going away too soon."

"You don't?" His voice was a faint squeak, so raspy he could barely understand his own words.

"Told ya I liked ya." She pressed him down on the bed, then pushed aside his suspenders and freed the buttons on his shirt.

"When I like somebody I treat 'em real nice, so's they'll come back real often."

Pritchard was glad, as she stripped his shirt off him, that he hadn't worn any undershirt, and that he'd worn clean drawers. Matters were moving so fast he didn't have time to worry how he might perform. It was all he could do to believe he was not merely imagining the girl and the warm knowing hands that were moving over his body with tantalizing frankness. When her fingers closed over the aroused flesh straining at the front of his trousers, his whole body jerked and he groaned.

Nettie giggled. "Ooh, you hot fer me, Pritchard? That's good, 'cause I'm hot fer you, too. Wanta see how hot I am?" Without waiting for his answer, she put his hand on her breast so he could feel the hardened nipples through the thin fabric of her dress. "They want you to touch 'em, only without no dress on. They wanta feel your mouth on 'em, too."

Pritchard groaned. He writhed in joy when she slipped a hand inside his trousers. Then, with sudden, grievous clarity he knew he was going to do the one thing he had feared most.

"Oh no," he whispered in a half-whine, "gonna strike out again." With a howl of combined joy and misery, he spilled his seed in his drawers. Shaking with humiliation, he rolled onto his stomach and tried to stem the tears that abruptly filled his eyes.

"Hey, Prit?" Nettie's hand stroked down his spine. "Don't feel bad. You ain't the first man couldn't wait 'fore he come off."

"I'm not?" Pritchard's head came up off the bed.

"Gosh an' golly, no." She eased him onto his back and brushed away his tears with her thumb. "I don't know why you men wait so long to find a gal you can ease yerselves with. Never fails to turn out thisaway when you do that. Simple matter a-waitin' too long is all it is."

Pritchard cupped her face with his palm, his heart filled with gratitude and relief. "You're about the prettiest thing I've ever seen."

Nettie giggled. "Aw, you don't mean that. You're jest glad I ain't mad at you fer cheatin' me outta a good time."

"Holy Hector, Nettie, I wouldn't have done that to you in a thousand years if I could have helped it."

"I know. Don't fret over it, Prit." She rolled on top of him, rubbed her body seductively against him and kissed his nose. "I bet it won't take two shakes of a coon's tail 'fore you're ready to go at it again, and then you can make it up to me real nice."

No sooner had she spoken than he felt himself growing hard again. His eyes widened and a grin spread across his face. "You know what? You're not only the prettiest girl I've ever met, but you're more exciting than hitting a home run with all the bases loaded and everybody in town watching."

"Hey, that's baseball talk. I jest love baseball, Prit."

"You do?"

"Gosh and golly, yes. All them men running 'round in them snug little uniforms." Her eyes lit up and she said, "Hey, you're one o' them Tillamook Kings, ain'tcha? That's where I seen you afore. I go to all their games."

"You do?" Pritchard's chest expanded to its full breadth. "Well, I'm their new first-string striker."

"Oooh, and Nettie Tibbs has you right here in her own little bed. Why, I'm downright honored, Prit." She kissed him hard. "I'm gonna show you such a good time, you ain't never gonna forget me. And I don't want no money for it, neither."

Pritchard kissed her back, his hands going to her lush breasts. "I could never forget you anyway, Nettie."

Her hand moved to his trousers. "That's good, Prit, 'cause I think you're ready fer your turn at bat again."

He couldn't have said later how they got rid of the rest of their clothes. All he knew was that they were soon rolling over the bed, both of them stark naked, legs entwined, their mouths and hands greedily devouring every inch of one another's flesh. Nettie wasn't shy about telling him what she wanted him to do, or in acting on her own impulses.

The hot, wet feel of her closing around him as he slid inside her was more heavenly than he'd imagined. So good he knew he'd never again think of a home run with the bases loaded in quite the same vein as he had before he met Nettie Tibbs.

At the same time Nettie was teaching Pritchard some of the finer nuances of making home runs, Bartholomew was entering the home of Dr. Abraham Wills on Third Street.

"What is it I can do for you, Bartholomew?" Dr. Wills motioned his visitor to a chair across the cluttered desk from his own. "You're not ill, I hope. You certainly look fit."

"I am, thank you. I appreciate you seeing me on a Sunday like this." Bartholomew eased himself into the comfortable armchair with its puffy, buttoned upholstery, and hung his keeper's cap on his knee. "It's Hester I've come about."

"You didn't bring her with you?"

"No. I'm afraid Hester has some odd notion about sickness having a direct correlation with sin. She insists that since she does not sin, she cannot be ill."

The doctor chuckled. The movement of his three chins made his frizzy red beard shimmy like a jellyfish. "She's an exception to most folks I know, then, if she never sins. Refused to come, I take it."

"Vehemently, no matter how I attempted to persuade her." Bartholomew shook his head with mixed disgust and wonder. "She is an obstinate woman, but I'm worried about her, Abraham. She's lost weight, I suspect her vision is failing and her legs seem to give her constant pain."

"Is she eating?"

"Like a half-starved boy. She drinks constantly, too, water mostly, though I'm afraid she's also taken to drinking a so-called tonic she bought from a patent-medicine salesman. Supposed to cure everything from childbed fever to gout." His disgust was evident in his voice.

"Ah, yes, predominantly alcohol, no doubt." Dr. Wills took up a pen with his stubby left hand, dipped it into the inkwell and made some notes on a tablet in front of him. "Damned leeches, preying on innocent people. Half of the poor devils can't even read." He slammed down the pen. A dark splotch spread across his desk blotter the way an epidemic goes through a town. "I'd give anything to see a few of those bogus doctors strung up from the highest tree. They've caused unnecessary deaths, you may be sure, simply by preventing folks from seeking real medical help."

"Are you saying the tonic may be causing Hester's illness?"

Wills shook his head. "In this case, probably not. Tell me, is she urinating excessively?"

"Yes, and she seems tired all the time."

"Hmmm. Any vomiting or diarrhea?" Dr. Wills reclaimed his pen and made a few more notes, his left hand giving his spidery script a slight backward slant.

"Not that I know of, but it's possible, considering how much time she spends in the water closet. What do you suspect, Abraham? Is it serious?"

Wills made no reply as he continued to write on his tablet. When he finally put down the pen, he swiveled about in his chair and took a book from a shelf behind his desk.

"I read an article in a medical journal recently, about a disease called diabetes. Its cause has not yet been discovered, but the article did mention enough of the symptoms you describe to make me suspect this may be what your wife suffers from. Ah, here we are." Wills found the page he had been searching for and copied something onto a clean piece of paper. Then he handed the paper to Bartholomew.

Mix three drops of alum to four pints of milk and drink one pint of this posset three to four times a day for eight to ten days, the note read. Bartholomew folded the paper and tucked it into his pocket. "Will this truly cure it?"

" 'Seldom fails to cure in eight to ten days,' it says here, but according to the article I read, they believe there are two types. One of them is almost invariably fatal. This type advances rather quickly toward the end, making it difficult to determine the seriousness of the patient's condition until it's too late. Not very encouraging, I'm afraid, my boy, but there it is."

Not bothering to hide his distress, Bartholomew rose and extended his hand. "Thank you, Abraham. I appreciate your time and trouble. I'll bring Hester in as soon as I can manage it."

"Do that, my boy, do that. I understand that young nephew of yours got married the other day," Wills said as he walked his visitor to the door. "Word is his bride is a beauty. She's not from around these parts, I take it?"

"No, Cincinnati."

"Hester must enjoy having another female on the place, considering how isolated you are there at the lighthouse."

Bartholomew gazed out the open door at the broad green plains that surrounded Tillamook, and thought of the mixed joy and agony Ariah's presence brought him. And what it did to Hester. "Yes, well," he said a bit guiltily, "thank you again, Doctor."

Hester vehemently refused the alum and milk posset, along with a visit to the doctor. She pushed more and more chores onto Ariah and spent her time reading the Bible and praying.

Ariah doubled her efforts to be helpful and friendly, reminding herself that Hester was ill and deserved care and understanding, not animosity. But it was nearly impossible not to feel resentment when everything she did earned only criticism and open malice from the woman.

This morning, thinking it would please Hester, Ariah had served her tea in one of the lovely cup and saucer sets she'd found in the oak cupboard in the dining room. The moment Hester laid eyes on the delicate china, however, she had let out the most vile invectives she could think of, startling Ariah so the tray leaped from her shaking hands. The hand-painted cup and saucer landed on a strip of bare floor and shattered to bits. When Hester ordered her out, Ariah had gladly gone.

To restore her spirits, she fixed Pritchard's lunch and carried it down to him at the light, remaining to visit while he ate, a habit she was coming to enjoy. Pritchard loved showing her the light. The first day she had joined him there, he'd taken her up the spiral staircase to the top floor to see the hand-ground crystal lens made in Paris by Henry LaPaute in 1887.

"There's only one other eight-sided light like this in America," he'd told her proudly. "It weighs over two thousand pounds. They had to bring it by ship around the horn, then hoist it up to the tower from a ship below."

The lens was so large they could walk around inside, reaching it through a crawl space off the stairs. As the day keeper, it was Pritchard's job to keep the thick prisms of the bull's-eye lens cleaned and polished to prevent sea spray from pitting the precious crystal. It terrified her to watch him hang by a metal handle as he did the upper panels, the wind trying to pluck him off and fling him into the sea. Together, they trimmed the five wicks of the kerosene lantern. Then Pritchard taught her how to operate the clockworks by the complicated system of gears and weights that kept the lens turning from sunset to sunrise.

Days had passed since he had even tried to kiss her, and Ariah felt pleased, certain it meant that he was coming to respect her because of their growing friendship.

The only thing she enjoyed more than standing on the open catwalk outside the glass tower, feeling the wind in her hair and watching seabirds wheel and soar above the waves, was wandering the beach or the lush tranquil forest. Often in the woods she had an eerie sensation of being watched. She waited for Bartholomew to show himself, longing to be with him, but never even caught a glimpse of him.

She sensed him everywhere. In the strength and tenacity of ferns and saplings rooted atop jagged trunks of trees felled by lightning or wind, in the gentleness of the spongy moss that coated earth and growing things alike, in the laughter of the wind soughing in the tree tops. Being in the wildness of the forest was like being in his embrace, comforting, yet arousing.

In her journal she jotted down the birds and animals and flowers she saw each day, along with other observations:

March 23—A rare day of sunshine and clear skies. Saw a Western tanager, yellow with red head and black wing— breathtakingly beautiful.

March 24—Too wet to venture out today. Took Hester a book of poetry I thought she would enjoy. She threw it at me, making me wonder if perhaps she doesn't know how to read. How awful for her if she doesn't. I feel so bad, but don't know what I can do about it.

March 25—Cloudy but warm. Found an enormous Sitka spruce Bartholomew claims was a ceremonial tree where Tillamook Indians buried dead chiefs in canoes slung like hammocks from the branches. The base is over ten feet thick. Limbs, three to five feet thick, go straight out before curving upward, like some giant's fantastic candelabrum. A trail nearby leads to the rocks where Indians used to fish, and where Bartholomew still does. I peered eagerly from the edge of the cliff but saw only a male rufous-sided towhee.

The warm days in the woods brought thoughts of Easter. Her mother had always made the holiday a celebration, from Palm Sunday through Easter itself, and Ariah saw no reason not to carry on the tradition, even if she was married and thousands of miles away from her hometown.

Busy planning a menu for Easter Sunday and studying the lush growth along the path, she had no warning until she heard the first deep throaty growl. Her head snapped up, but she saw only bright green foliage and rich dark shadows in the filtered sunlight. Then a shadow moved and she found herself staring into the small, ebony eyes of a bear.

The beast took two lumbering steps toward her, massive head lifted, nostrils flaring to catch her scent. Jagged teeth showed as it opened its mouth to issue another testy growl. Talons of fear dug into Ariah, sending her pulse soaring as the blood drained from her face and her body turned to ice. A scream rose in her throat and lodged there. Then, in her peripheral vision she caught a blur of movement as something leaped onto the path between her and the bear.

A wolf!

For the length of one breath—stretched to eternity by tension and fear—Ariah thought the wolf was about to attack her. Her terror doubled. Then she realized it was challenging the bear, not her.

The wolf lunged at the bear, its snarls answered by the frenzied growls of the larger animal. Ariah thought everyone at the lighthouse must be able to hear the racket. Yet no one came. The bear slashed the air. The wolf dodged and attacked the bear's flank, sinking its teeth deep into the huge animal's tough hide. The bear spun about, breaking free. With a last growl it lumbered off.

The wolf watched his enemy retreat, lips drawn back in a savage snarl, before he turned to Ariah. She stepped back, braced to flee. To her surprise, the wolf merely sat down on his haunches. His tongue hung out one side of his mouth, and he almost seemed to smile. Baffled, she hesitated. The wolf whimpered, then turned and vanished into the dense forest.

Ariah's legs trembled as her terror slowly receded and she realized she was safe. She slumped to the ground and wiped perspiration from her brow and the back of her neck. Then she gathered herself together and headed home as quickly as her wobbly legs could carry her.

Bartholomew was planting peas in the large vegetable garden when he saw her bolt from the woods as though the hounds of hell were at her heels. He quickly got to his feet, instinctively aware that something was wrong. The moment Ariah fell, he dropped the sack of seed and took off at a run, his heart in his throat. She dragged herself up, and fell again.

"Ariah, what is it? What's wrong?" he shouted as he rushed to her.

She cried out when she saw him, a small throaty sound that spoke of terror and relief. Her legs turned to mud; she stumbled and fell into his outstretched arms. "Bear . . . in the woods," she got out between pants. "A wolf drove it away."

"A wolf? Are you certain?" He knelt down and sat her on the grass, supporting her back with his knee. "Were you attacked? Are you hurt?"

He didn't wait for her to answer. His hands flew over her body, feeling, testing, searching for wounds. Having assured himself she was unharmed, he pulled her into his arms and cradled her against his chest. "What happened?" he said, his voice calmer now. "You say the wolf drove the bear off?"

She nodded, still gasping from her headlong flight. He framed her delicate face in one large hand and kissed her with a tenderness that brought tears to her eyes.

"Oh, God," he murmured. "To think I could have lost you."

He kissed her tears away, oblivious to the fact that they were out in the open where they could have been seen by anyone.

"The wolf," she said, looking up at him, "it's starving. I could see its ribs, in spite of its thick fur." She could feel his heart pounding against her shoulder where she leaned into him. It matched the racing beat of her own.

"Are you sure it was a wolf? I haven't seen one in these parts in ages."

His panic had faded, but he experienced no compulsion to release her. She felt too good in his arms. Too right.

Ariah traced the sensuous curve of his mouth with a finger. "It was white with black markings and a bushy tail that curled up over its back. How did you get back here so fast? I sensed you there in the forest only minutes before the bear appeared."

He stared at her. "I haven't been in the woods for days."

"But someone's been watching me. I could feel it on the back of my neck. I thought it was you, but . . ." Her voice trailed off. If it wasn't Bartholomew watching her, who was it? Goose bumps rose on her arms and she shuddered.

He felt her tremble and drew her closer against him, his mind searching for an answer. If someone was lurking about in the woods, Bartholomew would ferret him out. And beat him within an inch of his life for frightening Ariah. But who . . . ? Her uncle came first to mind, but she was safely married now, so the man was no longer a threat. Then it came to him. He might have chuckled, if he hadn't known that fear would prevent her from sharing his relief.

"It wasn't me, little nymph. I suspect it was the dog."

"Dog?"

"Shortly before I went to Portland there was a shipwreck. One of the survivors had a dog aboard that looked like a wolf. It had a tail that curved up over its back. Part wolf, part Alaskan malamute, part chow, specially bred for a sled team. I had forgotten until now. We assumed it had drowned."

"And you think it was that dog that scared the bear away?"

"He's probably been foraging in the woods all this time. And not doing too well, from the way you describe him."

"There are rabbits and mice in the woods. You'd think a dog would do well enough."

"Not necessarily, if it's raised as a pet and unused to hunting for supper."

"But why has he been following me? Why didn't he simply come to the station for food?"

Bartholomew shrugged. "He may have been hurt at first. Perhaps after all he endured—the shipwreck and everything—he's a bit wary of humans now. He's been living wild for over a month."

She leaned into his strength as she considered the idea. "A dog. A pet dog," she murmured. Then she struggled to her feet. "I must find it. It saved my life. I can't let it go on suffering."

His mouth curved in a gentle smile. "I don't think you'll have any trouble. If he is the one who's been trailing you, all you have to do is let him come to you."

"I'll get some meat scraps to take with me." She started for the house.

"Aren't you forgetting something?"

Ariah stopped and glanced back at him. "What?"

His smile broadened. "You're terrified of dogs."

"Oh." She frowned in confusion. "But this one saved my life. He could have attacked me today if he'd wanted to, or at any time in the last few days, if what you believe is true and he's the one who was watching me. Should I fear him?"

"No. Me maybe, but not him." His voice had grown husky, his gaze heated, as he came toward her.

She smiled, knowing that look and loving it. "Why should I fear you?"

"Because I have an insane desire to draw you down right here and make love to you the way I've wanted to since the first moment I laid eyes on you."

Ariah glanced about, and her smile slid from her face. "Oh, Bartholomew, what were we thinking to embrace here in the open like this? What if Hester saw us? Or Seamus?"

"I'm not sure I care if anybody sees us, especially Hester. *Philotimo,*" he murmured, gently touching her face. "I've let it rule me all my life. It bound me to Hester when I should have simply turned my back. And it kept me from taking the woman I love and escaping with her while I could."

Ariah merely stood there gazing at him. His words had been soft, so soft she wasn't sure he meant for her to hear them. *Philotimo,* Greek for love of honor. How ironic. It was honor that had killed her father. Honor—in the form of Uncle Xenos—that had threatened her life and sent her running to Oregon. Now Bartholomew was telling her it was honor that had denied her the man she loved.

A tortured look entered his dark eyes before he shuttered them and set her away from him. "Go and get your meat, little nymph, while I still have some honor left. We'll see if we can find your wolf."

For a moment she struggled with a desire to beg him to cast aside his damnable honor and run away with her, now, this very minute. But it would be wrong. He would never be able to live with himself afterward if he abandoned the scruples on which he had based his life. They were his soul. He could learn to live without her, but no man could survive without his honor.

Twenty

"There she goes again. Just like yesterday, the little trollop."

Hester winced as she limped to the next window, where she could see better beyond the assistant keeper's house. On the far side of the clearing, Ariah, in a cobalt blue dress, was vanishing into the forest. At least this time Bartholomew wasn't sniffing along behind her, like a dog after a bitch in heat. Hester had made sure of that by insisting he catch them some fresh perch for supper. With Pritchard at the light, Hester was alone at the compound, except for that old fool, Seamus, who was asleep. It was the chance she had been waiting for.

Hester stepped outside and looked about to make certain no one was around. Her feet and legs, especially the bad one, throbbed with pain as she hobbled across the lawn to the other house, aided by a broken broom handle she used as a cane. The blister on her heel had become infected, and the whiskey she had poured over it to cleanse it had done no good. She wasn't about to waste any more of her precious supply. The blister would heal eventually. Her health would return then.

When no one answered Hester's knock next door, she opened the back door and slipped inside. This time she would get rid of that slut for good.

Ariah found the forest dim and shadowy. Night rain had left the cape shrouded in mist so thick the tip of the bluff where the light stood was completely hidden. All that had been visible from Ariah's window that morning were gossamer wisps of gray, giving her the illusion of having awakened in a strange and alien world. Even the normal cries of the sea birds had been hushed, and an eerie, surreal quiet lay over everything.

The fog had cleared by midmorning, leaving low-hanging clouds and a somber gray ocean that battered angrily at the solid mass of the bluff. Bartholomew had been accompanying her on her trips into the woods, armed with a rifle, but last night Hester had created such a scene over the matter that today Ariah had stolen away an hour earlier than usual to avoid causing more trouble.

She placed some food on the trail and settled down a few yards away to wait. Suddenly she realized she was no longer alone. There was no warning. The dog simply appeared, as if he had materialized out of the vanished mist.

He hovered hungrily over the food she'd brought, afraid to take his eyes off her long enough to eat. Ariah went stock-still. A wave of her old fear washed over her, and she fought an impulse to run. For an eternity they stared at each other, the half-starved dog and the woman, and in that moment, Ariah's fear fled. He needed her, and she him, for in spite of her crowded days, she was lonely. Only when she was with Bartholomew did she feel truly alive and happy, but those stolen interludes were painfully rare.

The dog snatched up a piece of gravy-soaked bread, his piercing gaze never leaving the woman.

"Good boy," she murmured softly. "Go on, eat your fill. I won't hurt you."

As if taking her at her word, he laid down with the food between his front paws and ate greedily. When the food was gone, he stood. Slowly, she stretched out her hand, praying she had been right in her assessment of him.

"Come here, boy. I won't harm you. Let me pet that lush fur and show you I want to be your friend."

The dog cocked his head, listening, but made no move toward her. A reflection of her own searing loneliness stared out at her from the large sable eyes in the regal, black and white head. Then his ears twitched, and his gaze shifted to the trail behind her. Ariah turned to see what he was looking at, seeing nothing. When she glanced back, he was gone.

"Ariah? Be ye there, lassie?" a voice called.

Old Seamus shuffled into view around a bend in the trail, the rolling gait of his bowed legs giving him the appearance of a man still struggling to adapt to land after months at sea. His corncob pipe protruded from the salt and pepper bristles of his mustache. Suspenders held up his baggy trousers, which had seen better days and not nearly enough soap.

"You plan on burnin' down the house?" he drawled without preamble in the blunt way he had. "Or was that fire on the stove accidental-like?"

Ariah's eyes widened with alarm. "The beans! But how could they have boiled dry enough already to catch fire?"

"No water on 'em fer one thing. Fire hot enough to melt the plaster off the ceiling, fer another."

"But the fire was low, and I put the beans way at the back."

Seamus harrumphed. "Weren't when I found 'em. An' ye left that doctorin' book ye're allus a-readin' right next to the blasted pot. Good'n singed it be now."

"That can't be, I left the book on the table."

As she rushed toward home she heard him muttering behind her: "Told Bartholomew that hen crowin' this morning boded no good. He never listens. It's them hellfast witch's doin's people a-gone so bilge-brained over. 'Lectric lights an' tele-a-phones. Bah! Come to no good, wait an' see if it don't."

"Did you put it out?" she asked, thinking of the fire.

"Don't do no good to put it outside, cussed old hen," he said indignantly. "She'd jest go on crowin'. Woulda kilt her, was it up to me, but Bartholomew wouldn't hear of it."

Confused, Ariah lifted her thick brows to the sky. He was always talking about superstitions and reciting old tales of bad luck or good.

"I meant the fire, Seamus. Did you put it out?"

"O' course I did, lass," he shouted. "Ye think me a total fool?"

Ariah hid a smile. For all his idiosyncracies and orneriness, she liked the old man.

They had nearly reached home when Bartholomew came toward them with a string of fish. "Brought you some fresh perch, Ariah. The fishing was good today. My bait can was full in no time." He nodded to Seamus who was lighting a match by scratching the tip with a broken thumbnail.

"On the way back I noticed that the pheasant cocks are displaying for the females," Bartholomew continued to Ariah. "I thought you might like to go watch them."

Ariah rushed past him up the steps onto the back porch. "I can't now. I've ruined supper again. It's the third time this week. Pritchard will sulk all evening if I don't have something prepared on time, and Hester . . ."

Her voice trailed off and she cursed herself silently for bringing up the woman's name. It always angered Bartholomew to learn that his wife had been scolding Ariah. Torn between apologizing and explaining, she clamped her mouth shut and decided to do neither.

Behind her, as she ran into the house, Seamus muttered, "Tolt ye that cussed hen's crowin' meant trouble, lad. Woulda burnt the house down if'n I hadn'ta woke up early and smelled the smoke."

"The hen set fire to the house?" Bartholomew said with laughter in his voice.

"No, dagnab it! Yer woman done it, sure as I'm a-standing here."

Bartholomew surveyed the damage in silence, his mouth taut and grim. "Damn the woman! She's gone too far this time," he said, as he headed for the door. Ariah grabbed his arm, knowing instantly what he was thinking.

"Please, don't. She doesn't mean any real harm."

"You don't call this real?" he growled, pointing to the mess on the stove and the blackened wall behind. "What if Seamus hadn't woke up in time? He could have died."

Ariah blanched. "She wouldn't. No one could do such a thing. I'm sure she knew I'd be back long before that could happen. She must have been counting on it."

He shook his head at her in wonder. "She doesn't deserve your kindness, Ariah. I told you once, never turn your back on her. There's a sickness in her you don't understand. Hell, even I don't understand it. And I'm not talking about her physical health, either." He brushed a hand through his dark tousled hair and down the back of his neck. "Maybe it's my fault, I don't know. Maybe I should have tried harder to . . ." He couldn't say the words. And, deep down inside, he didn't really believe it would have made any difference, not even if he had learned to love the woman who'd tricked him into marrying her. Hester would have seen such an emotion as weakness in a man. A weakness she would have used to her advantage, to make his life even more miserable.

At the table where he'd quietly seated himself, Seamus cleared his throat. "What's ailing that woman was in 'er long afore you come along, lad. Don't be puttin' blame where it don't belong."

"I can't just let her get away with this," Bartholomew answered, gesturing to the fire damage. "All the things Hester's done to sabotage Ariah's housekeeping and make her look bad: the cayenne pepper, the sand in the bed, the spoiled meat she slipped into the stew so Ariah would be blamed for making us all sick. And Harlequin," he added softly. "I've talked to the woman till I'm blue in the face. I've threatened her." Again he shook his head. "She actually believes she's doing right, trying to ruin her own nephew's marriage. Who knows what she'll think up next? Somehow I've got to put a stop to it. Any way I can."

His face hard and implacable, Bartholomew slammed out the door. Ariah took one step after him, only to find old Seamus standing in her way. "He's a good lad, lass. Let him deal with it as he sees fit. He'll not harm the woman, though the Lord knows she deserves it."

Ariah choked back tears. "But it's my fault. If I had never come here, none of this would have happened."

"Now there ye be wrong. Only difference 'tween now an' afore ye came was in who she aimed her poison at. Used to all fall on the lad. Sneaky, dirty, little things fer no reason anybody could name, 'cepting her."

The tears spilled over then, but she wasn't thinking of herself. She was thinking of Bartholomew, and all he had suffered in his life. Surely he didn't deserve all this pain. How she wished she could make it up to him, soothe and comfort him with her love. The love she couldn't seem to feel for her own husband.

Pritchard dashed into the house shortly after four that afternoon. He found Ariah in the kitchen, attempting to create a palatable supper for him, her eyes red-rimmed from crying.

"High tide in an hour," he said, as he rushed through the kitchen toward the stairs, oblivious to the blackened kitchen and the stench of smoke and burned beans. "The fellows will be working out playing positions at the poker game tonight, so I'll be going into town."

Seamus, seated at the table, muttered a quiet "Humph."

Ariah dried her hands on her apron and followed her husband. When she reached his bedroom he was pouring water into the wash basin with his right hand, unbuttoning his shirt with the left.

"I didn't know you played poker," she said lamely. It was the third time in the past week he had gone into town. Since he couldn't get back until the next high tide early in the morning, Ariah was left alone in the house most of the night. Not having to suffer his ardent, puppy-dog stares was a welcome relief, but did little to ease her loneliness.

Pritchard barely glanced at her, too busy stripping to the waist. "I don't very often, but if I don't go tonight they might leave me off the team."

"The team?"

"You know, the Tillamook Kings." He soaped up a cloth and began to scrub his arms. "Our baseball team. Stuffy Simms chose the name. He's a fisherman and king salmon is mostly what they catch here."

Ariah wasn't sure she understood. "Aren't you hungry?"

"If I take time to eat now it will cut short the time I can spend with . . . uh, in town with the fellows. Stuffy's wife usually serves sandwiches while we play anyway."

He finished washing, dried himself and rifled through his drawer for a clean shirt. Uneasy and unable to explain to herself why, Ariah returned downstairs where Old Seamus sat hunched over a cup of thick black coffee and an ancient copy of the *Headlight-Herald*. A few minutes later Pritchard pounded back down the stairs. He snatched his coat and cap off the hook and scurried out the door with a hasty good-bye.

Seamus slapped the newspaper down on the table, rose to his feet and ambled off to his own quarters. The last thing Ariah heard before total silence fell over the house was a mumbled, "Cussed hen."

The next day when Ariah took Pritchard his lunch, he was snoozing in a chair balanced precariously on two legs, the back braced against the wall beside the window. His mouth was open, his head lolling to one side.

"Pritchard?"

The chair slammed onto all four legs and Pritchard's eyes flew open. Guilt flitted through those hazel orbs before they focused on his wife's face.

"Lunch time already?" He rubbed his eyes with his fists, drowsy still. Nettie had kept him up all night, teaching him the many positions and methods of sexual stimulation, some he had never imagined possible. Under her tutelage, he had gained a new self-confidence that extended beyond the bedroom. Until today, he had never been brave enough to catnap on duty.

Ariah set the tray on the desk and removed the cover, releasing the spicy scent of mustard and fresh baked bread.

"The poker game must have lasted all night," she said, noticing his lethargy.

"Pretty much." Pritchard stuffed his mouth with a forkful of potatoes and chewed while he talked. "But they designated me first-string striker, so it was worth it."

Ariah turned away to avoid watching the food swish about in his mouth while she tried to remember what a striker was. "Does that mean you'll be first to hit that little ball?"

"The most important thing it means is I won't be stuck on the sidelines this year." He grinned cockily. The other team members had looked at him with new respect when he'd spoken up for himself and demanded a chance to prove his worth. "I'll be hurling, too, on a stand-by basis; you know, throwing to the strikers from the other team."

"That's wonderful, Pritchard."

Through the window, she could see waves breaking against the huge formation of basalt Pritchard called Hat Rock because of its shape. With binoculars, she could see the puffins and murres nesting on its rough surface.

"I think I'll go up top and watch the birds while you eat," she said. "Join me when you're finished."

It was odd, Pritchard thought as he ate a thick ham sandwich, that the idea of spending time with his new wife no longer sent him into shivers of joy or almost uncontrollable sexual urges. She was pretty and he liked her, but he felt more at home with Nettie.

In the wee hours of the morning, he had lain in Nettie's arms while she told him how she had run away with the first man who came along, a tinker nearly twice her age, in order to escape the beatings her father inflicted on her daily. The tinker had taught her how to please a man, telling her all the while how he loved her and would take care of her. One night he brought a man home and commanded her to show the man how nice she could be in bed.

Pritchard had actually wanted to kill the tinker but Nettie had assured him the man had been out of her life for a long time. The whippings it had taken to bend her to the tinker's will left her so bruised and ugly that business fell off. One day he brought home a younger girl and kicked Nettie into the street.

Circumstances forced her to sell herself to survive until a sick old man rescued her. She nursed Old Saul to his dying day, grateful for his kindness. In return he had left her the shack where she now lived. She might be poor, but she now had a roof over her head that no one could take from her, and vegetables from her garden to eat. She didn't need Pritchard's money, she'd said. Or any other man's.

To learn that Nettie wasn't the whore gossip made her out to be had meant more to Pritchard than he bothered to analyze. He basked in her admiration because of his new position on the team, and found that he wanted nothing more than to hurry back to her adoring arms.

At Ariah's shout, he leaped from his chair, dropping the last of his sandwich. When he reached her in the glass tower, she handed him the binoculars and pointed past Hat Rock.

"It's a whale, I'm sure of it," she said in excitement. "I saw a spray of water exactly as you described. Then something dark rose to the surface."

"Yeah, I see it," he cried. "There it blows again. Now, see its back hump up? In another minute—there! See its tail thrust up above the water?"

"Oh, it's wonderful. Do they ever come closer?"

Pritchard handed her back the glasses. "Not often."

She watched awhile longer as the whale swam northward, then she turned to the stairs. "I'd better get back. Hester isn't feeling well, so I have all the chores to do."

Pritchard followed her down. "Uncle Bart's worried about her. He said Dr. Wills thinks she has something called diabetes."

"He has good reason to worry. She seems to have gotten much worse in only the last few days. I think you should spend more time with her, Pritchard. You can't be certain how long she'll be around."

Ariah's hint of approaching death sent a shudder down his spine. He hated to think about death; it was much too frightening. Pushing the thought from his mind, he switched to a more pleasant subject. "The first practice game will be next Saturday. Do you want to come and watch?"

"I think we'd best wait and see how your aunt is doing. We may be needed here."

Pritchard pouted like a child denied another cookie. "I have to be at the practice, Ariah. If I miss, they might replace me."

Stifling the angry retort that came to her lips, she went to the desk and picked up the tray she had brought. "We'll talk about it later. I'd better get these dishes done up."

He leaned against the doorjamb and watched her climb the damp wooden stairs while balancing the tray and avoiding tripping on her skirts at the same time. Her ankles, in the fitted button boots, were slim, the calves above gently curved. Nettie's legs were long and lithe, and wrapped about him in a way that drove his blood wild. Maybe it would be just as well if Ariah stayed home to take care of Aunt Hester on Saturday. That way, he would be free to visit Nettie after the game. He closed his eyes and envisioned her naked breasts cradled in his palms. His body hardened. With a smile, Pritchard turned back inside and shut the door. He thought again of Nettie's plump breasts while his fingers freed the buttons of his trousers. Another virtue Nettie had taught him was self-reliance.

Bartholomew nudged his horse to a faster gait, surprised at how eager he felt to get home. He had spent three days, going to Tillamook to take care of business and visit his brother Calvin at the old Noon dairy farm. It amazed him how much he could miss a woman. But then, Ariah wasn't just any woman.

At last he broke from the trees and cantered toward the barn. Even the old mare under him was eager for home now, and for the oats she knew would be waiting. A tendril of smoke rose from the chimney of the assistant keeper's house, filling Bartholomew with the warmth of knowing that Ariah was there, preparing the morning meal for her men. How he wished he was one of them, that he could simply stride into the house and take her in his arms.

There was no smoke rising from his own dwelling, but he'd expected no welcome there.

After seeing to his horse, he hoisted a burlap sack over one shoulder and tucked a box under the other arm, then headed for the back porch. The kitchen door was locked. An oddity, for there was no reason to lock a door here. He set down the goods he'd brought home and stepped over to the door that led into the hallway. It, too, was locked. "What the hell?"

In her kitchen, Ariah heard him shouting Hester's name and pounding on the door. She raced to the window, her heart flooding with joy. The station had been horribly lonely without him, and he looked more handsome than ever now that he was back. Wiping her hands on her apron, she hurried out the door and around the side of the house, wanting to warn him about his wife's odd behavior while he'd been gone. She came to a skidding halt as his back door gave beneath the thrust of his hard-soled boot, the wood splintering with a loud crack.

"Hester? Damn it, where are you?"

He reached through the hole he'd made, unlocked the door and vanished inside. Even from where she stood Ariah could smell the awful odor that rushed out through the fractured door. Slowly, her hand over her mouth as a frisson of dread zigzagged down her back, she retraced her steps to her own kitchen.

Bartholomew found the house eerily silent. The stench was so bad he had to cover his mouth and nose with a handkerchief. He tried to brush aside the unease that had niggled at him since dawn, but it had lodged in his throat, threatening to choke him. Remembering Dr. Wills's warning about how quickly Hester's illness could escalate didn't help. He thought of the unnatural sheen of sweat on his wife's skin before he left, the fluttering pulse at the base of her throat and her sudden lack of appetite.

"Hester? Where are you, woman?"

God, the house smelled like something had died in it. Terrified at what he might find, he raced up the stairs to Hester's room. The smell was worse there, not unlike that of the dead whale that had washed up on shore once and gone rotten. There had been a trace of this same stink even before he had gone to Tillamook. Hester had blamed it on a dead mouse in the wall.

"Hester?" He rapped on her door. "Hester, open up."

Hearing no response to his demand, he tried the door and was surprised to find it unlocked. It swung inward on noiseless hinges he himself kept well oiled. The heavy drapes over the windows blocked out the light. Trying not to breathe in the foul odor, he lit the lamp on the bedside table. Hester lay huddled beneath the covers of her narrow bed, blinking at the bright glare with sunken eyes devoid of emotion. Her gaunt face was as white as the handkerchief he held over his nose, and she was beaded with sweat, though it was cool in the room. He was afraid to speak, afraid to find out what he was facing. Afraid he already knew.

"God, Hester, what's happened? You look two steps from death's door. I'm getting Dr. Wills out here as soon as possible."

He had expected her to argue, but she said nothing. Metal drapery rings scraped along the wooden rod as he yanked open the curtains. Though the day was gray with a coming storm, she squinted at the additional light. He raised the window, letting the room fill with a brisk wind.

"Just getting that stink out of here will make you feel better," he said, drawing an extra quilt over her so she wouldn't catch a chill. "I'll empty the chamber pot and bring you up something to eat."

The chamber pot was full. Though he wanted to feel surprised at finding only urine and no feces in it, he wasn't really. For a long moment he stared into the china pot while terror clawed up his spine. Then he stood and looked down at his wife. She turned her face toward the wall.

"What is it, Hester? You smell like . . ."

Without another word, he flipped back the covers, and nearly gagged. For a long while he stood there, gaping at his wife while his throat worked to keep from vomiting, and icy fingers of dread dug at his flesh.

Death itself looked back at him.

Twenty-one

Bartholomew's frantic bellow caused Ariah to scrape her knuckles on the washboard. She dropped the dress she had been scrubbing into the tub full of boiling-hot water and lye soap, brushed the hair from her brow with the back of a wet sudsy hand and rushed out the door.

He stood between the houses, his face white as seafoam.

"Hester is deathly ill. Have Seamus relieve Pritchard and send the boy into town for the doctor. Then come up to Hester's room. I'm going to need you."

Ariah didn't question him. His fear was as tangible as the cotton apron wadded in her still-damp fists.

Five minutes later, having roused Seamus and passed on Bartholomew's instructions, Ariah let herself into the head keeper's house. She pressed a hankie dampened with lily of the valley over her nose, and hurried up the stairs. At the open doorway of Hester's room she came to an abrupt halt.

Bartholomew was bent over his wife who lay on the bed. The covers had been thrown back and her gown drawn high up her thighs, exposing two legs that looked as though they should belong to two entirely different people. The right foot was black, the leg swollen to twice its normal size. Above the black, angry red streaks ran from the ankle to the knee. The foot appeared blistered about the heel and ankle, as though badly burned. A watery discharge oozed from open sores and the smell was so foul it brought Ariah's gorge into her mouth.

"My God," she whispered.

Bartholomew swung toward her. He watched the blood drain from Ariah's face. She swallowed hard, clapped a hand over her mouth and sagged against the door. Two strides took him to her side.

"Don't swoon on me, dammit, I need you." His voice was rough, edged with desperation.

Ariah gulped in air. When the nausea passed, she straightened. "I'm all right. Let's get her into a clean gown and change the bed linens."

They worked in silence, knowing this wasn't the time for questions or for answers. When he lifted Hester into his arms so Ariah could whip off the wet sheets, the woman opened her eyes and spoke in a cracked, high-pitched voice. "Get her . . . out. Slut. You . . . you'll have him soon enough, soon enough."

Hester looked more dead than alive. Her hazel eyes glared dully from sockets sunk in a skeletal face, the skin stretched tautly over the bones like dry, wispy paper marked by a network of lines as fine as the crackled glaze on an ancient vase.

"Get . . . out," she repeated, her screech whisper-thin.

Ariah went about her work, glad they had gotten her into a clean gown before she awoke.

"She stays, Hester." Bartholomew turned so that she couldn't see Ariah. "I must have help if I'm to take care of you."

"No, no, I—"

"Save your strength, you'll need it if the doctor ends up having to remove your leg because of your stubbornness."

Hester's eyes grew round and large as sand dollars, the whites an unhealthy yellow as she stared at her husband. "My leg? Remove my leg? No, no." She thrashed about in his arms until Ariah motioned for him to place her on the bed.

"Shhh, Hester," Ariah crooned as she tucked the clean bedclothes about her. "It's all right, he doesn't really mean it."

"Oh, but I do. I mean every word, and it's her own fault. She has gangrene, the stupid fool."

Ariah heard his anger and frustration, saw it in his dark eyes and in the harshness around his mouth, and understood. Men were never good at dealing with their own helplessness when someone was in danger. She well remembered her father's rage when her mother became so deathly ill and then died. Considering all Hester had put her husband through in the seven years of their loveless marriage, one might expect him to welcome the chance to be rid of her. But Ariah was too familiar with the depth of Bartholomew's integrity to be surprised. His honor would never allow him to stand by while another human—any human—suffered.

Hester was muttering the same words over and over: "My leg, don't cut off my leg."

"A blister." Bartholomew's disgust was apparent in his voice as he paced the floor. "A lousy blister on her heel she wouldn't take care of because of a foolish notion that illness is the result of sin."

"I tried," Hester whined. "Tried . . . Wouldn't heal."

"Please, Bartholomew, you're terrifying her." Ariah stroked Hester's damp brow and spoke of whatever came into her mind: how many peas she had picked in the garden that day; how the sky looked, all marbled with purple and gray as the storm built; the kid birthed by one of Seamus's goats during the night—anything to get the woman's thoughts off her diseased leg.

When Hester calmed and seemed to sleep, Ariah went to Bartholomew where he stood staring out the window. "I don't understand," she said softly so Hester wouldn't hear. "Blisters simply heal on their own, we've all had them. How did hers get infected?"

"I don't know. Maybe it has something to do with this diabetes Dr. Wills thinks she has. All I know is, once gangrene sets in, if it isn't taken care of immediately . . ." His voice trailed off, the words too painful to say.

Hester whimpered and cried out in her sleep. "Don't wanna die. Didn't know, didn't know. Don't wanna die."

Ariah sat on the edge of the bed and took the woman's frail, fluttering hands in hers. "It's all right, everything will be all right."

"Damn Lenny Joe, his fault," Hester muttered. "He did it to me, he's the one."

Ariah glanced up at Bartholomew. "She's not making sense anymore, I think she's delirious."

He slumped down in a chair and said nothing.

"Damn 'im, damn 'im." Hester's head tossed back and forth on sweat-soaked pillows. "Don't want baby, curse it to hell, curse it to hell, and Lenny, too."

Ariah covered her mouth with her hand as she looked at the woman, then at the man in the chair. "Gracious Sadie," she whispered, "she had a baby?"

"No, Papa, no. I'll get rid of it, I'll get rid of it. Damn Lenny Joe, damn him to hell."

Wearily Bartholomew rose to his feet and motioned for Ariah to follow him into the hall. He shut the door behind them, but Ariah could still hear Hester ranting, sobbing, cursing. Her heart went out to the woman. "Oh, God, poor Hester, no wonder she's so bitter. Did you know, Bartholomew? Did you know about the baby?"

He hugged her to him, loving her for her concern. Ariah glanced up. Seeing the guilt on his face, she guessed what he wasn't saying. "This was the threat you held over her. You were going to expose her secret, weren't you?"

"Yes," he said miserably, "but you know how little good it did."

She stepped away, her eyes wide with shock. "How could you? Think what that poor woman has suffered. She was probably young when it happened, and innocent."

"Sixteen," he said with a sigh. "Her family disowned her for it. She was going from family to family, working for her keep when Ma sent for her to come and help us out. She was twenty-five then." He rubbed the back of his head as though it pained him. His face was a mask of anxiety. "But that's all in the past now. I only wish I knew what to do for her until Dr. Wills gets here. She hasn't a moment to waste. If something isn't done about that leg soon, she'll die."

"Are you sure it's that bad?"

He took her back into the bedroom and forced her to look at the swollen, discolored leg. "See those red streaks? That's the final stage of gangrene. For all I know, it may already be too late to save her."

At his raised voice, Hester stirred. Her body writhed as though she fought with imaginary foes, and she muttered incoherently. Ariah felt the woman's panic crawl down her own spine, slither into her and curdle her warm, vital blood.

Footsteps pounded up the stairs and Pritchard burst into the room, holding his nose. "Aunt Hester?" He stopped halfway into the room, his gaze going to his aunt's hideously swollen and discolored leg. "Holy Hector! What happened?"

"What in the hell are you doing up here?" Bartholomew growled between clenched teeth. "Didn't Seamus tell you to go for the doctor as though your life depended on it?"

"Yes, but—"

"There isn't a second to waste, damn you. It's gangrene. If you don't get the doctor here immediately, she's going to die."

"Oh, God. But the tide's going out, how—"

Taking the boy's coat lapels in both fists, Bartholomew hauled him to the door, letting anger block out the fear and guilt he found it more difficult to deal with. "Drag the damned boat over the mud if you have to. Crawl, *but get Dr. Wills.* If you aren't back in a few hours, I'll have to take the leg off myself."

Pritchard gulped as he stared into eyes like black ice. "Take the leg off?" Managing a nod, he glanced once more at his aunt's flailing body, then tore down the stairs.

After that began a period of waiting which threatened to drive Bartholomew insane, until Ariah, remembering Dr. Chase's book, raced to her house, returning with the tome in hand. In a low, calm voice, she read aloud the description of gangrene and its symptoms. When she came to the section on treatment, she exclaimed, "Oh, Bartholomew, this says that in order for the treatment to be at all effective, it must be given *before* the blisters appear."

He nodded as if unsurprised. "What's the treatment?"

"It says to raise the temperature of the skin, first by a succession of warm poultices and bottles of hot water, then with stimulants, wine, quinine and opium, to rouse the circulation. There's a recipe for a poultice."

Bartholomew expelled his breath and shook his head. "It's too late to worry about improving her circulation."

"But anything is worth a try, isn't it? It would certainly be better than pacing the floor and twiddling our thumbs while we wait."

"All right, I guess we could try the poultice. What do you need for it?"

"Camphor water, aromatic confection, carbonate of ammonia, laudanum, aromatic tincture, tincture of bark, and spirits of sulfuric ether."

"Aromatic confection? What in thunder is that?"

"I believe a confection is merely something sweet, but I would suppose that here they would mean a particular sort of sweet medicine."

"I'll bring sugar and honey," he said, heading for the door. "It's all we have, we'll have to hope it's close enough. The rest should be in Hester's medical supplies."

While he was gone, Ariah sat beside Hester and soothed the older woman when she became agitated.

Outside, rain pelted the earth, driven by fierce winds that whistled about the houses and through the forest, reminding Ariah of her wedding day. How ironic if Hester should die now. Now that Ariah was married to someone else. The Fates were not above playing nasty little games, it seemed. She wondered what more they had in mind.

In the barn, Pritchard leaped bareback on the first horse he came to, panic riding him as surely as he rode the startled horse. With both of the boy's booted heels jabbing him in the ribs, the buckskin bolted out the open barn and up the road. When the steep wet trail began its descent into Barnagat, the horse slid most of the way down.

At the dock, Pritchard leaped into a rowboat and took up the oars. The small skiff bobbed and pitched on the waves, seeming to go nowhere. Before he could reach the deeper water of the river channel the bay became so shallow that the oars whapped into the muddy bottom on each downward swing. Frustration drove him hard. No matter how he hurried he would never make it back before the tide receded, leaving the bay empty of everything but mud. He cursed, knowing the trip home was going to be long, difficult and—for his aunt—deadly.

By one in the afternoon, three hours after Pritchard's departure to fetch the doctor, it became obvious that Dr. Chase's suggested treatment was having no effect. Bartholomew went downstairs, leaving Ariah to change the poultices and to force hot tea, laced with laudanum and quinine, down Hester's throat.

Ariah supposed he was going for coffee and hoped he'd bring a cup back for her. Thanks to the opium, Hester had quieted. Ariah rose from the chair she'd placed at the side of the bed and went to the window, where she parted the drapes to gaze out into the gloom of the gathering storm.

A single gull hovered and swayed with the violent wind, a slash of white against the purple-gray sky as it struggled to reach the shelter of the bluff. The wail of the wind under the eaves was like the crying of restless spirits for release from their eternal struggles. Or for Hester to come and join them. Ariah shuddered at her morbid imaginings, and the house trembled as gusts battered its ungiving bulk, as if to remind the impotent mortals inside of the power of God's wrath.

"I'm going to carry Hester downstairs."

Ariah whirled, startled by Bartholomew's voice. She had been so lost in her thoughts that she'd failed to hear him come up the stairs and into the room.

"Downstairs. Why?"

He went to the bed, flung back the covers from his wife's frail body and lifted her in his arms.

"Even if Dr. Wills gets here in the next hour, he'll have no recourse but to remove the leg," he said, as he started for the stairs. "To do that, he'll need her on a firm surface with plenty of warmth and light. The kitchen will work much better than here. We might as well have her ready."

As Ariah followed him into the kitchen she noticed the neat arrangement of supplies on the counter near the table: rags, disinfectant, bandages, leather straps, three knives—the edges gleaming from being honed to a razor sharpness—and a hand-saw. Steam rose from a large kettle of boiling water on the stove. More filled the reservoir at the side of the stove. Bartholomew laid Hester on the table and tucked a blanket around her.

"Is all this necessary?" Ariah motioned to the grim instru-ments on the counter. "Won't Dr. Wills have his own imple-ments?"

"Yes . . . But if he doesn't arrive soon, I intend to do the job myself. Those red streaks are almost to her groin. If they go any higher, it'll be too late."

"Oh, Bartholomew, how can you? Such a drastic—"

"Would you rather I simply let her die?" he snarled.

"No! No, of course not."

She covered her mouth with her hands. Could he actually believe she would want Hester dead? It was true that with her marriage to Pritchard unconsummated, a quick annulment could easily be obtained. Then, with Hester out of the way, she and Bartholomew could be together. But she would never want that at the cost of someone's life. Not even Hester's.

"What's happening?" a weak voice said from the table.

They turned to see Hester looking at them through eyes glazed with pain and the fading effects of the opiate. Ariah's gaze flicked to Bartholomew, as she waited to take her cue from him. The look he gave her was one of fear, guilt and pain.

"The doctor isn't here yet, Hester, but we can't wait any longer. It may be too late already."

Hester blinked. "Too late for what?"

He took her hand. It was icy cold. He rubbed it between his, wishing there was any alternative to the course he knew he must take. "We can't save your leg, Hester. The only thing to do now is to remove it. If we don't, you'll die."

Hester's brow furrowed, her eyes filled with confusion. "Remove my leg? No, no, let me die. Don't—"

"I can't do that, Hester. I can't sit here and watch you suffer until the poison has invaded your entire body and finally ends your misery."

"Don't deserve to live. Sin . . . God punishing me . . . for sin." Hester's face was flushed with fever. She struggled to rise and fell back, defeated by a weakness she could not fight.

Bartholomew had never seen his wife cry before. She was a hard, intractable woman, but no less so with herself than with others, though he doubted anyone else realized that, since only he knew all the secrets of a past which tormented her. To see her this way transformed her from a scheming, unfeeling bitch to a pathetic human being, twisted by life's unforgiving cruelty. How much of that cruelty had he dealt her? And how would he ever forgive himself for it . . . if she died?

Ariah sponged Hester's face to bring down the fever and soothe her. Hester's fingers clutched fitfully at the blanket, and her head tossed back and forth. For a moment Bartholomew watched, seeking deep into his soul for the courage to face what must be done. Then he dropped the knives and the handsaw into boiling water.

"Fetch Seamus." One by one he lit the lamps he'd placed about the room. "We may need him to help hold her down while we put the straps on her."

When Ariah turned to go, he waylaid her with a hand on her arm. For a long moment he stared at her. His face gentled then, and he almost smiled. "It's windy. Be careful and keep hold of the cable."

Ariah saw in his tormented eyes the words he had not said: *Don't make me have to deal with losing you, too.* Through the hand that so tenderly embraced her cheek, she felt the trembling of his body.

"Bartholomew, are you sure you're doing the right thing?"

"I've never been more sure of anything."

But the trembling of his body said differently. He was terrified. Terrified at having to attempt the awful surgery that might save Hester's life, terrified not to attempt it. Her heart ached for him, yet there was no way she could help him, except to give her support in every way she could. At the door, she paused. "Bartholomew, what happened to the baby? Hester's baby?"

"That's where the real sin comes in, I'm afraid," he said softly. "She gave birth in the woods, then she took it to the town dump and left it there. It was a girl."

Ariah gasped. "But . . . didn't someone find it, didn't they look for it? They would have known she'd had it."

"Life is hard in that part of Georgia, too hard," was all he said.

Afraid to ask any more questions, she let herself out, closing the door softly behind her.

When everything was ready, they strapped Hester to the table with the leather bands, one across her shoulders, another across her hips. She struggled feebly, mumbling about sin and love and Lenny Joe. Bartholomew forced Hester's mouth open, dribbled in brandy laced with laudanum, then massaged her throat to make her swallow. It would numb the pain, if nothing more. Ariah bathed the rotten leg with boiling hot cloths dosed with carbolic acid to kill germs and infection.

Bartholomew laid the sterilized instruments, rags and bandages on a small side table for easy access. Suddenly, Hester froze. Her eyes went wide as she stared at the handsaw, the hazel orbs surprisingly lucid. Then she opened her mouth and screeched at the top of her lungs. Foam dribbled from her mouth and down the sides of her face.

"No, no, no." The room reverberated with her cries.

Bartholomew glanced at the clock. Even considering the weather, Pritchard should have been back by now. Rain spattered the glass panes, while wind whistled through minuscule cracks between the sills and window frames. Outside, the afternoon had grown dark as night. The storm was by now a full gale. He flexed the hands he had bathed in alcohol and hot water. At his side, Ariah waited quietly while Seamus finished fastening the leather tourniquet.

Bartholomew closed his eyes and his lips moved in silent prayer. His Adam's apple bobbed once, then he opened his eyes, glanced briefly at Ariah and at Seamus, who was standing near Hester's good leg, prepared to use his old man's strength to hold it still. Everything was ready. He picked up the knife.

Hester was sweating profusely. A muscle in her jaw flexed nervously like a tic. She gabbled something incoherent, staring at the corner of the ceiling as though seeing monsters there. Then her eyes rolled back in her head. A thin, birdlike whistle was emitted from her throat. Her mouth yawned open, then snapped shut on her tongue. Bloody, foaming saliva dribbled onto her chin, and her limbs began to jerk violently.

Ariah's hand flew to her mouth as she stared in horror. "Oh my Lord . . . what . . . ?"

"She's havin' a fit." Seamus moved quickly to the head of the table and tore at the strap binding Hester's shoulders. "Gotta turn 'er over or she'll choke on 'er own spit."

Bartholomew dropped the knife and reached for the strap around her waist, his heart thundering in his ears. "Damn," he muttered softly. "Ah, Hester . . . damn, damn, damn."

"Turn her head to the side." Even as Ariah cried out the words, she was taking care of it herself.

Hester's face was yellow. Her body arched against the loosening straps as her limbs continued to jerk. Suddenly she went still. For an instant, her eyes appeared normal, then the lids slowly closed. The stench of feces and urine tainted the air. The three people frantically working over her froze.

"Hester?" Bartholomew jiggled her shoulder. There was no response. He felt for a pulse in her neck.

"She gone?" Seamus asked.

"No." Relief was evident in his voice. "She's breathing."

"Plumb passed out then, thank the Lord."

Silence fell over the room. Even the storm seemed to abate

as they stood there staring down at the woman on the table. It was Ariah who first heard the pounding hooves, then the slamming of the gate. Before she could open the door that gave access to the back porch, Pritchard burst through the other door into the hall. He started up the stairs, the doctor close behind.

"In here, Pritchard," Bartholomew called.

The footsteps reversed themselves and the two men appeared, dripping wet, in the doorway. Pritchard's glance went to the still figure on the table, and he paled.

"Are we . . . are we too late?" His chest heaved from his difficult labors of the past few hours. His legs shook.

Dr. Wills shoved his way to the table and examined Hester's leg. "Good Lord. How did she let it get so bad?"

There was no answer, and no one tried to offer one. Wills turned to Bartholomew. "Why didn't you bring her to see me?"

Bartholomew bleakly shook his head. "She wouldn't listen. I didn't know about her leg until this morning. I . . ." Pain and guilt darkened his expression. He looked ready to collapse.

"It's all right, son, you did what you could." Dr. Wills lightly squeezed Bartholomew's shoulder.

But Bartholomew went on, as though he needed to get it all out. "She never said a word about her leg. Not one goddamned word." He dragged in a deep breath and turned away to hide the moisture gathering in his eyes.

"Is there anything you can do, Doctor?" Ariah asked.

Wills checked Hester's vital signs, and removed the tourniquet. "She's in a coma. I doubt she'll ever come out of it. Did she go into convulsions before she went into the coma?"

He looked from Ariah to Bartholomew, who was staring out the window. In the background, Pritchard sobbed quietly.

"Had a fit, if'n that's what ye mean," Seamus offered.

"That's what I mean, all right." Wills straightened and heaved a weary sigh. "It's the diabetes. According to the letter I received from my medical friend back East, in answer to my inquiry, this was to be expected. My guess is, she was too far gone before you ever even came to see me, Bartholomew. The vital organs go first, the patient slips into a coma, then dies. The coma is a blessing, actually. Doubly so, coming when it did. She'll go peacefully in her sleep now, no more suffering."

Bartholomew turned from the window. He had aged five years in the few days since Wills had last seen him. Guilt was etched as clearly on his face as the grain in a slab of water-polished driftwood. Wills pursed his lips.

"I see you were prepared to take off the leg," Wills said, glancing over the instruments laid out on the side table. "Have to commend you, Bartholomew. Not many men could even contemplate carrying out what you had already made up your mind to."

The doctor covered the angry, swollen leg with a blanket. "But it would have been a waste of time. Plain fact is, the woman sealed her own fate, hiding her condition the way she did. That gangrenous wound wasn't any new injury. If you'd gotten her to let me examine her the Sunday you came to see me, I might have saved her life by amputating the leg then, exactly as you were going to do today. Even so, it would have been only a stopgap measure. The diabetes would have gotten her anyway, in time."

"But she was fine only a few days ago," Pritchard objected, then added, "I mean, she was sick, but . . ."

"Once infection sets in, it moves frightfully fast," Wills explained. "In this case, I'd say she did amazingly well to last this long. The infection must have set in five or six days ago. I've seen patients die of gangrene poisoning in three days."

"How long will she live?" Bartholomew asked.

"Minutes, hours, a day at the most."

For an instant, before his gaze dropped away, Ariah's eyes met Bartholomew's across the room. His look was filled with a guilt she knew would not be so great, if not for her. A flash of insight told her not to expect him to forgive himself—or her—any time soon. The reality was like a blade thrust into her heart.

Twenty-two

White-faced Herefords scattered as the dark green surrey rolled toward them at a good clip behind a matched pair of sorrels. A killdeer flew up from under the cows' trampling hooves, faking a broken wing to lure her adversaries from her nest. The bird's plaintive cries did little to raise the spirits of the wagons occupants.

From her seat between Bartholomew and his widowed brother Calvin, Ariah inhaled the sweet fragrance of the lush grass, ignoring the more pungent odor of manure. Intermingled with the other scents were the ever-present tang of the sea and the earthy essence of an approaching storm. Overhead, the sky was a seamless curtain of gray, unmarred even by the flight of birds, for they had already sought out shelter.

A few drops of rain pelted the roof of the surrey as Calvin turned the buggy onto a narrow dirt track. In the distance, a red-roofed barn came into view over the crest of a low hill. A dog ran out to greet the wagon with sharp-bitten barks. Calvin slowed as they rounded the white barn. Beyond stood a two-story house painted white, its red trim matching the outbuildings. On the porch waited a portly woman garbed in black.

A crow, Ariah thought. But the minute Cal's housekeeper raced down the steps, she became a chickadee, chattering away in a cheerful, melodic voice as she fussed over each passenger alighting from the surrey.

"Bartholomew! Oh, Bartholomew, you poor dear man. Such an awful thing, losing a wife so young and so tragically. Do forgive me for not being at the funeral, but I didn't dare leave my stove for that long."

"Thank you, Goody," he said, using Cal's nickname for the woman. He bent down and kissed her soft, peach-blossom cheek. "Don't think a thing about missing the funeral. It was kind of you to go to all this trouble fixing us a meal. Knowing you, I'm sure it's a feast."

"Now how could I have done anything else but provide you a meal on a day like this? Funeral or no funeral, you must eat and keep up your strength. I even baked you your favorite— apple pie. And I expect you to do it justice, too. No excuses about lack of appetite. The soul needs food every bit as much as the body, you know."

"If that's the case," Cal said, winking at Bartholomew, "you must have one of the healthiest souls around, Goody."

Mrs. Goodman smacked his hand away as he gently pinched her plump arm. "Enough of that, young man."

Cal laughed. "Young man! Hell, Goody, you talk like you're old enough to be my mother, instead of only five years my senior."

"Sometimes I feel like your mother," she said, blushing. "Lord knows, you need one."

As if she'd not noticed Ariah's presence before, Mrs. Goodman exclaimed, "The bride! Oh, our little bride is here. Hello, hello. I'm Amy Goodman, but you just call me Amy."

Ariah found herself enveloped in motherly warmth redolent of flour, lard and vanilla. Sensations she had not enjoyed since she was thirteen rushed over her, and she found herself blinking back sudden tears. Embarrassment reddened her cheeks, but Amy Goodman was too busy hurrying her charges up the steps and into the house to notice. Ariah dawdled in the parlor to surreptitiously wipe her eyes with the backs of her hands. She sniffled under the guise of smelling a purple-blossomed African violet on a lamp table.

From the kitchen came the sounds of chairs scraping on a wood floor as Mrs. Goodman seated the men and Cal's two teenage sons at the table. The murmur of deep, masculine voices formed soothing background music, punctuated by the house-keeper's soprano chirping and the clatter of utensils as she dished up the meal.

Alone and seemingly forgotten in the front parlor, Ariah was overcome by a feeling of emptiness. In the other room a family was sitting down to an early supper, a family that did not include her. Not truly. For a moment she deeply regretted having let Pritchard go off to see his friends without her. She felt as though she belonged nowhere, not here at Bartholomew's family home, not with her own husband and his baseball buddies, not even at the lighthouse station which was now—for better or worse—her home.

Once more she wondered if she would be better off to search somewhere else for her place in life. Even in Greece. How could she be certain she would not love it there? But it took only the memory of her father, bleeding against the white sheets of his bed, to convince her that she could never be happy among a people who saw their women as bargaining chips for bettering the family's position or wealth. A people who cared little for the love in a young woman's heart.

And if Uncle Xenos found her, nothing would ever matter again, because she would no longer be alive.

If Bartholomew knew everything—her real danger at Uncle Xenos's hands and how easily she could get an annulment—would he whisk her away, marry her and guard her with his life? Not as long as he was bent on punishing himself for not saving Hester. And for loving a woman not his wife.

Since yesterday, when Dr. Wills pronounced that Hester would not live through the night, Bartholomew had spoken only when necessary, and to Ariah not at all. Alone, he sat by Hester's bed, holding her thin, worn hand until at last she had been freed of her mortal body, and her mortal pain. This morning, before the stench of her rotting body could worsen, Hester was buried in a casket Bartholomew insisted on building himself. On the lid, below her name, he had carved To Err Is Human, To Forgive

Divine. Yet he would not forgive himself. Nor, Ariah feared, would he forgive her.

"Ariah?"

At the sound of the deep voice, coming so close on the heels of her thoughts, her heart somersaulted. She whirled to face him. But the man standing before her was not Bartholomew.

"Are you all right?" he asked.

"Yes, Cal, thank you. I was merely admiring these lovely African violets."

"Goody grows them. You be sure and tell her you like them; she'll be thrilled. Since her husband passed away a couple of years ago, raising them flowers and fussing over my family has sort of become her life. Now, how about coming in for a bite to eat? We were wondering what happened to you."

Disappointment that it had not been Bartholomew who had missed her enough to come looking for her weighted Ariah's feet as she followed Calvin into the kitchen. She was directed to a chair between Mrs. Goodman and Cal, who sat at the head of the table. Bartholomew sat at the foot, the boys ranged on either side of him. His gaze, when she glanced at him, centered on his empty plate, making her fancy that he wished to avoid looking at her.

Amy Goodman passed her a bowl of steaming mashed potatoes. "Here, dear, fill up your plate, you're too thin by far. In fact, you look a bit peaked. Not breeding already, I hope? A newly married couple needs time to get used to each other before taking on the responsibility of children."

That brought Bartholomew's head up. Heat flooded Ariah's face.

"Where is that young devil you're married to, anyway?" Mrs. Goodman asked, oblivious to the girl's discomfort. "He should be here with Bartholomew and you on a day like this."

"He had something he needed to discuss with his friend, Stuffy, before we have to catch the tide for home."

"Stuffy Simms? Why, I saw his wife at the druggist's yesterday and thought sure she said they were going over to visit his folks in Bay City today." Mrs. Goodman shrugged. "Reckon they must have changed their minds."

Ariah murmured an answer, but her mind and her gaze were on Bartholomew who was scowling like an eagle whose supper had just slipped through his talons.

Pritchard rolled across the rumpled bed, taking Nettie with him. Coming to rest on his back, he lifted her with his hands under her arms until her breasts dangled above him like ripe peaches on a tree. His tongue snaked out to lave first one rosy peak, then the other. Nettie moaned and wriggled against him where she straddled his hips.

"God, I've missed you," he whispered.

"Have ya truly?"

"You know it." He scooted her back until the tip of his erection nosed the moist warmth between her legs. His voice grew more husky. "Doesn't this feel like I missed you?"

Nettie giggled. "It sure do, Asa."

"Now, Nettie, you shouldn't call me that. I wish I was as good a hurler as old Asa Brainard, but I'm not, and you know it."

"But you pitched a flawless game last practice."

"That doesn't make me an Asa, honey."

Grinning, she lowered herself until her breasts brushed teasingly against his chest. "Well, you're an Asa to me. You got perfect aim, you never strike out"—in one smooth movement she impaled herself on his waiting shaft—"and your bat is the biggest and the best in any league."

Pritchard didn't bother arguing with her. He was too hot, too ready to show her how well he had learned his lessons at her private school of loving. His hands dug into her hips as she carried him to new heights, her body moving on his as fast as the fleetest pitch Asa Brainard ever hurled. When it was over and they lay curled together, too sated to move, Nettie ran her fingers over his nearly hairless chest. Tipping her head back where it rested on his shoulder, she kissed his jaw.

"Lord, Pritchard, I wish you didn't have to leave."

"So do I, honey."

After a moment of silence, she said, "You sleepin' with her yet?"

He didn't have to ask who "her" was.

"I haven't touched her since I met you, Nettie. I haven't even wanted to."

"That's good." She nipped at his chin. " 'Cause I'd slug yer lights out, if'n you did."

Her voice went from threatening to weepy. "I ain't never cared 'bout no man the way I care 'bout you, Prit. I couldn't bear knowing you was going home to sleep with another woman."

He drew her tighter against him, his eyes shut, jaw clamped tight. "Ah, Nettie, it's you I love. Not her."

His words surprised him almost as much as they did Nettie.

Flushed with pleasure and excitement, she lifted herself onto her elbows, her upper body half-draped over his as she stared him in the eye. "Do you really love me, Prit?"

"Yeah, I really do." He smiled, realizing it was true.

"Then you gotta ask her to let you go. I didn't want to say nothin' till I knew how you felt about me, but . . . well, I think maybe you're gonna be a daddy, Prit. It's too soon to be sure, but I was pregnant oncet afore. I lost that 'un, but I feel the same now as I did then. Are you glad? Oh, please say you're glad. I couldn't bear it if'n you decided you didn't want us."

"God, Nettie, I . . . I didn't expect anything like this. I thought you'd know . . ." His voice trailed away as her face squeezed up as though she were getting ready to rain tears all over him. "Aw, it doesn't matter. Of course I'm glad, honey. I told you I wanted my own baseball team, didn't I?"

"Yeah, but that doesn't mean you want me to be their ma."

"Who else would I want to have my kids if not the woman I love most in the world?" He kissed her and wiped away the moisture beading at the corners of her eyes.

Good Lord, what do I do now?

Would Ariah let him go if she knew? She was a good woman.

He'd come to know her well enough these past weeks to believe that. She didn't act as though she was so enamored of him that she would try very hard to hang onto him. Still, she was his wife and he had been unfaithful to her. How would he ever find the courage to tell her?

For the first time since he realized Aunt Hester was going to die, he was glad she wasn't here. She would have boxed his ears good for what he'd done. Aunt Hester had been the most pious woman he had ever known. She'd been harsh at times, but there wasn't a woman around more godfearing than her. He thanked God he wouldn't have to face her when it came out that he'd fathered a bastard.

"Nettie, I have to ask you something."

"Go ahead, Prit, honey."

She had settled herself back down beside him, her hand rubbing lazy circles around his navel. Even though his mind was on other matters, his body was already reacting to her ministrations. Her hand drifted lower, barely brushing his sex. Desire bolted through him. Determined to get at least one problem straight between them before he allowed himself to succumb again to her allure, he clapped a hand over hers and said, "I have to know if you've been with any other men since the last time we were together."

"Aw, Prit, you know I promised I wouldn't. You been real good to me. I ain't needed no money or nothing. Besides, I don't want no other man touching me now I got you." She lifted her head and kissed him. "I love you, Prit. Don't you believe me?"

He kissed her back, lost in her special taste. A taste he craved more and more every day, almost as much as he craved her body.

"Yeah, I believe you."

He nudged her hand lower and groaned when she wrapped her fingers around his hot, turgid length. Tonight, when he went home, he would find a way to tell Ariah he wanted to be free. He would get an annulment, marry Nettie and move her to the lighthouse station. Then he could have her in his bed every night, all night, and know she was his alone.

Ariah had barely climbed into bed that night when there was a knock on her door.

"Can I come in, Ariah? Please?" Pritchard called.

She squeezed her eyes shut as fear and pain fractured her fragile peace of mind. Was this the moment she had dreaded ever since the morning after her wedding? Had Pritchard tired of waiting to make her his true wife? She wanted to bar the door, to bury her head beneath her pillow and pretend she hadn't heard him. She wanted to tell him to leave her alone. But it would be unfair not to face him honestly, and, in truth, she had done enough running from her problems lately. "Come in."

The door opened and her husband stepped inside, wearing a long white nightshirt that made him look like a little boy, lost and embarrassingly afraid of the dark. He halted just inside while Ariah fumbled to light the lamp.

As the wick caught, banishing the restless shadows to the far corners, Pritchard glanced about. The room was an echo of Ariah. Dainty. Feminine. Tidier than Nettie's place.

"You've fixed it up nice in here," he said. "Homey."

Ariah's gaze followed him to the dresser where he picked up the photograph of her parents. She sensed his reluctance to broach the matter he'd wanted to see her about, and hoped if she offered no encouragement, he would give up and return to his bed. Alone.

"Are you happy here?" he asked.

Here in Oregon? Or here in this bedroom? she considered asking. Yet she knew exactly what he meant. She hesitated, torn between honesty and prevarication. If she said she was happy, he might use that in his argument to get her to make a final commitment to their marriage. If she said no, would he suggest an annulment?

"I love the ocean, and the forest," she said evasively. "I've never seen a more beautiful country, and the people are kind—Calvin and his boys, Dr. Wills, Reverend Ketcham and his wife." She purposely left out Bartholomew, fearing he would detect the yearning in her voice. "Mrs. Goodman went out of her way to make me feel welcome today. Did you see the African violet she gave me? I put it in the living-room window. The light should be perfect for it there."

Her prattling stumbled to a halt. Pritchard hadn't once looked at her since entering the room. He had buried his aunt today, his only blood kin in the entire West. Was it possible he was feeling lonely and a bit melancholy? While she thought only of herself. Hating her lack of sensitivity, she rose and padded across the icy floor to him.

"Pritchard, I'm sorry about Hester. I know you must have loved her and—"

"Not really."

He turned then and gave her a smile that was shy and chagrined at the same time. "I used coming to stay with Aunt Hester as an excuse to get away from Missouri." He leaned against the dresser, running his slender fingers over the soft bristles of her baby brush as he talked.

"See, every time Aunt Hester's name came up when I was a boy, I was sent from the room and everybody would start talking in whispers. I wanted to know what the big, awful secret was about her, so when a letter came from Oregon addressed to Ma, and Ma threw it away without opening it, I stole it out of the trash and snuck it up to my room.

"Aunt Hester had written to let the family know she was married to Bartholomew. I think now that she was hoping her marrying so well would win her their forgiveness for whatever it was she'd done to rile them so. She wrote a lot in that letter about Oregon and how beautiful it was here. In Missouri there were a lot of trees, but she made the trees here sound the biggest, thickest, tallest." Pritchard put down the tiny brush and waved his arms expressively, moving away from the dresser.

"The creeks were clearer, the mountains higher, the sky bluer.

There were more deer, more bears, more of every critter imaginable. It sounded like the most wonderful, exciting place in the world."

He sat down on the foot of Ariah's bed. Caught up in his tale, Ariah sat down, too. She leaned back against the headboard and tucked her bare feet under the covers while Pritchard went on talking.

"And Uncle Bart, she was always writing about the things he did. He was so strong. All the farm work, I suppose, and having to lift his mother and father in and out of bed all the time. Aunt Hester thought him the kindest, most giving man she'd ever known." He shrugged. "At least, that was how she wanted the family to see him. She sure convinced me. Did you know that when he was younger, before his mother got bad, he spent an entire summer timbering with his brother-in-law over in Bend?"

Ariah shook her head and leaned forward, eager to hear the story. Pritchard scooted across the bed until he was seated next to her. The air was chilly, and she automatically pulled the covers over their legs.

"The lumbermen held contests to see who could cut down trees the fastest, scale a standing tree the quickest, throw a hatchet the farthest, things like that." Pritchard grinned. "Uncle Bart was only fourteen, but he put those full-grown men to shame. There they were, experienced lumbermen, and he tied their best man in half the events."

"Oh, Pritchard." Ariah laughed. "Are you sure Hester hadn't exaggerated a bit?"

"Maybe, but to me he sounded better than Paul Bunyan. I think I came mostly to meet Uncle Bart, hoping somehow I could get to be a little like him."

The wistfulness in his voice touched her. Without thinking she placed a hand on his arm. "You have your own good points, Pritchard. You don't need to be like Bartholomew."

"You mean that?" He took her hand in his while he gazed intently into her eyes, the yearning in them plain to see.

"Of course I mean it, Why, you're . . ." Desperately she

searched for an honest compliment she could give him. "You've
been very kind to me, and understanding. You're strong, too,
and, well, I'll bet you play stickball better than him."

"Baseball," he said sadly.

Seeing Pritchard's vulnerability heightened the guilt she felt
for having denied him a true wife. He had married her in good
faith and . . .

The awful realization came to her that she had, in her own
perhaps gentler and more innocent way, done to Pritchard what
Hester had done to Bartholomew. She had denied her husband
her bed only one day after their marriage.

Shame shafted through her like lightning through clouds.

Pritchard squeezed her hand, reclaiming her attention. "What
is it? Is something wrong?"

Very wrong. So very, very wrong. How could she have done
this to him? His only real failing was that he was *not* Bartholomew. She had never given him a chance to show her who he
was, or could be. Staring at him, face to face, she found herself
overwhelmed by guilt and sorrow and dread.

"Oh, Pritchard, I . . ."

They were sitting so close, their shoulders almost touching,
and she was looking up at him, her beautiful face full of concern
and what he thought might be desire. Pritchard's body suddenly
tautened, and grew hard. Her fragrance, sweet and clean, filled
his nostrils. Shadows that were her nipples showed through the
thin fabric of her gown. Nipples he had never gotten to see, to
touch, to taste. His *wife's* nipples.

The fear and inexperience that had unmanned him on their
wedding night was gone now. He knew how to put his lips to
hers, how to move them with exactly the right amount of moisture and friction to heighten the sensation. He knew how to
nudge her lips apart with his tongue, how to dip inside and
mimic the action his body wanted to enact inside hers. Desperately wanted to enact. With Ariah. With his wife.

Lowering his head, Pritchard took Ariah's mouth. Stunned,
both by his action and his gentleness, she made no move to

rebuff him. He deepened the kiss, the tip of his tongue running lightly around her mouth, then tracing the indentation between her lips. The way Bartholomew had so often done before. Ariah's eyes drifted shut, letting her sink into the lovely memories buried but not forgotten within her heart. Desire burst inside her. A tongue slipped into her mouth; the same moment a hand found her breast, and he moaned.

The flavor was wrong. The pitch of the masculine moan was wrong. The touch on her breast was wrong. Ariah's eyes flew open, and she jerked back her head. For a long second they stared at each other, panting as their bodies clamored for more. Then Pritchard leaped from the bed and ran to the door.

Pausing with his back to her, he said, "I-I don't know what got into me, Ariah. Please . . . I didn't mean to break our bargain. Forgive me."

He vanished into the hall, leaving the door ajar behind him. Alone in the bed, Ariah listened to the click of his own door shutting, then silence. Her heart was still pounding. She knew she should go to him, tell him there was no need to feel guilty for what happened. She should climb right into his bed and show him that she meant to keep the vows exchanged on their wedding day. But she couldn't.

Collapsing onto the pillows, she buried her face beneath her arm and cursed her stubborn love for Bartholomew. If only Pritchard would decide he did not want her. If only he would ask for an annulment. Lord knew, she hadn't the heart to ask him for one, though she knew it would be more honest.

In his room, Pritchard leaned his forehead against the cool glass of the window and stared out into the black night, wishing Nettie were there to ease the ache in his groin.

What had happened in Ariah's room? He had gone in there determined to ask for an annulment so he could marry Nettie and keep his son from becoming a bastard. Had he lost his mind?

It was Nettie he wanted, wasn't it?

Nettie with her sweet, giving body and her childlike worship of him. Nettie, the first woman who had ever made him feel truly wanted, truly a man. Of course it was her he wanted.

But Ariah was his wife. Ariah was educated, cultured, a real catch for a man from the backwoods of Missouri, a man who could do barely more than read and cipher. A man who . . .

He hadn't been completely honest with Ariah tonight. The main reason he had fled Missouri was because he was a coward. No other man back there would have turned his back on a simple challenge that required nothing more of him than to fight with his fists. In his hometown brawling was a way of life for men. But the thought of being struck, of suffering a broken nose or losing his teeth—of being hurt—terrified Pritchard. It made no sense, he knew that; he could suffer the same injuries playing baseball, but that seemed different somehow.

The reason his cowardliness hadn't been found out yet here was because of the lack of communication between Aunt Hester and the rest of his family back home. What he had told Ariah about coming here in the hope of learning from Uncle Bart how to be a man was true.

It simply hadn't happened.

But Nettie loved him anyway. Since meeting her, Pritchard had convinced himself he felt no desire for Ariah. She made him feel clumsy, stupid, inadequate. With Nettie, he felt at home. But he knew how to enjoy a woman's body now. And tonight, he'd nearly had a chance to enjoy Ariah's. He wouldn't have humiliated himself the way he had on their wedding night.

Nettie might be carrying his baby. But did that have to mean he couldn't have her *and* Ariah?

All he had to do was convince Nettie that Ariah wouldn't give him an annulment. He could say Ariah had insisted that they consummate the marriage, then and there, and that he'd had little choice but to give in. He would promise to keep coming to see Nettie, and to support her and their child. What more could she want? Nettie had been a whore, after all; she couldn't expect a decent man like him to actually marry her, could she?

* * *

Bartholomew was avoiding her the way a rabbit avoids a hawk. Ariah was certain of it. He had taken over the care of the domestic animals at the station, thereby ensuring that he would not run into her while she milked cows or fed chickens. She had to content herself with a glimpse of him going or coming from the outbuildings, while she weeded the garden or watched from the windows of the house.

He had spoken less than a dozen words to her since the day of the funeral, making it obvious that he did not want her attention. He cooked for himself, did his own laundry, cleaned his own house. Even her invitation to Easter supper, extended through Pritchard, came back with a polite refusal. His rejection of their friendship hurt Ariah more than she could bear, but she hid her pain in her preparations for the holiday.

Her mother's precious iconostasis, with its gold-etched image of the Virgin, was brought out from its sanctuary in Ariah's trunk and hung in the eastern corner of her bedroom. This part of the Easter tradition she would share with no one; it was too personal and seeped too thoroughly in sorrow.

Ariah did not cross herself in front of the iconostasis each morning and evening as her mother had, but she carefully unwrapped each of the items her mother had kept inside the small, glass-fronted, triangular, wooden box, and placed them exactly as Demetria had left them. A red easter egg, dyed by Demetria's own hand lay before the Virgin, along with a brittle, dried sprig of laurel from the last Palm Sunday mass Demetria had attended in Greece so many years before. The tiny bottle of water blessed by the priest on that long-ago Epiphany was empty now, its contents evaporated, but Ariah gave it its honored place anyway.

Pritchard and Seamus were badgered into digging a pit where the lamb would be roasted over hot coals. She insisted the pit be placed between the two houses. Bartholomew might not attend her special supper, but he would at least smell the food and hear their laughter.

Special ingredients were ordered from Portland and her old Cincinnati neighborhood: ouzo, a Greek liqueur her father had never learned to like; feta cheese; grape leaves; a rice-shaped pasta called orzo; rich Greek coffee; walnuts, almonds, pistachios, olives, figs and dates. The cooking began several days before Holy Saturday and required all of Ariah's concentration to prepare properly.

An entire day was spent making the special pastry needed for baklava, cream puffs, fruit tarts and other delicacies. The filo dough had to be rolled paper-thin, a difficult project for anybody, let alone someone as incompetent in the kitchen as Ariah. Several batches had to be thrown away, but she finally managed one that satisfied her.

"Who you invitin', the whole town?" Seamus asked one afternoon while she painstakingly wrapped dabs of spinach and cheese in layer after layer of the special dough and lined the results up like tin soldiers on a baking sheet.

Her floured hands went still, and she stared first at him, then at the mound of *kourambiedes,* her favorite butter cookies, cooling in the window, the trays of *baklava* waiting to be baked, eggplant she would make into a tart dip and a mountain of hard-boiled eggs dyed a brilliant red to represent the blood of Christ. There would be enough for an entire town.

Pritchard burst into the warm, fragrant kitchen. When he reached for one of the cookies, she quelled the impulse to slap his hand away, and smiled instead.

"Pritchard, are you going into town tonight?"

He hadn't planned to, having put off his confrontation with Nettie, but since he hadn't found the courage to invade Ariah's bed yet either, he was feeling randy. "The fellows wanted to practice again, but I reminded them I'm a newlywed yet and need to spend *some* time at home. Why?"

She began wrapping another spoonful of spinach and cheese.

"I wondered if you would have time to stop over to Calvin's to invite them to Easter supper. It's short notice, with Easter being only two days away now, but Mrs. Goodman will be spending the holiday with her son, so Cal and the boys might like to eat here." She glanced up and added, "I'm hoping Bartholomew will join us, too. He's punished himself long enough for not discovering Hester's condition sooner."

Seamus lit his pipe and said, "Good idee."

"It might cheer Uncle Bart up to have some of his family here, all right," Pritchard added.

"Good. Ask Dr. Wills, too, and what do you think of inviting Reverend Ketcham and his wife?"

Pritchard licked powdered sugar and cookie crumbs from his fingers, frowning. "I think having them around would only remind Uncle Bart of the funeral. How about Max Hennifee from the Pickled Eye? He and Uncle Bart have always been good friends, and Max won't have anywhere else to go on Easter."

Ariah grimaced. "The Pickled Eye?"

"Saloon . . . Near the dock," Seamus explained in his typically abbreviated manner.

"Oh. Well, invite him then. Four healthy male appetites should make a good dent in all I'll have prepared. Anyone else you can suggest?"

Pritchard munched another cookie while he considered. He might have invited Stuffy Simms and his wife, but that would risk Ariah's learning the truth about certain nonexistent practice games. "No. I reckon most folks will be tied up with their own family doings."

"All right. Do you want something to eat before you go? Besides cookies, I mean," Ariah called as he headed out.

Halfway up the stairs, he yelled back, "No thanks. I'll eat with Stuffy."

Seamus snorted and opened the back door. "Eat with Stuffy. My Aunt Patootie's hind end!" he muttered as he went out to see to his goats.

Twenty-three

When Holy Saturday arrived, Ariah had no trouble keeping busy until the magic hour of midnight. As the evening waned, she imagined her mother working alongside her, reciting tales of Easter in the old country.

Everyone in Demetria's village would be crowding inside the Church of the Holy Trinity now, with unlit candles in their hands and anticipation in their hearts. The lights would soon be extinguished. Then, at the stroke of twelve, the church's main doors would be thrown open. Incense would curl around the white-vested priest as he emerged from the cryptlike silence of the darkened church, carrying a single lit candle.

"Come and receive the light," he would call, while bells pealed out the news that Christ had risen. Firecrackers would flare, hiss and explode in a shower of sparks. Joyous voices would shout.

"*Kristos aneste,*" the priest would intone as the holy flame was passed from candle to candle. "Christ is risen." And the people would answer: "*Alethos aneste,* He is risen indeed."

Hands would shelter candles from the wind as worshipers strode home to mark a cross on their ceilings with the smoke in honor of another triumphant return from the dead.

Ariah had no holy flame, but she lit her own candle and placed it in Demetria's iconostasis, whispering the words to herself: "*Kristos aneste.* Christ is risen."

Finally, Easter Sunday arrived.

The pit was ready. Good smells filled the kitchen, and Ariah's spirits were higher than they had been since she fled Cincinnati. Only Bartholomew's participation in the day's activities could make the day better.

As soon as Pritchard relieved him from his watch that morning, Seamus departed for Tillamook to fetch Ariah's order from the fish market and to pick up the dressed-out lamb from Cal. After he left, Ariah went out to pick fresh garlic, celery, onions, tomatoes and parsley from the garden for the dishes that had yet to be cooked.

Bartholomew emerged from the barn. Holding her breath, she willed him to look her way, but when he did, it was only to stare for a moment, then disappear around the side of the barn. Her shoulders sagged as she filled her lungs with air and tried to banish the pain of his unwarranted rejection.

Two weeks had passed since Hester's death, but Bartholomew obviously hadn't yet come to terms with his guilt. She had shared that guilt until she faced the fact that his marriage had failed long before he met her. Had she never come to Oregon, nothing between Bartholomew and his wife would have changed. Hester would still be dead and he would still be condemning himself for not having loved her.

Frustration seethed inside Ariah. She wanted desperately to help him. What he was putting himself through now wasn't fair to him or anyone else who had to live with him here at the lighthouse station. It wasn't even fair to Ariah, though she accepted the blame for enticing him into acts that undoubtedly had made him feel unfaithful to his dead wife. She understood his grief, but she also knew that punishing himself only worsened matters.

And she refused to allow it to ruin Easter.

Leaving her herbs and vegetables on the ground, she brushed off her apron and skirt and stalked toward the barn. She found him exactly where she'd expected to—in the pheasant pen. Without a moment's hesitation, she marched up to the door and let herself inside. "Bartholomew?"

Except for the stiffening of his back, he ignored her.

"Do you hate me so much? Is it Hester's death you blame me for . . . or only your guilt?"

"I blame no one for her death—except myself."

"What nonsense. If anyone was to blame, it was Hester herself. Why do you insist on playing the villain?"

When he made no response, she grabbed his arm and forced him to face her. Eyes as hollow and ravaged as a beehive after a bear has been at it gazed down at her. His face had grown thin, accentuating the bluntness of his features and lending him a vulnerability she had never seen before.

Her voice softened as her fingertips moved lightly over that beloved face, longing to wipe the shadows from his soul.

"Oh, Bartholomew. How Hester must be laughing, to see you destroying yourself this way, because of her."

He wrenched from her grasp and turned away. "She might not be dead, if not for me. I was her husband, for hell's sake. I saw her limping about the house, I knew she was suffering. Yet I never even bothered to determine the cause of her pain. I was too busy lusting after . . ."

He left the word unsaid, but she knew what he'd left out. "If you were lusting after me, it was no one's fault but Hester's," Ariah said quietly.

He spun about, his eyes blazing. "What are you talking about? Damn it, she was my wife. I had no right to cast my eyes on another woman."

One more step and he would tromp her into the manure-speckled earth, but she held her ground. Her face was as calm as his was ravaged; her voice was soft and sure.

"She tricked you into marrying her, Bartholomew. She let you into her bed once, only to consummate the marriage so you couldn't have it annulled. Then she locked you from her room. What right has such a woman to complain if her husband turns to another? You gave her far more kindness than most men would have, and she knew it, in spite of her eternal nastiness."

Bartholomew jerked as though struck. "How did you know? I never told you any of that."

"She bragged of it, as though to dare me."

Ignoring his expression of shock, Ariah picked up a long, barred tail feather and stroked it as she spoke. "After hearing all that, how could any woman who loved you resist trying to make up to you for all Hester put you through? How could she deny the woman the pleasure of catching her husband in sin so she could ruin his name and then elevate herself to the level of martyr when she forgave you? Once the trollop who had lured you into sin had been banished, of course."

Bartholomew turned away. How naive he had been. Hester had always been manipulative, but he'd never guessed her capable of sinking to such depths. Yet, he could not doubt that what Ariah told him was true. Hester had wanted him to betray her. Somewhere in her twisted mind she had believed that his plunge into sin would erase her own. Had he driven her to such desperate measures by throwing her past into her face? By threatening her with it?

The same question that had haunted him the past two weeks and more came back to rattle about in his brain, like a pebble in a clam shell: If he had wooed his wife seven years ago instead of turning his back on her, would their marriage have traveled the same ugly path? If he'd offered her love rather than hate, would she have learned to love him in return? Hester had been badly misused by the men in her life before coming to Tillamook. And he had done her no better. He should have treated her with understanding and compassion, not intolerance and enmity.

Ariah was still there, behind him. He could smell her, feel her warmth, hear her soft breathing, sense her longing for him. Steeling himself against his physical reaction to her, he dragged up the bootstraps of his anger and said icily, "She still didn't deserve to die as she did."

"No, but it was she who chose to keep her condition a secret, she who refused to let Dr. Wills examine her. Bartholomew"— her voice became intent, each word spaced for emphasis—"you did not cause Hester's death."

His only response was a disgusted grunt.

Ariah tried again. "Don't you believe what Dr. Wills told you? She had a deadly disease. There was no cure. Even if her leg hadn't become infected, she would have died before the year was half over, probably sooner. There was nothing you could have done to prevent it."

He made no reply, as if he hadn't even heard her.

Ariah released her breath in a long, weary sigh. Then she retraced her steps to the door, oblivious to the handsome birds strutting about the pen or the duller females crouched on their nests. After letting herself out and latching the door behind her, she gave the man inside one more glance. He stood with his back to her, hands on his hips, head bowed.

"I've invited Calvin and the boys to supper," she said. "I thought you might like to know."

Then she went back to the garden, her heart so heavy that even the thought of the Easter festivities she had so looked forward to failed to cheer her.

The guests joined Seamus on his return trip, arriving shortly after noon. Ariah greeted them with a smile as big as the ocean, glad for the distraction of their company. In her hands she carried a tray bearing glasses of water, a spoonful of blackberry jam spiked with almonds balanced on the rims of each tumbler.

"This is *glyko* which means spoon sweet," Ariah explained as she passed them out. "In a Greek home, it's traditional to greet guests with a drink and a sweet. If anyone is hungry, I'd be happy to fix something more substantial. Meanwhile, think of this as an official welcome to a Greek Easter feast."

Seamus took one look at the small treat and opted for his pipe instead. "Don't give me none o' that cat-lap, lass. All I want is some o' the grog Max brung."

Jacob swallowed his in one gulp. "We already ate, but this is good. I'll take Seamus's."

Calvin cuffed the boy on the head and everyone laughed.

Then a thin whisker of a man stepped forward to offer Ariah a bottle of French wine. He towered above her, perhaps as much as two inches taller than Bartholomew.

"I be Max, ma'am. Appreciate the invite."

The spikes of a well-waxed mustache quivered as he spoke through lips as red as the wine he held. Bony wrists hung far below the sleeves of a threadbare sack coat.

"I'm glad to make your acquaintance, Mr. Hennifee, and to have you join in our celebration."

The middle-aged tavern owner blushed to the roots of his hair. "Don't be a-hanging that handle on me, ma'am. Nobody's called me nothing but Max in nigh on thirty years now. Don't reckon I'd think to answer to mister."

"Then you must call me Ariah."

Max bobbed his head. " 'Tis honored I'd be, ma'am."

She turned to Seamus and held out the wine. "If this is the 'grog' you were looking for, you'd best open it and pour some for whoever wishes to partake with you."

"That ain't grog," he growled. "That's fer women and lob-lolly lads, like them two o' Calvin's."

"Aye," said Max. " 'Tis rum he be wanting, ma'am."

"Oh, well, if we have any, it would be Seamus who'd know where to find it. You can help yourself as soon as you get the lamb on the spit."

"Arg," Seamus groaned. "Now it's crumb bosuns she's wantin' to make us into."

Ariah chuckled. "If that means what I think it does, you're exactly right. But remember, he who helps the cook, gets first cut of the meat."

"Aye. Suits me," Max retorted, playing the sailor under a ship's cook. "Jest show me to the galley."

After instructing the men on how to prepare the lamb for roasting, Ariah took the wine Max had brought, and the other parcels Seamus had gotten her, and returned to the kitchen. Watching the men through the open window, she heard Calvin ask where his brother was.

"Weepin' and wailin' like a dang female somewheres, likely," Seamus replied.

"Uncle Bart's at the light, if that's who you're talking about," Pritchard said as he joined them. "He offered to relieve me so I wouldn't miss the feast. He didn't seem to want to be around the rest of us."

Cal frowned. "He took Hester's death surprisingly hard."

"Huh! Woman was a Jonah, sure as I ever sailed a bloody ship to sea." Seamus spat into his left hand and Ariah knew it was for good luck, as if even the mention of Hester's name might bring him ill fortune. So much for her efforts to entice Bartholomew out with the smells of her cooking.

"Won't find her on no Fiddlers' Green, I tell ye," the old salt added.

Cal laughed. "I doubt we'll find you in any sailor's heaven either, you old barnacle."

The voices drifted away on the breeze as the men set about roasting the lamb. Ariah turned her attention to her cooking, hoping Bartholomew hadn't heard Seamus's unflattering comments. The chances of him joining them today were slim enough without ill feelings making matters worse.

Her heart ached. For Bartholomew, and for herself. The man she loved was free now, but he obviously wanted nothing more to do with her. She understood his remorse, shared his guilt and pain, yet she hated letting Hester win. And as long as the woman's death was allowed to keep them apart, the way her living presence had, then Hester had indeed won.

Checking the schedule she'd prepared to ensure that all the food would be ready on time, Ariah measured flour into two large bowls, mixing dough for apple fritters in one, bread in the other. Guilt, sorrow and frustration were shoved aside. Today was a day for hope and new beginnings. She refused to knuckle under to the painful emotions seething inside her.

While the dough raised, she put rice and ground lamb on to cook, then rinsed the brine from the bottled grape leaves. Scraps were set aside for the wolf-dog, whom she had named Apollo, after the Greek god of goodness and beauty, the inspiration of muses. There had been no time to steal off into the forest the last few days, and she worried that the dog would be starving.

When everything was nearly ready, she went outside to ask the men to bring out the large table and chairs from the dining room. The morning breeze had fled, leaving the day calm and warm. Much too lovely to spend inside. Soon the table was set with a crisp white linen cloth, napkins and the best china. Jacob and Robert helped her carry out the food, while the men took the lamb from the spit and began to carve it. After depositing a covered dish on the table, Ariah took Calvin aside.

"Cal, would you see if you can get Bartholomew to join us? I invited him, but . . ." She let the words trail away, uncertain how to go on without exposing her feelings for his brother.

"No one knows better than me how stubborn he can be." Cal patted her on the shoulder and gave her a conspiratorial wink. "I'll see what I can do."

Cal found Bartholemew at the keeper's desk, a logbook in front of him. "Hey, little brother, Ariah's put a fine-looking supper together up there," he said, motioning to the top of the bluff.

Bartholomew stared sullenly at the man leaning against the doorjamb, grinning as though all was right with the world and Bartholomew should have nothing on his mind save food and the pleasure of family and friends. It rankled, yet he did not want to be churlish to his brother. Lord knew, they saw little enough of each other as it was. The last thing Bartholomew wanted was bad blood between them simply because Calvin couldn't understand what he was going through, even though Cal had lost his own wife six years ago.

As though he had read his brother's mind, Cal said, "You know, for a while after Ellen died, I hated myself for being the cause of her death—"

"What do you mean? You didn't cause—"

Cal held up a hand.

"She died trying to birth a baby I put in her body, Bart.

Knowing that made me feel lower than a slug's belly, till one night Ellen came to me in a dream. 'You're a dang fool, Calvin Noon,' she said."

Cal chuckled, remembering. Ellen was always calling him a dang fool. "She reminded me that she had wanted that baby every bit as much as I did. No one understands the risks of childbearing better than a woman, she said. She chose to take those risks, and I was a pompous, overbearing ass to consider my part in that decision weightier than hers. She was right. From then on I concentrated on remembering the love we'd shared and on being grateful for having her as long as I did."

Cal pushed away from the doorjamb. He leaned both hands on the desk in front of Bartholomew and stared his brother hard in the face. "We all know what you've suffered, but there comes a time to put grief aside, and today seems like a good day for it to me. What do you say?" Cal straightened and held out a hand.

Lines from the Bible filled Bartholomew's mind: *"To every thing there is a season, and a time to every purpose under the heaven: A time to be born, and a time to die . . . A time to weep, and a time to laugh; a time to mourn, and a time to dance . . ."*

Perhaps Ariah and Cal were right; he'd kicked himself long enough. He gripped Cal's hand and allowed himself to be pulled to his feet. But Cal didn't stop there; he drew Bartholomew straight into his arms, embracing him openly and without shame.

"Sometimes, little brother, we have to ask ourselves if we're truly grieving or simply feeling sorry for ourselves."

Bartholomew punched him softly in the ribs. "Don't push it too far, old man," he muttered, but his tone lacked venom.

Cal chuckled and hauled him out the door.

Ariah avoided Bartholomew's gaze when the two brothers came to the table, afraid the hope in her eyes would reawaken his need to punish himself. When Cal suggested Bartholomew give the blessing, she wanted to kick the man.

Bartholomew gave them each a long, searching look, then

nodded. The prayer was brief but succinct, asking for a blessing on the food and on each participant. Then he added, "Help us, Lord, to always know thy will, to remember thy commandments, and to find the strength to obey. Amen."

Ariah felt kissed and cursed in the same breath. His choice of words admitted that he might not always know the right thing to do, but they also reminded her—as they had been meant to do—that what was between them was forbidden and that he meant to refuse her apple of temptation. Swallowing the emotion that swelled in her throat, she stood. Her voice quavered only slightly as she said, "Since this is a proper Grecian feast, I think it fitting to give an old Greek toast." She raised her glass and saluted each guest. "May God bless you all with male children and female goats."

As she had hoped, the awkward moment that had followed Bartholomew's solemn prayer dissolved into laughter.

Taking her seat, she helped herself to sliced potatoes cooked in olive oil and seasoned with lemon juice and oregano, then passed the dish on. Sensing an intense gaze upon her, she glanced up to find Bartholomew staring at her from across the table. Barely lifting his glass, his soft words intended only for her ears, he said, *"Kali orexi."*

That gentle reminder of another Greek meal shared in a cabin on the Trask River, and the night that had followed it, surprised and pleased her as nothing had in a very long while. He had forgiven her for whatever part she had played in his guilt. Blinking back tears, uncaring of the love exposed in her smile, she whispered, *"Kali orexi,* good eating."

Silence reigned over the table, except for the clink of silverware against china and a few grunts of approval.

"Hey, this is good," Pritchard exclaimed, biting into a succulent morsel in a crisp, golden brown crust. "You sure you cooked this, Ariah? I didn't think you had it in you to come up with anything this tasty."

Bartholomew quelled the urge to slug the boy. "You have real class, Pritchard."

"Thanks, Uncle Bart. Pass that bowl in front of you."

"Yeah, I'll take some more of that too," Jacob put in. "I don't know what it is, but I wish you'd teach Mrs. Goodman how to make it, Ariah."

Ariah waited until both men had full mouths. "I'm glad you like it. It's fried squid."

Pritchard stopped chewing. His face turned a sickly green. "It's what?"

"Fried squid." She smiled. "Is something wrong?"

He shook his head, muttered, "Excuse me," and raced from the table.

Everyone except Jacob laughed. The boy chewed, swallowed and pursed his lips. "Squid, huh? Sounds awful, but it sure tastes good."

"Here, try this." Ariah handed him a tureen of bite-sized chunks of meat cooked in tomatoes, wine, onions and celery.

Jacob gamely forked a bite into his mouth. "Ummm, this is even better than the squid. I suppose you're gonna tell me this is octopus or sea lion or something."

"You're right. Octopus."

"I'll be danged."

Cal was sternly rebuking the boy for his language when a shout from Robert cut him off and ended the laughter that had followed Jacob's exclamation. Leaping to his feet, Robert pointed toward the forest.

"It's a dog. How'd you get Aunt Hester to let you have a dog, Uncle Bart? She hated dogs."

Ariah turned. There, standing beside the fence not more than a hundred yards away, was Apollo.

Pritchard returned, hugging his stomach, his face still pale, though no longer green. Seeing that everyone was staring off toward the trees, he looked to determine what had captured their attention. "That's the dog from the shipwreck," he said.

"You mean that wreck a couple of months ago?" Robert asked. "Gosh, he must be hungry."

In spite of his queasy stomach, Pritchard smiled. "Ariah's been leaving him food in the woods to make friends with him."

"Can we pet him?" Too eager to wait for an answer, both of Cal's boys left the table and headed for the gate.

"Wait!" Ariah jumped to her feet. "He was half-wild when we found him and he's still wary of people. Stay here, please. I'll take him some food."

The disappointed boys flopped down on their seats. Seven pairs of curious eyes followed Ariah to the house. Moments later she reappeared with a newspaper-wrapped packet. When she reached the gate, Apollo's tail began to wag. Ariah slowed her pace, afraid she would frighten him away. The dog watched her every movement, his big chocolate eyes shrewd and intent.

"Hello, Apollo. Did you get hungry enough to come looking for me?"

Six feet away, she stopped, hoping to make the dog come to her. "Look here, I've got something for you."

Ariah parted the folds of the paper to reveal the food scraps inside and held it out for him to see. Apollo's nose twitched. His tail went still. His mouth opened and a coral tongue swiped at his chops. Ariah set the packet on the ground and crouched beside it. The dog craned his shaggy head toward the food and sniffed. He pranced nervously in place and whined.

"It's all right." Ariah eased back a few inches to give him more space. "Come on, I won't hurt you."

Chocolate eyes searched blue ones questioningly. He inched closer and whined again.

Ariah waited, barely breathing.

Apollo eyed the food hungrily. Two more steps. His gaze flicked from her to the food. Seeming to make up his mind, he snatched a chunk of meat and darted away. When Ariah didn't contest his action, he hunkered down to gobble his prize. Now he came to the paper less warily. His tail swished in short, choppy swipes. He seized a bite and ate without moving off.

Ariah waited until half the food was gone. Then she began to talk in a quiet, soothing undertone. When he had eaten nearly everything, she inched her hand toward him. He flinched at her first touch. Food was forgotten as he watched her reach toward him again.

"It's all right, Apollo," she crooned. "You have a home now, you won't ever be hungry again. And I'll love you, the way a big, beautiful fellow like you should be loved."

Her hand sank into thick coarse hair almost as long as her fingers. She stroked his head where dark markings came down over his eyes, her touch light and caressing. "In a way I'm as alone as you are, Apollo, but now we have each other."

The dog eyed the last morsel of food on the paper and whined.

"Go ahead. I'm not going to hurt you."

He dropped his head and ate. Easing herself onto her knees, Ariah continued to stroke his matted, dirty hair. She longed to pull out the burrs, but was afraid to try.

Suddenly something wet and rough sloppily laved her cheek. Startled, she drew back. Apollo's tail wagged double-time. He gave a short bark and licked her again.

Ariah's heart swelled and her eyes prickled. Throwing caution to the wind, she hugged him. He accepted the weight of her arms around him as he continued to lick her neck and face.

Behind her rose a round of cheers. She looked up to see that the men had left the table and come into the yard to watch. Every face held a smile, but the only one that captured her gaze—and her heart—was Bartholomew's. It came to her then that Apollo was not only the god of goodness and beauty; he was also the bringer of catharsis—the purification of guilt-ridden consciences—and the god of peace.

Twenty-four

That night, when Ariah put away her mending and doused the lamp by her chair, Pritchard tossed his newspaper onto the sofa and followed her up the stairs.

"Did you know Abraham Lincoln was playing baseball when he got the message that he'd been nominated for President?" he asked as they rounded a corner of the stairwell and climbed the last few steps to the second floor.

Ariah heaved a silent sigh. The routine had been the same since the night they had sat on her bed, when a harmless discussion had ended in a not-so-harmless kiss. Every night after that he had managed to get some sort of conversation going so that it seemed perfectly normal for him to follow her right into her room.

At first, when she made it obvious she was ready to change into her nightrobe and go to bed, he had nonchalantly kissed her on the cheek and left, closing the door behind him, the perfect gentleman. But after a week, the kiss on the cheek became an embrace and a full kiss on the mouth. It was his right; she was his wife. Yet, no matter how she lectured herself about the necessity of becoming a true wife to Pritchard, she was fast coming to dread bedtime.

"No, I didn't know Lincoln played baseball."

"He was one of its biggest supporters, actually."

"How interesting."

He followed her into her room. "I was reading in the *Head-*

light-Herald that they're going to allow substitutions of players now, any time during a game."

"That's nice, Pritchard."

He sat down on the side of her bed and watched as she poured water into the washbasin. Ariah felt his gaze crawling over her like ants on her flesh. She splashed cold water onto her face and prayed for patience. Pritchard Monteer was her husband. He was a good man, for all his childishness and insensitivity. In her wedding vows, she had promised to obey. No, more than that; *love*, honor, and obey.

If honoring him meant being faithful, then she had at least managed that much, in body if not in heart. The love she had hoped would come in time. Even if she never learned to care for him the way she did his uncle, she still believed she owed it to Pritchard to honor her wedding vows to the best of her ability.

And that meant granting him the use of her body.

Steeling herself to do what she must, she dried her face and turned to him.

"Pritchard—"

"Ariah—"

Having spoken at the same time, they laughed nervously.

"Ariah," he began again, his young face a study in hope and trepidation. "I hate sleeping alone. Let me stay with you tonight. I promise I won't do anything but hold you. Please?"

She tried to tell him that he was welcome in her bed, and to do more than hold her, but the words would not come. "All right," was all she managed to get out. Then, feeling awkward and foolish, she rushed to the dresser and pulled out her nightrobe. "I'll slip into this while you change into your night-shirt . . . in your room."

"That's great. I'll only be a minute."

When he was gone, Ariah collapsed onto the bed, the gown clutched to her breasts. What would she do if he broke his word and tried to make love to her? She would let him, of course. It was his right.

Pritchard returned so quickly she barely had time to pull her gown down over her hips before the door swung open and he stepped inside. His bare feet, sticking out from under the voluminous nightshirt, were small and narrow. He had been her husband now for over six weeks. Yet she had never seen before how slight his feet were. He shuffled from one to the other as though the floor were exceedingly cold.

"Either side all right?"

She blinked in confusion and he motioned to the bed. "Oh, yes, either side is fine."

He climbed in, leaving her to close the door and put out the lamp. Instead, she stood beside the bed, one hand gripping the front placket of her gown.

"I-I usually give my hair a hundred strokes."

Pritchard propped himself on an elbow. "Go ahead. I didn't mean to interrupt your routine."

At the dresser she pulled the pins from her hair and let it cascade in honeyed waves down her back. Then she took up her brush and went to work. In the mirror she could see Pritchard watching avidly from the bed, the way Bartholomew had at the Uphams' cabin. She pushed the memories of that other time from her mind and concentrated on counting her strokes, entirely too aware of the growing sensuality on her husband's face. When the hundred strokes became a hundred and twenty and she could no longer delay the inevitable, she put down the brush and went to the bed. Sitting on the edge, she extinguished the lamp. Then she slid beneath the covers and lay stiffly beside her husband, her back to him. His voice came out of the darkness, breathy with desire, hesitant with fear.

"Can I hold you?"

"Yes."

At once his arms came around her, one under her neck, the other curled over her waist, one hand coming to rest dangerously close to her breast. All along her back, she felt his warmth.

"Good night, Ariah."

"Good night."

For an eternity she lay there, rigid as a board. Though he

carefully kept his hips from touching her, the heat coming from that part of his anatomy, and the difficulty he was having getting to sleep, told her he wanted to do more than hold her. Only when the arm wrapped around her waist became heavy and his breathing slowed to the deep, measured breaths of slumber did she relax and finally drift off to sleep.

In the morning she awoke to find him gone. Too relieved to question her good luck, she rose swiftly to dress before he could return. When he came home that afternoon, he went straight to the stove and reached for the lid on a pot.

"Do I smell what I think I smell?"

"Careful!"

"Ow!" He dropped the hot lid and stuck his fingers in his mouth.

"Let me see." She pried his hand away from his mouth to examine the burn, ignoring his whimpers of pain. The skin was red and angry but not as bad as she'd feared.

"You'll live," she assured him. "Run cold water on them to ease the pain, and next time, use a towel to lift the lid."

Over the sound of the running water, he asked again about the aroma he had noticed as he entered the house.

"You guessed right," she said. "It's your favorite of *Mana's* recipes; chicken in brandy cream sauce, with beans."

Pritchard was always especially pleased when she cooked Greek; that meant it would be good because she always made sure she did it right. She took out three plates and set them on the table. "I'll call Seamus so we can eat."

"He won't like eating this early."

"He wants to go into town with you."

"What for?" Pritchard turned off the faucet and studied his scalded fingers.

"I didn't feel it was my place to ask. Is there some problem about his going along?"

"No, but . . ." He hadn't planned to go out tonight; he had planned to seduce his wife.

"I want you to buy me some gardening gloves," she said over

her shoulder as she went to call the old sailor. "And flower seeds."

"Flower seeds? But Aunt—"

"I know Aunt Hester didn't countenance wasting time on something as useless as flowers." Ariah stepped back into the room. "But she is gone and I am still here. Will you get the seeds or not?"

"Sorry. Of course I will. I guess I still find it hard to believe she's dead."

Not me, Ariah thought, unable to shove aside her guilty relief at being free of the woman's querulous presence.

Pritchard wasn't happy about having the old man go along. Though Seamus wasn't likely to follow him around the whole time they were in town, his very presence meant a visit with Nettie would have to be extremely brief. The men would have to return on the same tide so that Seamus could relieve Uncle Bart at midnight.

Nettie hadn't been at all pleased to hear that Ariah had refused to grant him an annulment. Only his promise to keep trying had smoothed her ruffled feathers. He intended to keep trying, all right, but not for an annulment.

Waking up this morning with Ariah in his arms, one full breast cupped in his hand, had been almost as wonderful as the first time he had thrust into Nettie's hot sweet body. In that first moment of wakefulness, he had thought it *was* Nettie in his arms. If Ariah hadn't pushed his hand away in her sleep as he began to explore her body, he might have made a bad mistake. Reminding himself how hard he had worked to get into Ariah's bed, he had forced himself to leave it before temptation overcame him, but that hadn't kept him from wishing she was Nettie so he could satisfy his need then and there.

Was it Nettie he missed or only her willing body?

At midnight, Seamus shuffled into the lighthouse and set down the lunch tin Ariah had fixed for his four A.M. meal.

"Evening, Seamus." Bartholomew closed the logbook he had been writing in, and rose from the chair at the desk. "Did you learn anything in town?"

Seamus took his time answering. He retrieved his corncob pipe from his pocket, filled the bowl and lit the tobacco. Perfect rings of smoke emerged from his mouth as he exhaled. Bartholomew watched them drift toward the ceiling, then vanish, knowing it would do no good to rush the old man. Seamus's favorite from Ecclesiastes was ". . . a time to keep silence, and a time to speak . . ."

Finally, Seamus said, "Seems we was right to suspect the lad. Hennifee says the young cock's building a harem, all right. Girl on the far end of the slough, name o' Nettie."

Bartholomew stared at the frothing sea, jade green in the bright morning sunlight, and tried not to think of Ariah. An impossible task. Would he ever be free of her hold on his heart? On his soul? A part of him prayed not, because with her inside him, he was at least alive. Yet it hurt. It hurt to have and yet not have her.

His nymph.

She had cast a spell over him, fed him a love potion more potent than wine, administered by the mere spreading of her lips. How could a smile be so powerful? To make a life that had seemed, until she came along, unworthy of the effort to keep it going, suddenly blossom with glory and ecstasy and promise. As though, as he had so often wished, he were being reborn.

She was a song in his soul that never ceased to play. Awake or asleep, at work or at leisure, her love whispered in his heart. Like the whisper of the sea in a shell long stolen from the watery depths of its birth. Like the echo of a lover's flute on a windswept bluff, devoid of tears or sorrow or pain. Like the stirrings of hope.

As the wind lifted the heavy drape of sable hair off his forehead, and rainbow-hued seafoam coolly kissed his naked toes, it came to him that until he freed himself from the bewitching allure of his intoxicating nymph, he would be like the pebbles on the beach, dragged willy-nilly by the undertow, then spat back onto the shore, impotent and alone. The thought left him feeling helpless and dejected.

Overhead, a gull hovered, its wings dipping negligibly to one side, then to the other, as it played the wind like the airholes of a flute, creating a song of lazy grace and summer sunshine. The wind switched direction. The gull plunged for a heart-wrenching instant before a few indolent flaps of its wings halted its fall. A moment later, catching another updraft, it soared high above the surging tide, effortlessly, the way Bartholomew wished he could, leaving behind the moorings of his beleaguered soul.

As if to argue the ramblings of his mind, the gull gave a keen, melancholy cry. At the same moment, Bartholemew's scalp prickled with awareness. His body tingled and a frisson fingered his spine in a symphony of hope. He spun about and saw on the rise behind him the quintessence of his dream.

Ariah.

Their eyes met across the windblown distance, and his soul awakened.

Ariah hesitated at the lip of the low bluff, enthralled by the sight of Bartholomew on the hard, flat beach below. His hair was longer than usual and brushed against his collar as the breeze riffled the dark strands. Excitement tingled low in her abdomen. Had she known he would be there, she would have honored his solitude. Fortunately, his presence was a surprise, like a pearl in a clam shell, and she felt no compunction to retreat.

Though separated by about thirty yards, the air between them sizzled with emotions left naked by their astonishment at the unexpected encounter. Joy. Need.

Desire.

A warmth, beyond the sun's ability, flooded Ariah as her feet carried her down the slope toward the man below. She wanted to throw herself into his arms, to wrap herself about him and beg him to keep her there forever. Unfamiliar shyness held her back. So much had happened in the weeks since he had brought her to this place. She was Mrs. Pritchard Monteer now, and Bartholomew was a widower. Hester's death had been hard on him. He had all but made himself a recluse at the station and, for all Ariah knew, might not welcome her company today.

A sudden, unnatural hush descended as he watched her descend the narrow path, all the world waiting as breathlessly as he did. Even his heart seemed to have stopped beating.

So beautiful she was, his nymph. Her hair lifted and fanned out around her delicate face like strands of sunshine trailing upon the wind. Her skirt whipped above her ankles, awarding him a tantalizing view unhampered by the petticoats she had had sense enough to abandon for her long hike to the beach.

She came to a halt in front of him, half a dozen feet away, her eyes as bright as sun sparkles on the sea. Slowly, her lushly defined mouth spread into a smile as she stared up at him. Not the smile of startling, heart-stopping radiance that he had fallen in love with, but one more subdued, less assured.

"I needed the sea today," she said simply.

As though awakened by her voice, sound returned—waves crashing upon the shore, gulls crying overhead, a crow cawing in the trees on the bluff—unduly loud after the eternity of silence. Blood pulsed in Bartholomew's veins and his heart surged.

She was waiting for him to reply, but his throat had closed up on him. The air seemed to shimmy around them, tense, expectant. All he could think was how desperately he loved her. All he could do was stare at her, as though she might vanish like morning mist if he were to do more.

Then Apollo came bounding out of the trees above them. The dog raced full-bore down the slope and leaped repeatedly at Ariah. She backed away, swatting halfheartedly at him while Bartholomew chuckled. It was as if the dog were trying to herd her into Bartholomew's arms, a notion the man minded not a whit. His arms fairly ached to hold her.

"Down, you naughty dog," she scolded, laughing.

Apollo jumped then at Bartholomew and laved his face with

a swipe of his tongue before running off after a red-beaked oystercatcher standing at the edge of the surf.

The moment fractured the tension between the man and the woman. Together, they watched the dog scurry out of the way of a wave as the bird took to the air. When Bartholomew glanced back at Ariah, her gaze was on him, her forget-me-not blue eyes filled with a longing that she banished at once with a flick of her lashes.

"Do you want to be alone?" she asked.

"No."

His tone was so sharp it brought her gaze back up.

"You needed the sea today," he said softly. "I needed you."

Her old smile flashed to life then, as radiant as a summer sunset. "I'm here."

A period of awkwardness followed, both afraid to speak their minds, yet unable to find a subject to fill the gap. Apollo had left sandy pawprints on Bartholemew's shirt. She longed to brush them away, but although he'd said he needed her, he'd made no move toward her, leaving her feeling as uncertain as before. Ariah tore her gaze from him and glanced about the deserted beach.

"I wanted to look for seashells," she said.

"Have you found any agates yet?" He turned and walked toward the cape where the beach was littered with rocks. Ariah fell in beside him.

"What are agates?"

He paused to gaze down at her, his perfectly sculpted mouth solemn, his eyes as dark and deep as the sea.

"Agates are rocks as translucent as your skin and almost as beautiful as your eyes," he said huskily.

"You take my breath away when you say things like that," she said, blushing.

There were other, better ways he would like to take her breath away, but he did not confess them. "I said nothing that isn't true."

"Oh, Bartholomew." She swayed toward him, needing to touch

him, then resisted. "You'll turn my head. Help me find a pretty shell. Or one of your agates."

Hunting shells was the last thing he wanted to do with her, and although he reminded himself that she was Pritchard's wife, the admonition did little good in light of what he had recently learned about the boy. Still, he followed her meekly enough as she headed down the beach.

"Wait." She sat down and removed her shoes and stockings, then stood and wriggled her toes in the sand. Her feet were small and slender, like her frame. "The sand isn't as warm as I expected, but it feels wonderful just the same."

Leaving her footgear where it lay, she raced toward the water. A shallow incoming wave met her, its edges scalloped with seafoam. Laughing, she danced away. Apollo bounded over to join in the fun. When the water receded, Ariah darted after it, the dog at her side. With her skirts held high, she allowed the next wave to catch her.

Bartholomew grinned as he watched. She was a nimble sea sprite, as enticing as a Lorelei. Childlike in her play, all woman in her allure.

"Come on." She waved for him to join her.

Like a truant school boy eager to cast off everyday cares, he rolled his trousers to his knees, then tossed aside shirt and shoes. Wearing only the shortened trousers, he sprinted toward Ariah. She fled, giggling, water splashing in her wake, her skirt hem at midthigh. Gulls scattered as he pounded after her, Apollo at his heels now.

Suddenly, she stopped, her attention captured by something on the bluff. Bartholomew all but ran over her. It seemed only natural to catch her in his arms.

"Look, a waterfall." She pointed to a trickle of water that tumbled down the sandstone wall. It streamed across the sand at their feet and into the ocean.

"There are a couple of them actually, if you could call those dribbles waterfalls."

"It's water, and it is falling." Her gaze moved on along the line of the cliff where it curved out into the sea. "Oh, there are caves, too."

"Sea caves," he said, as they walked on, arm in arm. "The tide is almost low enough for us to get out to them, but not quite. It will be coming in again soon. Perhaps we can explore them another day, if you'd like."

"I'd love to. What are they like inside?"

"Dark, wet, mysterious."

She laughed up at him. "Like you?"

"Do you find me mysterious?"

"Sometimes."

He stooped and plucked something off the sand. "Here. Your first agate."

"Oh, it's beautiful."

Lying on his palm was a wet stone the size of a robin's egg, its color ranging from milk white to nearly clear. She turned it over, examined it from every angle, then held it up to the sun to let its brilliance show through. "I've never seen anything like it. It's the most beautiful stone I've ever seen, like a jewel."

"They're thousands of years old, created before the ice age and buried in the basalt until the eroding sea frees them for us to find."

She clutched it in a closed fist over her heart and flashed him a smile. "Thank you, I will treasure it."

His sensuous lips curled upward in a teasing smile. "Enough to reward me if I find you another one?"

"Reward you with what? I have no money," she said, purposely misunderstanding the innuendo in his tone.

His smile remained, but his gaze became heated. "You could give me a kiss."

Ariah's own smile faded, his words too close to what she herself wanted at that moment. Then she forced her errant thoughts aside and matched his teasing smile. "You must find another agate first. A very special one."

"Will this do?"

With cocky assurance he took a much larger stone from his

pocket and deposited it in her hand. It was a dark bluish gray, one side smooth and glassy as though broken cleanly in half. An "eye" marked the center, a round depression encircled with faint lines of a lighter color, radiating outward.

"Oh," she cried, "you deserve two kisses for this one."

"I would take them . . . gladly."

She stared at him, her eyes a passionate shade of lavender now, filled with the moisture of emotions too close to the surface. "Oh, Bartholomew . . ."

Knowing full well that he was insane to do it, Bartholomew caught her to him and took her lips with his own in a kiss almost as violent as his need. Rather than resisting the hard pressure of his mouth on hers, she pressed closer. Her arms twined around his neck. Her lips parted and their tongues met in furious, desperate demand.

After a long while the kiss gentled, as fear of someone tearing them away from each other faded. Only Apollo's frantic barking broke them apart.

Bartholomew shoved her behind him as his gaze raked the beach for whatever had aroused the dog. Fifty yards up the strand, Apollo was racing back and forth along the edge of the surf. Out a few feet in deeper water, a seal calmly watched the dog, seemingly unconcerned. The rest of the beach was deserted except for gulls and an oystercatcher or two.

Relief shattered the tension rippling through Bartholemew. Turning back to Ariah, he swung her in a circle, happier than he had been in weeks.

"Good hell, but I've missed my nymph." He brought their dance to a halt, and his gaze devoured her face. "You'll never know how much."

"Yes, I would."

He scoured the depths of her expressive eyes and his heart smiled at what he saw. Need—every bit as desperate as his. But more than that, love. His pulse accelerated.

"Maybe you do." He took her hand. "Come with me."

"Where?" she asked.

"Into the woods. I know a special place."

The true question, left unsaid, was implicit in the hoarse, sensual tone of his voice. Anticipation sent her blood rushing. Her heart fluttered like the wings of a dragonfly. She made a halfhearted stab at sanity. "Now?"

"Yes, now. I feel as though I've waited forever."

"No longer than I have."

He drew her with him toward the path that climbed the bluff above the strand, gathering their clothing as he went.

"Look," he said, pointing to the sky as they neared the top of the bluff. "A bald eagle."

Ariah watched the bird circle above them, the sun glinting off its white head. "It has a fish in its talons."

"He's taking it to a nest in a snag up there on the edge of the cape, I've watched him before. See?"

Just as Bartholomew said, the great raptor landed in a dead tree farther along the edge of the bluff.

"It's magnificent," she said. "Like you."

Bartholomew grinned. "Like me?"

Glad to have her thoughts distracted from where he was taking her and what they would do when they got there, she gave him a teasing smile and said, "From the first, I thought of you as an eagle. So proud and beautiful . . . and rare."

His eyes darkened with passion. He took her hand and drew her to him. "Come, we'll watch my brother eagle another day. I want you. More than anything else in this world. And I want you now."

Ariah's breath caught at the intensity of his words, and the depth of need visible in his eyes. Fear, as well as excitement, coursed through her veins. They were insane in what they were doing, this flaunting of morality. She worried about how it would affect Bartholomew later, after their passion was spent and reality returned. Honor meant too much to him.

Twenty-five

Bartholomew's special place was a clearing in the midst of the dense, moss-draped wood, towered over by three giant trees that had long ago been stripped of branches. Primitive carvings, like those on totem poles Ariah had seen in pictures, decorated the tall trunks. At the perimeter of the clearing, trilliums and red bleeding heart nodded in the breeze above pink wood sorrel and yellow violets. Hemlocks creaked and rustled. But inside the circle, all was hushed, and so still she felt she stood before the altar of a holy cathedral. Sunbeams slanted through the leafy ceiling in golden prisms to spotlight the sacred trees and the azaleas blooming at their feet. The floor was a carpet of false lily of the valley, sprouting from a bed of thick, spongy moss.

Though the air never stirred, Ariah sensed movement around her and fancied that she could hear ancient voices chanting in the timeless rhythm of prayer. Yet, she felt no fear. Here, there was only peace and a feeling of reverence that heightened her awareness and made her heart ache with a fullness she'd never known before. Slowly she turned to face Bartholomew. In spite of her smile, a tear trembled on her lower lashes. With his fingertip he caught it and brought it to his own mouth.

"You feel it too," he said in a voice soft as a whisper.

"There's magic here," she answered. "I feel I've been enchanted by some ancient mystic."

"It's a sacred place, a ceremonial ground."

Ariah glanced nervously over her shoulder. "Won't we anger the spirits by being here?"

Bartholomew cupped her face in his callused palms. "What I feel for you is as sacred as this glade, Ariah. I can't think of a more fitting place to express that feeling."

"Oh, Bartholomew, I love you so." She put her hand over his and turned her face to kiss the warm hollow of his palm.

Emotion roiled inside him. Awe and disbelief that he was actually there with her, that she had said the words he had just heard. That soon a dream would be fulfilled. Guilt was momentarily swept away in the wake of an excitement so fevered he feared he might die of it.

"My eagle," she said, as she planted a kiss on his other palm. "And what kind of bird are you?"

"A wren."

He remembered wondering, that first day he saw her, what it was that attracted him to her so. His answer had altered little since then; inside, she was as gracious as a swan, as capricious as a chickadee, as ethereal as a hummingbird. As vital as life itself.

"You're no wren," he said huskily. "You're a nymph, one I am about to ravish."

She cocked her head as she looked up at him. "How does an eagle ravish a nymph?"

"The same way Leda was ravished by the swan. Shall I show you?"

Her gaze drifted below the waistband of his trousers. "But a swan is a waterfowl and probably equipped sexually like a man. An eagle lacks the . . . essential equipment."

Bartholomew's gaze followed hers and saw that his arousal was plainly visible beneath the taut fabric of his trousers. When he looked up, Ariah's chameleon eyes had changed to smoky amethyst, her hunger for him almost as evident as his was for her. With a low growl, he grabbed her to him, kissing her with an urgency as savage as his raging need. The small moan that lodged in her throat sizzled through him like a lit fuse, threatening to annihilate him.

He was dangerously out of control with wanting her, a sensation that was not new to him, though he had never felt it so strongly before. All his life he had been holding back, reining in his passions, denying himself. Since the moment he laid eyes on Ariah, the chore had become a near impossibility. Now he sensed himself revoltingly close to ruining everything. A moment such as this must not be rushed, but prolonged, savored, exalted. Yet Ariah was not cooperating. She was raining kisses over his face and pleading for more, not less.

"Love me, Bartholomew. I need you, I need the magic of your hands. I need to feel you inside me. You. No one else, only you."

Her hands tugged at the buttons of his shirt and her mouth on his was as hot as an August sun. When he succumbed, and the shirt was tossed aside, she splayed her hands over the hardness of his chest. She kissed the pulse beating an erratic tattoo at the base of his throat. Her lips trailed along the ridge of his clavicle and down the bearded plane of his breast to a small dark nipple. Bartholomew shuddered as her teeth closed gently over the nub.

"You turn me inside out, woman. If you do that again, I'm likely to shatter at your feet."

"Then you touch me instead."

"Gladly."

He kissed her neck, her ear, her temple and her eyes while his hands freed her hair and spread it around her shoulders, stroking its silk. Beneath the thick strands the texture of her dress felt wrong, out of place. One by one he unfastened the buttons. As the fabric fell open, he drew it down, pressing his lips to the skin thus exposed. Moments later the dress lay at her feet. Her chemise followed, and he said a silent prayer of thanks for her dislike of corsets.

When she stood before him, as naked as God had created her, he stepped back and let his gaze take its fill. She endured his perusal quietly, only the throbbing pulse at the base of her throat exposing the turmoil inside her.

It surprised him to realize he had expected her to look different from the last time he had seen her naked. Less innocent somehow. That she didn't pleased him more than he could explain or justify. If anything, she was more beautiful than he remembered, though that didn't seem possible, for he had lived on his memories for weeks now and would have believed them stretched beyond reality.

His hands shook as he peeled off his trousers. When he would have gone to her, she stopped him. "It's my turn now."

The experience of standing still while a woman scrutinized his physique was unique to him. And extremely arousing. His patience dissolved beneath the heat of her avid gaze.

"Enough, nymph, unless you wish to unman me."

He closed the distance between them and drew her down with him onto the bedding of their clothes, his mouth devouring hers, as greedy for her sweetness as a bear for honey. Bartholomew's hand found a breast. He swallowed the soft moan she breathed as he stroked her rounded flesh to a taut peak.

Against her lips he whispered, " 'I had been hungry all the years; my noon had come to dine; I, trembling, drew the table near, and touched the curious wine.' " Then he replaced his hand with his mouth. Ariah's breath caught in her throat and she arched against him.

When she could breathe again, she said, "You've been reading Emily Dickinson."

"Ummm. Keeps you close to me."

She drew his face back up to hers and kissed him. "I've missed you so."

"Me?" he teased. "Or this?" He laved her breast, then gently scored her nipple with his teeth.

"You . . . this . . . everything." Her fingers were buried in his hair, her voice breathless, yet firm. "Most of all, you. Don't tease me, Bartholomew. I want you too much."

He lifted his head and gazed at her with dark solemn eyes. "You are my soul, do you know that? The blood that pumps through my heart, the vessels that keep me alive, the marrow of my bones. Living without you, without being able to express my need for you, and my love, has been like blundering through fog, an endless, meaningless, blind hell."

"Oh, Bartholomew, if only I could have known that Hester . . . I never should have married—"

"Shhh. No one exists here except you and me."

He captured her hand and nibbled the tips of her fingers, then trailed his tongue across her palm until she shivered. "Warm me," he said. "I've been so cold without you, and so empty."

"I'll warm you, but before we're done, it's you who must fill me."

She drew his lower lip into her mouth, bit and suckled it, while her hand moved down over his chest, the fingers plowing furrows in the dark hair. He shivered when her nails lightly scraped his small nipple and she smiled, enjoying the chance to give back some of the sweet torture he had bestowed on her, now and in the past. His hands refused to remain still, however, and busied themselves painting ecstasy on her naked flesh, the same way his tongue etched her breast with images of rapture, but Ariah knew how to get the upper hand, and she took it.

" 'I gave myself to him, and took himself for pay,' " she recited as her hand closed over his most sensitive flesh. " 'The solemn contract of a life was ratified this way.' "

Bartholomew groaned. His body tensed and ceased moving as he savored her touch.

"Don't talk of contracts, nymph. It reminds me of the one that says you'll never be mine."

"I am yours, Bartholomew. My heart has been yours since the moment we met, and after today my body will be yours as well. No man but you will ever touch me this way."

Her words were music. Even though he knew she was in no position to make such promises, his need for her was too great to keep him from hoping they would be kept. He pushed aside dark thoughts and let only the pleasure she was giving him fill his mind. An inferno blazed inside him. God help him, he had no defense against his desire for her. At this moment, he believed himself capable of killing, if necessary, to have her. The thought terrified him, but did not quench the flames.

"How can you be so soft and so hard at the same time?" she murmured as she explored the secrets of his masculinity.

Bartholomew could not answer. He was hanging by a thread. The sweetness of their aromatic bed blended with the fragrance that was her own—hot, passionate, womanly—bathing him in scented mist. Balanced tipsily on the edge of control, he buried his face in the hollow of her neck and let the aroma and the feel of her silken flesh honey-coat his senses. The raspy sound of her rapid breathing was a mere echo to his own.

Ariah's hand on him, though clumsy with inexperience, still managed to send him spiraling upward in dizzying assent as passion soared within him. Paradise lay just around the corner. Bartholomew snatched her hand away and brought it to his lips. "I pray you are as eager for me as I am for you, little nymph, for I don't think I can hold off any longer."

"Oh, yes, Bartholomew, I am. Very eager."

He claimed her breast with his mouth, while his fingers drifted over her flat belly to her thighs. The sultry softness he discovered waiting for him wrenched a groan from deep inside his throat. She was more than ready. His intimate touch alone nearly unraveled her.

"You taste like a warm sea, alluring and illusive and sweetly salty," he said huskily as he lifted his head, "and you feel like a sunbeam; hot, sensuous, mellifluous.

Her chuckle was hoarse with passion. "And you are like life; hard, mysterious, stingy."

"Stingy?"

"Yes. How much longer are you going to torment me?"

"Is that what I'm doing?" he said, his fingers continuing to explore her heated femininity.

"Yes. Right now I feel as though I am about to die of the pain and pleasure you are inflicting on me."

Bartholomew's heart thundered in his ears. His control had been stretched beyond its limits, turning his face into a grim mask. Knowing he could not wait any longer, he moved over her. Her heat nearly scalded him as he positioned himself. The tightness that met his probing flesh both daunted and intoxicated him.

"Open for me, nymph, and we'll die together."

"I-I don't know how."

Bartholomew grimaced, fearing that he would explode before attaining his goal. From Pritchard's red-faced dejection the day after his wedding, Bartholomew had guessed that the boy had lost his own bid for consummation to a premature release. Bartholomew was a master in controlling his body, yet he found himself clinging by a single thread of spider silk, in danger of doing little better than his nephew.

What confused him was the shocked gasp he had elicited from her with the gentle pressure of his blunt flesh. Her unschooled reactions enthralled him as much as her uninhibited ardor. At least Pritchard's fumbling efforts had not ruined her for passion. But had the boy pleasured only himself, and left Ariah alone in the cold? The thought caused Bartholomew to grit his teeth in a greater effort to hang on until he could bring her a full measure of relief. He eased back and, with his fingers, caressed her until she trembled and tensed with an approaching release.

"No!" Ariah shoved at his hand. "Not without you inside me. I never want to take my pleasure at your expense again."

"I only want to make sure you're ready for me."

"I'm past ready. Now, Bartholomew, now."

He brought her legs up around his hips, making her as available to his purpose as he could. Then, drawing a deep breath, he drove into her. Ariah's gasp of pain was nearly drowned beneath his kiss, yet he heard it. He felt her flinch, felt the pressure and the tearing of an encumbrance he hadn't expected, and he froze in horror.

"God, Ariah, why didn't you tell me?"

He tried to withdraw, but her legs tightened about him and her nails sank into his arms, refusing to let him leave her.

"It's all right," she said, "the pain is gone now."

"How . . . ? What happened? How can you still be a virgin?"

"I asked Pritchard to give me time."

Ariah's arms slid up around his neck and she pulled him down to her, planting wild kisses over his face. "Please, don't let it ruin everything. This is what I want. It's how it should be . . . you and me. I never wanted Pritchard to touch me, and now he never will."

"It's wrong," he murmured against her temple.

"It is *not* wrong. In fact, nothing has ever been more right." She lifted her hips and with her heels drew him even more firmly inside her.

Bartholomew groaned. Not even the shock of finding her still chaste had diminished his desire for her. If anything it inflamed him more. She felt so good, he knew he could be happy simply lying there, buried in her welcoming warmth forever. Though his body might demand more. Was even now demanding more.

"Bartholomew? Please."

His conscience told him he should pull out of her that very moment and go away. He deserved no gratification for the crime he had just committed. But he was too far gone in his lust to heed such a demand. Reality, except in the sense that she belonged to him and to him alone now, had no place in the tiny world he had created for them there in the forest.

Ariah clung to him, her ardor telling him that she wanted him as badly as he wanted her. Her body was wrapped tightly around him and her fingernails were digging half-moons into the flesh of his shoulders, urging him on. And he was inside her. At last, gloriously, miraculously, imbedded deep inside her. There were no words beautiful enough to do the feeling justice. It was more than physical, more than cerebral. It was hot, liquid poetry. It was song. The tremolo of a flute, plied by lips of passion and accompanied by the sibilant voice of the sea.

Ariah whimpered beneath him.

"Patience, nymph." He ran his tongue about the perimeter of

her luscious mouth, pausing to reacquaint himself with the tiny mole he so adored. Then he moved on to trace the seam between those lush lips. They parted and his tongue stabbed into the warm chasm of her mouth, tasting paradise on the satin inner surface of her lower lip. Her tongue met his, not shyly this time, but wildly wanton in its intrepidity.

As their tongues danced the rhythm their bodies would come to know, Bartholomew began to ease out of her. Ariah whimpered and clutched him to her. Her agonizing need incited his own. To his surprise he found himself hardening even more. In that moment he knew his own patience was at an end. He plunged into her sweet, tight channel and heard himself groan with a prurient pleasure that surpassed anything he had ever experienced before. He was caught in an avalanche of sensation, powerless against the concupiscent force of his own lust. And he did not care. All that mattered was that he take Ariah with him, that she share the prize at the end of their sensual rainbow.

And she was there.

Together they soared like eagles racing to the sun in a courtship ritual older than Adam and Eve. Dipping and swaying, captured by crosscurrents of emotion and ecstasy.

Ariah met each of Bartholomew's plunges and gripped him in a rising rapture that drove him higher and higher. Even as he felt himself pitched into a wondrous inferno and muttered her name in a guttural cry that was half-prayer, half-praise, fearing he was about to leave her behind, she stiffened. Her flesh pulsated around him in tight, shimmering heat. Nothing could be more glorious.

That was his last thought before her high, keening cry of release reached inside and plucked him over the edge into sublimity. Thought ceased, suffocated in a blazing sea of sensation and seething emotion.

A long time later Bartholomew became aware of the wind on his back, kissing his damp flesh and leaving behind a trail of goose bumps. Trees creaked and sighed overhead. The scent of evergreens, lily of the valley and passion drifted to his nose. Reality had returned to the small glade.

He lifted himself onto an elbow and gazed at the woman lying partly under him, fearing that he would find her crushed by his weight. Her eyes were closed, her lips slightly parted. Yard-long tangles of hair spread out around her, framing her delicate face in shades of honey and gold. Freckles winked from the bridge of her pert nose. Emotion knotted in his throat. She was so beautiful. And she belonged to him. Or would, once he spoke to Pritchard and an annulment could be arranged. His heart constricted with a joy as fragile and rare as sunbeams in a sea cave.

The half-moons of her lashes flickered, then her eyes opened. Her smile, as she gazed up at him, outshone the sun, giving him a glimpse of the slightly crooked tooth he loved.

"Did I sleep?" she asked, yawning.

"I think we both might have."

"Might have?"

He smiled enigmatically. "I dreamed that I finally made you mine, in the most primal of manners."

Her gamin grin widened as she raked her fingers through the hair on his chest, drawing his eyes to the plumpness of a breast partly flattened against him. "Are you certain it was only a dream?"

Bartholomew kissed her. "It was too fantastic for reality."

She wrapped her arms about his neck and drew him down for another kiss. "Then perhaps I had better love you again so you can learn the difference between dreams and reality."

The mere thought had him quickening with a resilience he hadn't known since adolescence. Ariah felt the movement against her thigh and reached for him. Bartholomew closed his eyes and surrendered to her ministrations. While she stroked and caressed, he found a breast and teased it until she squirmed against him, trying to bring him into her.

"Relax, nymph, there are easier ways."

He rolled onto his back, taking her with him. His hands lifted her so she might straddle him.

"Now," he whispered huskily.

Ariah moaned on an exhaled breath as she slid down over him. There was soreness, but it was nothing compared to the accompanying ecstasy. She drew her legs alongside him and sat up fully, ensuring a deep fit.

Tight, wet heat enclosed Bartholomew. The only way possible to enhance the rapture was to take her firm breasts into his big hands, draw her down and parade kisses over them. As he suckled a swollen nipple, she sighed.

"Oh, I like this." She moved and smiled at the groan of pleasure she elicited from him. "I like having this kind of power over you."

She eased upward, paused until he murmured against her breast with impatience, then lowered herself back down. The softness sheathing him pulsed in the same rapid rhythm as his heartbeat. The intensity of the hunger racking his body, as though he hadn't finished making love to her only an hour ago, shocked him. When he could speak again, he said, "You've had me in your power since the moment I first laid eyes on you, nymph. I fear you always will."

"I thought I was the one under your spell. But this is different. It's physical, rather than emotional."

As if to prove her point she raised up again, until their bodies nearly separated. Before he could make the desperate move necessary to keep them joined, she sank back down, creating a fever of friction that nearly unhinged him. He closed his eyes and gritted his teeth against a guttural moan.

Ariah's voice came to him in a throaty purr. "Yes, I like this very much. I can drag this out as long as I like, torture you until you plead for mercy."

Bartholomew's eyes opened. He was ready to plead now, but what he said was, "Is that so?"

He looked very much the predator in that moment, with his hooded eyes and feral grin. Ariah knew an instant of vulnerability as hands of steel clamped about her waist and he began to move beneath her. In her. She was helpless to stop him, or even slow his pace. Didn't want to. The sensations splintering through her were too intense, the pleasure too great. Her hands clawed at his shoulders as she felt the beginning tremors she knew now would carry her to paradise.

Bartholomew's hands glided up her rib cage to mold her breasts in the hollows of his palms. Her rhythm as she moved with him never faltered. Her eyes were closed, her face tense with concentration. When he flicked her nipples with his thumbs, she moaned. The sound sent hot shivers over his body. Every change of expression on her face was beautiful to him. Her artless enjoyment of their coupling pleased him beyond measure. To see her with her head thrown back, her spine stiff, the nipples of her swollen breasts taut, the tip of a pink tongue barely visible between her luscious lips as she abandoned herself completely to passion's demands, heightened his own pleasure to a level he had not known possible.

When he drew her down and took her breast in his mouth, she gasped. Her thighs tightened around him like a vise, in the spasms of her release clenching and unclenching until he could no longer keep his own response in rein. White hot ecstasy flooded through him as she melted around him, bathing him in liquid heat.

Ariah's frantic movements ceased. Her chin dropped onto her chest. Her fingernails sank into the hard muscle of his upper arms. The woods echoed her primal cry of rapture, a cry that went straight to his heart and filled a portion of the emptiness he had lived with so long.

Then the world spun away as pleasure burst repeatedly inside him, and with a ragged cry that was her name, he was flung across the threshold into Elysium.

Twenty-six

Bartholomew paused outside the lighthouse, dreading the coming interview with Pritchard. He thought of the long day he had spent with Ariah, beachcombing and making love, and smiled. However unpleasant his talk with Pritchard might be, the end result would be well worthwhile if it meant having Ariah as his own for the rest of his life.

Pritchard was putting away the brass-polishing supplies in the storage cupboard when Bartholomew entered.

"Hello, Uncle Bart. I suppose Old Seamus has been spouting omens for foul weather all day. It definitely looks like it's going to blow up a storm." Pritchard glanced out the window at the calm sea and blue skies as he slipped his logbook into a drawer. "Can't gripe about the day, though. It's been sunny and warm."

Bartholomew's eyes hid secret pleasure. "Aye, it was an exceptional day."

"I'll be off then. Everything is in order."

"Are you in a hurry?"

"I thought I'd go into town. Was there something you wanted to speak to me about?"

Bartholomew busied himself storing away the metal tin which held his lunch and then taking out his own logbook, while he contemplated the best way to approach the delicate subject on his mind.

"You've had to go into town more often than usual lately," he said finally. "It must be difficult being away from your new bride all night. I'm surprised Ariah tolerates it."

Seconds ticked by while he waited for his nephew to answer.

"Has she said something about it?" Pritchard's tone was both defensive and wary. "Did she complain? I—"

"No, Ariah said nothing," Bartholomew interrupted, eager to avoid causing more trouble. Doubt suddenly plagued him. Maybe he should have let Ariah handle this, as she had wanted to before he'd insisted it would be better discussed man to man. "I simply wondered how things were going for you. I gathered from the way you talked the day after your wedding that you were having difficulty consummating your marriage."

Pritchard turned red as ripe beach strawberries. He quickly turned away. Bartholomew took a deep breath and plunged on. "This isn't an uncommon problem, Pritchard, and easily resolved, usually in only a few days, as I'm sure you've already found out."

"She wanted time, Uncle Bart." Pritchard's voice was muffled as he stared at his feet. "She said we needed to get to know each other better; then everything would be easier. I've been trying to be patient."

"Is that why you've been seeing a certain young woman in town? To help you be patient with your wife?"

Pritchard whirled, caught a glimpse of his uncle's stern face, and collapsed against the wall, one arm over his face. "God, Uncle Bartholomew, how'd you find out?"

"It's a small town, Pritchard. People talk."

The young man flung out his arms, beseechingly. "I swear I only meant to go once, just to get some experience so I'd know more what I was doing when Ariah was ready to . . ."

Unable to bear the guilt and misery on his nephew's face, and fearful now of how this interview would end, Bartholomew glanced out the window. A formation of cormorants was flying low over the gentle swells of the blue-green ocean. As boys, he and John Upham called them shags. Once, when they'd failed to bag a goose for their supper while they were hunting, they tried to cook one of the big seabirds. Even after twelve hours over a campfire, the meat was still tough and inedible. Like the sponge cake Ariah had baked for supper one Sunday.

"You realize this gives Ariah grounds for annulment," he said softly.

"Please, don't tell her, Uncle Bartholomew. I promise I'll . . ." Pritchard stumbled to a halt when he realized what his uncle would expect him to do. He couldn't give up Nettie. Not yet. "Just don't tell Ariah."

Bartholomew closed his eyes. The knuckles of his big hands gripping the chair back turned white as a puffin's breast. "Are you saying that you still intend to consummate your marriage after all this time? Are you sure marriage with Ariah is what you want?"

"Yes, I . . ." Again Pritchard paused. "She's a lady, Uncle Bartholomew. She's educated and well mannered, the kind of mother I want for my children."

"What about love, Pritchard?" Bartholomew's voice grew cold and hard. "Do you love her?"

"Yes, I-I love her."

Pritchard crossed his fingers behind his back to nullify any bad luck his lie might bring down on him. He wasn't sure what love was, but Ariah was his wife and he wanted her. Surely, making love with her would give him the same feelings for her that he already had for Nettie.

Silently, Bartholomew released his breath. He felt tired. Tired and ill clear to his soul. "I won't tell her, Pritchard. Go on home now."

When Old Seamus showed up at eight bells for what he called the churchyard watch, he found Bartholomew hunched over the desk. Unaware of the older man's arrival, Bartholomew cursed, crumpled up the paper on which he had been writing and tossed it to the floor where it joined several others like it. Thick, blunt fingers raked through long sable hair and his expression was as bleak as the now-cloudy sky.

Seamus tactfully banged the door shut, announcing his presence.

Bartholomew glanced up at him, then at the mantel clock on a shelf above the wooden pegs which held their rain gear. "You're early. Still deny that you love this pile of brick and iron and glass?"

Seamus grunted as he set his lantern on the floor. Smoke from a well-chewed pipe streamed from between yellowed teeth and the strands of a bristling mustache. One gnarled hand caressed the ball-topped newel post of the circular stairway.

"Whore is what she be, blast her purdy hide," he said softly. "Catchin' up yer log, are ye?"

Bartholomew's mouth was a grim slash. "No, a letter."

Without another word, Seamus trudged on up the stairs. Bartholomew sighed and resumed his work. The clock chimed the half-hour. Outside, the beam from the bronze, five-wick lantern switched from white to red, then back to white, conspiring with the clock to taunt him with the hours wasted at his hateful chore.

Seamus shuffled back down the stairs, filling the room with the scent of tobacco. "Brightwork's shipshape," he said, speaking of the gleaming brass gears and fittings Pritchard polished each day.

Bartholomew answered with a disgruntled snort.

"Vexed with the lad, are ye?"

Bartholomew tore his letter into shreds and scattered them on the floor.

Seamus's wise old eyes studied the other man for a moment, then he shook his grizzled head. "Got the weight o' the world on them shoulders o' yourn, haven't ye, lad? Wanta talk 'bout it?"

Bartholomew sat back in his chair and squeezed his eyes shut with a thumb and forefinger. Stress lined his forehead below his mop of dark hair. A button was missing from his shirt. After a moment, he stood, flexed his stiff back, and handed the old man a piece of paper. "Here, read this."

In the silence that followed, the first rain drops peppered the window. When Seamus finished, he handed back the letter with a single word: "Why?"

"It's best."

Seamus yanked the pipe from his mouth and plunked it down in the brass ashtray on the desk with a clunk. "Fer who? You or that loblolly boy up to the house? Clap onto yer mind, man. The lass don't want him, and he dadblamed don't deserve her."

Bartholomew let his mouth curl in a grim smile. "She got to you too, eh?"

"Aw, put it up," the old man growled. "I'm right and ye know it."

"He says he loves her, Seamus. And intimated that he'll do the right thing about the Tibbs girl."

"Money'd no doubt get that flash packet's jaw working good, should ye need 'er words to win the lass a divorce."

Bartholomew sank wearily into his chair. "There's no need to get Nettie to testify against Pritchard. The marriage hasn't even been consummated. Ariah could get an annulment."

"Then heave to, lad. Make off with her on the morrow, while that lubber she's tied to plies his polishin' rag. He'll be napping half the day, anyway, no doubt, since he's gone adrift on the evenin' tide an' won't be back till dawn."

"He went into town?"

"Aye."

Bartholomew swore under his breath, furious that the boy had gone to his doxy in spite of their conversation that afternoon. Perhaps he had gone to end it with Nettie Tibbs. A part of Bartholomew hoped not. Yet it made no difference to the decision he had made this night.

"No matter what he's done, I can't run off with his bride before he's had a chance to make his marriage work," he said.

"Yer brain's cast off fer Fiddlers Green, lad, an' left yer body here to flounder about without it. What if he manages to plug 'er, good an' clean, and the marriage still don't fare well? 'Twill be too late then fer easy measures."

"To do anything else would be less than honorable, and I've

enough on my conscience. Just promise me you'll look after her. She has an uncle who has it in mind to take her to Greece and sell her off to some rich, old duffer. That's why she came here. She's sure the man will give up his scheme once he sees he can't get legal guardianship over her, now that she's married, but it won't hurt to keep an eye out. You know she can't count on Pritchard."

Seamus nodded. "I'll guard 'er like she was me own ship. You gonna be around in case yer needed?"

"Yes. For a while anyway."

Seamus shook his head and picked up his cold pipe. " 'Tis a sad day, lad. A powerful sad day."

Bartholomew watched the old man drag himself up the stairs, looking almost as old as Bartholomew felt. As always, Seamus had perceived the goings-on at the cape with a clear and unbiased eye. He had seen straight into Bartholomew's soul and sensed not only the turmoil there, but the cause as well. But to Bartholomew "sad" seemed too small a word to describe the torment inside him.

It was ten after eight when Ariah looked up from the flower bed beside the front porch to see Seamus coming up the walk from the light. She waved before turning back to the fringe cups she had transplanted from the forest. The stalks of creamy, minuscule flowers rose as pertly above their maplelike leaves as they had at the clearing where Bartholomew and she had made love. The night's rain had done the plants good.

"Good morning," she said, as she dusted off her hands.

The old man stared at her so long she put her hand to her face, wondering if she'd smudged her cheek with garden dirt.

"Ye've a glow 'bout ye this mornin', lass."

"Why, thank you." The unaccustomed compliment surprised her. "The coffee's on the back of the stove. I'll be in to fix your breakfast in a minute. I thought I'd step over and invite Bartholomew to join us."

Seamus frowned. "Got somethin' ye'd best read first."

Puzzled, she followed him into the house. He sat at the kitchen table and fumbled in his pocket while she poured him a cup of coffee.

"What is it, Seamus?"

Though a sober man by nature, his manner today was more gruff than usual. Almost angry. Ariah's heart fluttered with unnamed fear. Something was wrong, something that had to do with Bartholomew. Had Seamus seen them together in the woods yesterday? Color flooded her face at the thought, but she was more concerned about what this gentle old man might be feeling toward the man he obviously saw as the son he'd never had.

Without another word Seamus handed her a sheet of paper and lumbered from the room, taking with him his coffee and the fresh apple fritters she had left on the table for him. Unease ghosted down Ariah's spine as she pondered the folded note. Her name was spelled out on the front in the slanted, spidery script she recognized as Bartholomew's.

Her vision blurred. She blinked moisture from her eyes and tried to dislodge her heart from her throat. Then she took her shawl from its hook and slipped from the house.

Apollo galloped toward her as she headed for the sheltering comfort of the woods. He slowed as he reached her, seeming to sense her mood, and sedately followed her up through the tangled, moss-bedecked hemlocks and spruces. The ground was wet and muddy from the night's rain and she regretted not putting on her rubber overshoes.

Only when she reached the clearing with its strangely naked trees towering overhead did she stop.

In the center, where she and Bartholomew had lain the day before, the false lily of the valley were bruised and bent. Like her heart, she thought. She knelt upon her shawl and tried to smooth the crimped edge of a satin leaf. The breeze carried the briny scent of the sea and the whisper of its roar. Sunshine arrowed through the branches to spotlight her in golden warmth, adding to the sense of peace and solitude in the small glen.

The serenity was welcome, the solitude was not. She keenly felt Bartholomew's absence.

Sighing, she pulled his note from her pocket with trembling fingers. Meticulously, she unfolded the paper and smoothed the creases, as she had tried to do with the leaf. The sight of her name scrawled at the top in his strong masculine hand brought moisture back to her eyes. She brushed it away impatiently and focused on the words.

My dearest Ariah,

I am leaving this missive with Seamus as I know I can trust him to get it to you discreetly. The tide which will return your husband to you this morn, will also carry me away.

Last evening Pritchard assured me that he loves you and wants to make his marriage work, which caused me to wonder how much my presence in your life has interfered with the success of your wedded life. On reflection, I find that I cannot in all good faith, steal his wife from him without allowing him the chance to win her for himself.

Therefore, I am resigning my post as Head Keeper. I apologize most heartily for leaving Seamus and Pritchard to take care of matters alone until a replacement can arrive.

I can almost taste your tears. Believe me, sweet nymph, I go not from you unscathed, for mine own heart has shattered into a thousand pieces. But I know that, once your tears have dried and you have had time to reflect upon my decision, you will understand and deem my actions not only fair, but necessary.

Yours Always,
Bartholomew

Ariah crumpled the letter in her fist and pressed it to her heart. He had abandoned her. How could he go off and leave her like this? Had he lied when he'd said he loved her? Now that he had finally sated himself inside her body, had he tired of her already?

"Damn you, Bartholomew Noon," she raged at the empty sky. "I won't let you do this to me. I won't let you . . ."

But he already had.

Did Seamus know where Bartholomew had gone? Instinct told her that even if he did, he wouldn't tell her. The old sailor would point out that, had Bartholomew wanted her to know, he would have told her in the letter. She could go to his brother. Even if Bartholomew wasn't there, surely Calvin would know where to find him.

When Pritchard had come home this morning, smelling of whiskey as he always did after a night in town, he must have seen Bartholomew at Barnagat, waiting for the boat. Unless Bartholomew had stayed out of sight in the trees until Pritchard left for home.

How clever of Bartholomew to sneak away in the night, telling only an old man as closemouthed as a clam.

"It's not fair, Bartholomew," she wailed, unaware of the tears coursing down her cheeks. "It's not fair."

Summoned by her ragged cry, Apollo came from the forest where he'd been sniffing out a hare. Whining, he licked the salty moisture from her cheek. Ariah wrapped her arms around the warm comfort of his furry body and wept. After a long while, she wiped her face on her sleeve and read the letter once more. Though her tears were now dry, she still didn't understand. Neither did she "deem" his actions "fair" or "necessary."

"Necessary." What a vile word. Worse even than "fair."

She lay back and stared at the sky, feeling Apollo's warmth and wishing the dog curled up next to her were Bartholomew. How would she live without him?

With her eyes closed she stretched out her arms until the cool satin of lily of the valley leaves kissed her fingers and sent their fragrance wafting to her nose. Tears ran unheeded down her temples while she relived the precious hours she had spent there with Bartholomew only the day before.

She ran her tongue over her lips and felt his kiss. His gentle hands stripped her bare and her body tingled at the remembered ardor in his gaze as he looked at her. Her mouth spread in a wan smile as she envisioned him standing before her again in all his naked, masculine splendor, so strong and proud and powerful.

Like his brother the eagle.

He had trapped her in the talons of his heart, ravaged her soul with his love. Now he was gone, leaving her broken and incomplete. Didn't he know he was taking her heart with him?

Half-blinded by her tears, Ariah leaped to her feet and ran down the trail, filled with a sudden need for action. Her feet slid on the slick mud, dumping her on her bottom in the muck, but she picked herself up and kept going. Behind her Apollo was barking. She had started down a steep grade when she glanced over her shoulder to see him racing after her.

Suddenly her feet went out from under her. Her body hit the ground with a thud and rolled down the steep slope. Twigs raked her hands as she scrabbled for something to stop her descent. When her sleeve caught, bringing her up short, she thought at last her fall had been checked, but the fabric tore free and she plummeted on down the sheer incline. Pain bolted through her as one knee struck a gnarled root protruding from the ground.

Apollo's wild barking became frenzied. She opened her mouth to cry out to him and tasted moss and dirt.

Then the trail zigzagged and Ariah's tumble came to an abrupt end as she slammed into a moss-encrusted log. Apollo slid to a stop beside her, whining and nosing her inert body. Slowly, she sat up. Aside from scrapes and bruises, she was unharmed. Bracing herself with a hand on the dog's strong back, she limped the rest of the way down until she stood on the bluff above the beach and the crashing, frothing sea filled her gaze, its wild, rumbling voice calling out to her.

* * *

Nestled in the gentle cavity between two thick roots of a massive uprooted Sitka stump, Bartholomew leaned back and gave himself up to the sights and sounds of the sea. The bleached wood cradled him like the arms of a chair, sheltering him from the brisk wind. Gulls wheeled overhead, their shrill screams sounding like children's one moment, wailing women's the next. Beyond the breakers a small fishing craft drifted south toward Pyramid Rock.

The day of the shipwreck, when Pritchard first told him he was marrying a young woman he had never met, seemed long ago now. So much had happened since then. Bartholemew no longer felt himself the same person who began that trip into Portland with a crateful of frightened pheasants and an empty soul.

Ariah had filled him with her beauty and generosity. She had given him back his will to live.

He hungered for her with an intensity that shocked him. In all the weeks he had forced himself to stay away from her, to remind himself over and over that she could never be his, he had thought it impossible to want anything more than he wanted her. But that was before he had sunk himself into her warm welcoming body and learned what joy truly was. When, for the first time in his life, he learned how it felt to be fulfilled, complete, whole.

Walking away from Ariah in the middle of the night had been the hardest thing he had ever done. For an hour he had stared at her darkened window, willing her to awaken and look outside, knowing he could never tell her good-bye if he had to do it gazing into those incredible blue eyes.

Forget-me-not eyes.

Bartholomew's throat tightened. If only he *could* forget her. And yet, even if that were possible, he would not choose to have it so. He was more a man now than before she came into his life. Through her eyes he had seen his weaknesses and his strengths. He no longer hated the part of him that had chosen to do right by Hester. Nor did he hate Hester.

Yesterday he had allowed his need for Ariah to convince him

that Pritchard's infidelity negated his wife's need to be loyal in return. He had told himself that they could make love with impunity. He had been wrong.

Pritchard had destroyed all his rationalizations with three small words: I love her.

The boy's transgressions, no matter how heinous, failed to justify Bartholomew in casting aside his own integrity, his own honor. Or to cause Ariah to violate hers.

"God forgive me," he murmured, and the sea murmured back.

He closed his eyes, straining to hear redemption in that soft rhythmic whisper. All he heard was the barking of a dog.

Bartholomew's head jerked up. Far down the beach where the trail began, two small figures were emerging onto the strand, one gamboling about the other on four sturdy legs, his companion stumbling toward the sea in a muddy, tattered dress.

Ariah!

Bartholomew's heart stilled. His soul soaked up the sight of her the way hot sand swallows water. This was what he had hoped for, what had kept him from leaving; a last secret glimpse. He drank it in hungrily, his heart surging, pulse racing, until finally it sank in that she was limping.

The sand on which she walked was not the loose sort one sank into, making walking awkward. It was smooth and hard with only a little give in it; it could not account for her stumbling gait. Without thinking, Bartholomew moved away from the enormous stump and stepped toward her. Three hundred yards of empty beach were all that separated them. He could reach her in a few short minutes.

Something halted him. Something forbidding in her appearance. Her dress was torn and covered with mud. A ripped sleeve fluttered in the wind. Loose, disheveled hair lashed at her face like silk ribbons. She reached the line that separated dry sand from wet and sank to the ground. Shallow water, marbled and edged with foam, rolled toward her invitingly. The dog, seeming to realize she was in no mood to play, sat down beside her. Together, they stared out to sea looking lonely and forlorn.

No words were necessary to tell him that Seamus had given her his letter, that it was his abandonment of her that had brought her to the state he saw her in now. She was suffering, because of him. He took another step toward her and stopped.

What good could possibly come from going to her now? He could never leave then. And if he stayed . . . ? To keep his hands from her would be impossible. To sleep alone while she shared the bed of her husband, would be intolerable. Torn between abiding by his heart and breaking it, Bartholomew stood there doing nothing, his hands clenched in helplessness, his throat aching from suppressing cries clamoring to burst free.

Ariah rose onto her knees. She brought her fists to her heart, her head fell back and she cried, "Bartholomew!"

Never had he heard a more eerie and soul-shattering sound. It drove with crucifying cruelty deep inside his being.

"Bartholo-mewww . . ."

Moisture clouded his vision, but he could still see Apollo pacing about Ariah where she sat on her heels, her head on her knees, her hair trailing in the wet sand. Could still hear the dog whimpering, still hear Ariah's sobs, soft and ragged like torn silk.

He had to go to her.

No, Bartholomew. You've done enough damage.

Ariah was hugging the dog now, letting his long, shaggy fur absorb her pain, the way Bartholomew wished *he* could.

She needs me.

Leave her be. She's young, she'll forget you and go on with her life.

What about me? What will my life be without her? Don't my needs count?

There was no answer.

Before he could move from the spot where guilt and agony held him, Ariah came to her feet. She gazed out to sea for a long moment. Then she turned and, with the dog beside her, limped to the path that would take her home, and out of Bartholomew's life forever.

"No." With a hand lifted as if to stop her, he moved forward.

His answer came then. His needs did not count, not when they interfered with hers. He had to do what was right. He had to let her go.

His hand fell. Like the shadow of the giant tree stump in which he had sat, he remained frozen, watching her walk out of his life, while his heart crumbled into pieces.

Twenty-seven

Ariah opened the door to the pheasant pen and stepped inside. "What are you doing here?"

Pritchard turned to look at her. In his hand he held a bucket of feed. "Good morning. Seamus said Uncle Bart wanted me to take care of his pheasants for a while. Do you know what's going on? I can't believe Uncle Bart would simply up and resign like this."

Ariah glanced away, afraid her husband would see the pain in her eyes and guess its cause. That Bartholomew had asked Pritchard to see to the pheasants instead of her deepened her agony. She felt as though a knife had been slipped between her ribs, straight into her heart.

"Give me the bucket, Pritchard, I'll take care of this. You'd better get to the light."

"Gladly." He handed over the feed. "I don't know how you can stand it in here. It stinks, and I'm always waiting for those darn birds to swoop down on me."

"They spend most of their time on the ground, Pritchard, so they aren't likely to 'swoop down' on anybody."

"Swoop up, then. Will you be bringing my lunch?"

"Don't I always?"

He looked at her askance. "Sorry, I didn't mean to upset you."

Ariah sighed. "No, I'm sorry. I seem to be a bit edgy today for some reason."

Sensing that he had the advantage for the moment, he bent and kissed her full on the lips. She tasted like marmalade.

"Ummm, you taste good enough to eat. I missed you last night. Why did you go to bed so early and lock the door?"

Ariah moved out of his embrace and began to scatter the feed. "I wasn't feeling well. It . . . it's my woman's time. You know . . ."

"Oh." Disappointment washed over him. He had hoped to make tonight the big night when their marriage would become real at last. Besides, after being with Nettie, it took days for his hunger for sex to diminish, and now that Uncle Bart was gone, it would be impossible to get into town again until a replacement arrived.

"Does that mean you'll be wanting to sleep alone until it's over?" he asked.

"I think it would be more pleasant for both of us."

He pouted like a child denied his favorite toy. "All right. I'll see you later when you bring lunch."

Ariah didn't bother to watch him go. Her vision had blurred with unwanted moisture. Was this how it would be the rest of her life? Making excuses, lying; to avoid intimacy with her own husband? She wasn't certain which she dreaded more, a lifetime with Pritchard or being found by Uncle Xenos. The only thing certain was that neither could be as bad as losing Bartholomew.

All night she had lain awake pondering how to get word to him that she would leave Pritchard. She even wrote a letter to be posted to his brother's house at the first chance. But there would be no opportunity until the next time they needed supplies, which was a week away. Unless she took it to the post office at Barnagat herself. It wasn't much farther than when she went to the beach; she could do it. And that way, neither Pritchard nor Seamus would know about it.

Pritchard kept his head down as he walked to the light. The shadows of half a dozen ducks crossed the boardwalk in front of him, colliding with his own shadow, but he didn't look up. There were always birds flying around. Loons, pinheads, grebes, murres, herons, gulls. Nuisances. Extra work due to the messes they left on the tower. More than once, seeing the reflection of the sky in the gleaming glass, one had smashed into the panes. Then, he not only had to clean up the carnage, he also had to replace the broken glass.

With Uncle Bart gone, Pritchard would have to work longer hours. It wasn't fair. Losing Aunt Hester must have scrambled the man's brains. Pritchard couldn't remember him ever being so selfish and inconsiderate. The Tillamook Kings would likely replace Pritchard if he couldn't get to the practice sessions and games. The mere thought made him damned angry.

Along with losing his place on the team, he would lose his excuse for going into town to see Nettie. That sure wouldn't make her any happier. Matters had been bad enough since he'd told her his marriage was consummated now and could no longer be annulled. He'd had to talk long and hard to get her to accept the new situation, what with her being so sure there was a baby coming and all.

At first he hadn't actually believed in the baby. It wasn't so much that he thought she was lying, as that he didn't reckon she could know so soon. But after his last visit, he had to figure she was right. She was vomiting into the chamber pot when he arrived, and he remembered Stuffy complaining how his wife did the same when she was carrying their boy. Pritchard had wanted to turn right around and leave, but Nettie begged him to stay. After a while she assured him she was feeling better and even began stroking him through his trousers.

"It's mostly smells what make me puke, not sex," she'd said when he'd objected.

After that, he didn't stop her caressing hands; they felt too good. But he did have something on his mind he needed to get off before he could really concentrate on the pleasure she was giving him. "Honey, are you sure . . . ? I mean, is there any chance this baby might, well, might not be mine?"

"Prit, how can you ask that?" Her face puckered up like she was going to blubber worse than a sou'wester. "I told you when you first come here that I didn't have no reg'lar fella. Once I met you, I never wanted no one else. Don't you believe me?"

He put his arms around her and drew her to him.

"Sure, honey, sure. I just had to make sure, is all. Don't cry. You know what it does to me when you start crying."

He moved her hand back to his groin. "See, your big sugar stick is going soft already."

"I can fix that." She opened his pants and freed him from his underwear. "Long as I know you still love me, I can show you there ain't nobody fer me but you." Then she lowered her head and began to prove her words.

"Oh, God, Nettie. I do love you, I truly do."

Afterward, at the game, she had screamed every time he appeared on the field. It had filled him with pride, yet he'd worried that she would lose the baby if she kept jumping up and down like that.

Since that night, he found himself thinking about the baby a lot. In little more than half a dozen months he would have a son. A thrill sang up his spine at the thought. Unless things changed, however, it would be a bastard he would be unable to claim, and that made him feel low.

Pritchard reached the wooden stairs to the lower level of the bluff where the light sat, and skipped down them, slipping slightly on moisture left behind by the night air.

The way things were going with Ariah, he feared he would never have any legal children. Somehow, when she was over her "woman's time," he would have to find a way to get her to let him make love to her, once and for all.

Maybe he should take her to another game. She hadn't enjoyed the one he'd taken her to in Astoria some weeks past, but it had rained and they'd had only an umbrella to keep the water off. Besides, the game had been a shutout so it hadn't been very exciting. She'd enjoy the next one a lot more.

The irritating thing was that they wouldn't be able to go anywhere until a replacement for Uncle Bart arrived. Of all the lousy times for his wife to be indisposed—on top of not being able to see Nettie. Damn Uncle Bart!

"Bartholomew, what brings ya in?" Max Hennifee wiped non-existent stains from the bar with a wet rag and smiled at his newest customer of the day. "Other than the mornin' tide, that is," he added in the way of a joke.

Bartholomew leaned an elbow on the polished mahogany and rested a foot on the brass footrail. As usual, Max's bony wrists were hanging out the bottoms of his sleeves. The man was so tall and skinny, there wasn't a shirt he could afford that had sleeves long enough.

"It's a long story, Max. Got any coffee?"

Max set a heavy stoneware mug of steaming liquid in front of him and shoved back the nickel he'd laid down.

"Best keep that nickel if this is all the business you're getting these days," Bartholomew said, glancing around.

Max stroked the long, waxed spikes of his mustache. "Well, hell, it's allus this way at nine of a mornin'. Give 'er an hour; reg'lars'll start showin' up then. Meantime, whyn't we sit down? Ya got the look of a man what needs to sweep the dust outta his mind."

They carried their coffee over to a corner table. Outside, Big Charlie was readying the *Henrietta II* for a trip to Bay City. The crew members were haranguing Charlie, saying that his latest female conquest was not only over the hill, but through the valley and halfway up the hill beyond.

"Goldurnit, you bilge-breathed bits o' barnacle shit, how in hell old do you think I am?" Big Charlie yelled. "You oughta carve my likeness in whalebone, 'stead o' hecklin' me. Ain't ever' man my age can still get it up, you know."

Max Hennifee chuckled. "Ol' Charlie reminds me o' that nephew o' yourn, Bartholomew. Why is it men never 'preciate what they got at home?"

Bartholomew sipped his coffee and said nothing.

"Dang it, Bartholomew, shouldn't o' said that, knowin' what it was ya lived with so long."

With a shrug, Bartholomew passed the comment off, as well as the unintended offense. When he still said nothing, Max eyed him speculatively.

"Run out on yer job, din't ya?"

Bartholomew's mouth stretched in a thin smile. "Have you taken to reading minds, Max?"

"Enough to know what yer pining for cain't be found in no graveyard, on account o' she's still alive and kickin'."

Bartholomew looked up in surprise at the gaunt, shabbily clothed man sitting across from him. The wisdom and insight of Max Hennifee never ceased to amaze him. "What makes you think that, Max?"

"Seen the way ya looked at 'er at Eastertime. Like she was ever'thin' ya ever wanted to eat or drink or own or hold dear to yer heart, all rolled up in one pretty package."

There was a slight increase in the sag of Bartholomew's shoulders. What had happened to the veneer of cool indifference he had worked so long to develop in order to hide his emotions?

Ariah. She was what had happened. The mere thought of her had blood pumping through his veins and his heart singing. His love for her was too strong to hide. The thought didn't make him feel very hopeful for his chances of living happily without her.

"Run out on 'er, too, haven't ya?" Max said.

"She belongs to Pritchard, Max. My presence there was interfering with their marriage."

"Why you suppose that be, Bartholomew?"

"What are you getting at?"

Max fetched the coffeepot. He refilled their mugs, set the battered old pot on the table and resumed his seat. Outside, the *Henrietta II* was steaming up the slough toward the bay, leaving wakes in the water behind, and a growing silence. A mongrel stuck its nose through the open doorway and gave a hungry whine. Max stomped his boot on the plank floor and waved a long arm. "Get, you ol' fleabag." The mutt vanished.

As if the long moment of quiet hadn't interrupted their conversation, Max said, "Seen the way she looked at ya, too, Bartholomew. If her marriage weren't goin' good, 'twas on account o' her feelings fer ya. Ya wanna call that interfering, I won't argy with ya, but what makes you think leavin' like ya done is gonna wash them feelings outta her, easy as rinsing suds from a dish?"

A customer sauntered in, giving Bartholomew an excuse to avoid answering. Max fetched the man a beer and swapped a few words with him before returning to his friend.

"Point I be tryin' to make, Bartholomew, is yer being there or somewheres else ain't likely to make a hoot 'n' a holler's difference to what's inside that gel's heart. Did ya love yer mother any less oncet she was in the ground? Hell no. Absence makes the heart grow fonder; that's how the saying goes, Bartholomew. Not t'other way around."

"That may be, Max, but the only way I could have stayed on there was to move her out of Pritchard's house and into mine. I couldn't do that to him. Say what you want, but the boy is still my nephew, and he never intentionally hurt anyone in his life."

"What's it gonna do to 'riah once she finds out what 'er husband's a-doin' behind 'er back? Don't know if you kin call that sort o' hurt intentional or not. But even if she don't care a fig 'bout Pritchard, 'er pride's gonna take a bruisin' from it, ya can count on that."

Bartholomew sighed. Max was right, as usual.

"At least that's one thing my leaving will accomplish," he said a bit testily. "Until the Lighthouse Board can get a replacement here, Pritchard's trips into town have come to an end. Maybe he and Ariah will grow closer then, and Pritchard will no longer need to come to town for his . . ."

He couldn't finish. His insides spasmed with pain at the thought of Pritchard and Ariah together that way. Suddenly restless, he walked to the doorway to fill his lungs with clean, seasalty river air. The stench of fresh dog feces filled his nostrils instead. Turning back inside, he asked, "When's the next steamer due in?"

"Twelve noon from Astoria. One-thirty from Portland. Expectin' yer replacement this soon?"

"Not really."

He had sent Biggs into town yesterday morning with a wire for the Lighthouse Board, and although he wished they could take action this fast, he knew better than to expect it. Only if they happened to have a man already free and handy, could they have gotten him on this morning's steamer, and that was about as likely as Pritchard being named the Father of Altruism.

Maybe next year they'd be able to take care of such matters over the telephone and would see results a great deal sooner. But Tillamook didn't have phone service yet. Or electricity. It was probably what city folks would call a one-horse town, but that suited Bartholomew fine. He had never cared for big cities.

Over the next few days, he tried to keep himself occupied helping Cal around the dairy. There was always plenty of work for another pair of hands, and he liked to feel he was paying for his room and board. But as morning rolled sluggishly toward noon, with the predictability of the tides, he inevitably found himself standing somewhere, a shovel or a harness or a milk can in his hand, staring off toward town. At that point, Cal would take the shovel away from him and tell him to ride into Tillamook to meet the boat from Astoria or the stage from Yamhill.

A letter had arrived from Ariah three days after he'd left the station. Bartholomew had stared at it a long time before he'd torn it into tiny pieces, unopened. She would have pleaded with him to return or to take her away with him, and he didn't trust himself to resist. He knew she believed with all her heart that she loved him, but she was young, and he had all but seduced her before she'd even met Pritchard, which meant the boy hadn't had a fair chance. Bartholomew prayed everything would turn out for the best, eventually. Still, he worried whether or not he was doing the right thing.

All the distance in the world could not stop him from missing Ariah. He thought about her every waking moment, dreamed of her at night. He caught himself listening for the sound of her voice, and sniffing the wind like a hound to detect her scent. The only way to survive giving her up was to go somewhere new, where he wouldn't be reminded of her.

"Bartholomew."

"What?" He looked up from the breakfast table into Amy Goodman's worried face.

"That's the creamer you're drinking out of," she said, nodding to the container he held to his lips.

He flushed with embarrassment. She took the creamer and placed it back on the table. Jacob and Robert snickered, but Mrs. Goodman remained sober.

"Yesterday, right there in the washroom, you were trying to shave with a butter knife," she said. "Now, you aren't a stupid man, Bartholomew. What is it has you so all-fired preoccupied that you can't tell cream from coffee?"

"He's pining," said Jacob.

Robert jabbed his brother in the ribs and they giggled.

From the head of the table, Calvin sent his sons a stern look of disapproval. "You boys appear to have had enough breakfast. Why don't you go fix that fence the bull kicked in?"

"Aw, Pa, that old bull'll rip us to pieces if we go near that field, same way he did Grandpa. You know he hates us."

"Only because you tease him half to death anytime he's penned up. Maybe by next year when we get a new bull, you'll have learned to leave well enough alone. Now, get."

After the boys were gone, Calvin turned his compelling gaze on Bartholomew.

Of all Martha Noon's sons, Calvin most resembled their pa. Considering that, Bartholomew often wondered how he could love Cal so much. Their father had been a hard man who believed only discipline kept a man on the straight and narrow. And the way to discipline for his boys lay in the razor strap, which he applied freely and with vigor. Bartholemew being the youngest and the last of her children, Martha had tried to protect him. But the more she'd sheltered and petted the boy, the more liberal Jacob had become with the strap, so that Bartholomew came to know its sting far more intimately than had his brothers.

Though Cal had the look of their father, his temper was entirely different. Cal was a good man, kindhearted and gentle spoken. So, out of respect, Bartholomew now remained quiet under the man's piercing scrutiny.

"You're a fool, little brother," Cal said at last. "Why don't you go back and get her? She loves you. You know it, I know it, everybody knows it. Except that dolt she married."

"She's his wife. I have no right to interfere."

"You have no right deciding what she should or shouldn't do, but that's exactly what you're doing. Pa beat his code of honor into you so thoroughly that now you're forcing people around you to abide by the same rules that trapped you in a cold, loveless marriage for over seven years. Is that what you want for Ariah?"

Bartholomew raked both hands through his dark curls. His voice was ragged and tortured. "Dammit, Cal, I don't know what I want anymore. I don't know what's right. I only know I didn't have the heart to tell Pritchard I was taking the woman he loved away from him."

Cal shook his head in disgust. "That boy doesn't know the difference between love and what satisfies the itch in his crotch. I never thought to see the day you refused to fight for what you wanted."

"You saw that day a long time ago, Cal," Bartholomew said wearily. "Two days after I married Hester, when she barred me from her room and I let her."

To Ariah, the days had never moved so slowly. With Bartholomew gone, there was more work than ever. Enough to keep her busy from sunup to sundown, with not a moment in between for pining over him. Yet he was never off her mind. She fed the pheasants and wondered where he was. She sank her arms to the elbow in hot sudsy water and thought how feverish his touch made her body. She bottled sweet English peas and remembered his kisses. She yanked weeds from tidy rows of snap beans, carrots and onions, and cursed him for ignoring her letter.

When she was able to break away from the station, she escaped to the woods or the beach, accompanied only by Apollo. Her journal bulged with bird feathers and pressed flowers. A jar of water holding agates and red and green jasper sat on a window sill where sunlight displayed their gleaming colors and translucency. Japanese glass floats lined another sill.

"Holy Hector, Ariah," Pritchard complained, "why in hell do you have to keep dragging in all this junk? It's getting sand in everything."

"As long as you don't find sand in your food, your bed or your underpants, I don't think you've much to complain of," she retorted.

"Except that pretty soon we won't have room left to move around in," he said, unchastened by her words. "At least throw out the snail shells. I can't imagine why on earth you'd want them."

She looked at the limpets that reminded her of tiny Chinese hats, at the chink, unicorn, whelk, and cockleshells that littered a table, the sand dollars, piddock fossil and water-polished petrified wood set among knickknacks on a shelf, and said nothing, knowing he would never understand the beauty she saw in them.

Yet all the beauty in the world couldn't fill the gap Bartholomew's absence left in her heart. She lived for only one thing; the arrival of his replacement. As long as Pritchard and Seamus were shorthanded, she couldn't abandon them, but the moment they no longer had to work extra hours and could see to their own meals and laundry, she would pack her bags, endure the horror of the boat ride to Tillamook and track down Bartholomew. Then, no matter what he said, she would never allow him to leave her again.

Twenty-eight

From his favorite corner table at the Pickled Eye Saloon, Bartholomew watched passengers from Astoria disembark from the small steamer which had just docked. He nodded to Pete Maddux, Ed Fischbocker and Ed's wife, who waved greetings to him through the window. Another day he might have invited the men in for a drink, but he was aware of the curiosity about his resigning his post and in no mood to answer questions.

Max Hennifee appeared at Bartholomew's side. "See anyone what looks to be yer replacement?"

"Not yet."

Bartholomew tipped back his head and guzzled the last ounce of ale in his glass. It was his third and had done little more than the others to alleviate the sense of doom with which he had awakened that morning. Without a word, Max picked up the empty glass and headed back to the bar.

For once, Bartholomew knew the cause of his premonition of death and destruction. A week had passed since he'd wired the Lighthouse Board for a replacement. The man would be arriving any day now. Which meant Bartholomew was about to run out of excuses for hanging around Tillamook, doing nothing but drinking coffee—or ale as it was today—and watching the comings and goings of townspeople and strangers.

Never would he admit that what he had truly been watching and praying for, was old man Biggs rowing up to the dock with Ariah and her luggage in tow. Common sense argued that it was a foolish long shot, yet love had never been reasonable and

Bartholomew was no longer certain he wanted to be. The truth he had been trying to drown this day at Hennifee's saloon was that he had lost his gamble. She was not coming. To him that was a sort of death; the death of hope and of dreams.

Truth was a far more bitter brew than what Max served him. He took the refilled glass and drank deeply. If luck was with him, he'd be drunk enough by bedtime to sleep through the night without dreams haunted by the sight, smell, taste and feel of Ariah.

A small wiry man stepped off the steamer. Bartholomew studied him as the stranger looked about. A satchel sat at the man's feet. He wore dark, sensible clothing, with a cap set forward on his forehead, a bit jauntily to one side as if daring a man to knock it straight. His dark-tanned skin, crinkled about the squinted eyes and the hard mouth, gave him the look of a seaman.

For a moment, Bartholomew felt frozen. Cold dread sat on him, like sixty-five tons of killer whale. He shook off the weight of his reluctance and rose to his feet. The time to finally, irrevocably, give up his position as Head Keeper of the Cape Meares Lighthouse had come.

Before he reached the door, the wiry stranger stepped inside. The man looked about, then headed for the bar where Max waited. Bartholomew hovered nearby while the man ordered a mug of locally brewed ale.

"The Cape Meares Lighthouse, where is it from here?" the stranger asked in a heavy accent.

Hennifee glanced at Bartholomew over the man's shoulder. "West as far as ye can go, then south a couple o' miles."

"There is a road goes there?"

"Naw, gotta get Big Charlie to run ye 'cross the bay on the *Henrietta* to Barnagat. 'Tis a trail from there on, up over the mountain to the light."

The man quaffed his ale in one long gulp and clanked the mug back on the bar. He fished inside his shirt for his monkey bag, came up with a handful of change and carefully counted out the correct amount. A sailor from a foreign port, Bartholomew decided. One who knows that local brews will be cheaper, if not better tasting. One who'd been in the country long enough to understand its money system, not long enough to lose the flavor of his native tongue.

"Thank you, my friend. Tell me, can you now, where to locate this Big Charlie?"

Again Max Hennifee's gaze met Bartholomew's. Bartholomew stepped up to the bar next to the stranger.

"Right outside where you got off the steamer," he said, holding out his hand. "I'm Bartholomew Noon, the keeper you'll be replacing at the light. Welcome to Tillamook."

As if his spoon were a shovel, Seamus scooped hot mush into his mouth, smacking his lips between bites. "Eat up, lass." He pointed with his chin to her untouched bowl while he soaked up the last of his breakfast with a chunk of bread.

"I'm not hungry."

Seamus grunted disapprovingly. He'd not seen her eat more than a few bites since Bartholomew left. Indigo half-moons underlined her eyes, and her cheeks had begun to appear hollow. "Go on an' fill yer gullet, lass. Ye may need yer strength 'fore the night's o'er."

"Why do you say that?"

"Bad storm a-comin'."

Ariah no longer smiled indulgently at the old sailor's predictions; the man had an uncanny knack for reading weather signs.

That afternoon, when she went out onto the front porch to shake the rug from the vestibule, she saw Seamus standing on the boardwalk, flanked by his goats, all of them staring out to sea. Silhouetted like that against a dull, cloudy sky and the gray sea, nary a line between to mark the horizon, he created an image that made Ariah's fingers itch for paints and canvas, though she had never painted in her life. The bent old man in his baggy, short-waisted trousers and bright red galluses, his sleeves rolled high to expose tan, wiry arms, gave Ariah a sense of pensiveness and longing.

He had sailed the Pacific ocean half his life, and before that, other more exotic waters. He had witnessed strange lands and strange peoples, savored foreign flavors and wondrously exotic scents. Though he had never married, his hands, when young, had no doubt explored dark and forbidden feminine textures. It tantalized her to think of the tales those bewhiskered lips could tell. Yet he was stingy with his words. Perhaps he feared that the treasures buried in the calm harbor of his memory would lose their preciousness once shared. If she could paint the scene before her, Ariah decided she would call it *Remembering*.

Ariah went back inside, leaving the old sailor to decipher the cryptic messages of wind and cloud. She was late with Pritchard's supper. His eight-hour watch had been extended to twelve hours, ending at eight P.M. when Seamus took over. After preparing a tray, she hurried toward the light, Apollo dogging her heels until he spotted a rabbit and bounded after it.

Her husband was on the top level, polishing prisms, when she found him. "Pritchard, your supper is downstairs."

"Good, I'm famished." He dropped his polishing cloth and greeted her with a kiss, then scampered down the stairs, leaving Ariah alone to stare out the wall of windows at the sea below.

Row upon row of huge waves were rolling in to shore. As each wave crested, the wind kicked the frothing water into towering spumes of seaspray. Ariah watched the waves crash wildly into Hat and Sea Lion's Head rocks, until she could almost feel the cool spray on her face and taste the salt. The sky had grown dark and ominous. Seamus's prediction of a bad storm was going to come true.

Perhaps it explained the restlessness that had come over her the last few days. She resisted the urge to race down to the beach where she could more fully experience the storm's fury, knowing it would be foolish. The trail was difficult to hike in dry weather; in wet, it was often impossible. More so after dark. Instead, she allowed herself to drift into the dream world of her day on the beach with Bartholomew, of their lovemaking in the woods. So absorbed was she in her thoughts that she was unaware of her husband's return, until he encircled her with his arms and drew her back against him.

"Um, you always smell so good." Pritchard nuzzled her neck. "Are you through yet with . . . ?" He halted and tried again. "Tonight . . . Can I stay with you? Please? I want you so, Ariah. Surely your woman's time is over by now."

Ariah's heart sank. She had put him off for a week on the phony excuse. If she allowed him the intimacy he sought, he would soon know she had been lying. Worse, he would also know she wasn't the virgin she had been on their wedding night. Yet she could think of no way to deny him. Nor, except for her own reluctance, did there seem any reason to. The fact that Bartholomew had not answered her letters told her he no longer wanted her. Without him in her life, it seemed unimportant what happened to her.

Closing her eyes, and trying to ignore the hardness of her husband's arousal pressing into her bottom, she said, "Yes, Pritchard. I believe it is time we truly began this marriage."

Panic fluttered inside her the moment the words were out. She did not love this man. It was wrong for her to stay with him, wrong to fool him into believing their marriage might be a happy one. But, if she left him, where would she go? Who would protect her when Uncle Xenos caught up with her? And what if she was carrying Bartholomew's child? What would she do then? Unmarried and alone in a strange city somewhere, with no one to turn to, what would become of her?

Pritchard was nibbling on her ear with more finesse than she would have thought him capable of. One hand had found her breast and was kneading it rhythmically. Already his breathing had become ragged. She tried to push away from him. "Please, Pritchard, wait until tonight. Someone might see us."

"Who?" he breathed into her ear. "Seamus will be asleep by now and Uncle Bart is gone. Who else is there to see?"

His hands moved to the buttons on her dress. Shocked by the

intensity of his ardor after all the weeks when the attention he gave her was sporadic, and sometimes more brotherly than romantic, she jerked herself free and pivoted to face him, but the words she had been about to say died in her mouth. Two men were approaching the light; Seamus and a man Ariah had never seen before.

"Bartholomew's replacement," she murmured.

"Holy Hector! You're right, it must be Uncle Bart's replacement."

Ariah gave a dejected sigh. "He'll want to see his quarters and get settled in. No doubt that's why Seamus brought him down here, to find me."

Pritchard started down the stairs. "Maybe he's just eager to see the light."

The two men had reached the top of the stairs to the lower level by the time Ariah and Pritchard emerged from the tower. The stranger was past his prime, yet still fit. His step as he descended the stairs was brisk and surefooted, compared to old Seamus's slow shuffle.

Conflicting emotions roiled inside Ariah as she watched Bartholomew's replacement come toward her. She could no longer pretend that Bartholomew might return. Yet she would be free now to seek him out, if she dared. Would he greet her with welcome or rejection? As the world closed in on her, hope and despair vied in her mind.

Why did Bartholomew have to leave? This was his world. It was everything he loved: the sea, the woods, his birds. She was the one who should have left. Except that she, too, had come to love this place. The very thought of leaving it was painful, though she would do it in a heartbeat if that would reunite them. Her longing for him was like a living presence that haunted her day and night.

Now this new keeper had come to make everything irrevocable. He would live in Bartholomew's house, sleep in Bartholomew's bed. To Ariah it seemed she was being forced to look inside a casket, not knowing who she would find there, and terrified it would be her own soul staring, open-eyed, back at her, and in Bartholomew's clothes.

" 'Tis a good thing ye arrived when ye did," Seamus was saying as they walked up to the couple waiting outside the lighthouse door. "Sou'wester blowin' in, bad 'un."

Ariah sensed that the man was paying Seamus no mind; his attention seemed to be focused entirely on her. At Seamus's introduction, he pulled his cap from his head but did not smile. His blue eyes were cold as an arctic wind. Stiffening her spine, she held out her hand. "Welcome to Cape Meares, sir. I hope you'll be happy here."

"Thunderation, Bartholomew!" Max Hennifee muttered. " 'Tis beyond my ken that ye'd up an' leave us thisaway."

"Life is short, old friend, and over too soon," Bartholomew replied, undaunted by Max's dismay over his imminent departure. The ticket he had just purchased rustled in his pocket as he raised his glass to drink. The evening steamer from Astoria had arrived ten minutes before. Unless the foul weather scared the captain into waiting out the storm, Bartholomew would hear the call to board for the return trip at any moment now. From Astoria he would take a larger ship to Seattle, then go on to Alaska.

The saloon was far busier tonight than it had been this morning. Fishermen, celebrating the day's catch, lined the bar and overflowed onto the tables. Max moved down the bar, refilling glasses and cracking jokes.

"We might as well see all we can of this world while we're here," Bartholomew said when Max returned, "and enjoy what we can of life."

Cal, standing next to Bartholomew, placed a hand on his brother's shoulder. "I can't argue that, and I doubt Max can either. What we're trying to say"—he slapped that same hand over his own chest—"at least, what I'm trying to say, is that I don't see what the confounded hurry is. Wait a month. Wait a year. What can it possibly hurt?"

Bartholomew shrugged, unwilling to go into the reasons he felt impelled to leave as swiftly as possible. Whether Ariah's marriage to Pritchard had been consummated or not, what he had done with her that day in the woods was still adultery. If he stayed, he knew he would do it again. To expect him to keep away from her when she was only a boat ride away was like asking him to stop breathing. Outside, it was raining, but the sound was barely audible above the wind and the boisterous voices to be heard in the saloon.

"Runnin' sceered is what he's doin', Cal," Max accused.

Cal nodded. "Running from a blue-eyed angel named Ariah. Yeah, I figured that, but I still think he's foolish to go so soon. She's as taken with him as he is with her, if I'm any judge, and I'd bet my whole farm that she comes looking for him before the month is out."

"Leave it alone, Cal." Bartholomew downed the last of his ale and slammed the glass on the bar, irritated by the constant needling. Leaving was difficult enough without them making it worse. "I know what I'm doing."

"Huh! Coulda fooled me."

"Mr. Noon?"

Bartholomew and Calvin turned to the boy standing in the doorway. "Which one do you want?" they asked in unison.

The boy, one of Clyde Tavish's, judging by the carrot hair and beaked nose, studied the smeared ink on the wet telegram he held. "Bartholomew," he announced.

"Here, son." Bartholomew dug into his pocket for a coin which he dropped into the boy's grubby hand.

"What is it?" Cal watched his brother frown as he scanned the few lines that made up the message.

"Doesn't make sense," Bartholomew said.

"What doesn't make sense?"

"This." He thumped the paper with his fingertips. "It's from the Lighthouse Board, apologizing for the delay in getting my replacement here and assuring me that the man will arrive to-morrow morning."

"Well, if that ain't the goldangedest . . ." Max stared at Bartholomew in bewilderment. "If yer replacement's still on his way, then who was the feller ya sent up to the light?"

Bartholomew's eyes glinted like black ice as he frowned. "I don't know. It has to be some kind of mistake."

An older gentlemen, trim but stocky, who had been standing on the other side of Cal, leaned over the bar and spoke to Bartholomew. "Excuse me."

The man was vaguely familiar; something about that generous mouth, Bartholomew thought. Yet he was certain he'd never seen him before. Twin streaks of white marked the man's thinning hair at the temples, but his face was virtually unlined, his mustache dark and full.

"Forgive me, but if I overheard you correctly," the stranger said, "I may have the answer to your question. Once you hear it, perhaps you'll be willing to help me, for I fear that the people at your lighthouse are in grave danger."

The hair at the back of Bartholomew's neck rose. The man's words, coming at the end of a long day filled with the dread that always accompanied his premonitions of disaster, were too timely to be coincidental. Already, adrenaline was pumping into his veins. Fear tautened his muscles and his voice came out sharp and deadly as a skinning knife.

"I don't know who you are, mister, but you've got thirty seconds to spit out what's on your mind."

The stranger did so, quickly and succinctly, in the manner of a man well accustomed to persuading men to his own thinking.

Two hours later, Bartholomew was galloping through the darkness across the Tillamook plains, a small rescue party behind him. Wind drove the rain into his dark face, obscuring his vision and slowing the pace of the horse Cal had lent him. He jabbed his heels into the chestnut bay for more speed, and ground his teeth in frustration. If anything had happened to Ariah, he would never forgive himself for not being there to protect her. Cal was right, his and Ariah's was a love too rare to let slip away. He never should have left her.

He cursed the bad luck that had flung a sou'wester at them tonight of all nights. Again and again he prayed they wouldn't be too late.

Though he was not greatly experienced in horsemanship, his natural affinity for dealing with animals forged a bond between him and the mount struggling to carry him to the woman he loved. Man and horse moved as one, in graceful, efficient harmony. Between his thighs, he could feel the horse's powerful muscles bunching, stretching, reaching, bunching again. The bay staggered slightly as a fierce gust buffeted them. Bartholomew bent lower over its neck to give the wind less bulk to catch and batter.

If not for the storm, he and his party would have landed at Barnagat by now. Bartholomew cursed Big Charlie's faintheartedness in refusing to attempt the boat trip across the bay. Valuable minutes had been wasted in arguing with the man, more in rounding up Dr. Wills, weapons and horses. In this weather, the usual eight-hour trip over the mountain to Netarts and then up the coast to the cape would take double the time. Barring complications. But the storm wasn't expected to let up for two or three days. And he couldn't afford to wait.

The chestnut bay slowed to cross a stream and Bartholomew cursed again. Already the water was rising, which boded ill for the condition of the many streams they had yet to ford. He prayed for the rain to let up, then cursed it for existing at all.

Please, God, keep Ariah safe until I can get there.

The new keeper held Ariah's hand overlong, caressing it with a gnarled thumb. Uncomfortable at the unwonted intimacy, she tried to free herself, but he held fast.

"Your mother, she is in your eyes," he said in a heavy accent.

A chill that had nothing to do with the icy rain skimmed

Ariah's flesh. The one thing she had feared more than any other had happened.

"A pretty one, Demetria, the hope of us all, until that misbegotten English dog shamed her. *Katalavenis?*" He spoke in Greek, then repeated the last in English. "Do you understand, child?"

Stiffening, she said, "I understand."

"Ah!" he exclaimed, pleasured by her use of the Greek language. "At least your whore of a mother did not deny you your native tongue. And you know me, though we have never seen each other before. I am happy. You will restore the family honor, in spite of being a bastard."

"Don't call my mother that. And I am not a bastard," Ariah blurted out, this time in English. "My parents were legally married."

"Not legal!" Xenos shouted. "Not in eye of church."

"The church isn't God, Uncle Xenos," she retorted, wiping the rain from her face. "And neither are you. You've no right to exact vengeance. That is for God to do. Not you."

Seamus had been glancing back and forth between them. Now he said angrily, "Ye lied, man? Ye ain't here to replace the Head Keeper?"

"No, he is here for me," Ariah said. "Pritchard, Seamus, would you leave us alone? My uncle and I have much to discuss."

"Wait a minute, Ariah," Pritchard objected. "This is the first chance I've had to meet any of your kin."

He extended a hand to the small man, oblivious to the dark undercurrents swirling about them. "I'm Pritchard Monteer, Ariah's husband."

Xenos cast him a disdainful glance and ignored the hand. "I am too late?" he asked Ariah. "You are married to this man?"

"Yes, and there's nothing you can do about it, so you may as well give up your vendetta, Uncle Xenos. Go home to Greece. You've done all the damage you can do to my family."

"You marry in Greek Orthodox Church?"

"No, but—"

"Then it is illegal and of no consequence."

"Hey!" Pritchard cut in. "What do you mean by that?"

Xenos ignored the young man. Hatred fired his blue eyes and sculpted his mouth into a sneer. "I return to Greece, yes. But only when I can once again face my *papou,* my grandfather, with pride. This cannot be until Polassis family has retrieved honor stolen so long ago by English dog who got you off my fool sister."

"Papa stole nothing from you," she cried. "He loved *Mana,* and she loved him."

"Love!" Xenos Polassis spat on the ground. "That is what I give for love. You are child, what do you know of love?"

Ariah stiffened. Her brilliant blue eyes, so like his, darkened. "I know more of love than you ever will. Your heart is too empty, too frozen, to feel love, but I have suffered its pain." Tears blurred her vision. She blinked to clear them, her head held high. "And known its ecstasy."

Grinning, Pritchard grabbed her hand. "Ariah, are you saying that you love me?"

She yanked herself free. "Stay out of this, Pritchard. It doesn't concern you."

Hurt and perplexed, Pritchard stared at her. "But you're my wife, who else . . . ?"

Xenos glared at him. "You forget you ever had wife, eh, little man? You find another." He crooked his hand at Ariah, motioning for her to come to him. The look he gave the other two men dared them to interfere. "Come, you go with me."

"No!" She spun out of his reach, moving closer to the edge of the bluff. She could not trust Xenos. He would kill her the minute they were out of sight of the station.

Her skirts billowed in the fierce wind, pressing against her legs so that she had to lean into the gale to keep from being forced backward. The wind whistled shrilly in her ears, seeming to taunt her. The crazy notion of giving in, of letting the wind carry her over the brink to the wild, crashing waves below, coursed through her head.

Xenos started toward her. "You do as I say. No woman defies Xenos Polassis."

"No Greek woman, maybe," Ariah snarled back. "But I am American, and free. I choose my own husband, my own home and," she added, glancing over her shoulder at the sea so far below, "if I am to die today, then I will choose my own way to go."

Xenos raised his hand. Whether he would have struck her or aided the wind by giving her a gentle nudge, she would never know, for Old Seamus stepped forward to grab the man's arm.

"Belay that, lad. Don't like to shove me oar in where it don't belong, but I won't be havin' ye hurt the lassie."

Xenos shook him off with a Greek curse.

"I don't understand," Pritchard protested. "What's going on here?"

" 'Tis clear as sunshine to anybody but a corkbrain," Seamus muttered. "The lassie's uncle here has it in his noggin' to make off with yer wife. It's why she come here in the first place, to hide out. Bartholomew told me 'fore he cut an' run."

Pritchard looked at Ariah. "You came here to hide from your uncle? I'm your husband, Ariah. Why did you tell Uncle Bart and not me?"

Ariah gave an exasperated sigh. "I didn't want to frighten you, Pritchard. Your advertisement for a bride explained that she would be living in a very isolated spot; I hoped Uncle Xenos wouldn't be able to find me here."

All he heard was that she had worried about frightening him. The words struck his most vulnerable spot. Did his cowardice show so plainly that even she had noticed it? She hadn't hesitated to tell Uncle Bart her fears. Anger surged through him. Anger toward his wife for seeing through him so easily. Anger toward his uncle for being the man Pritchard wished he could be, and wasn't. Most of all, anger toward himself.

"I'm sorry, Pritchard. As my only living relative, he could

easily have gotten the courts to assign him as my legal guardian." Her gaze focused guiltily upon her young husband. "I needed a husband, a man who could protect me."

Pritchard straightened and firmed his spine. Whatever her reasons for answering his ad, whatever she thought of his courage, she belonged to him now. For once in his life, he was going to prove that he could act with honor and bravery.

"And that's what you got, a man to protect you." He stepped beside her and faced Xenos. "I'm sorry, sir, but you're not taking my wife anywhere."

A barrage of angry Greek words burst from Xenos. With one hand he snatched at Ariah's arm, with the other he reached inside his coat. When Seamus moved to interfere, Xenos pulled out a gun and whacked the old man on the head. Seamus slumped to the ground, his corncob pipe falling into the mud. Ariah screamed. She tried to go to the old seaman, but Xenos held her back.

"Get away, unless you want the same," Xenos warned Pritchard. "Almost twenty years I have give of my life to restore family honor and appease *Papou,* for not watching my sister closer and letting her shame herself. Many times I go back to Greece in disgrace because I no find Demetria. Now I am old. I deserve to go home, sit in plaza, drink ouzo with friends, dance, watch grandsons grow big. Is right."

Pritchard swallowed hard as he stared at the cold steel barrel of the gun pointed his way. His knees began to shake, but he did not move. "Ariah is my wife, sir. You can't just take her from me."

"You did not marry in church; in God's eyes this is not legal. Now get aside or I shoot."

"Please, do as he says." Ariah tried to nudge her husband away from her, but he was rooted to the ground. The fool would get himself killed, just as her father had.

Rage boiled inside her. Knowing that to spit on a Greek was the worst insult she could offer, she said, "I spit on you, Uncle Xenos. I am your *zonia,* your kinswoman, yet you value your goats more than me. Why should I give up my life to make some old man in Greece happy, and get him off your back for you?"

"*Arketa!* Enough, woman!" he shouted back. "I am elder. To me you give respect."

"Why should I? You hounded my parents and denied my mother her homeland." Tears ran unheeded down her cheeks as she raved at him. "You helped put *Mana* in her grave, with all your hate and vengeance. Still, you weren't satisfied, so you killed my father. I detest you, do you hear me? All *Patera* ever did was love my mother with all his heart and make her life one of goodness and joy. What gave you the right to take his life?"

In fury, she threw herself at Xenos. She clawed at his rain-drenched face, too angry to fear the gun he held. "You killed him, damn you. You killed him."

Pritchard tried to pull her off, while Xenos shielded his face with his arm.

"Holy Hector, Ariah. You want to get us shot?"

"I don't care, I don't care." She leaned her head against him and let the tears, the pain and the animosity she had kept bottled up since her father's death burst free. "He took my father from me. My home, my friends, everything I ever knew in my life. I didn't even dare go to my father's funeral. Damn him! Damn him!"

"*Arketa!* Make her to be silent," Xenos demanded.

"How did you find me? Why did you show up now?" she cried.

Xenos smiled and tapped a forefinger to his temple. "I use cunning, sneak into house of man . . . what is American term? Lawyer, yes, in lawyer's house I find note, says Ariah Scott, Cape Meares Lighthouse, Oregon. I ask questions, find out where is this Oregon. When I arrive I go in tavern to ask how do I get to lighthouse. Big man comes up, gives me welcome to become keeper in his place. Thinks because I work my way here on ship and look like sailor, I must be man he is expecting. I say to myself, here is chance to surprise my slippery niece."

Ariah moaned. "Oh, Bartholomew."

"Yes," Xenos said, "That is name of man who send me here." He bowed arrogantly. "When I am home, I will pay for a blessing to be said for this Bartholomew."

His words brought to Ariah a memory from the stories her mother had told her of her people and of how they feared having curses placed on them. Breaking from her husband's grip, Ariah faced her uncle, glaring at him with all the venom she could muster in her wet, bedraggled state.

"I curse you, Xenos Polassis. It is wrong to visit the sins of the fathers on the heads of the children, do you hear me? Wrong. You are wrong, and you'll suffer for it, I promise you. Plutarch was right, your villainy will be your downfall. I only pray that I be allowed to witness it, and that your end be as bloody and senseless as what you inflicted on my father."

"*Okhi!* No!" Xenos paled. "I did only what was right."

Dramatically, she pointed an accusing finger at him. "You did the devil's work, and I curse you for it, Xenos Polassis. Only if you leave and never come back can you escape it."

Flustered, Xenos tried to regain the control he saw slipping through his fingers. "Curse me all you want, but I will see this finished. If you want the man you call husband, and the old one, left unharmed, you will tell them to stand away. Then you come with me."

"*Okhi!* No," Ariah stared at him in calm defiance.

Outraged, Xenos struck out. The air rang with sound as his hand made contact with her jaw. Her head snapped from the blow and she reeled backward toward the cliff.

Instinctively, Pritchard retaliated with a strength he hadn't known he owned. Xenos's trigger finger flexed as nose tissues and bones shattered beneath the young man's fist. The gun fired, drowning out Ariah's scream.

Twenty-nine

Fear rode him as Bartholomew cursed, prayed, cursed again. The muddy road was treacherous even for the surefooted bay, slowing their pace so that the other men were able to catch up to them. Cal, on a dappled mare, drew up alongside. He had to shout to be heard over the trees thrashing in the keening wind and driving rain.

"Doc's plumb tuckered out, Bart, and the horses will be dropping out from under us if we don't rest them soon."

"I know," was the growled reply. "Let's get off the road and into the damn trees where we'll have some shelter. I'll give them an hour, no more."

Cal did well to get Bartholomew to wait out the promised hour before the man was back in the saddle and on his way, the others plodding wearily along behind. Bartholomew chafed at every delay with barely concealed fury. The others kept their distance and spoke in low monotones, but he never noticed. He was too busy worrying and scrutinizing the inner workings of his mind and heart.

Cal was right; he had been an absolute fool to turn the woman he loved over to another man without even a whisper of argument. Self-denial and deprivation had been so thoroughly ingrained into him early in life, he never questioned the rightness of it. With the mute acceptance of a blind mule, he had allowed a false sense of honor to lead him astray. It shamed him to realize how little care he had given to Ariah's feelings, how little faith he had held in her ability to choose her own way. Her own man.

She had given him her heart, as well as her virgin's body. Why had he walked away from her? Cal had accused him of running because he didn't know how to handle happiness. There had been no bounty of it in his life, that was certain.

"All your life you've had to give, give, give, until you no longer knew how to accept, how to take," Cal had told him, poking a finger at his brother's chest. "You're right, it's time for a change, but inside here where it counts. Concern for others is good, but you can't let it rule your life. The Lord doesn't serve up happiness on a silver platter while we wallow in self-pity. We have to prove we deserve it by accepting nothing less for ourselves. And for those we love."

Pretty words that hid a mountain of truth.

Right now, as Bartholomew and the bay trudged in agonizing slowness through the thick mud, he felt as though that entire mountain had tumbled down on top of him. Fear weighted his shoulders and tore at his heart. When he wasn't cursing fate's trickery, Mother Nature's treachery or himself, he was praying. Praying they were wrong about what might be happening at the lighthouse. Praying that when they got there, he would find his nymph safe and well.

The explosion of the gun deafened Ariah. Smoke clouded her eyes. Through the haze, she saw her husband falter. The blast nearly knocked him from the bluff, but he managed to stay on his feet. With a grunt of pain, he grabbed his shoulder. Crimson liquid oozed between his fingers and down the back of his hand, to be quickly washed away by the rain. He paled at the sight. His gaze flew to Ariah, pleading as though he expected her to make everything right. Then his knees buckled, and he crumpled to the earth.

"Pritchard!" Ariah was trying to find his pulse when she was roughly snatched back to her feet, the cold metal of a revolver pressed into her temple. She caught a whiff of gunpowder before the wind whisked it away.

"Now, it is your turn," Xenos whispered close to her ear. "The dishonor of Polassis family will at last be wiped away."

Rain streamed down her face and plastered her dress to her slim body as she struggled to break free. "Let me go. My husband's hurt. I have to tend him."

"He would be well, if you did as you were told. His death sits on your pretty head, little English bastard."

"You're the bastard."

Xenos grunted as she landed a well-aimed blow to his shin with the heel of her boot. Greek curses filled the air. She lunged for the gun, but he snatched it aside. Her racing heart pounded in her ear, nearly obliterating the noise of the storm. He was a small man, but wiry and strong. Much too strong for Ariah. Her foot slipped in the mud and he managed to snare her about the waist with his arm.

Once more she felt the icy cold of metal against bare flesh. The click of the hammer being drawn back was drowned out by a blast of thunder that shook the earth. Lightning glanced off the rod on the lighthouse roof. In the glare, as she waited for Xenos's bullet to ram into her brain, she saw what she knew would be her last glimpse of the angry sea she had come to love. Bartholomew's sea.

Oh, Bartholomew, how can I bear never seeing you again?

Suddenly something large and solid flew between them out of the darkness, slamming against Xenos's chest. Ariah was knocked to the side. She fell in a heap on the ground.

Vicious snarls erupted around her. She looked up to see Apollo sink his teeth into the hand which held Xenos's gun.

Frightened that the dog would be shot, Ariah shouted for him to back off. Apollo ignored her cry.

Xenos danced backward to avoid the savage, slashing canine teeth. The low railing of the wooden guard fence the men had built in a half-circle around the light tower at the edge of the bluff caught him at the backs of his knees.

Ariah screamed.

For an eternity, Xenos Polassis teetered there, bent backward and flailing his arms in a desperate attempt to right himself. The wind howled around him like a thousand avenging souls. It billowed the fabric of the man's coat as if it were the sail of a ship. A look of horror spread across his dark face as a fresh gust launched him dispassionately into hell.

Crouched beside her unconscious husband, Ariah buried her face in her hands while Xenos Polassis's scream of terror slowly faded away. Apollo nudged her shoulder, whimpering.

"Oh, Apollo, what would I have done without you? Thank God, Bartholomew couldn't find the man who lost you." She hugged him tightly, oblivious to his wet, muddy fur.

Pritchard moaned. She released the dog and bent to examine her husband's wound. The bullet was lodged in his shoulder under the collarbone. His eyelids flickered and blinked open.

"God, Ariah, it hurts."

"I know. It's bleeding badly." She pulled up her skirt, tore a length of ruffle from her petticoat, and folded it into a thick pad. After placing it against the wound, she pressed his hand over the bandage. "Hold this tightly to slow the bleeding. I have to check Seamus."

"He shot me, I can't believe he shot me."

"I know, but you'll be all right. I'll take care of you."

A corner of his mouth curled into a crooked grin. "I stood up to him, though, didn't I, Ariah? I stood up to him."

"Yes, Pritchard, you were wonderful."

He grimaced at a particularly fierce pain and closed his eyes. "Wonderful . . . stood up to him."

Ariah moved to where Seamus lay in the wet grass. She breathed a sigh of relief when she found his pulse beating steadily, if shallowly, beneath the tough, weathered skin of his throat. The wound at his temple was shallow, but bleeding profusely. She ripped another piece of ruffle from her petticoat and bound it in place.

"Ariah?"

She turned to see Pritchard peering at her through the rain. "Is he okay?" he shouted over the wind.

"The injury doesn't seem bad, but he's still unconscious." She gazed at the steep stairs that were the only way to the upper level of the bluff. "I've got to get the two of you to the house somehow. It's so dark now, and the storm is getting worse. We have to get the light going."

"Wouldn't it be easier to take him into the tower? We can get him to the house later, after the storm lets up. Maybe he'll be able to walk home by himself, by then."

Ariah stared at him in amazement. What had happened to the whiny little boy she had married? Not only was he concerned for someone other than himself, he wasn't even complaining about the pain she knew he must be suffering.

"What if he's hurt worse than he looks?" she asked. "You'd both be more comfortable at the house, and that's where all the medical supplies are."

"Get a horse, some rope and a couple of blankets. We'll drag him home on a litter." Pritchard tried to sit up and blanched as waves of pain coursed through his chest. Ariah hurried over to force him back down.

"You'll get it bleeding again if you move around too soon. Lie there and rest while I fetch a horse and blankets."

"You need help."

"I'll be fine. Apollo can help me."

The time it took her to traverse the thousand feet that separated her from the houses, to collect blankets and rope, round up one of the horses that had taken shelter in the barn and get it saddled, seemed like hours. She didn't bother to change into dry clothes, knowing she would be soaked again by the time she reached the light. She tied the horse to the railing at the top of the stairs, then unloaded the blankets and carried them down to the men.

"Did you think to bring some brandy?" Pritchard shouted as she knelt to bundle a blanket around him. "I'm frozen clear through."

She held out her hand and Apollo dropped a leather flask into her palm. Pritchard drank, coughed and drank again before handing it back. "Pour a bit down Old Seamus. It'll help keep his body temperature from dropping any lower."

Nodding, she crawled to the old man. It was difficult to tell how much of the brandy she got into Seamus's mouth and how much was washed away by the rain. Pritchard hitched himself over beside her as she struggled to pull Seamus onto the blanket she had spread out beside him.

"Take his shoulders," Pritchard told her. "I'll get his feet, we'll roll him on."

"Your shoulder's too bad, I'll have to do it alone."

"I'll be careful. Come on. We're fighting time here. If the storm gets any worse, we'll never get to the house. And I'm sick of this damned rain."

Together they worked the old man onto the blankets, then bound them around his frail body.

"Tie the end of that last rope under his arms." Pritchard's voice was growing weak and strained from pain and exhaustion. "We'll attach the other end to the saddle horn."

When everything was ready, Ariah helped her husband climb the slippery stairs. Once he had managed to haul himself into the saddle and to wrap the rope securely around the horn, blood was flowing freely again from his wound and his color was as gray as the barrel of the gun Xenos had dropped into the mud. Ariah prayed the saddle was secure; she wasn't at all sure she had done up the cinch right. If Pritchard tumbled off, she knew she'd never get him back on, and the fall wouldn't do his wound any good.

With Pritchard commanding the horse from above, Ariah guiding the bulky weight of Seamus's wet body from below, they dragged the old man to the foot of the stairs. The wind whipped Ariah's skirts about her legs, hindering her movements. Her teeth clattered so loudly she missed half her husband's shouted instructions.

"Watch . . . from bumping."

"What?"

"Don't let . . . head bump."

The stairs were too narrow for Ariah to walk beside Seamus. She had to sit on the step, haul his head and shoulders into her lap, hitch up a step, haul him up, hitch, haul, hitch, haul.

Exhausted, dizzy and weak, it was all Pritchard could do to stay in the saddle as Ariah finally led the horse, with Seamus in tow behind, up the long walk to the house.

"Pritchard? Pritchard, we're here. Give me the rope, I'll help you down."

He mumbled something in reply, dragged his leg over the horse and slid into her arms. They ended up on the ground. Drained by now and shivering with cold, Ariah used a combination of physical strength and threatening demands to force him to his feet. She wouldn't remember later exactly how she got both men into the house. Somehow she managed to get their wet clothes off them. A pallet was made up for Seamus on the living-room floor near the fire. Pritchard lay on the couch. Their mud-splattered faces were bathed, their wounds tended, their bodies warmed.

Ariah yearned to crawl into her own bed and let sleep erase the horrors of the past hours. But out on the tip of the bluff sat a darkened lighthouse, luring unsuspecting ships toward the dangerous, rocky shoreline. No matter how she yearned to ignore that responsibility, she couldn't. Because of her, a man had tumbled into the raging sea and two more lay near death at her hearth. Her conscience couldn't handle being the cause of more grief. So she bundled herself into the warmest coat she could find and dragged herself back out into the storm.

Eager for his own warm bed, the horse had headed for the barn. Ariah found him with his tail to the wind, his head hanging dejectedly over the fence that blocked his path. She got him into the barn, gave him a bucket of grain and covered his wet coat with a blanket, apologizing for being too weary to rub him down properly.

She was halfway down the steps that led to the lower bluff

when she slipped and tumbled the rest of the way down, landing in a muddy, tangled heap at the bottom.

The lantern she had brought with her had gone out. In the pitch-black night the whitewashed tower was a faint blur of lightness. Bruised and soaking wet, Ariah hauled herself up and limped toward the door at the base, praying she would make it before she was swept into the sea.

Safe inside at last, she leaned against the closed door and shut her eyes while she caught her breath and allowed her pulse to slow back to normal. Finally, she pushed away from the door and felt her way across the room to the storage cabinet where she found matches and the spare lantern. Within minutes a warm yellow glow flooded the round, whitewashed room.

Taking the lantern with her, Ariah climbed the stairs to make certain Pritchard had trimmed the five wicks and filled the heavy bronze kerosene lantern before Xenos's disastrous visit had altered their lives. Assured that everything was in order, she lit the wicks, creating an 18,000-candlepower flame, and, to equalize visibility, the 160,000-candlepower light behind the red filters, thus providing that alternating white and red beams would flash their warning throughout the night for anyone caught at sea within twenty-one miles of the cape. That done, she descended to the second floor where she set the clockwork system of gears and weights which would keep the lens turning. Every four hours she would have to reset the clockworks, but for now she could return home.

Rain whipped to a frenzy by the wind, peppered the windows in an erratic rhythm as Ariah bathed Seamus's still face. In some ways she was more worried about him than she was Pritchard. A blow to the head such as the old man endured could cause serious internal damage. At the very least, she figured he must have suffered a concussion or he would be awake by now.

She turned away with a sigh. There was no help for it; she would have to operate the light herself. Thank heaven, Pritchard had shown her so much about how it functioned. But how would she survive, running the light at night and tramping back and forth to the house to tend the men, cook, clean, milk cows and feed animals until Seamus or Pritchard recovered enough to help? Or until Bartholomew's real replacement showed up.

She wished she could simply climb onto a horse and let it carry her to Barnagat. Another trip across the bay was the last thing she wanted, but it would be worth it if she could find Bartholomew and take refuge in his sheltering arms. The temptation was almost more than she could resist.

Seamus had wet himself. Feeling like a sneak thief, she went into the forbidden room off the vestibule, then climbed the box stairs to his bedroom. After finding a nightshirt in one of his drawers, she yanked a blanket off the bed and returned downstairs where she proceeded to strip off the old man's clothes and dress him in the nightshirt—no easy chore. She replaced the wet blanket under him and covered him with another. Deciding that the room seemed cold, she built up the fire in the fireplace.

While she worked, Pritchard slept peacefully, his skin dry and slightly warm, but not feverish enough to alarm her. She bathed his face, neck and arms with cool water, then went upstairs to change out of her wet, muddy clothes and wash up.

In the kitchen she brewed a pot of coffee and forced herself to eat a sliver of ham stuffed into a folded slice of bread.

Boots entwined her sleek furry body around Ariah's legs, mewing plaintively. The cat had long ago cleared out the mice in the pantry. At first, Ariah had kept her merely to aggravate Hester and to impress upon the woman that *she* would decide who and what came and went in her kitchen. In time, Ariah had grown used to the cat, and so it remained.

Although the storm still raged, inside all was dead quiet, intensifying Ariah's loneliness. In all her weeks there, she had never sensed the station's isolation more intensely. Nor had she felt so vulnerable. She broke off a piece of her sandwich and fed it to the cat, glad for its company.

After replacing the compress on Seamus's injured head, she

checked Pritchard's shoulder. He squinted up at her from under eyelids heavy and swollen with fatigue.

"Is it bad?" he asked, working his tongue against the dryness of his mouth and throat.

"It could be better." She smiled to hide her own fear. "The bullet doesn't seem to have hit anything major, which is good, because I don't have the slightest idea how to get it out. You've lost a lot of blood, though."

He dragged his hand out from under the covers and noticed he was naked. "Who took my clothes off?"

"I did."

"Damned rotten timing," he muttered.

"What?"

"The one time you take an interest in getting me naked and I'm unconscious."

Ariah's smile was genuine this time. "Is that all you ever think about?"

"Guess it has been on my mind a bit lately."

"How about some hot tea?"

"Sounds good."

She evaded his gaze as she hurried from the room, but he noticed the flush on her cheeks from his teasing. Nettie never blushed.

Suddenly it struck him that he had come very close to dying that day, and never seeing Nettie again.

Until that moment out on the bluff when the bullet thudded into his chest, he had avoided thoughts of death. He was young. Old age and death happened to other people, older people like Aunt Hester, not to him. There was so much more he wanted to enjoy during his lifetime.

Like seeing Nettie grow round with his baby. If he had been killed, he would never have learned if it was a boy or a girl. It startled him to realize that mattered.

Ariah returned with the tea. Her skin looked so soft as she bent over him to hold the cup to his lips. He put up his hand to touch her. She cast him a quick glance, saying nothing. If he touched Nettie like that, she would coo like a dove and snuggle into his hand, not turn away as though it meant nothing.

"Who's Plutarch?"

Her thick brows lifted in surprise at his question. Then she remembered mentioning the man in her argument with Xenos. "A Greek essayist who lived around one hundred A.D. He wrote the famous line, 'Wicked men who congratulate themselves on escaping immediate trouble receive a longer, and not a slower, punishment.' "

Pritchard frowned. "Figured he'd be someone like that."

He was lightheaded and woozy, yet even clearheaded he knew he would be no match for her in a discussion on the teachings of a bunch of old Greeks who'd lived so long ago that none of their words could possibly still be valid today. Uncle Bart, though, he would have loved to share that sort of talk with her. They would make a good pair.

Ariah held the cup to his lips again. He tried to take it and found his hand too shaky. The wind was whistling under the eaves, making Pritchard glad he didn't have to go back outside. The Tillamook Kings had a practice game scheduled for tonight. No doubt it would be canceled because of the storm; a lucky break for him since he would have had to miss it. He gave his wife a long, piercing look.

"You don't like baseball, do you?"

"What's to like, Pritchard? A bunch of grown men knocking a ball around with sticks and seeing how filthy they can get, sliding in the dirt?"

For a while after Ariah left to reset the clockworks at the light, Pritchard thought about things he had never spared a thought to before, until finally, sleep overcame him.

The wind had abated somewhat, making Ariah's trip to the light easier this time. After setting the clockworks, she tied a piece of wood to the bottom of one of the weights. Then she wrapped herself in a thick wool blanket she had brought from the house and curled up below the block of wood. When it descended enough to touch her, waking her in the process, it would be time to reset the works for another four hours.

Thus she passed the night, napping in between her duties as temporary lighthouse keeper. By morning, the storm had eased, but instead of finding clear sunny skies, she awoke to a dismal fog that blanketed the cape and muted the sounds of the sea. For a while, Ariah stood outside, wrapped in her blanket as she listened for the whistle buoys at the mouth of the bay a few miles north. The silence was eerie and absolute. A gull rose to its feet in the scrubby ground cover where it had nested for the night. It stretched its wings and stepped toward her with a cry that sounded like a mournful "Please," as if hoping she had a spare fish in her pocket.

Ariah went back inside, her spirits dampened by the fog. She raised the wicks and measured the remaining kerosene oil, finding only enough to last a few more hours.

At the house she found Pritchard awake and worrying about the light. Ariah assured him she had seen to everything.

"But the lantern will have to be filled," he pointed out. "The kerosene oil is in the storage sheds just above the light. It has to be strained several times, and I can't imagine you handling those five-gallon cans by yourself. They'll have to be lugged down the stairs, into the tower, then upstairs to the lantern."

"I'm strong, Pritchard. I'll manage. How do you feel?"

"My shoulder hurts more than it did last night, if such a thing is possible. It's so stiff I can hardly move my arm."

"It will loosen up as you exercise it. Are you hungry?"

Ariah frowned at his negative reply. Pritchard normally had a very healthy appetite. She put her hand to his brow and found it overly warm. "You may have a slight fever. I'll bring you some hot tea to sip while I give you a cool sponge bath."

"You're going to give me a bath?" He managed a suggestive smile. "That sounds good."

"And about all you're strong enough to handle, Pritchard."

"I might surprise you, if you gave me a chance."

"Just concentrate on getting well before I collapse from exhaustion, please."

At once he sobered. "I'm sorry all this had to fall on you, Ariah. Isn't Seamus any better yet?"

"He's still unconscious. I'm worried about him."

"I'll watch him, and try to help with the meals, too."

Surprised, she gave him a smile that immediately brightened the cheerless room. "That's thoughtful of you. Now, let me help you into these." She waved a pair of clean underpants. "It'll make bathing you less . . . improper."

"We're married, how can seeing me naked be improper?" he asked, thinking how different she was from Nettie.

"It just is, Pritchard."

With Pritchard perched on the edge of the couch, his lap covered by a blanket, she eased the underwear up his legs, then helped him to stand so she could pull it into place. "Steady yourself with your hands on my shoulders."

He did as she suggested, but even with a blanket between them, she could not help noticing that he was aroused. Gruffly, she shoved him back down onto the couch. Pritchard stifled the complaint he had been about to make because of the jarring pain of sitting so abruptly. Instead, he apologized. "I can't help it, Ariah. I don't do it on purpose."

"I wouldn't think you'd be well enough for such a . . . thing," she mumbled as she tucked his blankets around him again.

"Being well enough to get hard is one thing, Ariah. Being strong enough to act on the impulse is another. And even if I could . . ." He let the sentence fade into the silence of the foggy morn, uncertain that he was ready to talk about the decision he had made during the night when the pain in his shoulder kept him awake.

"Ariah . . ."

She turned and looked at him questioningly. "Yes?"

"May I ask you something terribly personal?"

"I suppose so." She managed a weak smile. "After all, I don't have to answer, do I?"

Pritchard failed to rise to her halfhearted teasing. His pleasant young face remained as solemn as Reverend Ketcham's in the middle of a Sunday-morning sermon.

"Do you love Uncle Bart?"

Her mouth opened, then closed. Her cheeks flushed rose red, and she spun away from his anxious gaze. "Why on earth would you ask such a thing?"

He watched her arrange and rearrange the medical supplies on top of the table beside the couch.

"I spent a lot of time wondering why he went away so suddenly the way he did. He talked to me about you the evening before, you know."

She became very still.

"No, how would I have known? I never saw him again that day." She placed the roll of bandages beside the scissors, moved them next to the laudanum, then set them by the scissors once more.

"Again?" he asked. "You were with him that day?"

She gripped the beveled edge of the table and stared at her reflection in its gleaming surface, her cheeks as pale as the bandages she'd been toying with. "I saw him. Why do you ask?"

Her tone was defensive. Pritchard released a long sigh, then tried again. "Ariah, I think there's something you should know. After the way I . . . well, after the disaster of our wedding night, I made a foolish decision to get some experience before I tried bedding you again. There was a girl I'd heard about in town, and I went to see her."

He paused so long that she turned to look at him, almost holding her breath as she waited for him to finish.

"I think I love her, Ariah." He met her gaze with an apologetic shrug that ended in a grimace of pain.

"You . . . you fell in love with a girl in town?" she said in a daze. Pritchard nodded.

"She thinks she's in a family way. I promised I'd ask for an annulment. Remember the night I came to your room and ended up kissing you? It felt so good, I guess it sort of threw me off kilter. Ever since, I haven't been sure who I wanted, but realizing that I might have died yesterday put things more in perspective. Nettie and I are a good match." He tilted his head and peered at her questioningly again as he added, "The way you and Uncle Bart are."

Ariah blushed and looked down at her hands.

"Don't feel guilty, Ariah. I understand, and it's okay. Really."

"How did you know?"

"The pain gave me a lot of time last night to think. I got to remembering looks I'd seen pass between you, a yearning in Uncle Bart's eyes when he'd watch you. I had told myself it was envy, because things weren't as good between him and Aunt Hester as they should have been. Last night I realized it was a whole lot more, and that you felt it too."

Ariah lifted her hands and let them fall. "I never meant to hurt you, Pritchard."

"You didn't." His face glowed with enthusiasm. "This is perfect, don't you see? We can get the annulment, I can marry Nettie and give my son a name. And you can marry Uncle Bart."

She rose and walked to the window to stare out into the fog. "Except that I don't know where he is, or if he'd want me as his wife."

Pritchard grinned, self-confidently. "He'll want you. Believe me, we men know these things. Now, fix us something to eat, I'm hungry as a whale."

As she hurried into the kitchen, Ariah thought with wonder that her young husband no longer seemed so young. He'd grown up overnight, and all it had taken to bring it about was a bullet and the threat of death.

Thirty

Precious hours were wasted when the rescue party had to make a long, arduous detour because the road was washed out. They rode miles out of their way to find a place to ford the swollen stream that had caused the damage. A horse went lame when the creek bottom shifted beneath him, injuring his leg. Bartholomew remained unnaturally quiet as they searched for a homestead where they could trade the animal for a healthy one. As morning approached, his hopes rose. Even if the storm lingered, they would be able to travel faster by daylight.

But he hadn't counted on the fog.

They straggled into Netarts hungry, wet, half-frozen and so weary Cal was certain they could all sleep standing up, if Bartholomew would let them stop long enough. Old Doc took the matter into his own hands.

"Son," he said to Bartholomew, "I know you're fretting over the folks at the lighthouse, but without food in our stomachs and dry clothes on our backs, we're going to be in too bad shape to help anyone by the time we get there. Now Portugee Joe lives no more than a quarter-mile up the bay and I know he'll feed us. You do what you think you must, but I for one am heading for Joe's."

As Dr. Wills trotted away on his old swaybacked horse, Cal heard Bartholomew mutter something under his breath about the good it might do Wills to lose a couple of the chins he had bobbing under his big mouth. Yet when Portugee Joe handed out tender sticks of dried elk meat, Bartholomew ate as greedily as the others did.

After changing into the dry clothes they had brought in waterproof bundles, the party once more got under way, this time heading north along the coast road. Fog forced them to maintain a snail's pace where the road edged along the cliffs and there was danger of walking off into the ocean below. A mile beyond Netarts they found a tree lying across the road. While Cal searched out a saw big enough to handle the four-foot-thick trunk, Bartholomew shouted the vilest expletives he could think of and kicked impotently at the hapless spruce.

Shortly after noon the wind rose up and swept away the fog. The air smelled of rain, and the temperature fell ten degrees.

Standing at the top of the light-tower, looking out the windows at the white-capped sea, Ariah listened to the wind whistle and sough and moan eerily beneath the domed metal roof. The sound set her hair on end and caused her to shudder. She told herself there was no such thing as ghosts, and certainly no reason for one to haunt a lighthouse little more than a year old.

Unless it was Hester.

The Greek people would say that Hester had not died at peace, that she was a vampire now, wandering. Ariah gave a faint laugh and shrugged off the image of Hester floating through the air sporting long, jagged teeth. If anyone could come back to earth and haunt those left behind, it would be Hester, but Ariah was not about to accept what her educated mind told her was only a fantasy for frightening children on stormy nights.

The enormous lantern was nearly out of fuel. As she entered the storage shed where the extra oil was kept, a spider scurried out of sight from directly in front of her face. Ariah couldn't stop the frightened yelp that escaped her mouth. She clasped a hand to her suddenly pounding heart and scolded herself for being scared of a tiny spider, after all she'd endured the past two days.

Maneuvering one of the heavy five-gallon cans of kerosene in order to strain the oil so it wouldn't clog up the lantern was difficult and exhausting work. To get it down the stairs to the tower, she had to lower it a step at a time until she reached bottom, then reverse the procedure to get it up to the lantern. Her shoulders and arms ached from the strain. Dirt, spiderwebs and oil stains covered her dress. Exhausted, she returned to the house.

By evening Ariah knew she had a full scale sou'wester on her hands, even more violent than the one the night before. The wind howled about the eaves, more like a hundred maddened wraiths than merely one. It rattled the windowpanes and whipped the hemlocks and spruces about as though they were thin saplings.

Pritchard was feverish and cranky. Seamus awoke finally, for which Ariah said a silent prayer of gratitude. His head ached fiercely, though his mind seemed clear. A dose of hot broth containing laudanum sent him back into a deep, healing sleep.

As she hurried back to the lighthouse along the walkway, tightly gripping the guide rope, Ariah feared that the thunderous roar of the waves crashing against the bluff, the wind screeching in her ears, would deafen her.

But her danger was far greater than that.

The wind whirled beneath her skirts, filling them like a bellows and lifting her off her feet. Xenos's last moments were vividly brought to mind. The bluff here was less than forty feet across, and while Xenos had been much closer to the edge when he'd been carried over, she knew her chances of suffering the same fate if she let go of the rope were very high.

Inch by inch Ariah forced herself to keep moving toward the light, crawling now on hands and knees. Her skirt became shredded from the wooden planks of the walkway. Her left hand was scraped raw by the rough hemp of the guide rope, her right was riddled with splinters. Maintaining her hold on the lantern was not only difficult, but dangerous. She needed both hands to hang on for dear life, so she left it behind.

At times the gale became so fierce she could move neither forward nor back for fear of being torn from the rope and swept right off the bald bluff.

A silent litany ran through her head then, while she fought off terror and panic. *Bartholomew, Bartholomew, Bartholomew.*

With one arm wrapped about a sturdy post, Ariah did the one thing open to her; she clawed at the buttons of her dress. When they resisted her efforts, she literally ripped the skirts threatening her life from her body, leaving only her bodice, chemise and drawers to cover her. Tattered bits of her garments swirled and snapped and tumbled across the bluff until, finally, they vanished into the void.

Then the rain began. It pelted her naked flesh, poured down her back and between her breasts beneath her chemise. The pins had long been ripped from her hair. Now the long wet strands slapped against her like a thousand stinging whips. They filled her mouth and covered her eyes. They tangled in the guide rope and tore free at the roots.

Stumbling—half-walking, half-crawling—clinging to the rope with all her might, her knees skinned from falling again and again, Ariah inched toward the lighthouse. She descended the stairs on her bottom, one step at a time, then crept to the door of the tower.

Inside at last, she slammed the door shut and lay on the cold floor, her breasts heaving as she gasped for breath. When she recovered enough to move, she fumbled with half-frozen hands for the spare lantern and matches. After several tries, she set the wick aglow, and cloaking her chilled body in the blanket she had left there that morning, she thawed her hands in the lantern's meager warmth.

The immense lens would need cleaning and polishing to keep it from being pitted by the salt spray, but Ariah was too weary to care. Knowing she should at least check to make sure everything was all right, she forced herself up the stairs. As soon as she stepped onto the platform that surrounded the slowly rotating lens, the strong beam swept over her. She flung her hands over her eyes to shield them from the blinding glare, unaware that a rock, tossed by the tremendous strength of the towering waves, was at that very moment hurtling toward her.

Bartholomew had blessed the wind that swept the fog away and allowed them to work more quickly at clearing the road of the deadfall. Since he was the only one among them with lumbering experience, it took most of the day to saw the log through, cut a stout pole to use as a lever, then pry, kick, shove and threaten the cursed spruce over the side into the brink.

Before they were done the wind had become a full-blown gale and the clean clothing they had changed into that morning was no longer dry.

Discouraged and disgruntled, the men pressed onward.

The rock crashed through the glass wall in a shower of shattered glass. Ariah screamed and tried to throw herself clear, receiving a glancing blow on her hip that knocked her to the floor. The rock bounced off the platform, nicked one of the lower prisms of the lens, then rolled harmlessly to her feet.

Ariah groaned in despair. Her hip might be bruised and her chemise and her drawers torn, but she was more concerned about the broken pane. Though extras were kept in the oil sheds for such mishaps, she had no idea how to install them.

Thank God the precious lens itself had not been badly damaged. The light would continue to operate.

Downstairs Ariah searched for something to cover the broken pane until it could be repaired. All she found was a pile of old newspapers she had no way of fastening over the hole. Unable to come up with anything better, she wadded them up and stuffed them into the gap as tightly as she could. When she was finished, her hands were crosshatched with scratches from the broken glass.

Overhead, wind rattled the fitted metal gores of the pitched roof as though bent on snatching them away. The sea boiled like an old crone's cauldron, foam-capped swells as far out as Ariah could see in the brilliant beam of the giant lantern. During the long night, other rocks thudded into the tower as the horrendous waves plucked them from the ragged cliff and flung them furiously through the air, but none struck the glass and for that she was grateful.

At midnight, she knew she had no choice but to fetch kerosene from the storage sheds again. Burning the lantern night and day used up the fuel much more rapidly than on a normal day when the candles were extinguished during daylight. The trip would be cold and wet and perilous. She considered tying the blanket around her neck and waist, then decided she would need a dry blanket more after her trek than the meager protection one would provide during it.

An eternity later, she dragged the oil can inside and sank to the floor. Aware that she must get dry and warm at once, she rested only a few seconds before seeking the comfort of the blanket left behind. All night she worried about her patients, alone at the house, but the keening wind and her near nudity reminded her that it was entirely too hazardous to attempt the trip again until the storm diminished.

In the wee hours of the morning she awoke from a fitful nap to realize that the lens had stopped turning. "Please," she cried, exhausted and cold and discouraged. "No more problems."

No one was listening. She reset the clockworks. Nothing happened. The lens remained immobile. When several minutes of work brought no results, she accepted the unpleasant fact that there was only one way the great lens could be kept rotating— she had to turn it by hand.

Dawn brought only a faint lightening of the sky, and no relief from her lengthy hours of labor. The storm had eased but not enough to allow her to extinguish the light.

Like the muscles of her overworked arms, her bruised hip was stiff and sore. Splinters from the boardwalk, rope burns, and scratches from broken glass swelled her hands until she could barely use them. Sleeplessness and worry over Pritchard and Seamus puffed her eyes. Their lids felt as though sand had become trapped beneath them. Still she cranked and cranked and cranked, keeping the lantern turning.

When the discomfort of a full bladder became too great, she let the lens slow to a halt while she limped downstairs to the chamber pot. She slaked her thirst with fresh water piped down from the same spring that supplied the houses. Then she dragged her weary body back up the stairs.

Rain tinkled steadily on the metal roof and streaked the windows, but the gale had nearly blown itself out and the surf was calmer now. Ariah was debating whether or not she dared let the light go out when she heard a distant sound. Hester's ghost howling again, she told herself. Then the sound moved closer, grew louder. A voice, deep and masculine, not high and piercing as Hester's had been.

Someone was calling her name.

And barking, she heard barking. Turning from the lens, she peered toward the houses through the gloom. There, coming down the walkway, were two men, followed by Apollo.

Both the men were familiar, yet neither was Pritchard nor Seamus. One was stocky, the other tall and . . .

Tears pricked her eyes at the same moment her heart gave a flutter of joy and a name clogged her throat. Nose and palms pressed childlike to the misty glass, she cried out soundlessly.

Bartholomew! Bartholomew! Bartholomew!

Thirty-one

Ariah forgot her state of near nakedness at the sight of Bartholomew walking toward the lighthouse. She forgot her duties as lighthouse tender, forgot the painful throbbing of her bruised hip, her scraped knees, her lacerated hands. Oblivious to everything except her desperate need for him, she raced down the stairs and flung open the door. Feeling neither the chill wind nor the icy rain, she tore up the wooden steps to the top of the bluff.

He saw her and waved.

"Good hell," Bartholomew muttered as he stared at the disheveled woman coming toward him. What little she wore was tattered and filthy. Her hair was a riot of snarls flying out around her bare arms, tangled about her waist. One hip, where her chemise was torn, bore a reddish brown stain Bartholomew thought looked suspiciously like blood. "It looks as though she's fallen down the damn cliff and crawled back up it."

"Go to her," said the man beside him.

Bartholomew hesitated. "But you—"

"Right now, she sees only you. Go on, I'll wait here. I believe she's had more than enough shocks to deal with lately. We'll take this one slow and easy."

Ariah was running toward him, holding out her arms as she cried his name. Without another word of argument, Bartholomew went to her.

Ariah laughed out loud. Even muddy and unkempt, he looked so beautiful she wanted to cry. So big and brawny and alive.

He hadn't deserted her. He was here, coming for her, bringing solace and safety and joy. Within minutes she was throwing herself into his strong, capable arms.

"Bartholomew. Oh, God, it's really you."

"Aye, little nymph, it's me."

He hugged her tightly, his eyes closed as he let his body and soul absorb the warmth of her, assuring himself that she was truly alive and well. Her arms were entwined about his waist, their fierce grip telling him her feelings for him had not changed. After a long moment, he gently disentangled himself and held her away so he could study her face. Tears mingled with the rain on her cheeks, but her smile was radiant.

Then it faded. "Uncle Xenos came," she said. "We thought he was the new keeper. He shot Pritchard."

"I know, I know."

He hugged her again. Her chemise was soaked clear through. He could see her nipples pressed against the thin fabric and felt himself harden. Impatient with his body's inappropriate timing, he took off his heavy coat and wrapped it around her.

"We brought Dr. Wills with us. He and Cal are tending to Pritchard and Seamus now. Come on, let's get up to the house before you catch your death of cold."

He took hold of her hand. Ariah winced and jerked away. Tenderly, he forced her to let him examine her palms.

"Damn! Ah, Ariah, what in God's name have I done to you, leaving you here at the mercy of that bastard? That blasted husband of yours is as helpful in a fight as a—"

"He's not going to be my husband much longer." She put a silencing finger to his lips. "And he was wonderful, defending me against Uncle Xenos as best he could."

Bartholomew's heart stood still. "What did you say?"

Her smile broadened and he had a sudden impulse to kiss the impudent mole perched on her upper lip.

Though cognizant of what he wanted to hear, she couldn't resist teasing him as she slid her arms into the sleeves of the coat he'd put around her, and inhaled his scent. "I said he defended me—"

"No, the other."

"You mean, that he won't be my husband much longer?" She was cool as seawater. Then she laughed and bobbed up onto her toes to kiss him. "He's in love with someone else, Bartholomew. A girl in town. Her name is—"

"Nettie," he finished for her.

Ariah's smile faltered. "You knew?"

"How else could I ignore the vows you exchanged with him and make love to you that day in the woods?"

Ariah's amazement switched to anger. Her eyes sparked like flint on steel. "Then why did you leave me? Why did you go away without a word, in the middle of the night like a thief?"

"I gave Seamus a letter to give you. Didn't he—"

"Oh, yes, a letter . . . The coward's way out. He gave it to me." She marched away, pivoted and pointed an accusing finger at him. It was barely visible inside the long sleeve of his coat. "You shredded my heart with that awful letter. I thought you loved me, I—"

In two strides he reached her and drew her close, muffling her words against his chest. "I do love you. Lord, nymph, you're my heart and soul, my very life. Don't you know that?"

Her arms snaked about his waist as she nuzzled into his warmth. "Yes, I know," she said with a sigh.

Bartholomew caught her chin on the edge of his hand and forced her to look up at him. "You know?"

"Marry me, Bartholomew. Promise you'll marry me."

Her unforgettable blue eyes pierced him straight to his soul. "Ariah, I—"

She gripped his shirt front and gave it a jerk. "No excuses, Bartholomew. You just said you love me, and I love you more than life itself. We're free now, both of us, and I want to spend the rest of my days with you."

Deep laughter rumbled up out of his chest. "I'm not trying to give you excuses, nymph. Don't you know it's the man who's supposed to propose marriage to the woman, not the other way around?"

"Only if she's too cowardly to take things into her own hands. I'm not taking any chances on letting you get away. Please, stop teasing me now and say you'll marry me."

He sobered as he stared into her bottomless eyes. "Aye, I'll marry you," he said huskily. "And I'll spend the rest of my days worshiping you." He kissed her nose. "An hundred years to praise thine eyes, and on thy forehead gaze." While his lips brushed hers, his hands slid inside the coat, upward over her ribs until they met the fullness of her breasts. " 'Two hundred to adore each breast, but—' "

A throat was cleared loudly behind them.

Bartholomew's hands fell away, and he turned to face the man he had forgotten waited his turn to greet Ariah.

"Sorry, Bartholomew, but it's getting a bit wet out here, and besides, I was growing impatient," the man said.

Beside Bartholomew, Ariah uttered a gasp, then moved hesitantly forward. "Papa?"

Scott Jefferson, alias Jeffrey Scott, smiled. "Yes, poppet, it's me." He held open his arms. "Do I get a hug, or do you save them all for Bartholomew?"

"Oh, Papa." She threw herself at him. Tears poured down her face.

For a long time, Scott rocked her in his arms while she stroked his beloved face and sobbed. The moistness glistening in the distinguished attorney's eyes brought a lump into Bartholomew's throat. Finally, Ariah's sobs quieted.

"I thought you were dead." Her voice vibrated with emotion. "Uncle Lou—"

"He knew you'd never leave me otherwise, Poppet. He held a funeral with an empty casket to throw Xenos off the trail and went along with your plan to come to Oregon so he could be sure you were safe." Scott held his daughter away from him and stared down at her sternly. "Had he known about your idiotic scheme to marry a total stranger, he never would have let you go, however. Now, can we get in out of this rain?"

Unchastened, Ariah glared back at him, refusing to move. "He should have been honest with me. Do you know the agony I suffered, thinking you were dead? I could strangle him with my own hands. How could he do that to me, Papa?"

"We do strange, unaccountable things sometimes when we think we're protecting the ones we love." Over her head, his gaze met Bartholomew's. "Don't we, young man?"

Bartholomew nodded. "Aye, sir, that we do."

Ariah smiled, first at her father, then at Bartholomew. "Gracious Sadie, what am I whining about? Last night I wasn't certain I would even survive until this morning, yet here I am. And, best of all, the two people I love most in the world have come back to me."

"Well," her father said in his best courtroom voice, "now that your world is all golden and glorious again, let's go to the house, and while we walk, I expect you to explain to me why you're running around in your unmentionables, and why you look as though you've been dragged by a rope over ninety miles of hard ground."

"I'd like to hear the answer to that myself," said Bartholomew as he swooped her off her feet and started up the path.

"I can walk, Bartholomew," she objected lightly. "And, in case you hadn't noticed, it's even stopped raining."

"Aye, but the way you look, I'm not sure you'd make it all the way before you collapsed. Besides, I haven't yet had my fill of having you in my arms again."

From her safe, warm nest in Bartholomew's arms, Ariah beamed at her father. "Don't be shocked, *Patera*. He's not my husband, yet, but he is the man I intend to spend the rest of my life with."

Scott smiled indulgently as he walked along beside them. "A good decision, I would say. Your young man and I had a long talk on the way here. I told him he was a fool for going off and leaving you. When a man finds the woman he loves, no means are too extreme to make her his, even when he knows he may pay for that privilege some day. I know." His smile faded and his expression became wistful.

"Oh, *Patera*," she cried.

"Don't go getting all weepy again," Scott scolded. "The only regret I have is not being with you when you needed me most. But that's enough on that subject. I want to know what went on here, and I want to know now."

"So do I," Bartholomew said, "but talk fast because the minute I get you into that house, I'm taking you up to bed—"

"Bartholomew!"

"Let me finish. I want Dr. Wills to give you a thorough examination, and then you're to get some rest."

"I'm hungry, and I'm not going to bed without a bath."

"Good hell, but you're a stubborn woman."

"I come by it honestly." She flashed her father a wicked smile.

"I refuse to be your scapegoat, young lady," Scott objected. "Your mother was the stubborn one. Now start talking. The way Bartholomew's long legs are eating up ground, we'll be at the house before you get even a sentence out. Pritchard and Seamus already told us what happened when Xenos showed up, and that you've been tending the light ever since. Start with what happened to your clothes."

So, in a precise description, she told them all she had endured in the past two days. She had reached the point at which the clockworks broke down and stopped turning the giant lens when Bartholomew carried her through the gate and headed for his own porch instead of hers.

"Bartholomew, this is *your* house."

"I'm aware of that," he calmly replied, not even winded after his rush up the gentle slope with her in his arms. "From now on it's also your house. You're not spending another night with Pritchard, and I'm not spending another night without you. In separate bedrooms, of course," he added for the benefit of the older man following them.

Scott gave Bartholomew an understanding smile and discreetly cleared his throat. "Why don't I fetch Dr. Wills while you argue it out with your future wife as to whether it's going to be a bath first or bed?"

"It will be a bath, Papa," Ariah said, "so bring him in half an hour."

"Bring him *now.*" Bartholomew's tone was dangerously soft.

As he carried her into the house, he said huskily, "I am the eagle, remember, little nymph? Which means I am bigger as well as stronger."

And she answered pertly, "But which of us is the most stubborn?"

That night, after Ariah's father retired to the garret, Bartholomew let himself into his old bedroom and eased the door shut behind him. Going to the bed, he gazed down at the woman asleep beneath the covers, barely visible in the subtle light of the myriad stars that filled the clear, dark sky in the wake of the passing storm.

Dr. Wills had pronounced Ariah's wounds superficial. He had prescribed a day or two of bed rest, then had returned to his patients at the assistant keeper's house.

Seamus had suffered a concussion, but was on the mend and would suffer no lasting results. The bullet had been removed from Pritchard's shoulder. His fever had ebbed, and he and Bartholomew had held a very satisfactory discussion about their respective futures.

Bartholomew sat on the edge of the mattress and lightly brushed the enticing mole on Ariah's upper lip. Her eyes opened and she smiled.

"Feeling up to company?" he whispered hoarsely.

Her smile broadened. "As long as it's you, I am."

Anticipation curled pleasantly inside her as her gaze followed the movements of the large hands unfastening the buttons of his shirt. Muscles rippled in his arms and under the dark hair of his chest as he removed that garment and tossed it to the floor. When he reached for the placket on his trousers, liquid warmth jetted through her. Her lethargy fled.

Bartholomew saw her eyes begin to smolder, saw her squirm beneath the bedclothes, and the smile curving his sensuous mouth became the primal grin of a predator who knows his mate is eager for him. A smile of possession, and of pride.

The breath caught in Ariah's throat as he kicked off his trousers and paused beside the bed, her gaze taking in his savage beauty. When she could breathe again, she lifted the covers in silent entreaty, and he slid in beside her.

For a long moment they stared at each other, her slender, pale body, bared to the waist, graceful and glorious; his muscular, broad-shouldered form like some pagan god's.

"Bartholomew," she whispered finally.

In answer, he placed an open palm over her breast to let her feel how he trembled. "I'm shaking, I want you so. I feel as though the gods are testing me, and if I fail you'll vanish before my eyes, like the fairy nymph that you are."

Her voice came back, soft but sure in the darkness. "I'm neither fairy nor nymph . . . only a woman who has given her heart to a man and who now wants to give him her body as well."

"Lord, how I love you."

His lips found hers then. His ears caught the throaty sound she made, like the contented purr of a cat, and he quivered deep in his loins as his body quickened in response. That light touch was all they needed to bring the coals of desire, damped for so long, into flame. The sensual memories and fantasies that had haunted their dreams since their idyll in the Uphams' cabin— embellished and reinforced by their day in the woods more than a week before—now came alive as lips and hands sought, found, teased and pleasured.

Though in reality they had exchanged their hearts long ago, they belonged to each other now in a new way—openly, honorably—and because their love was no longer bridled by guilt or shame, the passion flaring between them seemed achingly new and infinitely precious. For Ariah, it was the culmination of a dream, for she knew what she had won in the form of the strong, compelling man sharing her bed: provider, protector, friend, lover, soul mate. Wherever Demetria Scott was at that moment, the woman was smiling.

For the man in bed with her, years of loneliness, of unwanted entrapment, of frustration and need, fell away like the chaff that protects a seed until it is ready to germinate, to flourish and grow into something green and strong and beautifully enduring.

And as he sank himself into the heated haven of Ariah's welcoming body, he knew that life—*that he*—would never be the same again.

Bartholomew Noon had just been reborn.

Epilogue

"Mama, Mama!"

The screen door slammed shut as a small girl barreled into the kitchen.

"What is it?" Ariah Noon turned from the sink where she was shelling peas.

"Look, Mama, I brunged you some flowers," the five-year-old announced, holding up a dirty fist.

Ariah's grin softened with sentimentality as she accepted the bouquet of tiny white flowers. "You *brought* me some flowers, Demi. And they're very pretty. Where did you find them?"

"I can't tell you, Mama. It's a secret."

Ariah chuckled softly as the youngster skipped out the door to join her sister on the porch where three tiny raccoons were nestled with their mother in a padded box. The two heads bent over the box below the window where Ariah stood were as opposite in coloring as the personalities of their owners. Eight-year-old, blond Martha Anne was as well behaved and trustworthy as dark-haired Demetria, lovingly called Demi by her mother, was rash, reckless and impudent.

Lounging nearby was Apollo, the girls' ever-present guardian. The dog had grown sedate in the nine years since Ariah found him in the woods, starved and half-wild. As if hearing her thoughts, he lifted his regal head to glance at her, gave a dignified yawn and replaced his chin on his paws.

Ariah didn't truly need to hear where her daughter had found the blooms. Though they were common enough in other locations, there was only one spot in which they grew on the cape, a spot she well knew. And loved.

Wood nymphs. How she and Bartholomew had laughed to find the flowers growing there almost a year to the day after their tryst in the secluded glade when they'd first made love.

So much had happened since then. Bartholomew was Head Keeper again. Pritchard had married Nettie and was well on his way to having that baseball team he wanted. In order to be close to his daughter and grandchildren, Jeffrey Scott had settled in Tillamook and opened a law practice.

The titillating details of his first case were still being whispered behind gloved hands over dainty tea trays, for it was said that his client stood brazenly before the judge and unashamedly testified that although her marriage had never been consummated, she suspected she was carrying the child of another man. Furthermore, the woman's husband was the confessed father of a child conceived by one Nettie Tibbs who had been known in the town for some time as a "scarlet woman." Mumbling over the decadent and irresponsible behavior of today's young people, the judge had immediately declared the union of Ariah Scott and Pritchard Monteer null and void. On Friday, July 3, 1891, Ariah had become Mrs. Bartholomew Noon.

Old Seamus, as though determined to resist being forced into accepting the new century and all the changes it would bring to the country, from "tele-a-phones" to horseless carriages, died peacefully of heart failure on Christmas Eve, 1899, his corncob pipe still clutched in his weathered hand. The memory still brought tears to Ariah's eyes.

But the year 1900 marked a change even more monumental to the Noon family than the coming of a new century, for in a few short weeks they would be leaving their lighthouse home behind. Having finally completed a correspondence course in veterinary medicine, Bartholomew would be taking up a position at Robert Noon's veterinary clinic, specializing in birds and wild animals.

Ariah had mixed emotions about the move. Cape Meares had

become more than a home to her over the years. It was a way of life. It was freedom. It was love. Yet life in town offered opportunities she would enjoy. Her work as a woman's rights advocate would benefit, and she would be able to take Hester's old spot with the Tillamook Women for Temperance Coalition as well.

"Woolgathering again, are you?"

Ariah turned to find her husband standing in the pantry doorway. Her lips spread in a grin. Here was one thing that had not changed, for he was as handsome as the first day she'd laid eyes on him, standing on a railroad platform while steam billowed around them from the puffing locomotive that had brought her to Oregon to marry a man she had yet to meet.

Watching her now, Bartholomew's sable eyes darkened in a very familiar way. Deep inside, she felt an answering tingle as heat pooled between her thighs.

Slowly he crossed the room until he stood directly in front of her. "You're looking at me with fire in your eyes, Mrs. Noon."

"Oh?" she retorted saucily. "What sort of fire?"

"The sort I like best." He lowered his gaze to take in the flowers she held, recognizing them instantly. "Have you been to the glade without me?"

"Ummm. And if I have?"

Bartholomew drew her tightly against him. His voice was low and hoarse as he nuzzled her neck. "You better have been alone. Better yet, you better not have gone there without me at all."

Tilting her head back to give him better access, she wriggled against the hard bulge pressing into her. He moaned and slid a hand over her breast.

"Do we have to wait until our anniversary to go back to the glade this year?" He ran his tongue up the side of her neck to her ear and chuckled at the shiver he elicited from her. "I could use a whole afternoon of naughty nakedness with my sweet nymph. No hiding under the covers, no choking down moans to protect inquisitive little ears."

"Those little ears are just outside the door, Mr. Noon."

Bartholomew's arms fell away from her, and he glanced guiltily toward the back porch.

"And as far as the glade is concerned," Ariah continued, "I'm afraid it's not our secret anymore. Demi brought me the flowers."

She squelched his groan of dismay with two fingers pressed to his lips. "It just so happens, however, that Nettie has invited the girls next door for George's birthday. I rather imagine they'll be too busy to notice if we slip away into the woods."

Bartholomew grinned. "When?"

Breaking away, Ariah went to the door and opened it. "Demi, Martha Anne, it's time to go next door. Be sure to wash your hands first. Nettie's serving chocolate cake and ice cream."

The moment she stepped back inside, her husband grabbed her and planted a kiss on her willing mouth. "I love you, Ariah Noon."

"And I love you, Bartholomew."

In spite of the changes wrought by the years, gulls continued to wheel and soar over the sea as Ariah and Bartholomew raced each other to the path through the woods. Whales and seals, puffins and sea lions came and went. Storms battered the buildings and the indomitable bluff on which the lighthouse station sat. Summer followed spring, and the sun set in glorious color on the Western horizon.

In the glade hidden in the forest where three limbless totems reached for a sky as blue as Ariah's unforgettable eyes, the scents and sounds of the towering Sitka spruces, the flowers and the sea filled their senses as they renewed the love that never once wavered but grew deeper each year, as it had been fated to do. As it always would, beyond life into eternity.

A love too rare to forsake.

Author's Note

Although the characters in *Forever Mine* lived entirely in my imagination, everything mentioned about Judge Owen Denny and his efforts to establish Chinese ringneck pheasants in Oregon is true. Today, thanks to Judge Denny and breeding farms established in 1911 near Corvallis and Hermiston, Oregon, Chinese ringnecks can be found in nearly every state of the nation, and are as American as Bartholomew's favorite apple pie.

The Cape Meares Lighthouse was lit for the first time on January 1, 1890. In 1895 a much-needed, heated workroom was erected between the light-tower and the sloping rise of the upper bluff. That same year, the slippery wooden stairway was replaced by one made of steel. The light was replaced by an incandescent oil-vapor lamp in 1910, and electrified in 1934. On April 1, 1963, an automatic light was installed and the old light forever retired.

Today, the barn, houses, oil-storage buildings and original workroom are gone. Only the ghosts of a colorful past, which will never be known again, inhabit the windy bluff and the whitewashed tower of Cape Meares Lighthouse—except in the minds of those imaginative enough to hear the old voices, and to sense the passions that might once have stirred within.

About the Author

Forever Mine is Charlene Raddon's tribute to an area of the country for which she holds a very special affection, a place of beauty, romance, and mystery. Each year she answers the call of the sea and pays a visit to Cape Meares where she walks the beach, hunts agates, and writes, writes, writes.

Charlene resides in Utah with her husband and two cats, and is currently working on her next historical romance, which Zebra Books will be publishing in 1997. Her previous Zebra historical romances include *Taming Jenna* and *Tender Touch*.

Charlene loves to hear from her readers and you may write to her at 1816 Tramway Drive, Sandy, Utah 84092. Please include a business sized self-addressed stamped envelope for a book mark or reply.